Aki McKenzi grew up by the coast and spent the first 18 years of their life down by the beach, hanging out by the pier. After moving farther inland for university, they made sure to stay less than an hour away from the sea. They have a small garden outside their flat and enjoy spying on the neighbours' cats. *Edge of the Empire* is their debut novel.

To my 18-year-old self who first came up with this idea; we did it kid.

Aki McKenzi

WORLD'S END: THE LEGACY OF THE NEO WARRIORS

Book 1: Edge of the Empire

AUSTIN MACAULEY PUBLISHERS
LONDON * CAMBRIDGE * NEW YORK * SHARJAH

Copyright © Aki McKenzi 2024

The right of Aki McKenzi to be identified as author of this work has been asserted by the author in accordance with sections 77 and 78 of the Copyright, Designs and Patents Act 1988.

All rights reserved. No part of this publication may be reproduced, stored in a retrieval system, or transmitted in any form or by any means, electronic, mechanical, photocopying, recording, or otherwise, without the prior permission of the publishers.

Any person who commits any unauthorised act in relation to this publication may be liable to criminal prosecution and civil claims for damages.

This is a work of fiction. Names, characters, businesses, places, events, locales, and incidents are either the products of the author's imagination or used in a fictitious manner. Any resemblance to actual persons, living or dead, or actual events is purely coincidental.

A CIP catalogue record for this title is available from the British Library.

ISBN 9781035839766 (Paperback)
ISBN 9781035839773 (Hardback)
ISBN 9781035839780 (ePub e-book)

www.austinmacauley.com

First Published 2024
Austin Macauley Publishers Ltd®
1 Canada Square
Canary Wharf
London
E14 5AA

A huge thank you to everyone who has been involved in making this novel a reality: to Alice, Caro, Emma and Shay for reading whatever draft I thrust at you without complaint and for keeping me motivated throughout this whole process. Thank you to my uncle, Andrew, for helping me finance this publication and to everyone who has helped me over the last 15 years, including those no longer here. Lastly, a huge thank you to my mum for everything you've done for me. This clumsy paragraph doesn't even come close to expressing how much the support of all of you has meant to me. I love you all!

Brax, the second largest of the five Worldwide Kingdoms and home to the most influential royal family in the world. Once a small country of only twelve hundred, the Braxian Empire expanded and now there are that many people living in the royal palace alone.

The desert to the south is home to the ruined kingdom of Dracon, once the largest of the five and now only large in the land it covers. Since the fall of Dracon, the people of Brax are now the only magic users left in the world; something that has caused the Braxians many problems over the years. Heading east from Brax is Alsta, the smallest, and even further east is Eriadal. Across the sea to the west is the kingdom of Cimmerian. The relationship between the kings of Brax and Cimmerian has always been rocky at best to say the least and it is considered a time of peace between the countries if they are not baying for each other's blood.

It first began eight hundred years ago when the eldest son of the king of Cimmerian fell in love with one of the princesses from across the ocean. The king of Cimmerian was superstitious: he hated the Braxians' use of magic, believing that it would one day mean the end of the world. He deemed the Braxians thoughtless for using it so lightly, after learning what had happened to the Draconians and how their magic had ultimately destroyed them, and wanted to put an end to all magic users forever. So, when his heir told him that he was in love with one, he gave his son a choice: either give up the woman he loved and take his throne as the new king of Cimmerian or be exiled to Brax and die along with the rest of the heathens.

The prince chose love over his father's will and left for Brax to be with the princess. They were married shortly after his arrival and the princess fell pregnant with their first child—a boy named after his father—a few months later.

Braxian custom stated that the first child of each family would be raised as a magical high priest or priestess and the child possessed magical abilities despite being half-Cimmerian. Determined to leave behind his roots as a Cimmerian and fully accept Braxian culture, the prince took part in rituals to ensure that any other children they were to have would also be born with the same abilities.

The princess and the prince had a further twelve children after the first; although each of them, unlike their eldest brother, only possessed one specific magical skill that their mother and other priests and priestesses taught them to hone. Each child was named after the ruling planet their magic was associated with and, as they grew into adults in their own right, each of them married and began to pass on their specific ability to their children until only those descended from their brother possessed more than one magical ability.

While their eldest brother was versed in the way of politics by their father and was to be next in line for the throne, the twelve were each given their own land to govern and eventually became the heads of the Twelve Houses of Brax. Each of the Houses was represented in the Royal Court by the head for the running of both House and country. The prince and the princess were eventually crowned king and queen and, along with their children, began to expand the country. In a few short years, Brax blossomed into a thriving and fruitful empire by setting trade routes and building relationships with the other kingdoms that the king of Cimmerian had never even considered. Thus, the Braxian Empire was born.

~ *** ~

Years after the Braxian king's exile from his homeland, word reached him that his father had passed away and his younger brother had taken up the throne. He sent a message to his brother to offer his condolences in the hope that he would be able to rebuild their relationship and unite their kingdoms once again.

But his father had been a cruel man.

After the king of Brax had left Cimmerian, his father had taken all of his frustration out on his brother, who now was filled with anger and hatred for the older brother who had abandoned him to this fate and the heathen princess who had bewitched him into leaving. The king of Cimmerian responded to his brother's message by declaring war on Brax, vowing not to rest until their heretical trickery was at an end and his brother was dead by his hand.

War Broke Out. All those willing and able to fight for their country took up arms against the invading armies of Cimmerian. Brax was strong but the hatred of the king of Cimmerian was stronger and, after a gruelling battle, the king of

Brax fell. It was then that his eldest child—now a strapping young man of twenty-five—took up his father's throne and, along with his siblings, devised a new tactic that would ensure their victory.

He told his brothers and sisters that he wanted the strongest and most gifted member of their growing Houses to represent them. All of them wanted to avenge their father's murder so each of them took up the proffered position. They were to use the gifts that they were born with, however meagre they might seem compared to other members of the army, to overcome their enemies. They were a new kind of fighter: one who trained and honed their one skill until they were the strongest in the world. They were the Neo Warriors.

With the Neo Warriors unleashing their full potential, the Cimmerian army fell and the king was captured. He was to be sentenced to death, but the new Braxian king and his siblings found that they did not have it in their hearts to kill their uncle, despite the atrocities he had caused. He was shown mercy and allowed to live but on the condition that he abdicate and turn his throne over to his eldest child: his daughter. The Cimmerian king reluctantly agreed and negotiations of peace began between the two kingdoms that lasted for a good few decades before another king took the throne and they both decided to try to kill each other once again.

With the war over, the Neo Warriors returned to lead their Houses as they had done before but they all agreed that they needed to be prepared for the next time the Cimmerians decided that the fiendish Braxians should not be allowed to live. One member of each House between the ages of eighteen and thirty was selected to represent their House as part of the king's army: young enough to fight, old enough to die.

When a Neo Warrior turned thirty-one, or if they were killed in action, they would be replaced by the next, to be selected between those ages, more often than not the next member of their family. They continued to train themselves to be the strongest in the world; that way, if war were to break out again then they would be ready to fight for their king and country.

This is where I now find myself...

Part One

Chapter 1

"Ari…" a whispering voice sings. "Ari…"

I hear my door creak open a little more, surprisingly loud in my otherwise silent room.

No!

None of this! I don't want this!

I pull my covers over my head, trying to block out what's happening and make it go away. If she thinks I'm asleep, maybe she'll leave me alone…

No such luck.

"Ari…" Soft footsteps pad across the floor before a heavy lump jumps on top of me with a quiet squeal of delight. "Ari!"

"What do you want, Trista?" I groan into the sheets. She rolls onto her back, still on top of me, crushing me underneath her.

"Are you awake?" she asks.

"You know I am," I grumble in response.

"Good." I can hear the grin in her voice…bitch.

"Why are you here? You have your own room down the corridor—go back to it!"

" I wanted to talk to my best friend," she says as if that should have been obvious. Best friend… She isn't my best friend; she's a demon who likes to wake me up at ungodly hours of the morning.

"But it's…" I turn as best as I can with her on top of me, so I can blearily look at the clock on my bedside table, just able to read it in the moonlight coming through my windows. My jaw drops. "Oh my god! It's four in the morning!" I shove her off and roll onto my back. "Go back to bed, Trista!"

"Don't want to." She flops back down on top of me again, not perturbed by being pushed off in the slightest. At least this time I just have a face full of hair rather than one of her knees in my spine. "The ocean is calling me so I must respond."

Shoving her off again, I roll over onto my side so that my back is to her. She won't want to drape herself over me when there's a chance that I can shove my elbow into her stomach.

"Then, by all means, answer it; leave and let me go back to sleep."

I wait, hoping to hear her go but she doesn't. Instead she wriggles under my covers and rolls over, so that her chest is pressed against my back. She slings an arm over me and leans her head on my shoulder before hooking one of her feet between my calves and I'm instantly hit by how freezing cold her feet are. I try to wriggle free but she tightens her hold so I can't get away. "Get off me!" I hiss. "What do you want?"

"Aren't you excited?" she asks, hugging me tighter. I really don't want to play this game right now. Not when she's woken me up, climbed into bed with me, made me cold and, most definitely, not at four in the bloody morning!

"No."

"Oh you're no fun! Why not?" she asks. Her grip slackens, giving me enough room to roll over to face her.

"Because, and I believe I've made this point already, it's four in the morning!"

Trista just sighs and rolls her eyes. "How can you not be excited?"

"Because I *was* sleeping!"

"But it's a big day tomorrow!" She looks horrified that I'm not as excited as her before thinking for a moment. "Or today I suppose it is now."

"You're like a child," I sigh.

"Oh don't pretend you're not excited," she says giving my shoulder a playful shove.

"I'll be excited at a reasonable hour," I groan. I'm not very good first thing in the morning and Trista bloody well knows this—we've known each other since we were babies!

Trista is my best friend (despite what I say about her when she wakes me up in the small hours of the morning to talk about stuff that really could wait until after dawn). We practically live together; we've been inseparable since we were about five years old and she's almost like a second sister to me. We're quite different though: Trista is a lot more outgoing than I am, despite being a little over a week younger than me—especially around new people—over the years she's made me more sociable and she is one of the people that I would do absolutely anything for, even if she does keep waking me up in the middle of the night.

She rolls over onto her back and stares up at the ceiling for a moment, sighing wistfully, before she turns back to me. "Do you realise that in a few short hours one of us could be engaged to one of the most eligible sons of the De'Latore family and one of us could be the new Neo Warrior to represent the House of Neptune?" she asks. She grabs the edge of the covers and hugs them to her chest, barely able to contain her excitement.

I smile at her and roll my eyes. She's such a kid sometimes, especially when she gets excited—which is all the time. She's like a puppy and hasn't changed at all in the last thirteen years.

"Yes," I reply, "I do." It hasn't escaped my notice, no. "And one of us could also become the new Head of the House."

"I know which one I'd rather be," she says, staring up at the ceiling again, completely ignoring what I've just said. "Can't you just picture it? Me walking down the aisle to become Mrs Jackson De'Latore? Oh god, I'd love it! We'd have a huge wedding and eight beautiful children."

"Eight?" I ask in astonishment. She knows where these hypothetical kids are all going to be coming from, right?

"Well," she says after a moment's thought, tapping a delicate fingertip against her lips, "maybe not eight but we're going to have lots and all the other girls will be really jealous because I'll have a gorgeous important husband."

I laugh quietly and roll onto my back so I'm also staring up at the ceiling. "Yeah well I know which one I'd rather have."

"Oh yeah?" Trista asks. She rolls over to stare at me and leans her head on her hand, propping herself up on her elbow so that she can grin cheekily down at me. I can't see her very well—the moon must have gone behind a cloud—but I can tell that she's grinning. She knows me too well. She knows exactly which one I want to do and she knows why too. It's not like I've ever made a habit of keeping it a secret, not from Trista anyway, and considering the vast amount of Neo Warrior memorabilia decorating my room it's incredibly obvious. Trista and I tell each other everything and have done for years so of course I would confide this dream in her, she just wants to hear me say it out loud.

"I'd rather be a Neo Warrior," I say. Get married at eighteen and settle down for the rest of my life or go off, travel the world and have loads of really cool adventures? It's a no-brainer.

"You only want to be a Neo Warrior so you can meet Luciana Van Garret and the rest of them," Trista teases, giggling.

I glare at her. "That's not the reason," I say.

"It totally is and you know it," she giggles. I scowl at her in return. "Oh come on! You know I'm right, you've told me so on numerous occasions that you want to meet her and your room is like a freaking museum with all this crap."

"It's not the *only* reason," I mumble, turning to meet the eye of one of the posters that practically cover my walls, which also just so happens to be of Luciana. It's not but it's definitely up there on my list of reasons why I want to be a Neo Warrior.

Luciana Van Garret, the representative Neo Warrior for the House of Mercury, is one of the coolest people in the world! She's a sky pirate Captain with her own airship, that she commands! She has the coolest clothes, she's ridiculously gorgeous and (from what I've heard and read about her) she's really nice and funny. Luciana Van Garret is my idol! I have pictures of her up on my bedroom walls, I read everything about her and know practically everything that has been published in interviews, so getting to meet her in person would make my life!

If I could be half as cool as she is, then I'd be happy and if I got to not only meet her but travel around the world with her and the rest of the Neo Warriors, it would be so amazing! To be considered in the same league as them would be one of the biggest accomplishments of my life; they're all so powerful, talented and everybody loves them. Not only that, my grandma, my aunt and my cousin, Michael, have all been Neo Warriors so it would be amazing to be able to continue the family tradition. I think my granddad would like that too so it will either be me or my older sister, Harmony.

"You know there is still every chance that Harmony could get any of those positions, right?" I sigh, tearing my eyes away from Luciana mid-flight and turn back to Trista. "Plus tradition states that the line of Neo Warrior succession should be passed down to the next oldest person between the age of eighteen and thirty in the family."

"I guess so but she's *way* older than us so if they did pick her for the Neo Warrior position she wouldn't be one for very long because she'd have to retire and come home in a couple of years," Trista says.

"Five years is still quite a long time," I reply but Trista does have a very good point. Harmony is twenty-five at the moment, soon to be twenty-six, so if she were to be chosen as the next Neo Warrior it wouldn't be all that long before they would have to think about reselecting. "Do you really think they'd gamble on one of us though?"

"I would have thought it would be in their best interest *to* gamble on one of us," she says with a shrug.

"How so?"

"Think about it," she says, "we've both *only* just turned eighteen. That means, unless something were to go horribly wrong, they won't have to reselect for like another thirteen odd years."

"I guess so." I hadn't thought of it that way before. Realistically, I still think it's incredibly unlikely that either of us *will* be picked for Neo Warrior (as much as I would like to be) but she does have a point. That would probably be my granddad's way of thinking anyway. It's the way she said 'unless something were to go horribly wrong' that has my stomach knotting. 'Horribly wrong' is why we're even being considered for this in the first place…

Also, I'm not super happy with the prospect of suddenly becoming someone's wife at eighteen and not getting a chance to get off this island and see the world, because I probably wouldn't be able to do so for a good few years if I did get married; there's loads of rituals and ceremonies I'd have to take part in. At the same time, I don't want to stay here and become Head of the House (not that I think it's particularly likely I'll get that either but they've got three positions they need to fill with the three of us to choose from). Really, I want to be a Neo Warrior…

"Can we talk about something else?"

"I thought you wanted to go back to sleep," Trista teases and I can see her grinning as the moon shines through the window again.

"Are you going to let me?" I ask in return.

"Nope," she giggles.

"Then I guess I'm awake now."

Trista squeals softly with delight again, flopping back down onto her back starting to make plans for the potential wedding she might have to Jackson De'Latore if she is selected for the inter-House marriage. I have every intention to listen and engage but I can already feel my eyelids drooping again. Leaning back against the pillows, I get comfy and let Trista's chatter wash over me. She doesn't seem to be expecting me to answer her and appears content with my hums of agreement so I let her chatter lull me and I slowly drift back off to sleep.

I hate formal wear. Ever since I was little, I have always hated formal wear. It's too damn uncomfortable and there's always something that doesn't quite fit properly, which makes breathing, leaning forward or sitting down virtually impossible. I also find that, no matter what I do or how I stand, I always end up with some part of my underwear riding up my butt and today's full length, too-tight dress (an old hand-me-down from Harmony) is no exception.

I try not to fidget as I stand between Harmony and Trista (with little success) lined up in front of all twenty members of Neptune House's High Council along with high standing members of the public who have been personally invited to witness today's meeting. It's a little unnerving that there are so many people here who have come just to see how the rest of my life is decided but I should have expected this being one of the daughters of a prominent Neptunian family.

Every household in Brax has a High Council. They are twenty people strong and mostly made up of members of the most influential and prominent families (ex-Neo Warriors, their families and the like) and their sessions tend to be kept private apart from grand announcements like this. The High Council oversees what happens in the household and the surrounding land owned by that household. I'm not in front of them very often but when I am it's very rare that there is someone present who doesn't know who I am. Considering that both of my parents are on the council it's hardly surprising. Two out of my three aunts and all three of my uncles are members. Both Trista's mother and her older brother, Maxwell, are members along with both of her aunts. My granddad is the Head of the House and my grandma used to be on the council as well, after she retired from her position as Neo Warrior, until she died about three years ago. I guess having this many family members making up the High Council sort of makes me, Trista and Harmony quite important in the grand scheme of things and we will probably all end up on the council at some point.

I don't want to be a council member though, not yet at least. It will be so boring—lots of arduous meetings in stuffy rooms meeting even stuffier people from the other households, the mainland and the Royal Court. I want more out of my life than sitting in the same room forever. I want to go places but not to spend my time looking at the world out of windows. I want to meet new people and immerse myself in their cultures, not spend my entire time in meetings discussing topics I have no real interest in and wishing the time away.

I really should be concentrating on what my granddad is saying—considering that it's about my future and all—but I'm so tired from Trista climbing into bed with me and proceeding to talk my ear off until dawn broke (not to mention that she hogs the covers), and I'm distracted by the fact that my underwear has decided that it wants to live up my butt crack, that I'm not really here anymore. My brain has jumped off the itinerary train and is already off travelling the world, being anywhere but here.

God, I want to be out there! Out on the road with nothing but a map, a compass and a change of clothes. There is only one way I can see this meeting ending with a desired outcome for me: I become the next Neo Warrior, get to escape the island and see the world, Trista gets to marry the De'Latore guy (which will make her very happy) and Harmony… Well, who knows what Harmony wants out of this.

She barely said anything to me as we were getting ready this morning aside from to give me a smack around the back of the head and to tell me to stop fidgeting with my dress. Anyone would think I was eight, not eighteen. Harmony and I used to get on really well when we were younger and then she hit fifteen and stopped spending time with me: she threw herself into training and seemed to spend all of her time shunning the fun things that we used to do. I don't know what made her change. She very rarely spoke to me about her feelings and, not going to lie, it still hurts a bit. I tried talking to her as I got older but that never amounted to anything.

We were like best friends and every moment that wasn't spent with Trista was spent with her. She used to read to me before we slept, do fancy things with my hair when we had to get dressed up, and let me come into her bed when I was scared. I used to idolise her as much as I now idolise the Neo Warriors. When she suddenly changed like that, I thought it was something I had done but I didn't really understand; I was only eight at the time. Eventually, after unsuccessfully trying to find out just what I had done wrong and simply getting snapped at in response, I gave up and spent more of my time with Trista.

Harmony does look really pretty though, in a long, figure hugging pale blue dress with all her hair pulled back into a high ponytail and radiating confidence, like she already knows the outcome of this meeting. Both her and Trista are stunning. Trista's dress is a sea green colour and comes down to her knees with a puffed out skirt and she has her hair (the same colour as the dress) hanging about her shoulders in ringlets. I probably scrub up quite nicely too, in one of Harmony's old ice blue dresses (also a similar shade to my hair, which I've left loose), but I'm trying too hard to remove my underwear from between my bum cheeks without being noticed to really think about it too much.

My god, this is uncomfortable!

"Now, the reason why we are all present today," my granddad says. "We will fill the open positions for three newly appointed officials of the House of Neptune."

Finally, the moment I've been waiting for! I stiffen slightly but I don't think it's noticeable. I can feel Trista practically trembling with excitement beside me and I'm right there with her. I take a deep breath and try to keep my face relatively neutral. It does help that my granddad has a very soft and lilting voice, which is incredibly calming. There is something so comforting about his voice—even though he's about to hand me a fate that will determine the rest of my life I feel strangely at ease.

"After much deliberation, the High Council has unanimously decided which of the three standing before us—Harmony Sirenia, Ariana Sirenia and Trista Alantisté—will fill the post of the new Head of the House, who will be joined in matrimony with our esteemed friends from the House of Pluto, the De'Latore family, and who will represent us as the next Neo Warrior among the ranks of the royal army," my granddad says.

"First the post of the new Head of the House, taught to follow Neptunian law as well as Braxian law and will take over the position currently held by Arthur Sirenia, when he steps down in a few months' time," Trista's mother says. "Step forward Harmony Sirenia."

Say what?

I try not to let my jaw drop and keep my face neutral. I don't know what I had expected but it wasn't that and I'm clearly not the only one as whispers begin to start spreading around the council chamber.

Honestly, I had sort of expected Harmony to be chosen as the new Neo Warrior. She's older than both me and Trista, has more experience and has had longer to prepare for it, not to mention she's been training for the last ten years plus there's the whole tradition thing. She's also hot as hell so it would have made sense if she had been chosen for the marriage too. I mean, who in their right mind is going to turn her down? She's practically goddamn royalty on this island (I mean all three of us are but that's not the point). Harmony is quite literally the best that we have over the age of eighteen so why is she being shoved to a desk job?

I watch as Harmony gracefully makes her way over to stand in front of the council's bench, the train of her dress flowing behind her as if she were walking through a river. For a moment, I wonder if she is actually using magic on it to make it do that. It seems a little excessive but at the same time totally something that Harmony would do as she knows people are watching.

The prospect of Harmony becoming Head of the House is weird. I'd never thought about anyone other than my granddad being Head of the House and now that it's going to be my sister it's strange, to say the least. Trista said last night that it would be stupid for them not to pick her for this—give the other jobs to fresh blood and all that—but I guess I still expected tradition to be what decides our futures more than anything else. Realistically I didn't think about it until now because I never wanted to think of the prospect of having to sit through this whole ceremony as it's quite nerve racking.

A few feet away, Harmony stops in front of the huge council bench and dips herself in a graceful curtsey before looking back up.

"Do you, Harmony Sirenia, accept this position of future Head of the House of Neptune along with all the responsibilities that go with it and will carry out the position to the best of your abilities until you are of retirement age or death takes you?" one of the council members asks (amazingly not one of the ones directly related to me).

"I accept this position and all the responsibilities that go along with it until I reach retirement age or death takes me and I thank you greatly for your consideration," she says. She told both Trista and I this morning that we have to be polite when we speak to the High Council (again Harmony treating me like I'm eight, not eighteen) and that script seems as good as any so when it's my turn I'll probably just say something similar. Up in the centre of the bench my granddad nods at Harmony and smiles.

"You will be granted a provisional position on this council, where you will learn our ways, customs and traditions, until you are ready to take over from me and your training will commence at the beginning of next month," he tells her.

Harmony gives the council another small curtsey before she turns and makes her way back to where Trista and I are standing. I smile at her but she won't meet my eye and when she comes to stand beside me she's stiff, closed off and there is a hardness in her eyes like she's trying to hold in anger; a complete contrast to how she was a few moments ago. I should do or say something to her but I don't think I can without drawing attention to the both of us and that will just annoy her even more. She's not happy about this, no doubt about that (just one look at her face is enough to say that she's not), but I don't know what I can do.

Nothing right now, I'll just wait until afterwards when we can talk.

"Secondly," my mother says, her gentle voice lightening the tense mood that has descended between Harmony and I and some of the crowd behind us, "for the proposed marriage to Mr Jackson De'Latore: first son of the House of Pluto. Step forward Trista Alantisté." Well, that *was* to be expected.

Trista gasps softly beside me. She casts a quick glance in my direction, eyes wide with shock and confusion. Clearly she has no idea what she's supposed to do or how she's supposed to react; getting exactly what she hoped she would and not knowing how to deal with it. I can't fault her for that. I gesture with my eyes towards the council's bench and she seems to snap back to herself. She gives me a tiny nod before she makes her way over to stand in front of them, looking completely composed on the outside but I can see the slight tremor in her legs, the only thing to show her nerves.

"Please step forward Mr Jackson De'Latore," my uncle Christian says.

There is movement from the back corner of the room and a tall, well-built man comes forward to stand next to Trista. I hadn't even realised that he was there!

Guess that's Jackson… He *is* quite the hunk—standing a head and shoulders over Trista he's all hard defined muscle that can be seen quite clearly under his shirt with his long dark hair scraped back into a low ponytail. He's also got cheekbones and lips to die for. I can't see his eyes from here but if they're anything like the rest of his face they're probably gorgeous as well. Trista turns to face him and, even from over here, I can see her jaw drop and her eyes light up as she looks up at him.

That extra foot and a half he's got on her must be making her incredibly happy.

I smile to myself, I'm glad she's happy with this outcome.

"Do you, Trista Alantisté, accept this decision to be joined in matrimony with Mr Jackson De'Latore of the House of Pluto?" my father asks.

"I accept this decision and thank you for your consideration," Trista says, her voice a little more breathy than normal.

My father nods before he turns to Jackson. "Do you, Jackson De'Latore, accept this decision to be joined in matrimony with Trista Alantisté?"

"I accept this decision and thank you very much for your consideration," Jackson replies smiling down at Trista. Oh, he has a nice voice: all resonant and masculine and powerful.

I can see Trista trying not to visibly shiver at the sound but still prickling and blushing slightly all the same. I must admit this man is a hunk and if I had a voice like that whispering in my ear then I would probably find it very hard not to blush too (especially with the kind of things Trista's mind will jump to).

"The two of you will have a formal announcement in both the House of Neptune, the House of Pluto and in the Royal Court before completing a trial period of living together for two months to see if you will work as a match without fatal disagreements," Mum says. "If you survive that then both Houses will begin preparations for the wedding."

"Thank you for your consideration and thank you for granting me this honour," Trista says, inclining her head at the council. Mum nods at her and Trista turns to look at Jackson. He takes her hand and presses a gentle kiss to the back of it and even from here I can tell that she's blushing profusely. Jackson is everything she could have possibly asked for and more—tall, dark, handsome and built like a barge. Hell if this is what *he* looks like, and he's not a soldier, I can't even begin to imagine what the Neo Warrior from the House of Pluto looks like in real life! Guy must be built like a fortress! I mean I have pictures of Ellis De'Latore up on my wall but pictures won't do the real thing any justice.

Jackson smiles down at Trista, still holding onto her hand, and he seems very pleased with her too. I can't imagine having to live with someone for two months if there wasn't at least a spark to begin with. When I finally get married, I certainly want to do it because I'm in love with the other person, not out of some political obligation. Not that I think Jackson and Trista won't end up falling in love: everyone who meets Trista loves her and, judging by the way she's looking at him, Trista's already diving in head first with Jackson.

I guess that's why they do trials first though. It would do no one any good to have a political marriage between people who have the magical abilities to kill each other if they hate each other enough. That would only lead to sparking a civil war and, though things have been peaceful lately, we still have the Cimmerians to worry about without fighting against the other Houses.

Trista comes back to stand with me and Harmony while Jackson retreats to his previous position at the back of the room. I lock eyes with her and she's practically screaming with joy through the look on her face. Grinning back at her

I'm also trying to hold my excitement in. I know that look: that look means she wants to jump around with me and scream until neither of us have any energy left. Unfortunately we have to be prim and proper and behave with decorum at a formal ceremony like this. No time to go crazy, especially as there's only one position left and only one of us standing here without one. It feels like my heart is going to explode out of my chest: I'm so excited and I don't think I'm ready for this. By process of elimination, I know what I'm about to be handed but there is a good chance I could just be dreaming.

"Finally for the position of the next Neo Warrior to represent the House of Neptune in the Royal Army," my granddad says. This is it! "Step forward Ariana Sirenia." Oh my god!

I'm not ready for this! I'm *so* not ready for this!

I take a deep breath and pinch the side of my leg just to make sure I'm not dreaming. It hurts. This is real.

I should have expected this as soon as Trista was announced for the inter-House marriage. I should have mentally prepared myself while I was watching her and Jackson. Really I should have mentally prepared myself for the potential of every position long before now, as soon as I found out this would happen, because right now all I can concentrate on is trying to remain as calm as possible and not freak out.

I want to look at either Trista or Harmony for extra confirmation that this is actually happening and I haven't just fallen asleep but I don't. Harmony is practically seething beside me so I definitely don't want to look at her and Trista will probably be trying to keep calm like me. Taking another deep breath I slowly make my way over to stand in front of the council's bench. Muttering starts up from the crowd and there are a few gasps but I try to ignore it.

Every step feels as if I'm travelling miles; the distance stretching much further than it actually is and I become more and more painfully aware that every eye in the room is now on me. Well, they already had been but now I'm even more aware of it. It feels terrifying but the more I walk the easier it starts to become. Confidence begins to seep through me. These people are putting all their faith in me that I can do this. Check me out, I'm a Neo Warrior!

Having said that just walking that short distance also makes me so painfully aware of everything else as well: how hot it is in this room, despite the high ceiling and the fact it's so poorly insulated most of the time. I'm especially aware of it in this stupid dress, which seems intent on clinging to all the wrong places and sticking to my skin. My palms are sweating and the back of my neck is sticky underneath my hair (really I should have worn it up but I didn't want to look any more like a younger version of Harmony than I already do) and my underwear is still up my butt! I feel like crying, jumping for joy and throwing up all at the same time and I'm not quite sure which one I want to do first.

Finally I stop in front of the council's bench—have they always been that high up? It feels like I'm standing in front of a mountain—and curtsey clumsily. Am I shaking? It feels like I'm shaking. I hope no one else can tell if I am. Oh god that would be embarrassing! Oh god! This is actually happening! I am actually standing in front of the Neptunian High Council and a room full of witnesses and I am going to be named the next Neo Warrior. It's all I've wanted since I first saw Luciana Van Garret fly over the island when I was ten and she had first become a Neo Warrior. Of course I didn't know her name back then but I knew she was a Neo Warrior and I knew she was someone cool.

I'm so overwhelmed I have no idea what I'm supposed to do so I take another deep breath and concentrate on actually breathing, getting my words out and not making a total idiot of myself in front of everyone.

"Do you, Ariana Sirenia, accept the position of representing the House of Neptune among the Royal Army as our new Neo Warrior along with those of the other Houses until you reach the age of retirement or death takes you?" Trista's mother asks. I take another deep breath. I'm desperate to settle my nerves because I'm pretty sure that if I don't consciously keep breathing then I'll forget and pass out and that would be so uncool, especially if I do before I've accepted the post. They might reconsider after that.

I slam my hand over my heart in the salute of the Braxian army, hardened eyes staring up at them. I'm a soldier now, this feels right. "I accept this position and thank you very much for your consideration. I am deeply honoured," I say, my words tumbling out in a slightly garbled rush to leave my mouth. I'm too giddy to think about what I'm saying and when I drop the salute and go to incline my head I go down a bit too far so that I'm practically bowing.

Nice one moron!

Wincing I feel heat creep up the back of my neck again. I'm sure Harmony is internally sniggering at me and Trista more than likely wants to roll her eyes and smack herself in the face. God, I am such a loser! I can't even hold it together for the three minutes it takes to do all the formal stuff without making a complete fool of myself! Must try harder and work on that before I meet the others…

"You will begin preparations to leave for Mainland Brax and the capital by the end of the week where you will begin your military training under Commander Caspian Feioré of the House of Mars," Granddad says. "Once that is complete you will be given the title and duties of Captain along with the other Neo Warriors if Commander Feioré is happy with your performance and progress."

"Thank you again for the opportunity," I say and curtsey again. I turn and make my way back to Trista and Harmony before I can embarrass myself further.

I lock eyes with Trista and give her a pointed look. She gives me one back that seems to say 'I know right'. I don't think either of us can quite believe that we have gotten exactly what we wanted and we both just want to jump and scream in excitement but still can't for propriety's sake so I don't try to stop the grin that spreads across my face. Glancing over at Harmony she seems to be purposefully not looking at me so I ignore her and slip into the space between her and Trista before turning back to the High Council.

"All three of you step forward," my father says.

Really? They couldn't have got Trista and Harmony to come to me rather than making me go back and forth?

We step forward to where I was only moments before and stare up at the council's bench. This must surely be the end, there can't be a whole lot left for them to say to us now. I really want to get out of this dress and burn off some of this excitement.

"Each of you has been granted a position of great honour and you have chosen to accept them," Granddad says. "You will carry them out with the honour and decorum befitting a member of the House of Neptune and you will not bring shame upon the great name of our House, carved by generations before us."

"We will do as you wish and we will not let you down," we all say in unison. I try not to giggle at how absurd the three of us sound all speaking at the same time. That would be so inappropriate right now.

"That I do not doubt," my granddad says smiling. "The three of you are dismissed to begin your preparations. Council will take a short recess and will commence with just members of the High Council in five minutes. All rise."

Everybody in the room stands along with us and raises their right fist to the ceiling in the salute of our House.

"For the honour of Neptune: glory under the seas," the entire room chants before dropping their hands.

There is a shuffling and scraping of chairs against the floor as everybody moves and, as one, Trista, Harmony and I turn and make our way out of the huge hall, all eyes still on us even though everyone is heading to leave themselves. We head back to the large room we had been waiting in before going into the ceremony. It's not very far away, which I'm thankful for, because I don't think I can contain this excitement for much longer. As soon as the heavy wooden doors close behind us I let out a long breath that I didn't realise I had been holding while Trista lets out a high-pitched squeal of excitement. She throws her arms around my neck and hugs me tightly, giggling. "Can you believe it?" she squeaks in my ear. "I'm getting married!"

"I know," I laugh and hug her back.

"And you're a Neo Warrior!"

"I know!"

"This is so amazing!"

"I know!"

"We have so much that we need to think about now," Trista says. "This is the first day of the rest of our lives."

"I know," I say. It's all I can seem *to* say at the moment. "This is—"

"Will you two give it a rest?" Harmony snaps, cutting me off.

Both Trista and I turn to look at her. She has her arms folded over her chest (making her boobs look enormous, no idea why she's doing it like that—we're the only people here) and she looks down her nose at us like we're a pair of annoying children who are acting up.

"We're just celebrating, that's all," I say.

"Well, do it later, we're officials now," she says. "There is a certain way you should be acting and squealing like pigs is not one of them."

"Harmony…" I begin. I don't know what to say to her. She looks really angry and I still can't figure out why. She's been standing there seething since she was told she is the new Head of the House. This time she doesn't even bother to answer me, just clicks her tongue in disgust and heads over to the door, wrenching it open, her heels clicking angrily against the marble floor. "Hey Harmony…" I call after her.

"Save it," she says giving me a furious, fleeting look over her shoulder, "I have a new position to prepare for, I suggest that you do the same." With that she leaves the room, letting the door slam behind her.

I stare at the closed door, not knowing what to do. Should I go after her or would that just make things worse? What *is* her problem? I continue to stare until I feel Trista wrap her arms around my neck from behind and she places her chin on my shoulder.

"What's up her butt?" she asks.

"I don't know," I reply quietly, my voice thick with the tears starting to prick the corners of my eyes. I thought this moment would have been different…

Is Harmony angry because I was made the new Neo Warrior? Or is she angry at Trista because she wanted to marry Jackson? I'd always thought she didn't care that much about either of those things, but she obviously did.

"So what do you want to do to celebrate our newfound roles as Neptunian officials?" Trista asks, breaking the tension.

I shake off any thought of Harmony and turn to grin at her. "First I want to get out of this stupid dress," I say, "and then I want to eat my body weight in food."

"Then clearly, we are on the same page," she says, linking her arm with mine.

"Great minds think alike," I say.

"True."

"To the kitchens then!" I point theatrically in the direction we're heading.

"Hey," Trista asks as we round the corner at the end of the corridor, "is your underwear up your butt too?"

"Oh god, so much," I groan.

"Oh good, I thought it was just me."

Chapter 2

The rest of the day passes in a surreal blur. I spend most of it with Trista, celebrating and relishing being back in my own clothes again. We don't really go in for a lot of ostentatious clothing out here on the island of Neyara (not like they do in some of the other Houses) so anything super fancy that's only likely to be worn a few times that used to belong to an older child inevitably gets passed down to the younger ones. As someone who receives clothes like this it's annoying as nothing ever fits completely right but you get over it as formal occasions are few and far between. However there is also the celebratory dinner tonight held in our honour that I need to look presentable for.

Dinner is a horrendous affair. Everyone spends their time congratulating Trista, myself and Harmony but every time someone brings up me being a Neo Warrior I can practically feel Harmony glaring daggers at me. Trista is up the other end of the table to me talking to Jackson, the two of them making eyes at each other. It's rather adorable and they are going to have no trouble hitting it off when they start their trial. I spend most of the night talking to my ex-Neo Warrior aunt, Carla, about what to expect when I get to the mainland: basic training and such. It sounds like hard work but, by the sound of it, Neo Warriors also party hard as well.

After dinner is over, I retreat to my room to start packing my things. I say packing…what I end up doing is actually closer to staring at my empty suitcases with all of my clothes strewn around the room trying to work out what I'm going to need, what still fits me and what I should just throw away. I've been at it for a good half hour and all I've managed to accomplish is shoving every single pair of socks and underwear I own into a pile on top of my pillows. Then I have the sudden realisation that I don't have anything that looks even remotely appropriate for combat. I have one kit I use as sparring gear but not a lot else.

A soft knock at the door catches my attention making me turn and see my mum standing in the doorway smiling at me. I've been told that I look the spitting image of her when she was my age and I'm okay with that. She's gorgeous: tall and willowy with a smile that makes you instantly comfortable and soft turquoise eyes. Her hair, which she keeps out of her face by pulling the top layer back and up, is a tiny bit greener than mine is—I take after my dad in that respect—but other than that we basically look the same. We still get that 'are you two sisters' joke from market sellers trying it on when we go down to the docks together. I smile back at her, a little embarrassed at my clear lack of organisational skills.

"Need a hand?" she asks, her voice as lilting and soft as it has ever been. I don't think I've ever heard her raise her voice once, she can just silence people with a look if she has to.

"Nah," I lie, waving her off confidently. "I've got this."

"Do you really?" she asks, raising an eyebrow at me and folding her arms over her chest.

"Totally," I say, grinning.

"And this is what?" she chuckles. "The elimination process?"

"Something like that."

Laughing the same musical laughter I've heard all my life she pushes herself off the door frame and comes over to stand next to me. Moving some of my clothes she sits me down on the edge of the bed and brushes a lock of hair behind my ear.

"Do you want me to help speed it up?" she asks as she picks up an old pair of oversized shorts that I stole from my dad for the huge pockets.

"Yes please," I concede as she folds them and puts them into the suitcase. I move some more of my clothes so I can sit behind the suitcase and cross my legs on the mattress. The old stuffed duck I've had since I was a baby, that used to be a bright yellow but is now rather faded, is lying on my pillow so I pick it up and hug it to my chest, watching Mum as she continues to pack. "Hey Mum," I begin after a pause.

"Yeah baby?"

"Is Harmony pissed off at me?"

I can't shake this feeling that it's me in particular and it's been plaguing me all day. The way she acted after we left the council chamber, how she was with me at dinner and the fact that she's been avoiding me ever since sure makes it look as if she is. I haven't tried to talk to her again (apart from to ask her to pass the butter) because, knowing Harmony, it won't get me anywhere aside from dirty looks and snippy comments.

Harmony is stubborn and always has been, especially when it comes to someone younger than her beating her at something. She was furious when our cousin Laurie beat her in a sparring match when she was fifteen and Laurie was thirteen and didn't speak to her for a month. She also seemed annoyed when Laurie got married and announced that she was pregnant about a year ago but didn't quite go as far as to not speak to her. I guess it's something she still hasn't quite grown out of yet.

Mum doesn't say anything for a moment, just continues picking up clothes I'm likely to need, folding them and placing them into the suitcase, obviously thinking over her answer very carefully. "Harmony just needs some time to adjust to the idea of being the new Head of the House," she says.

"Okay…it just seems like she's really angry because I'm the new Neo Warrior," I say, fiddling with the faded blue ribbon around the duck's neck. Ironically it was Harmony who gave me the ribbon when I was five to make Ducky look prettier.

"She'll come around to the idea," Mum says. "The council picked each of you for your positions for a reason."

"What do you mean?"

"Okay, so take Trista," she says. "She was picked for the inter-House marriage to Jackson because she's likeable, pretty and easy for people to talk to without being a push-over. Trista is strong willed, gracious and takes no nonsense if someone tries to underestimate her pleasant nature for weakness. Her marriage to Jackson will further a relationship between both of our Houses and strengthen the bond between their families as well."

"Okay that makes sense." Trista has always been the likeable one, ever since we were little. She was the friendly one and I was the shier one. Little did they know that Trista was (and still is) very good at showing her distaste with people behind barbed compliments that you wouldn't notice unless you were paying close attention.

"Plus she is a hopeless romantic and will adore Jackson," Mum says.

"I think she does already," I say.

"You noticed it too?"

"Everyone noticed," I laugh. "And what about Jackson?"

"Jackson is a very thoughtful, very pleasant man. His extra years have given him experience and earned him respect from his peers. He will take good care of Trista and will treat her like an absolute queen," Mum replies.

"Good," I say. I'm so glad Trista is going to end up with someone decent. "What about Harmony?" I ask after a pause.

"Harmony is also very strong willed and takes no nonsense from anyone. She is objective enough, most of the time, to make decisions based on the facts in front of her rather than her own personal feelings or biases," Mum says. "Underneath her hard exterior she is also very kind and understanding to the plights of others and will put the needs of the many over the needs of the few for the benefit of the House. Once she has gotten round to the idea, accepted it and has been trained by your granddad then she will make a fine Head of the House."

Again that makes sense. Both Harmony and Trista's qualities seem almost obvious now that I think about it. Maybe I'm just too close to the situation to know what I'm supposed to be looking for in a wife, a Head of the House or a Neo Warrior.

"And me?" I ask hopefully.

"Well," Mum says, smiling at me, "you're my special little girl…and we had an extra position open."

"Hey!" I protest.

She laughs and leans over the top of my suitcase to gently flick me in the forehead. I let out an undignified squeak and rub the spot, even though it didn't hurt, pouting at her. This only makes her laugh more before she goes back to packing.

"If I just told you why we picked you then you wouldn't figure it out for yourself along the way and grow as a person and a Neo Warrior," she says.

"So is this like some sort of test?" I ask, cocking my head to the side. "And when I figure it out I'll pass?"

"If you want to call it that," she muses. "You'll work it out eventually but it will be much more of a benefit to you if you discover it on your own. It'll make you stronger, smarter and more prepared to deal with what life throws at you."

"Can you at least give me a clue?" I ask, grinning at her. Smiling, she throws the shirt she has been folding at my head and it covers my face. I pull it off, giggling. Her answer is to raise an eyebrow at me but she can't seem to stop herself from smiling back. She shakes her head and rolls her eyes.

"No I can't, you cheeky bugger," she says.

"Oh please!"

"No!"

"But...what if I mess up?" I ask, suddenly hit by that very unappealing thought and going serious for a second, my smile fading. I still have no idea what it is I'm supposed to be doing. All these years I spent wanting to be a Neo Warrior I never once *really* thought about what I would have to do if I actually became one. It's so much more than the celebrity world they inhabit but that isn't printed in the interviews.

"What makes you think you're going to mess up?" Mum asks. Does she want a list? I can give her a list.

"I don't know," I shrug, sighing. "Lots of reasons."

"Care to share?"

"Maybe because I have no idea what I'm supposed to be doing and I'm woefully underprepared for training with the big leagues. This will be the first time I've done anything that hasn't been on Neyara—hell, this will be the first time I've even *left* Neyara—and I don't want to let you all down and make a complete fool of myself in front of the rest of them." That isn't helped by the fact that they're all so much older than me. The youngest (bar me now) is Samuel Yonglass from the House of Saturn and he's a good three years older than I am.

"Oh baby," Mum laughs softly. She moves my suitcase to the floor and comes to sit down on the bed next to me, pulling me into a hug so I can rest my head on her shoulder. "We picked you for this role because we think you will be good at it. It will take you a little bit of time to find your feet; it does everyone when they're suddenly thrown into a position like this, but you will in the end and you'll do an amazing job. You'll probably even have a good stint as Commander too."

"You think so?"

"I know so," she says. "There's a good few years between you and Samuel so you'll have a couple of years as Commander before you have to retire and you can do a lot in that time if you put your mind to it."

"You think I'll be a good Commander?" I ask.

"I think so," she replies. "Just listen to Caspian and you'll learn from one of the best. He'll teach you everything you need to know. He'll push you because he knows you can do it and you can as long as you don't give up."

"Okay."

"Besides we wouldn't have picked you if we didn't think you could handle it," Mum says before she drops a kiss on the top of my head.

"Thanks Mum," I say, smiling, and hug her back.

"And you know you're going to have everyone on the island rooting for you, don't you?"

"Yeah," I say and feel a little better. Despite what it felt like after an evening of Harmony trying to reduce me to ash with her eyes, no one is waiting for me to fail. They're all behind me and will support me when and if I need it. "You're still not going to tell me the full reason you picked me, like you did with Trista and Harmony, are you?"

"Not a chance in hell," Mum laughs, giving me a shove as she gets up and continues with the packing. "I said you can figure it out on your own and I'm sticking to that. Anyway it would be no fun if I told you."

"Fine!" I groan as I flop down across a load of my clothes. "As long as you're not going to tell Harmony why you picked her either."

"Would I ever show that kind of favouritism?" she asks, smirking at me.

"I don't know," I reply, leaning up on one of my elbows and raising an eyebrow at her. "Would you?"

Mum doesn't say anything. She just fixes me with a slick grin and closes my first suitcase, putting it on the floor before picking up a second and putting it where the other was. My mother: always one for jokes.

~ *** ~

I lie in bed staring up at the ceiling. Honestly I tried to get an early night, but for a number of reasons I can't sleep. After Mum finished helping me pack she left so I went to bed. A combination of tossing and turning and watching the shadows from the moonlight coming in from the window, drifting across the ceiling in interesting patterns leaves me wide awake. Looking over at the clock again I groan: it's barely even midnight! At this rate I'll have another sleepless night and I'm already tired. Why couldn't Trista have crept into my room tonight? Although she's probably with Jackson if she isn't sleeping.

With a sigh I roll onto my side, staring out of the window at the night sky. Maybe I should give up with trying to sleep for now and go for a walk to see if I can tire myself out? At least that way I wouldn't be lying here waiting to fall asleep.

I've been thinking a lot about Harmony. It doesn't matter what Mum says about her needing time: she has a stick up her arse about me being the new Neo Warrior even if she won't say anything. My dad called a few people, including us, into one of the larger rooms for a nightcap after dinner and she barely said anything to me during that either. Having said that most of the conversation was directed at asking Jackson questions about the House of Pluto. He had answered them all dutifully but throughout the whole evening he barely took his eyes off Trista, totally infatuated with her already.

My thoughts then turn to what Mum had said as well about the three of us being picked for our new roles for a reason. I know that's true—she wouldn't have said it if it wasn't—but I'm still confused about the whole affair. I mean, sure, this is all I've wanted for so many years now but whether I actually have the capacity to do it is another story. I mean what if I don't even pass basic training? And what suddenly made the High Council decide to break tradition and pick the me over Harmony?

Sighing again I sit up, running my hands through my hair. Forget it! I can't sleep and I can't keep lying here hoping that eventually I'll drop off. So I slip out of bed and pull on an old pair of shoes I use for sparring and when I go running. Grabbing a jacket from the end of my bed I pull it on before running a brush through my hair. It's been quite chilly at night recently and I don't fancy roaming the corridors in just my pyjamas. I shove my hands into my pockets to keep them warm and leave the room.

Walking around the House at night is actually quite enjoyable. It's peaceful and there is rarely anyone else up which works out perfectly for me because I imagine anyone that I could run into will want to congratulate me and probably stop for a conversation. I'm not overly in the mood to talk to anyone as I'm still reeling a little from the day's events. Considering that I was woken up by Trista at four o'clock this morning I'm surprised that I'm having as much trouble sleeping as I am.

The House that I live in is basically an old converted palace where members of the High Council and their families all live and, considering that most of us come from the same family, it's not that weird for me. It's all I've ever known and I know that I have it really lucky getting to live in a palace with all my family and friends, so it's almost kind of strange that I want to leave when there are people out there who would kill for this kind of life.

People on the island live well though so we're all pretty lucky. We have a lot of resources for fishing and good open trading with both the mainland and the Cimmerians as well as with Alsta and Eriadal. There are some other Houses who have it much tougher than we do but then again the House of Neptune is surrounded by water: our life force, and main source of income and food. Even though it's not a small island by any stretch of the imagination, everyone treats everyone like family and everyone knows the names of all the members of the High Council and their families. Going out into the market, people wave at me and say hello. I always say hello back and if they want to stop and have a conversation, I do. I guess having the rest of Brax knowing my name and what I'm doing isn't going to be so hard to get used to.

Turning a corner I see that the light is still on in my dad's study. He's someone I wouldn't mind sitting down and having a chat with, mostly because we can talk about anything so I quietly make my way over to the ajar door. I don't want to disturb him if he's still up working but as I get closer I hear voices, quite angry voices—one male, his, and one female.

Sneaking closer, I make sure I'm even quieter as I've probably walked in on something I'm not supposed to be hearing. I should turn and leave but as I get closer I realise that the female voice is Harmony's and stop dead in my tracks. What would she want to talk to Dad about this late at night? I need to know so I lean against the wall next to the open door, listening intently.

"Look the preparations have already begun; this decision has been made," Dad says. I hear Harmony scoff and instantly I can guess what this conversation is going to be about.

"But your decision was wrong!" Harmony snaps.

"Oh you think so, do you?" Dad asks and he sounds surprisingly calm at having Harmony speak to him like that.

"I do, yes," she replies.

"Care to enlighten me?" he asks. Despite his calm tone, there is a definite edge to his voice. I have no idea how long they've been arguing but I can tell that he's starting to lose his patience with her.

"What?"

"If you think that our decision is so off the mark, then why don't you enlighten me as to why?" he replies.

"Because she's not right for the position," Harmony splutters. Of course: they are talking about me.

"Oh really?" Dad asks. "How so?"

"She's immature, woefully unprepared to handle herself in a fight, she is too impulsive to make decisions, she doesn't follow orders, she's disrespectful and she doesn't have the magical skill to be able to place herself in league with the likes of Caspian Feioré. He'll send her back to us a laughing stock and then where will we be?"

Thanks for that list, Harm, I wouldn't have said all of those were true but nice to know how you feel.

"She is young, she'll learn," Dad says.

"And what if she doesn't have time?" Harmony asks. "War could break out with Cimmerian tomorrow and if it does she'll come back in a casket."

"There hasn't been a war with Cimmerian for over two hundred years," Dad replies, "and while their current king is on the throne there won't be another either so that is an unnecessary concern. She has time."

"But Dad these concerns *are* necessary," Harmony says.

"And if Ariana had been made Head of the House then we would be standing here having the exact same conversation," Dad says.

"No we wouldn't," Harmony says.

"We certainly should be."

"What do you mean?" Harmony asks. She's going on the defensive now because she's about to get called out for this.

"The complaints you have about Ariana being made a Neo Warrior should be exactly the same as if she were made Head of the House, otherwise you're just being petulant."

"But—"

"So as far as you're concerned, you believe Ariana is unprepared and unfit to fulfil the job of either Neo Warrior or Head of the House and would have been better suited to the proposed marriage?" Dad asks.

"I can hardly see her as somebody's wife either," Harmony says with more than a hint of undisguised derision. Thanks Harm, thanks for that. Clearly she doesn't think I'm suited for anything on offer. I can't help but wonder what she *would* be happy with me doing but let's not open that door.

"That aside I imagine that you would be equally unhappy with the decision if Trista Alantisté were granted either of these positions as well?"

"Well, no but…" She's got no answer and it's totally obvious why.

"Just as I thought," Dad says.

Part of me wants to laugh; Dad's got her sussed and I got the confirmation I needed. She *is* pissed off because she wanted to be the Neo Warrior and instead got lumped with a desk job. Well, that's her problem. Maybe if she had done something beforehand then she wouldn't get called out for pulling this kind of stunt.

"Either way," Dad says after a pause, "our decision is final and we will not go back on it now."

"But Dad…" Harmony begins.

"I said our decision is final," he snaps. "We chose each of you for the positions you were assigned for a reason and we will not back down on that. You were selected to be the new Head of the House because you are well suited to it, much as Ariana is well suited to be our representative Neo Warrior. Of course both of you will require training, it is only natural. If you are unable to make objective decisions without putting your personal feelings before the good of the House, then you will need more training than we originally thought. You will see, in time, that you were both picked specifically to fulfil these roles for a purpose. We will leave it at that and say no more about it. Have I made myself clear?"

"Yes," Harmony says and there is a definite catch in her voice.

To be honest she's doing better than I would be if I received a dressing down like that from Dad. It's so rare that we ever hear either of our parents raise their voices but when Dad is angry he's a force to be reckoned with. It makes me wonder why he wasn't chosen as the next Head of the House but maybe it's because he's already on the High Council and they wanted some new blood coming in.

"Then we have nothing more to talk about," Dad says, his voice much softer.

"No," Harmony agrees begrudgingly.

"I'm glad we understand one another then," he says. "Now please go, I have some arrangements I need to make for both you and Ariana."

"Yes Dad," Harmony says.

I hear her footsteps against the floor, growing louder as she gets closer to the door. Oh no! She's going to walk out of Dad's office any second now and she's going to see me standing here. She'll realise that I've been listening in on their conversation and she's going to be even more furious than she already is! I need to get out of here before the resulting argument wakes up the entire House.

Darting down the corridor I try the handle of the first door I come to. Luckily for me it's unlocked so I slip inside, barely breathing. If she had found me, I would be for it. Not just from her but probably from Dad as well for listening to a conversation that was supposed to be private. I wait, pressing my eye against a tiny gap between the door and the frame so that I can see out into the corridor. I listen to Harmony stalk away from Dad's office, fury in her footsteps, and watch as she passes by.

When I realise I'm in the clear and can no longer hear her, I let out the breath I was holding and place my hand over my heart, leaning against the door, and wait for it to stop pounding. It feels incredibly loud in the otherwise silent room but, aside from Dad, there is no one else around to hear it so I'm still safe. That was way too close for comfort though. She would have screamed the place down if she had found me and probably never spoken to me again.

I think it's been long enough now that I shouldn't bump into her if I go back to my room (after that rush of adrenaline I'm exhausted and I'm pretty sure that I can sleep until morning…or next week). Rubbing a hand over my face I sigh, long and slow, before pushing myself off the door and open it. As I'm about to leave the lamp on the desk suddenly flicks on and I realise that I'm not alone and haven't been since I came in.

Slowly I turn, dreading who I am going to come face to face with and wondering who in the hell is sitting in a deserted room in the dark in the middle of the night, and see my granddad reclining in the chair behind his desk.

Oh balls!

I am in so much trouble!

I didn't even think about who was going to be in this room before I charged in. It should have occurred to me that it was a study (most of the members of the High Council have a study on this corridor) and I should have known that the only reason it was open was because someone was in here but, under the circumstances, I wasn't thinking. I'm going to be in such deep trouble for disturbing him while he was, presumably, asleep. (I mean why else would all the lights have been off?)

My granddad is a mystery to me these days; I sort of remember him from when I was little. He used to spend a lot more time with me and Harmony when we were younger, before he became the Head of the House, but mostly I just remember him as this imposing figure who was always busy and had final say in what goes on around here. It wasn't that he never had time for us after he became Head of the House but rather that that came first, as it should. I remember he used to be really tall—I thought well over six foot—but I don't know if that was just because I only came up to his knees.

Picking up his glasses from the top of the desk he puts them on. He sits forward and peers at me through them in the dim light. I close the door and step a little closer so he can see exactly who it is that came in and disturbed his sleep.

"Oh Ariana," he says when he realises it's me. "What are you doing in here?"

"I…um…"

Should I tell him that I was effectively spying on Harmony complaining to Dad that I'm unprepared to do anything that the High Council could want me to and then ran in here because I'm scared of getting into an argument with her? It's almost laughable really: the brave and fearless Neo Warrior is afraid of conflict with her older sister and runs at the first sign of it.

"I was out for a walk," I say finally. "I couldn't sleep and I thought it might help." It's half true. I just happened to stop, take a detour and listen in on a private conversation that was about me for a couple of minutes.

He nods slowly, clearly knowing that I'm not telling him the whole story. "Walking?"

"Yeah."

"I was working and thought I would rest my eyes for a minute but it seems I may have fallen asleep in my chair," he says, changing the subject. "I'm feeling a little on the stiff side. Would you mind helping an old man up so I can go and sit on the sofa?"

"Sure," I say, a little surprised, and go over to his side.

"Thank you." he says, smiling up at me. "Can you pass me my stick please?"

I pass him the walking stick that is leaning against the desk, just out of his reach. He takes it and, using that and a hand on my arm, he pushes himself to his feet. I walk over to the sofa with him and it's only now I'm closer to him than I feel like I've been in years that I see just how old he's looking. There are more wrinkles than I remember him ever having and, while he used to tower over me, we are now basically the same height. I don't know if that's gravity or I've just grown but I could have sworn he was a giant when I was a child. His movement is slower and it seems as if it takes much more effort now. This must be why he's decided to retire as Head of the House.

"I heard your sister down the hallway having a chat with your father," he says offhandedly, as if he were commenting on the weather, but it's obvious that he knows I heard.

"Oh really?" I ask after a short pause, trying to sound nonchalant. Deny all knowledge and walk away: that totally works, right? He doesn't *know* I heard her...

"Well, I say 'having a chat'," he says, putting his stick down on the small table in front of the sofa. "Harmony could wake the dead when she's angry."

I can't stop myself from snorting with laughter at that. He's not wrong. Harmony can be kind of a shrill bitch when she wants to be, especially when she's angry. That might not have been the most polite or dignified thing to do though. "Sorry," I say, trying and failing not to grin.

"Don't be," he smiles. "I imagine you heard her and what she was discussing with your father."

"Yeah," I say, suddenly becoming very interested in my shoes, "I did..."

"I thought as much," he says, nodding. He pats the vacant space next to him on the sofa and I sit down, perching on the edge at first but falling back into the cushions as he puts his arm around my shoulder and pulls me back down with him. It's such a comfy sofa and I could quite happily fall asleep on it. "Is that why you came tearing in here once she had finished?"

"Little bit," I reply. "I didn't exactly think she would be overly thrilled to see me again after everything that's happened today as well as finding out that I'd been eavesdropping on her conversation on top of that. Thought it was probably best to stay out of her way."

"That was probably a very wise decision," he says. "Harmony is up in arms at the moment but she will come around to the idea in time."

"So people keep telling me," I mutter, fiddling with my thumbnail.

Granddad chuckles. "She may act as if the world has come to an end right now but once she's settled into her own new position, after you've been away for a month or so, and people start referring to her as 'The Right Honourable Harmony Sirenia', she'll have calmed down."

"*The Right Honourable?*" I ask with a raised eyebrow.

"You'd be surprised just how much respect being Head of the House gets you," he says.

"I don't think I would," I laugh; considering how much respect people give the High Council they must love the Head of the House.

"What about you, *Captain*?" he asks.

A huge grin spread over my face. "I don't think I'll ever get used to that."

"You will," he says. "Once you've been called that by everyone for a couple of months and maybe one day even Commander."

Commander Ariana Sirenia… "Now that I *know* is going to take some getting used to," I chuckle.

"You say that now," Granddad says, "but you're young and everything is still very new to you. By the time you're Commander, it'll feel much more natural to have a title precede your name than not."

"It probably will yeah," I say. Honestly, listen to us: talking about me becoming Commander like I didn't just get the job of Neo Warrior this afternoon.

My granddad slowly reaches forward and opens a drawer on the table (one that I wouldn't have known was there even if I had looked for it) and pulls out a small square bottle filled with clear liquid and two small glasses. He opens the bottle and pours some of the liquid into each of the glasses before handing one of them to me.

"Here," he says.

"What is it?" I ask as I take the glass. I lift it to my nose to take a sniff but he stops me. "Don't smell it, just drink it," he tells me.

"Okay."

"Cheers," he says. He holds out his glass and I clink mine against it. In exact synchronicity we both drink, downing the contents in one.

The taste hits my tongue, making my eyes water and the back of my throat burn as I drain the glass. I cough and splutter once I've swallowed it, tears starting to fall down my face. It tastes like aniseed and paint stripper mixed together but with an underlying hint of the gin that Trista and I used to sneak from the kitchens when we thought we could get away with it.

"What was that?" I splutter, my voice hoarse from coughing.

"That was proper Neptunian gin," Granddad laughs as I wipe my eyes, "not that watered down piss that you and Trista have been drinking since you were fourteen."

"You knew about that?" I ask, unable to stop myself from grinning.

"Of course I did."

"How?" We always thought we were being so sneaky when we stole bottles from the stores or kitchen.

"I'm Head of the House," he says with a wink, "I know everything."

"So why the sudden introduction to it now?" I ask.

"Neo Warriors are notorious for liking a drink," he replies, "especially when they enrol a new member. You don't want to pass out on your first night and then spend your first day of training hungover."

I cough again. Wow, that stuff is strong! What if the stuff they drink on the mainland is stronger? God, if I can't even handle this then I'm going to be a mess every time a drink comes out. There's no way in hell I'm going to be able to keep up with the others if they've been drinking like this since they enlisted.

"Hey Granddad," I begin after a pause, when it feels as if my stomach has stopped burning from the alcohol.

"Yes?"

"Why did you decide to go against tradition and pick me?" I ask.

Taking my glass, he pours the both of us another drink without a word before setting the bottle down and rubs his chin. He's getting stubble: I can see, even in this light.

"Why do you think we chose you?" he asks.

Thinking back to what Harmony said to Dad and the list she gave of the reasons why I shouldn't have been chosen does make me question it. I asked out of curiosity but there is a niggling part in the back of my mind that wonders if Harmony might be right: I haven't trained for this, she has. "Because I'm younger than she is," I say after a moment's thought. "Go on?"

Oh god does he want a proper list?

"Well, I'm only eighteen, right? So that means I'll have a full twelve or thirteen years of being a Neo Warrior even though that goes against tradition," I say. "If you had picked Harmony then she would have had to have been replaced in about six years."

"And you think that's the only reason?" he asks.

"I know there are other reasons," I say, "I just don't know what they are right now. I asked Mum but she wouldn't tell me. She said I could figure it out on my own."

"Then we really don't need to be having this conversation," he chuckles. "Some traditions should be broken every once in a while. We decided to take each of your personalities into consideration before we made the decision rather than blindly follow a tradition that we all agreed was outdated. Becoming a Neo Warrior will help you discover your strengths and weaknesses and build on those and we will start by building up your alcohol tolerance."

"Okay."

"If it helps in any way at all," he says as he hands me the full glass again, "it was not a difficult decision to make for any of you, you especially."

"That does yeah," I say smiling.

"Good," he says, clinking his glass against mine before we both down the contents. I cough but not as much as the first time. "This is something you'll learn in time and when you realise it, it'll be so obvious you'll laugh at yourself for ever doubting."

"Any clues now?" I ask hopefully. "You know, to help me along the way?"

My granddad laughs again. "You always were the more entertaining one," he says. "You will fit in just fine with the rest of the Neo Warriors."

"You've met them?" I ask, intrigued.

"Of course," he says. "All the Heads of the Houses meet with the Neo Warriors. We like to know just who is fighting for our country."

Oh my god! My granddad has met Luciana Van Garret! Would he tell me about her if I asked? I'm sure he would: he's proven pretty easy to talk to about everything else I've asked him tonight. He could answer all of the questions I have about them.

But hang on… If Granddad has met the Neo Warriors and all the Heads of the House meet them then eventually Harmony is going to be introduced to them all and I'll have to see her again when she is. What if that's before I've passed my basic training? She'll be so smug and I'll never hear the end of it. That thought alone is enough to bring me back down to earth with a thud.

"So I'll have to come face to face with Harmony eventually then?" I say.

"You can't hide from her forever."

"I know," I sigh. "Can't I just hide from her until I've passed basic training?"

"Better pass quickly," he teases. "Harmony will be looking to finish her own training as fast as possible, probably for the exact reason of wanting to check up on your progress."

"Great…"

"I can see your grandmother in you; you'll pass quickly."

"I won't let you down," I nod, smiling at him. I've heard that she was an amazing Neo Warrior; I'll be fine. Granddad takes my glass, refills it and hands it back to me. He holds his out and I clink mine against it.

"Cheers," I say. I swallow the drink in one, a little more prepared this time for the taste and the burning to hit me now I'm on my third. It still makes me cough and my eyes water, but less so this time. Having said that I probably shouldn't drink much more.

"So," he says once I'm breathing normally again, "anything else you would like to talk about?"

"Can you tell me about the other Neo Warriors?" I ask hopefully. "Like stuff they wouldn't print in the magazines."

"Who do you want to know about?" he asks.

"Luciana Van Garret," I reply without even having to think about it. "Is she really like how she is in interviews?"

He chuckles, clearly not surprised by this in the slightest. "She is," he replies. "Luciana is tall, at least a good few inches taller than you are, and she has these beautiful smoky grey wings that span at least six feet and she likes to talk and have a joke with people…"

I listen with rapt, wide-eyed enthralment. Everything else can wait for tonight. Now I'm quite happy to spend the rest of the evening listening to him talk about Luciana and the others.

Dealing with Harmony can wait until tomorrow.

Chapter 3

The following morning (after my introduction into the world of real alcohol) I'm summoned in front of the High Council again. It's exactly the same as last time but in a slightly smaller room as there is no need for formal witnesses this time. I'm so glad that I'm not hungover for this: while giving me my first real drink Granddad also gave me advice on how to prevent feeling horrific after a night of drinking as well as being able to actually handle my liquor. I took that advice to heart so, thankfully, I'm not swaying where I stand.

Looking up at the council's bench I see Harmony sitting behind Granddad. Obviously the High Council wants her to start her training as soon as possible as much as she does. Can't say that I blame her really: I want to start my training the moment I get to the mainland. If it wasn't for having to actually go there first and getting specific military training then I would start here. I can feel Harmony glaring daggers at me so I don't meet her eye. If she thinks I'm so disrespectful and can't follow orders then I'll show her that I'm not and I can. I'll make sure I'm the best damn Neo Warrior the House has ever seen.

"Step forward Ariana Sirenia," Granddad says, breaking me out of my thoughts. Damn, I probably should have been listening to what was going on beforehand but, give me a break, I got distracted by Harmony. No, that's not an excuse! Off to a great start…I ignore my inner chastising and step forward until I am directly in front of the bench, looking up at them.

"Are you ready to begin your position as our new representative Neo Warrior?" my dad asks.

"I am, yes," I reply. See Harmony, I can be respectful.

"And are you ready to leave for Mainland Brax and the capital as soon as a ship is stocked with food, provisions and resources for our House to trade with upon arrival?" Mum asks.

"I am," I reply again, this time my answer coming out a little gushed. I can't stop myself from smiling up at her. She smiles back and winks at me. Honestly,

I don't think she would want me to be completely stoic in a situation like this—she knows as well as Trista just how much I've wanted this and for how long. I mean, come on, this is cool and she's always said that I look better when I'm smiling.

"Wonderful," Granddad says and he is smiling at me too, clearly proud that I managed to stave off the hangover like he taught me. "The ship should be ready to embark on its journey by the end of the week at the latest."

"I'm packed and ready to go at a moment's notice," I tell him.

"The journey should take you no more than two weeks if the tide is with you," one of the other council members says (a cousin of Trista's father). "We've had weather readers monitoring the tide and have been informed that you'll have a good ride unless there are sudden drastic storms out of our prediction."

"Thank you sir," I say.

"As soon as you reach the mainland you will be met by the Neo Warriors' Second Commander, Katarina Navroe," Trista's mother says. "She will take you from the docks to the capital and, from there, you will go on to complete your training."

"Of course," I nod. Okay so at least I know who I'm supposed to be looking out for. Out of all of them it makes sense that she would be the one to pick me up, being the Second Commander, and I can't wait to finally meet her in person. I can't wait to meet all of them in person but she's a good start. Granddad told me that it's true what they put in the magazines and that she's just as much fun as she is business so having her come to pick me up will be a real help. I don't know why I hadn't thought of asking him for advice before but it was one of the best decisions that I made last night.

"Your training will be intensive and at times it may even be difficult but I know that you'll do an excellent job," Granddad says, smiling at me again and I can see a little twinkle in his eye. It fills me with pride knowing that they're all behind me on this.

"I won't let you down," I say.

"Wonderful," he says again. He looks proud of me already. It's nice to know that he is and it makes me want to continue to make him proud. I can't let any of them down, not when they all believe in me so much. "You're dismissed," he continues. "You may do whatever you wish with the rest of your time on Neyara. We will send for you as soon as the ship is loaded and ready to depart. For now you are free to say your farewells and prepare yourself to start your new life once you reach the mainland."

"Thank you very much sir," I say, bowing slightly. It always helps to throw a 'sir' in there if you're speaking to a member of the High Council, even if they are related to you. Maybe I'm laying it on a bit thick but Harmony said I couldn't be respectful so I am going to show her that she's wrong. This is only ceremonial anyway: just extra pomp and circumstance as I've already accepted the job officially.

I look up at the council's bench and lock eyes with Mum. She winks at me again and I smile before I turn and leave the room. I can't stop that silly grin spreading even further across my face. Maybe I had some reservations about this whole thing last night (and after the way Harmony has been you can hardly blame me) but knowing that everyone else believes in me I know I'm going to be fine. I've wanted it for so long there is no chance in hell that I'm going to screw it up now.

As soon as I close the door of the council chamber behind me something—or more accurately someone—jumps on top of me and I fall to the floor, pulling them down on top of me as I go. I wasn't expecting that and landing on my backside is painful, especially as the person who jumped on top of me is pressing down on my lungs, squashing all the breath out of me and giggling. So of course I don't even need to look to know who it is, especially with the face full of turquoise hair I'm getting.

"Trista," I groan as I try to push her off but to no avail. She's shoving her entire body weight on top of me and she is not light, despite what the petite physique might suggest (probably all those years of swimming and climbing rocks).

"Ari!" she cries, wrapping her arms around my neck and hugging me tightly, cutting off even more of my oxygen.

"What are you doing?" I ask.

"I came to find you," she replies as if that explains everything.

"Okay," I say, "but did you really need to jump on me when you found me?"

"Always."

"You're terrible."

"Oh come on, I wanted to surprise you," she whines.

"Consider me surprised," I chuckle. "So what has prompted this assault?"

"Mum told me you're leaving at the end of the week so that means we only have a few days left with each other before you go. We need to do as much as possible while we still have time," she says.

"Don't you want to spend some time with Jackson?" I ask as she finally gets off me and gets to her feet.

"I spent all of last night with Jackson and I have the rest of my life to spend with him too. You I only have for a couple more days for maybe like the next twelve years or something so I want to spend it with you."

"I'm not going to be away from home for twelve solid years," I chuckle, pushing myself up to a sitting position. "I get leave and can come visit you sometimes."

"Good," Trista says, beaming at me. "I can't not see you for twelve years!"

"Right back at you," I say, holding out my hand to her. She takes it and pulls me to my feet.

"Plus you need to be at the wedding," she says, "both as our representative Neo Warrior and as my Maid of Honour."

"You want me to be your Maid of Honour?" I ask, smiling fondly.

"Of course I do," she replies. "Who else can I rely on to get the rest of the Neo Warriors as strippers for me?"

I laugh. "I don't have anywhere near that kind of influence yet."

"You might do by the wedding," she sings. "Seriously though Ari, you're my best friend. We've been through so much together and you've been a huge part of my life for as long as I can remember. I can't think of anyone else doing a better job and it would be such an honour if you would."

I wrap my arms around her neck and hug her tightly. "Of course I will," I tell her.

"I love you," she says hugging me back.

"I love you too," I whisper into her hair. Pulling away I grin at her "Did you really think I was just going to be gone until I'm thirty?"

Trista shrugs. "I don't know," she says. "I don't know how this works."

"Me neither," I admit. "Guess I'm just going to have to learn and find out when I get to the mainland."

"Guess so."

For a moment, I don't really know what to say and I can tell that Trista doesn't either; we just stare at each other. I'm going to miss her so much when I'm gone. I know I'll make friends with the other Neo Warriors and people I meet but there won't be anyone like Trista. Who else is going to sneak into my room at four in the morning to talk about nonsense?

"So," she says, breaking the silence and trying to lighten the mood, "you've got 'til the end of the week before you leave. That's about four days. What do you want to do first?"

"I don't know, I hadn't actually thought that far ahead!" I laugh, the solemn mood gone.

"Well, you're going to need to do something," she says, giving me a poke in the ribs. "You can't just spend your entire last week here in bed."

"No that would be a waste."

"So what would you like to do?"

"Firstly I think I want some food," I reply. "All these meetings are making me hungry. I was so nervous earlier I could barely eat anything at breakfast."

"Kitchen it is then," Trista grins. She links her arm with mine and together we head off in the direction of the kitchen, hoping to score some food from one of the nicer chefs.

~ *** ~

"Remember the last time we did something like this?" Trista asks as she passes me the bag of biscuits we stole from the store cupboard.

We went to the kitchen to get some food but the grumpy chef was in so the most we were able to do was steal biscuits (which Trista got me to grab while she distracted the kitchen staff, just like we always did when we were little) before going out to the fountain at the very back of the House gardens.

I take a biscuit from the bag before passing it back to her. "I don't know," I say, taking a bite. I kick my feet through the cool water of the pond underneath the fountain, watching the fish swimming away as I disturb them. "When we were fifteen, maybe, I think, although substitute the biscuits for gin."

"We did love that watered down gin." Trista smiles wistfully.

"I had the real thing last night," I tell her.

"How was it?"

"You know when we were little and we got sick and we had to have that god-awful medicine?"

"Yeah…"

"It tasted kind of like that."

"Gross," she says pulling a face of absolute disgust. "Maybe that was what they gave us when we were kids."

"Maybe."

She sets the biscuits down on the small expanse of stone between us. "Disgusting gin aside, we haven't had the time to do something like this in recent years."

"Yeah we've been so busy with school lately."

"Not to mention training for numerous possibilities."

"I've missed this," I say wistfully as I stare up at the fountain, watching the water cascading down into the little pond below and the ripples slowly making their way across the surface.

"Me too," Trista says.

She waves her hand in mid-air, pulling a small globe of water out of the pond, drawing it up into the shape of a heart, floating just above the top of the fountain. Once she is done I draw my own rivulet of water from the pond and manoeuvre it to circle around Trista's heart so there are two hearts in mid-air, one around the other.

"I'm going to have to get better at this if I have to go into battle," I say. "I mean little bits of magic here and there are fine on the island but they aren't going to cut it in the big leagues."

"You sound like Harmony," Trista teases.

I wrinkle my nose in disdain. "Thanks."

Trista giggles "Sorry."

"It's just that I don't think I could level a city with my magic," I say.

"Do you think you're going to *have* to level a city?"

"Don't know," I shrug. "I hope not."

"Yeah I can't imagine a situation where that would be in any way helpful," she says.

"Me neither."

"So why do you think you might have to?"

"I don't really," I reply, "but Neo Warriors are supposed to be the best of the best so I need to get better."

"Yeah but you can do more than just this," Trista says nodding in the direction of the water hearts. "You've always been really good at magic."

"Well, yeah," I say, rolling my eyes, "but I don't think I could do something huge like set up an impenetrable water shield or something like that. I know I'm good but I'm not that good. Not like the High Council or Harmony or Michael."

"Again, do you think you'll need to?" Trista asks.

"That one I might," I say. "It might be a thing I have to do in basic training, you know, to prove that I can or whatever."

"You're much more skilled at magic than you give yourself credit for," Trista says. "I've seen you do some super intricate stuff that I've never seen anyone else do. You just compare yourself to other people too much. Recognise your own magical talent!"

"Okay, okay, I will," I laugh, holding my hands up in defence as she pokes me in the side. "I will still need to practice though."

"Obviously."

"'Cause you know how when you want to do something big you think about what you're going to do and work out how you need to do it before you actually do it?" I ask. "Yeah…"

"If I think about it then I overthink and then I mess it up," I say. "If I need to do something, I have to just do it and let my body react on instinct."

"You'll be fine, great in fact," Trista says. "Just don't think too much…or at all."

She drops her hand and I catch all of the water into a ball together, moulding it into a kaleidoscope of water butterflies. I make them flap their liquid wings, fly around the two of us for a moment before they go to perch on the very top of the fountain. After a moment or two, I drop my hand and let them melt back into the rest of the water.

"Pretty," Trista says.

"First thing Dad taught me when I was old enough to use magic without creating total chaos: water butterflies. Closely followed by Michael trying to teach me how to write 'boobies' in the air with raindrops."

Trista laughs. "Michael always was a bit odd."

"Just a little bit," I agree.

"Do you know what happened to him?" she asks.

"Not really," I reply. "I'm guessing he got ill or something and never recovered. Everyone's being really tight lipped about it and I don't really want to ask, just in case it sets Aunt Annie off again."

Michael was the last Neo Warrior to represent the House. In theory, he should have had a good four years left in him, being roughly the same age as Harmony, but all of a sudden we got the message saying that he had died and that they were choosing a new Neo Warrior and nothing more was said on the matter. No one told us what happened to him and the council have barely said anything about Michael at all.

"So they still haven't told you anything?" Trista asks.

"Nope," I reply. "I did think about asking Granddad last night but I got a bit distracted." Distracted here being asking him about Luciana Van Garret when I should really have tried to find out why Michael suddenly died—if he would have even told me at all.

"It's just so weird how they won't say anything," Trista says after a pause. "I mean we need to know what happened to him. *You* need to know if no one else."

"I suppose so." It would be nice to know what I'm in for on that front.

"Does your aunt know?"

"I would assume she does," I say. "You know what she's like. If no one told her what happened, she would storm down to the royal palace and demand that the king himself tell her."

Michael's mother, my aunt Annie, was never a Neo Warrior herself but she is a force to be reckoned with, especially when she's angry. Not being told why her son had suddenly died with no explanation would have made her furious, so she must know even if the council doesn't. It's probably a good thing she's not on the High Council anymore—a few weeks ago she just up and quit, probably about the same time that Michael died—as I don't imagine the last couple of days have been overly easy for her.

"I don't know," Trista says, shrugging. "It just seems a bit on the fishy side if you ask me."

"What do you mean?"

"I mean he just suddenly dies and no one says anything about what happened to him," she says. "It kind of seems a bit suspect."

"I suppose so," I say. She's not wrong; it *is* weird.

"He might have been killed in action."

"What?"

Trista shrugs. "I don't know, I'm just guessing."

"I guess it could be possible but there's no action, so how could he have been killed in it?" I ask.

"No idea," Trista says. "He was always just so fit and healthy so I don't know how he could have suddenly gotten so ill that he couldn't fight it."

"Yeah…" She's not wrong on that front. I mean Michael was a Neo Warrior for god's sake—they're the fittest, healthiest of the lot plus they have the best doctors in the entire empire who should have been able to do something if he was ill.

"I just don't know why they would be keeping it from us," Trista says after a moment's thought.

"Me neither."

Both of us stare at the fountain, neither knowing what to say. I really should have asked Granddad last night. He might have told me as well, he seemed pretty willing to talk about everything else with me so he might have given me an answer.

Beside me Trista sighs and I hear her take another biscuit from the bag. "Everything's going to change now isn't it?" she asks with a sigh.

"I suppose so," I say, shrugging and taking another biscuit of my own, "but in a good way."

"It is yeah," she says, although she doesn't sound completely convinced.

"You're going to be getting married to a solid hunk of beef," I say, hoping to lighten the mood.

"And you're going to be a super famous Neo Warrior and eventually make Commander," she finishes.

"Let's not get too ahead of ourselves on that front," I laugh. "I haven't even passed basic training yet and I'm trying to pass with Caspian Feioré: he doesn't like anyone."

"Yeah but you will," she says. "I know you will."

"We're moving up in the world," I say.

"We're growing up."

"We finally get to start our lives properly!"

"I know right!"

"So how many kids are you planning on having?" I ask.

Trista thinks about this for a moment, tapping her half eaten biscuit against her lips. "Well," she says, a huge grin spreading across her face, "after seeing Jackson yesterday I'd say I'm going to have at least four."

"My god! What is wrong with you?" I ask, my eyes widening.

"Hey, even if we don't have four, it will certainly be fun trying," she giggles, winking.

I laugh. "I'll take your word on that."

"You'll change your mind when you meet the man of your dreams," she says.

"If you say so," I mutter, taking a bite out of my own biscuit.

"Oh you will," she says. "He's out there somewhere and when you meet him you'll know." She's probably right but so far my experiences with the opposite sex (that aren't members of the council or directly related to me) and with sex has been an awkward fumble at a formal function when I was sixteen. His name was Marco, he had freckles and way too much cologne. He was very sweet but a bit on the wet side and it kind of put me off the idea for a while. Having said that, if I had a husband who looked like Jackson then I would probably change my mind pretty quickly.

"So where am I supposed to meet this 'man of my dreams'?" I ask sceptically. "I'm going to be doing Neo Warrior stuff for the next decade or so—I won't have time to meet anyone."

"Everybody digs the Neo Warriors though," Trista says. "You can pick yourself up a fanboy easily and, you never know, it might end up being one of the other Neo Warriors."

"You think?"

"Oh yeah. The vast majority of them end up getting into relationships with each other because they spend so much time together," she replies. "It's where at least forty percent of the inter-House marriages come from."

"Did you research this or something?" I ask incredulously.

"Ever since I found out that there was an inter-House marriage being discussed," she says nodding. "I thought it was something that I should know just in case I did get picked—and I kinda wanted to get picked—and I did and now I know."

"Right…" I say, drawing the word out. It's a bizarre thought process to take but I can see her thinking. "Let me get through my basic training before I start scoping out the hotties. I'm sure I'll have other stuff that I need to concentrate on as I'm just starting out and the last thing I want is for Feioré to send me home because I'm useless."

"You're not useless," Trista says, swatting at my shoulder with the back of her hand.

"But from what I've heard Feioré is a hard-arse so I want to be on my best behaviour until I'm done with basic," I say.

"Well-behaved women rarely make history," she sighs.

"Well-behaved women don't get a court martial," I point out.

"How long do you think your training is going to last?" she asks, taking another biscuit and biting into it, changing the subject.

"Couple of months maybe," I shrug. "I don't really know but in interviews they say that's about how long it tends to take."

"When are you likely to find out?"

"When I get to the mainland, I guess," I shrug. "I imagine pretty much all of the questions I have are going to get answered when I get there."

"Do you know who's coming to meet you?" she asks.

"That I do know; apparently I'm getting picked up by Katarina Navroe," I say, "and I suppose I'll be eased into it from there."

"You say that like your training is going to be easy," Trista laughs.

"That would be nice," I say taking another biscuit. "I mean I don't imagine it will be but it would be great if I got a couple of lie-ins rather than up at the crack of dawn for drills every single morning."

"I don't see why it would be too hard," she says after a pause. "It's not like we're at war or anything at the moment and, from what my dad says, as long as the current king of Cimmerian is on the throne we're not likely to go to war any time soon."

"No…"

"So you could possibly spend your entire career as a Neo Warrior without actually seeing any action at all," she says.

"Yeah," I say, absently staring off into the distance, "I suppose I could."

It's true. It's *not* like we're at war or anything. If we were, then I guess my training would be a very different story as the Neo Warriors would actually be thrown into a fight. That is our whole purpose for existing. I'd have to learn how to defend myself and get on top of learning how to command a squad while doing my basic training, as well as any other magical training, all at the same time and pretty damn sharpish to boot. That's actually quite a scary prospect: learning how to do something that quickly will make you mess up and something will get lost along the way.

Thankfully, we haven't had a war with Cimmerian (and let's face it, they are the only people who are ever stupid enough to go to war with magic users when they don't have any magic themselves) in a long time. We're very lucky to have had such a long time of peace. From what I've heard from my tutors and what I've read in history books, there were times where the wars just kept going on and on for years. Kings would pass down their prejudice to their sons who would then pass it on to their sons, or a father would be killed on the battlefield and the son would demand revenge. It was an endless cycle until someone stood up and put a stop to all the needless violence and peace was restored between the countries.

If we continue to be lucky, the current Cimmerian king will probably pass on his wish for peace to his son, as his father did with him, and things will remain as they are for years to come. We could continue to reopen trade routes and all the damage done by the previous wars would finally be repaired. If that happens, Trista might be right and I may very well go through my entire career as a Neo Warrior without having to fight.

"Hey, you okay?" Trista asks, her voice pulling me out of my reverie.

"Huh?"

"You went off into a stare for a bit there."

"Oh sorry," I say, chuckling, "just started thinking."

"Dangerous."

I give her a playful bump with my shoulder. "Whatever."

"So what were you thinking about?" she asks.

"About wars with Cimmerian and stuff," I reply.

"What about them?"

"Just that it's a good thing we're not in one right now," I say, smiling.

"Obviously," she says, rolling her eyes. "With Neyara being so close to the Cimmerian border and everything, I don't fancy our chances much."

"It's not like we're completely powerless though," I say. "I mean we've got a good strong set of soldiers and everyone is competent with their magic."

"Yeah but they've never had to use it in a fight," Trista says. "You said so yourself; little bits of magic here and there are fine for everyday use but actually using it to defend the place might be a lot different."

"I suppose so," I say staring off into the centre of the fountain again.

Just thinking about it like this makes my stomach go a bit funny. Now that my grandmother has died and so has Michael we only have one ex-Neo Warrior who still lives here left on Neyara and maybe having a few more would serve us well if anything were to happen. Not that I think it would or anything: I guess

I'm just a little unsure because this is the first time I've ever left home before. It's just nerves because it's going to be a new experience; I can't worry forever though, otherwise I'd never leave.

"You nervous?" Trista asks after a short pause, her voice bringing me back to the real world again.

"What?" I ask, turning to her. I wave her off and give her a smile. "No."

"Not at all?"

"Not really," I say. "I don't *think* I'm nervous."

"Hell does that even mean?" she asks. "You're either nervous or you're not and normally you know if you are."

"Like you said, we're not at war so what does it matter how I feel at the moment?" I ask. "There's nothing for me to be nervous about."

"Not making any friends, messing up your training, tripping and falling in front of the king when you meet him, Luciana Van Garret turning out to be kind of a bitch," Trista says counting them off on her fingers.

"Alright," I laugh, giving her a shove. "Those things aside there is nothing for me to be nervous about."

"So you're not even the tiniest bit nervous that you're going to meet the king?" she asks grinning.

"Well, now you mention it…" Meeting the king is actually something that is going to be crazy scary! I've heard so much about him and just being in the presence of the ruler of the entire Braxian Empire is, I'm sure, going to be like standing in front of some kind of god.

"Told you," she giggles.

"You're supposed to be helping here!"

"I am helping," she says.

"Are you?" I ask. "Are you really?"

"I'm making you admit that you're nervous rather than bottling it up and working yourself into a state," she replies, grinning.

I roll my eyes. "Whatever."

"You'll thank me for this one day," she says.

"If you say so."

"Oh you will." She picks up the bag of biscuits and looks inside before holding the bag out to me. "Do you want the last one?"

"Nah, you have it," I say, shaking my head.

She takes the biscuit and takes a bite. "We're out of food," she says as she screws up the empty packet and pockets it.

"And I don't know about you but my feet are getting cold," I say. I stand up and step out of the fountain. I'm glad it's sunny out today because I didn't bring a towel with me. That would have been the sensible thing to do, so of course I didn't do it. It's quite warm so hopefully the sun will dry us off pretty quickly.

"That won't be the only thing that's cold," Trista giggles.

"What?" I ask, furrowing my brow at her.

"Take this!"

She bends down and scoops up a handful of water to throw it over my face with a laugh. I let out a cry of surprise and catch the water in a flat sheet before it has the chance to hit me. Looking at Trista through the water I can just make out her grinning wickedly at me. Wanting revenge I swirl the water into a ball and throw it back at her. She lets out a high-pitched squeal of mirth as she catches it. Laughing I don't give her the chance to fling it back at me before I throw a ball of water of my own at her.

"You can't stop it if you're already holding one," I laugh as she drops the water ball she's holding into her lap as mine hits her square in the face.

"You cheeky bitch!" she cries as she pushes her wet fringe off her face.

She jumps to her feet and flings more water at me. I scream with laughter and run away from her as we start our own water fight, barely bothering with the water from the fountain anymore and just conjuring our own, both of us getting in a few lucky hits when the other is occupied with either conjuring or defending; both sopping wet, laughing and splashing around in the sun.

Neither of us are paying attention to the world around us—we're only interested in making the other as wet as possible. We continue trying to get one up on the other when we hear a loud bang from the back door and it's then that we realise we're no longer alone.

Both Trista and I scramble to our feet, trying and failing to stifle our giggles as we catch our breath. As the door crashed open I thought it might have been one of our parents being a little overly enthusiastic but we're met with the stony face of Harmony as she stalks across the grounds to meet us. Great…just what I need right now—a lecture from my sister because, for reasons unknown, she seems to be pissed off with everything I do at the moment. She's got a face like thunder and if looks could kill then both Trista and I would be dead already.

"What on earth do you two think you're doing?" she growls as she reaches us.

"We're just having some fun," Trista replies.

"Is this an appropriate way for representatives of our House to behave?" Harmony asks, glaring down at the both of us. I'm only about four or five inches shorter than her but her elevated eye-level (and the fact that she wears heels all the time) makes her think she has the right to look down her nose at me.

"We're just having fun, Harm," I repeat.

"Fun?" she asks, scoffing incredulously. "Do you really think that you, of all people, have time for fun?"

"I've got some spare time before I leave for the mainland," I say, "and besides, there's nobody around so I wouldn't worry about us showing up the House if that's really what's got you shouting."

"I saw you out of the window," she spits. "What if someone else had seen you? Someone who isn't a member of our House, who will then start telling everyone that our Neo Warrior can't behave properly."

"If you're talking about Jackson," Trista starts to say, "then—"

"I don't think I was talking to you," Harmony snaps.

Trista looks down at the ground, the hurt evident on her face.

That's not okay. Harmony's really overstepping her mark this time. Just because she's angry with me doesn't mean she should be taking it out on Trista as well. I glare up at her; I'm not going to let her walk away from this without calling her out on it.

"Look I'm packed, I'm ready to leave, there is nothing for me to do but say my goodbyes and wait," I say. "I've got some free time to myself to do what I want."

"And shouldn't you be spending it learning how to do your job?" she asks.

"Maybe you should worry about doing your *own* job," I snap before I can stop myself. I most definitely shouldn't have said that but I'm so fed up with her that I can't stay silent any longer. The way she just spoke to Trista was the final straw.

"Excuse me?" Harmony asks, blinking at me in infuriated surprise and confusion.

Trista stiffens beside me and I don't even need to look at her to know that she's staring at me with her mouth open, probably wondering what the hell is wrong with me. I know I should have just kept my mouth shut and keep my head down but Harmony's still my sister and she's not Head of the House yet.

"You heard me," I say. I've already said it; no point in backing down now.

"I knew you weren't suitable for this position," she says shaking her head and crossing her arms over her chest. "You're disrespectful and you can't follow orders."

"I can follow orders just fine," I say, "but you're not giving me orders. You are bossing me around for no reason because you're in a mood."

"Really?" she asks. "Because all I can see is you messing around when you should be preparing yourself for your new role."

"I'm packed and ready, what more do you want from me?" I ask.

"I want you to take this seriously!"

"I *am* taking this seriously!"

"Are you though?" she asks. "Are you really?"

"I'll be gone by the end of the week so I wouldn't worry about me," I say. "I'll be out of your hair soon enough."

"And I can surely expect a letter from Feioré about your poor performance and your poor attitude shortly after you arrive," she says.

"Why are you so certain that I'm going to fail?" I ask.

"Because I know the standards that Caspian Feioré demands and you are so far from meeting them it's laughable," she says.

"But isn't that the whole point of my training?" I ask. "For me to get better?"

"He would still expect you to have been training your whole life as if you were going to be given this position," she says. "He'll take one look at you and think that the House of Neptune is a complete joke!"

"You say that as if he hasn't already met people from our House," I say. "He was Michael's Commander—he has a better impression of us than what you seem to think and I won't be the first impression he has."

"And I don't want meeting you to destroy whatever opinion he may have made of us," she says.

"Look I know you seem to have a problem with me being named the new Neo Warrior but I can do it!" I tell her. "I'll prove to you that I can do this and the High Council weren't wrong when they picked me."

"If you say so," Harmony scoffs.

"Like I say, I'll be gone at the end of the week."

"Fine," Harmony snaps. "Just stay out of my way until then."

"Believe me, I intend to," I reply.

Harmony turns and stalks away. As soon as she is back inside the House and has slammed the door behind her I sink back down to the edge of the fountain and put my face in my hands, all the energy going out of me. I want to cry and scream both at the same time, all the fight sinking out of me and into the water beneath me. Trista sits down next to me and wraps an arm around my shoulders, pulling me into a hug. Leaning against her I drop my hands from my face, letting them fall into my lap.

"You okay?" she asks.

"Yeah," I sigh. I rub my hand over my face to catch the few tears that have started to prick the corners of my eyes before she can see them. "Just Harmony making me crazy."

"She was out of order," Trista says.

"Yeah but, to be fair, I was too," I say.

"Yes what were you thinking? Going toe to toe with her like that? I mean she's the Head of the House, are you insane?"

"Not yet she isn't! I still technically answer to my grandfather until he officially passes it over to her."

"You could still end up in a lot of trouble though," she says.

"Maybe," I say, "but Harmony needs to realise that I'm not the only one who needs a lot of training. Neither of us are actually qualified to do our jobs yet— it's not just me."

"That's true."

I push myself to my feet and start pacing in front of the fountain. "I just wish she'd stop treating me like I'm this stupid little kid," I say. "How am I supposed to prove to her that I can do this if she won't even give me a chance?"

Trista pushes herself to her feet and pulls me into another tight, slightly damp, hug. "You'll get your chance," she says. "Just get through these next few days and then you'll be on your way. You can wow Feioré with how amazing you are and Harmony will have to eat her words when she gets a letter from him saying you've passed your basic training faster than expected."

"Thank you," I say, hugging her back and burying my face in her hair. Out of everyone, I'm going to miss her the most, second only to my mum.

"No problem," she says, "that's what I'm here for."

"I'm going to miss you so much."

"Hey, save that for when you leave," she says, pulling away. "You've still got the next four days here and we shouldn't waste a moment of it."

"What do you have in mind?" I ask.

"Whatever you want to do," she says, that famous Trista hell-raising grin spreading across her lips.

Chapter 4

Trista and I stay out late. We leave the House and go down to the coves around the side of the island to explore for probably the hundredth time. I don't relish the idea of hanging around the House because I know that there will be some sort of repercussion for tearing chunks out of Harmony. We catch our own dinner from the ocean and cook it over a small bonfire that we make ourselves and by the time we finally get back most people have gone to bed. The only person we meet is Mum, who asks us where we've been all day and doesn't chastise us for being out so late, but other than that no one, which I'm thankful for.

The following morning I'm up early—before everyone else—I don't want to run the risk of getting cornered by Harmony again so I pull on my shoes and go for a run. I'm really not one for crack of dawn activity but every minute I spend in the House I expect to be called into an office to talk about what happened yesterday. I'm really not in the mood for it because I know that it's just going to make me angrier (and when I think about the fact that I'm going to be the one who gets all the flack for it I feel the fury spiking) so I decide to put the excess energy to use and get some early training in.

By the time I get home, I'm hot and sweaty and in desperate need of a shower. I turn the corridor to where my room is and see someone standing outside my door. Freezing, thinking that it's Harmony or someone else I don't want to see but then I take a proper look and see that it's Trista.

Instantly relaxing I make my way over to her.

"Hey," I say, grinning at her as she turns and spots me, "what are you doing here?"

"You missed breakfast," Trista says, raising an eyebrow at me. "You never miss breakfast and naturally I was worried."

"Cheeky," I laugh at the obvious sarcasm and lead her into my room. "I went for a run."

"Why?" she asks, looking bemused as she goes to sit on the edge of my bed.

"Felt like it," I say, shrugging.

"Didn't want to have to face Harmony more like," she says.

"Why bother asking if you already know the answer?"

"Getting you to admit things, you giant coward," she replies.

"Thanks."

"Has anyone said anything to you about it?" she asks, absently tracing the pattern on my covers.

"Haven't been in long enough to find out," I reply as I begin to strip my sweaty shirt off and chuck it into the basket in the corner of my room.

"So I'm guessing you want to get out again as soon as possible then?" she asks.

"As soon as I'm showered if you want to come with me," I reply.

"Of course, why do you think I'm here?" she asks smiling at me. "What do you want to do today? We can go anywhere and do anything."

"I don't feel like I can have proper fun here with the threat of Harmony hanging around me waiting for another excuse to get into a fight," I say. "I don't know if she is waiting to catch me 'behaving inappropriately' or not but it's starting to feel that way. On top of that, there's still a chance I'm going to get some kind of repercussion from what I said to her that I also don't want to have to deal with."

"Well, we have all of Neyara to find something to do so we can easily avoid her if need be," Trista says with a smile.

"Who's in the kitchens today?" I ask.

"Still the grump," Trista replies.

"Urgh!" No chance of breakfast here then…

"Do you think that you could, you know, use your influence as a Neo Warrior and get some food that way?" Trista asks.

"I doubt it," I snort. "I've used every trick in the book on him and the fact that I'm the granddaughter of the Head of the House has never swayed him before so I doubt that he's going to suddenly change his mind now."

"Good point."

"We could go down the market," Trista offers. "Only place you'll get food now."

"Sounds good to me," I nod. It gets us out of the way in case Harmony is lurking around ready for another argument and I can have a look to see if there is anything that I might need when I get to the mainland. "I'll quickly hop in the shower."

"Please, you smell," she grins.

I fix her with an unimpressed raised brow. "I will throw my sweaty bra at you."

"I beg you not to."

Twenty minutes later I'm showered, dressed and Trista and I are heading out of the House in the direction of the market down the docks. "So do you have many plans for tonight?" I ask after we're out of the House gardens.

"Not much really," she says with a shrug. "Spending the evening with Jackson."

"Oh yeah?" I ask, smirking and raising an eyebrow.

Trista flushes and gives me a shove, not meeting my eye. "Nothing like that! We're just going to talk."

"Is that what you're calling it?" I tease.

"I'm serious Ari!"

"Okay!" I grin, raising my hands in surrender, "Sorry."

"You're such a bitch," Trista huffs, crossing her arms and pouting.

"I know," I reply, still grinning. I do love to tease her but I also know when to drop it. Trista has always said that she wants to save herself for when she gets married (which I think is admirable) and even though she and Jackson are getting married I know she's still going to wait until after the official ceremony.

"Did you know he's nine years older than we are?" Trista asks when she's finished being annoyed with me.

"No I didn't."

"He is, he's twenty-seven."

"Wow."

"It's not that uncommon for there to be large age gaps between inter-House marriages," she tells me. "It's often more common for there to be an age gap rather than there only be a year or two between them."

"I didn't know that."

"His brother's like you," Trista says after a second.

"How so?" I ask.

"He's a Neo Warrior and he's the younger one," she replies.

"Oh."

"So it's not just our council that fancied a break in tradition and decided to take a chance on someone younger," she laughs.

"Do Plutonians have that tradition as well then?" I ask.

"I think all Houses sort of do," Trista replies, "but it depends what it comes down to when they actually select…or so Jackson said when we talked about it the other night."

"I know they do in the House of Mars," I say. "It's only ever passed down to another Feioré. I don't think there's been a Neo Warrior that isn't from the Feioré family for three hundred years."

"They must train them for it," Trista says.

"They do," I reply. "Pretty much from the moment that they can do magic they start training for the possibility of one day being a Neo Warrior."

Trista wrinkles her nose in mild disgust. "I can't imagine having to train my entire life for something and never being allowed to have any fun," she says.

"I know, it sounds dull," I say. From what I've heard Caspian Feioré is the product of his upbringing: the perfect soldier and an excellent Commander. I can't imagine what it was like for him as a child: never being able to do anything other than train… Then again I could be reading this completely wrong as I don't properly know what goes on in other Houses.

"So what else did you and Jackson talk about the other night?" I ask.

"This was with other people around so nothing overly personal," Trista replies. "Although he told me all about the House of Pluto and where we're going to be living once we're married. They have a huge flower garden, I can't wait to see it."

"Where's the House?" I ask.

"On a big stretch of flat land about three hours from the Neo Warriors training ground."

"Sounds nice."

"Doesn't it?"

"Remember when we thought that Plutonians lived underground?" I ask, laughing at the memory. "We were so convinced that they lived under a mountain like in those old fairy stories we used to read."

"I know, we were, what seven?" Trista laughs.

"That seems like so long ago," I say.

"That's because it was."

"Oh god…"

As we come to the edge of the House grounds I hear Mum's voice call out to us and we both turn to see her coming down the path towards us.

"Are you two off to the market?" she asks as she gets closer.

"Yeah, I was going to get some food and have a look at what else is on offer," I reply.

"Would you mind picking me up some more of that perfume you got me for my birthday if they have any?" Mum asks. "I've nearly finished that bottle and have been meaning to go and get some more but I've been so busy recently."

"Sure thing," I say and smile at her.

"Thanks baby," she says and gives me a one armed hug. "You're such good girls."

"Is there anything else we could look out for?" Trista offers.

"I don't think so," Mum says. "Besides, if it's just the two of you, you don't want to be hefting a lot of stuff back from the market."

"Well, we asked," I grin.

"Exactly," Mum says, "and that's enough. What time do you think you'll be back?"

"Definitely in time for dinner," I assure her.

"Good, you've already missed breakfast," Mum chides.

"Sorry, I was distracted," I grin sheepishly.

"Training?" Mum asks.

"Yeah, I went for a run."

She chuckles and shakes her head. "Your dad's looking for you, by the way."

"I figured he probably would be," I mumble and look at the floor.

She seems to notice the look on my face and she gives me a squeeze. "I'll tell him I haven't seen you."

"You sure?" I ask, looking up.

She nods. "You'll go when you're ready."

"I promise." God knows when I'll be ready but I've said I would now.

"Good. Have fun out today and remember to have something to eat," Mum says tweaking the tip of my nose. "I can't believe I'm having to tell you of all people to remember to eat."

"Complete shocker isn't it?" Trista giggles.

"Oi!" I cry, affronted. I miss one meal after years of constantly being vigilantly punctual every time there's food on offer and…actually maybe it is deserved, I'm quite shocked at myself to be honest.

"Come on," Trista says linking her arm in mine as my stomach rumbles quite loudly, "let's go get you something to eat."

"Fine," I say and allow myself to be pulled along by her.

"Stay safe girls," Mum calls after us.

"We will," Trista calls back over her shoulder, grinning before turning back to the path in front of us, absently kicking a few blades of grass as she steps. "I might try and see if I can find something for Jackson while we're out today," she muses.

"Oh yeah?" I ask. "Anything in particular?"

She shrugs. "Not sure, just some kind of token from the island that he won't be able to get anywhere else."

"You're so cute," I say, grinning. "Just out of interest what's Jackson doing while he's here when he's not with you or in formal ceremonies and stuff?"

"He said that he's been sitting in on a few meetings with the High Council as his mother is Head of the House of Pluto," she replies, "and I know he's had a few meetings with just my parents to talk about marriage arrangements and things like that."

"Isn't that something you should be invited to as well?" I ask. "I mean if you're supposed to be marrying the guy shouldn't you know about marriage arrangements too?"

"To be honest I just like being alone with him," she replies. "He'll tell me what they talk about and then asks me my thoughts on it when we're together so it's not like I'm really missing out on anything. When I asked about it he said that he wants me to be able to spend your last few days with you before you leave and it's mostly financial stuff anyway."

"He seems like a nice guy—you know from the few conversations I've had with him," I say, smiling.

"He is," Trista says, a lovesick smile spreading over her face as she thinks about him. "I was so happy when they said that I would be marrying him but really it was just because he's attractive but now that I've spoken to him a few times and started to get to know him I can definitely see myself spending the rest of my life with him."

"Good," I say. "I'm glad you're happy."

"So happy," she sighs contentedly. "What about you?"

"What about me?" I ask.

"All this stuff with Harmony must be getting you down," she replies. "I don't know the whole story but she seems to have a real rod up her arse to still be this annoyed about the whole affair."

I sigh. When I stop to think about it, it does get me down but I've been trying to keep Harmony out of mind so that I can just focus on the fact that I'm a Neo Warrior and be excited. I get to leave and start my training soon and then I can show Harmony just why I was picked for this in the first place. "Kind of yeah, but I'm just trying to give her some time to cool off first."

"Sounds like a sensible idea," Trista says. "I never thought she'd be this petty."

"Me neither but I guess she can," I say with a shrug.

"I love it out here," Trista says, stopping to take a deep breath and close her eyes for a second.

"I know, so do I," I say, following suit. If I strain my ears hard enough I can just about hear the sounds of people chattering not that far away.

"You'll miss it when you leave," she chuckles, moving on.

"I know," I agree, smiling fondly.

It's not a long walk down to the market (thankfully as I'm starting to get hungry now) and as it's still early there aren't many people around. It's peaceful and I can feel the ocean singing when I close my eyes. The closer we get, the more noise starts to filter through from the docks and I can feel the excitement bubbling up. I love coming down to the docks because there's always so much going on, always so many faces that I've seen for years and some that I don't recognise at all—it's the liveliest place on Neyara and it never seems to stop. It's never the same when I come here either, something new is always afoot. As soon as we step into the crowded market I hear a voice calling my name.

"Ariana!"

I look over and see Marco waving at me, smile so bright it's almost blinding. Oh god, we haven't spoken in…a while (not quite as long ago as our first encounter but it's always embarrassing when we do talk). I raise an awkward hand and wave. "Hi Marco."

"Marco?" Trista asks so that only I can hear. "Isn't that…?"

"Yep, shut up," I reply before she can finish the question. Marco jogs over to us, huge grin still on his face. He's cute, kind of like a baby animal, with his soft brown eyes and freckles everywhere and he's sweet so I think that must be what attracted me to him in the first place. It really was one of those moments that I kind of regret now though. "Hey Marco," I say as he reaches us.

"It's so great to see you, Ariana," he says, flashing that adorable smile again.

"He calls you Ariana?" Trista mutters to me, still quiet enough that only I can hear, the question getting lost in the sea of voices to everyone but me.

"Yeah, drop it," I mutter back, still smiling at Marco. "What are you doing here?"

"I'm helping out on Dad's stall today," he replies, tilting his head back in the direction he came from. I look over and see an older version of him standing behind a market stall and talking to a tall, thickset woman.

"Oh of course," I say, shaking my head as if I should have known this. In all honesty, I barely remember anything about Marco at all: I don't even remember us talking all that much when we met. I mean we must have done for me to have thought it was a good idea to fool around with him in a deserted room in the House but, bless him, it was so unmemorable that I can't even begin to place any information about him.

"I heard about you being named the new Neo Warrior," he says. "Congratulations."

"Thank you," I say. "It's very exciting, I'm heading off to the mainland at the weekend and then I start my training as soon as I get there."

"That sounds amazing," he says and he sounds so genuine and sincere I feel guilty for thinking that he's a bit of a wet fish most of the time. "I'm sure you'll do a fantastic job."

"Thank you," I say. A subtle nudge in the side from Trista reminds me that she's still there and I see my opening to make this conversation a little less humiliating. I put my arm around her and shove her forward slightly. "This is my friend Trista," I say. "Hi," she smiles and holds out her hand to Marco. "Hello," he says, taking it. "Trista Alantisté isn't it?"

"It is yes," Trista grins.

"Trista, this is Marco," I say, thankful that I don't need to tell her anything other than his first name.

"So how do you know Ari?" Trista asks.

"We met at a gala held at the House a couple of years ago," Marco says (thank god one of us properly remembers).

"Oh yes, I remember that," Trista says. "A lot of merchants came and bought various members of their families with them."

"Yes I came with my dad," Marco says.

"And you met Ari," Trista says an innocent, blissfully ignorant smile on her face that only I know is total crap and I could throttle her.

"Er…yes, that is where we met," Marco says, blushing slightly. I can feel my neck tensing and my hand reaches down to pinch the back of Trista's thigh. She knows exactly what she's doing and thoroughly deserves this.

"So what kind of stall does your father own?" Trista asks, completely at ease. I know better though: she's not being friendly, she's checking him out because she knows that I (in a slight lapse of judgement) had sex with him.

"He owns a shellfish stall," Marco replies. "He specialises rather than having a broad range of seafood. He's incredibly knowledgeable about shellfish and that gives him the edge over some of the other merchants here who don't have that."

"Interesting," Trista says before turning to me. "We should go there and have a look before we leave today."

"Sure," I say.

"How long are you staying in the market today?" Marco asks.

"As long as possible," I reply, almost without thinking.

"Then definitely come over at some point," Marco says. "I'm sure my dad will be happy to sort out some kind of deal for the new Neo Warrior."

"Thank you," I say.

"I should probably go back but it's good to see you Ariana," he says.

"You too," I smile at him.

"It's nice to meet you Trista," he says, nodding at her.

"And it is *lovely* to meet you Marco," Trista says flashing him her usual winning smile. I will end her one of these days.

Marco barely notices how uncomfortable the conversation has been and heads back over to his father's stall. I turn to see Trista giggling so I grab her by the wrist and drag her off in the opposite direction so that he can't hear us.

"Are you trying to kill me?" I ask her when we're sufficiently surrounded by other shoppers so that we won't be overheard in and amongst the chatter.

"What?" she asks, feigning innocence but the grin on her face speaks volumes. "I don't know what you're talking about."

"You know exactly what I'm talking about, Trista Alantisté, and don't you damn well pretend otherwise," I growl.

She laughs. "Oh calm down I was just seeing what he was like, that's all."

"If you say so," I grumble.

"Babe he's sweet but you can do better," she says.

"Bit harsh."

"You know it's true," she says. "I mean he's nice *enough* but you're about to be spending a lot of time with the likes of Ellis De'Latore and Caspian Feioré. Develop better taste in men!"

"I already *have* better taste, that was two years ago!" I protest.

"I should hope so," she says, stopping in front of a flower stall. "Didn't one of them do a naked shoot at some point?"

"Yeah Renton Remelston got naked in one of the magazine interviews he did," I reply. "There was some tasteful censoring but there was a lot of skin on show."

"Please tell me you were thinking about him when you had sex with that guy," she giggles, jerking her head back in the direction of Marco's stall.

I give her a punch on the arm. "Will you keep your voice down?" I hiss. "What if he hears you?"

"That's not a no," she giggles and I can feel a heat rising up the back of my neck. "Ariana Sirenia you dirty little stop out."

"I hate you," I say, walking away to another stall. She is going to be the death of me one of these days. She laughs again and runs after me, taking hold of my arm when she catches me and hugging it to her chest.

"No you don't—you love me!"

"For my sins, yes," I begrudgingly admit.

"What about the others?" Trista asks. "That's three of them, there's still three unaccounted for."

"Dmitri Tavaron's quite attractive," I reply. "The other two I don't really know what they look like because neither of them do interviews or turn up on the posters."

"What about that one you got with all the silhouettes?" Trista asks.

"Haven't filled it yet," I reply. About a year ago one of the magazines I always get because it has huge articles about the Neo Warriors in it bought out a special poster with all of them on it but just in silhouette. That particular article came with a sticker of Caspian Feioré and the idea was that every so often there would be a sticker of another Neo Warrior in with the magazine so that you could eventually fill the poster. Even after a year mine still has a few gaps in and now I guess they'll run something new because this one still has Michael on it and I'll be replacing him on all of the merchandise.

"Oh my god Ari," Trista's voice cries breaking me out of my thoughts, "look!"

I look up to where she's pointing and pinned to the front of someone's stall is a poster with 'Our new Neo Warrior' written in huge bold letters at the top. Underneath the words is a picture of me from the ceremony the other day in that old dress of Harmony's, holding the Braxian salute and actually looking pretty cool. My jaw drops and all I can do for a moment is stare in disbelief at it. I'm actually on a poster!

I cast a quick glance around and I see that there are more of them. Store owners seem to be displaying them proudly and one of the stalls that carries newspapers and magazines has a bundle of them rolled up and is selling them. As I stare someone even walks up and purchases one of them. This is surreal! People are actually buying posters of me! This is just another thing that I'm going to have to get used to now that I'm a Neo Warrior. There's a certain amount of celebrity that comes with it and that has sort of slipped my mind with the excitement of actually being named.

Trista gives my arm a tug. "Come on," she giggles, "let's go get a closer look."

"Okay," I say, too stunned to argue. I let her pull me over to the stall where we first saw the poster to have a better look at it. Up close it's even more impressive. I stand out, vibrant colour against the dull yellow of the paper it's printed on and it reminds me of the posters that went round the island when Michael became a Neo Warrior. I stare up at myself, open mouthed, in complete and utter awe. I'm thankful that they picked a decent picture of me otherwise that would be incredibly embarrassing. I look cool: I actually look like a Neo Warrior should.

"Mummy, Mummy!" a voice cries, bringing me back down to earth. "It's her!"

Turning I see a young boy of about five or six pointing at me and tugging on his mother's skirt. His mother, who had been examining the fruit from the stall they're at turns to him with a long suffering sigh.

"Rayne, Mummy's busy," she tells him, not looking to where he's pointing. "What is it?"

"It's her!" the boy cries again, still pointing in my direction. "It's that girl from all the posters."

His mother looks up and her eyes lock with mine. She looks from my face to the poster behind me a few times before she gasps. "Oh my goodness you're right!"

By this point, quite a few people have stopped what they're doing and turned to stare at me. I can feel my face heating up but I stand my ground. People have always known who Trista and I are because most members of our families are on the High Council but this is new. This isn't just 'oh it's Arthur Sirenia's granddaughter' this is 'holy crap it's you!' I smile at the boy and give him a wave. He starts tugging on his mother's skirt harder, clearly ecstatic with this turn of events.

There's quite a lot of murmuring going on around us and now it's starting to feel real. People are comparing me to the poster and are saying my name as they look in my direction. This is crazy! I turn back to look at the poster and the stall owner catches my eye.

"Nice, isn't it?" she says with a grin. She's a very pretty woman with bright eyes and hair as dark as the bottom of the ocean.

"Where did you get it from?" I ask, my voice a little breathless.

"The guy who owns the newspaper stall was handing them out to everyone who wanted to show their support," she replies.

"Wow!"

"Better get used to it," Trista teases. "Going to be fighting off the boys with a stick at this rate."

"I guess so…"

"I'm glad they chose a lass this time," she says. "We need a bit of girl power and now the balance has shifted so that it's equal once again."

"And our little Ari's going to absolutely smash it," Trista says, beaming at me. She's looks so proud and so sure that I'm going to be totally amazing that I can't help but actually believe that she's right. I am going to do this because I *am* amazing.

"Isn't proper, carrying on like that," a gruff man's voice says. He's suddenly appeared behind the store owner; he looks like he could be her brother as he's not old enough to be her father and he's glaring down at me.

"Rich!" the stall owner hisses.

"What?" he asks. "I'm just saying."

"Can you refrain while I'm talking to customers?"

"No I'd like to hear this," I say before I can stop myself. He's a huge imposing mass so facing off against him is probably not a good idea but he already seems to have a problem with me so I might as well stick around and find out why.

"It isn't right that the succession of Neo Warrior be passed to the younger when the older is still of Neo Warrior age," he says.

"Rich!" the stall owner hisses again.

"It's tradition that it is passed down to the older sibling if they are of Neo Warrior age and Harmony Sirenia is still of age!" he says.

"Oh fuck you and your traditions!" the stall owner snaps and a few people turn round to stare at us.

"Traditions are the backbone of our society," he says. "If something has held up long enough for it to be a tradition then there is no point in breaking it."

"That's archaic and ridiculous!" his sister growls at him. "And I'll ask you not to insult my customers."

"Stating an opinion isn't an insult," he says but it sure as hell feels like it.

"It is when you're stating it like that," the stall owner mutters. She turns back to me and Trista. "So was there anything you were looking for in particular?"

"I was looking for perfume…" I say, mumbling slightly. Suddenly the idea of lots of people looking at me is not so appealing anymore. I can hear people whispering around me and whether they actually are talking about me or paranoia is telling me that they are I don't know but I just want to buy my stuff and leave.

"You're in the right place then." The stall owner smiles at me. I think she can tell just how uncomfortable I am and she's trying to distract me. "I have any and every scent that you can think of."

"And why pick the younger sibling when the elder has had more training?" her brother continues suddenly.

"Oh my…fuck, are you not done yet?" she asks him incredulously. He doesn't seem to be listening, in fact he seems to be on a bit of a roll.

"There's more of us who support Harmony Sirenia and the decision to make her Neo Warrior because that would have been the right decision for the House," he says, ignoring her completely. He's not talking to me either, he just seems to be talking *at* me, as if I want to listen to this. My jaw clenches and I can feel tears beginning to prick the corners of my eyes as he voices all my worst fears for everyone who will listen.

"And what makes you think Ari was the wrong decision?" Trista suddenly asks from beside me. I turn to her and she's glaring at him with a ferocity that I very rarely see from her.

"Excuse me?" the man asks.

"I said what makes you think that Ariana was the wrong choice for the Neo Warrior position?" Trista asks, still glaring at him.

"Because tradition states…" he begins.

"No, give me a proper answer that has nothing to do with tradition," Trista says, interrupting him. More people are turning to stare at this tiny girl facing off against this man with absolutely no fear at all.

"Well…I…" he flounders and it's suddenly very clear that he has no real basis for an argument. The only reason he supports Harmony is because she is older than I am.

"So what you're telling me is the only reason you don't support the *High Council's* decision in choosing Ariana is because she's the younger of the two of them?" Trista asks.

"She won't have had as much training," the man says, visibly cowed by Trista's fierceness but still holding his ground.

"And that is what her first few weeks on the mainland are for," Trista says. "No House trains their children to be Neo Warriors anymore, aside from the House of Mars. There are other factors that are taken into account when the line of succession is passed on."

"But—" the man begins but Trista doesn't seem to be giving him the chance to get a word in edgeways.

"Regardless of whether or not *you* think that Harmony would have been a better choice, the fact of the matter is that Ariana *is* our new Neo Warrior," she says. "She was chosen by the High Council because she is suited to it and she will fulfil her duties exactly as is required of her, as will Harmony in her role as Head of the House. If all you care about is traditions and how things used to be, then you really need to keep your opinions to yourself. You are a citizen of the House of Neptune and you will show the proper respect for your Neo Warrior."

A round of applause from the small crowd around us accompanies the end of Trista's speech and I let out the breath I didn't realise I was holding. I wonder how many people feel the same as this guy but judging by the applause I'd guess not that many here. He clenches his jaw and turns to me, clearly irate at being scolded by a teenage girl in front of a large crowd.

"Sorry, I spoke out of turn," he says but he doesn't sound sorry. I don't even care anymore, I just want this whole conversation to be over.

"It's fine," I mumble.

"Now go away Rich," the stall owner tells him.

"Fine." He walks away into the crowd, tail between his legs, and the people around us turn back to what they were doing before.

"I'm so sorry about him," the stall owner says, turning back to Trista and I.

"It's okay," I mumble.

"No it's really not," she says. "He shouldn't have been going on like that." After a pause, she smiles brightly. "Tell you what: anything you want, free of charge."

"Are you sure?" I ask, staring at her to see if she is joking.

"Yeah of course," she says smiling. "Think of this as my way of congratulations if you don't want to think of it as an apology."

"Okay," I say and grin back at her. I hold out my hand. "Ariana," I tell her introducing myself properly.

She takes my hand and shakes it. "Raphaella."

~ *** ~

The rest of our time at the market passes uneventfully, with most people I meet congratulating me on being named Neo Warrior. I think word must have spread about Trista's smackdown because if there are any people muttering near us then they immediately stop as soon as they see her. No one really bothers us after that first man, occasionally we get some free samples from the stall owners but it's mostly food (which is absolutely fine with the two of us). It's starting to get a little cooler later in the afternoon as the two of us head back to the House. Trista is her usual chatty self but there are too many things on my mind for me to properly listen.

I knew that there were people who were still very set on old traditions—hell, there are still people who worship the old gods when barely anyone else does these days—but I never realised that people would disagree with the decision of the council because of how set in their ways they are. Maybe the council should have kept to tradition and made Harmony Neo Warrior…but then they couldn't honestly have thought that I would be a good Head of the House, could they?

Maybe they are keeping up with tradition but because the Head of the House position had to be filled it just doesn't look like it? Maybe—

"My god you think loudly," Trista says after she clearly can't take anymore.

"What?" I ask, snapping back to the real world.

"I can practically hear you thinking—you're going crazy up there," she says and gently swats my forehead with the back of her hand.

"Sorry," I mumble, rubbing the back of my neck in embarrassment.

"Don't be sorry," she tells me, "just tell me what's on your mind."

"It's not important," I tell her. I don't really want to go into it, not even with her, because it feels ridiculous to let the words of some random man at the market affect my confidence and my excitement.

"We've never kept anything from each other before," she says and I instantly feel guilty.

"Okay," I say on an outbreath. "You didn't have to step in for me like that earlier."

She snorts. "Yes I did."

"Why?" I ask, stopping and turning to look at her.

"Ari you're my best friend—that should be enough if nothing else," she replies, "but I didn't like the way that he was running his mouth like that. Regardless of what he thinks we all need to respect the decision of the High Council and what they have chosen otherwise what's the point of even having one at all?"

"I suppose so."

"And you, missy," she continues, poking me square in the chest, "you need to respect that decision as well."

"What do you mean?" I ask, rubbing my chest: that was a surprisingly hard poke for someone so tiny.

"I mean you have to respect the council's decision in picking you and stop doubting yourself," she tells me.

"I'm not!"

"Don't lie, I know you too well."

"Okay fine but just knowing that there are more people out there who think Harmony would have been a better choice just keeps reminding me that she might have been," I say, looking down at the floor and scuffing the dirt with my shoe. I can't look her in the eye anymore because I feel silly even saying this out loud to her when I was so excited a few days ago. She believes in me so much that she's willing to shout down a man much older and bigger than herself on my behalf.

"Then become a Neo Warrior in your own right and make everybody forget that they ever doubted you in the first place," she says. "You think that anyone from the House of Pluto gives a damn anymore that Ellis is a few years younger than Jackson?"

"Probably not."

"No, because he's been a Neo Warrior for six years now and he's made a name for himself on his own," Trista says, ducking down so that I have to look at her and grinning at me. "So you just have to do the same."

I throw my arms around her and pull her into a hard hug. "Thank you," I whisper into her shoulder.

"What for?" she asks, giggling.

"Being you," I tell her. I can't put into words just how much it means to me to hear her say all that and for her to believe in me so strongly. Just knowing that both she and Mum are in my corner is a real help and, really, they're the only people who matter. They're the only people whose opinions have ever truly mattered to me.

She hugs me back. "You're silly."

"Thanks," I laugh, rolling my eyes. Clearly the moment's over and we're done with all the emotional talk. "Shall we head back home then?"

"Yeah I'm hungry," Trista replies.

"You're always hungry," I say as we begin walking back in the direction of the House.

"You're one to talk!"

"I know."

"Is that Jackson?" Trista asks, suddenly turning her attention to the large figure walking along the path towards us. It's a giant tower of a person who looks like he's carved out of rock—it must be Jackson, no one from the House of Neptune looks like that.

"Wow, he's huge!" Every time I see him again I'm reminded of just how big this man actually is. He's at least a foot taller than the both of us.

"Jackson!" Trista calls, waving at him. The man waves back; it is him.

"Good afternoon ladies," he says, smiling at us as we reach each other. "I hear you've had quite the eventful day at the market."

"What?" I ask, confused.

"Word made its way back to the House that my future wife is quite the little firecracker," he says, grinning down at Trista.

"Problem?" she asks with a smirk and a raised eyebrow.

"Not at all," Jackson replies. "So what was all the commotion about?"

"It was nothing," I say, wanting to just brush it off and forget about it.

"Traditionalists being disrespectful," Trista says, knowing exactly what I'm trying to do and, for better or for worse, not letting me do it.

"Okay fine," I admit, "there was this guy who was running his mouth, saying that Harmony should have been named Neo Warrior because she's older."

"Ah yes, traditionalists are a problem," Jackson says. "There was a lot of that going around when Ellis was first named Neo Warrior even though there are barely two years between us. He won't thank me for telling you this but Ellis was quite sensitive when he was younger so it got to him; the constant whispering from people in the halls of the House and in the surrounding grounds, people speculating that I would have been better just because I was older."

"How did he deal with it?" I ask.

"He got strong," Jackson replies. "He filled out as he was quite scrawny at the time, he made himself a soldier and he stuck to the training he was given. The shirtless photo shoots from a few years ago helped his popularity as well."

"And what about you?" I ask. "Did it bother you as well?"

"Only in the sense that I hated people talking about my brother like that," he replies. "It was hard because I felt like I should be looking out for him but then I realised, when he went off for his training, that he didn't need me to look after him—he was strong enough to manage it just fine on his own."

"Okay," I say, nodding. "So I just need to pass my training quickly and everyone will forget that they ever thought it should be Harmony?"

"Exactly," Jackson says with a smile.

"You could also do a naked photo shoot," Trista teases.

"Or not," I say with a wry smile.

"Spoil sport," she says, pouting.

"Now," Jackson laughs, changing the subject, "may I escort you two lovely ladies back home?"

"Did you come out here just to greet us?" Trista asks, taking the arm he offers her.

"I may have done," he says with a grin.

"I could get used to this," Trista giggles. "You coming Ari?"

"Sure," I say and take the other proffered arm. Ultimately Jackson is right and I just need to remember that. Once I pass my training and earn my proper rank as Captain then everyone will forget that they ever thought I wasn't the right choice in the first place. I'm even including myself in that one.

Chapter 5

The following morning, after a night of me sticking to Mum and avoiding both Dad and Harmony, Trista and I go down to the beach, opting to watch the sun rise before breakfast. We spend the early hours hanging around by the rock pools, looking at the vibrant wildlife and watching the ecosystems thriving. I used to come down here to look at the pools a lot when I was little but not so much in recent years and now that it's something I won't be able to do when I leave I want to do it more. The training grounds I'm going to be living in will probably be a fair way from the coast and the mainland is going to have vastly different wildlife than we do out here because of the soil and the water. This is also the last time I'm going to have any significant amount of time off to myself until I've at least completed my basic training.

We leave when the sun is finally hanging high in the sky, knowing that we should head back to clean up for breakfast. Both of us are covered in sand and grime from the rocks and dripping wet. Thankfully the walk back dries us off somewhat, the heat of the day still enough to keep us from getting cold. Upon arriving back home, we're both about to head up to our rooms when Trista's mum, Angelica, calls out to us.

"Nice out girls?" she asks, smiling at us as we meet her on the stairs.

"Yeah," Trista grins. "We've been down in the rock pools."

"Please tell me you didn't bring anything living back with you," Angelica says with a raised eyebrow.

"Not this time," I reply, stifling my giggles at the memory of when we were thirteen and bought hermit crabs back to keep as pets so that they didn't get eaten but the huge seagulls that had been hanging around. We were told no and had to take them back which we were both very disappointed about. "Just sand."

Angelica rolls her eyes and shakes her head. "Honestly is there ever a time when the two of you *aren't* covered in sand?"

"When we're in occasion wear?" Trista offers.

"Okay I'll give you that one, cheeky," Angelica chuckles and gives one of Trista's loose ringlets a gentle tug before turning to me. "Ari your dad said he wanted to see you as soon as you got back. He said to head up to his study as soon as you're ready."

"Oh…okay." Time to face the music I guess. Harmony clearly went to tell on me to him and Mum and it's high time I took the punishment. Mum will cover for me, I can't ask everyone else to do the same.

"You should probably go clean up a bit first," Angelica laughs, "you're a bit on the streaky side."

I look over my shoulder at one of the windows and just about manage to catch my reflection in the glass and she's right: there is quite a lot of grime from the rock pools smeared over my face (probably shouldn't have dunked my entire head in for a closer look). "Whoops," I laugh. "Yeah I'll go wash, then head over."

"Good luck," Angelica says as I head off up the stairs to my room. That sounds ominous; I'm definitely in trouble.

"See you later Ari," Trista calls.

"Later," I call back as I reach the top of the stairs and round the corner, darting off to my bedroom. I'd better not keep Dad waiting (especially if I am about to get told off).

I have a very swift shower upon returning to my room, getting off the grime and the sand in order to make myself presentable before dressing in something clean that I can stay in for breakfast afterwards, and head to Dad's study. With the exception of the other night, I really don't come down this corridor all that much and after the other night I would have liked to avoid it again. I pass my grandfather's study and see that he's in. He looks up from his work to wave at me and I give him a small wave back before carrying on.

When I reach Dad's door, it's closed (already a good sign) so I knock and wait. A few seconds later, I hear his deep 'come in' and open the door. Closing the door behind me I come to stand in front of his desk. Nerves bubble up inside me as I'm pretty sure that I'm about to get told off for having it out with Harmony and not owning up to it, not to mention for avoiding him 'til now.

"You wanted to see me?" I ask as Dad looks up from his papers.

"Hey kiddo," he says and he doesn't sound like he's too angry so maybe that's not why I'm here at all and I'm just jumping the gun. "Take a seat."

"Sounding very formal there Dad," I chuckle nervously as I perch on the edge of the chair opposite his desk. He gives me a tired, strained half a smile and I realise that I was right in the first place—I've only ever seen that look on his face a few times and that's usually followed by 'I'm not angry, I'm disappointed'.

"You've been avoiding me, kiddo," he says.

I think about lying for a split second but then I realise that there's absolutely no point—he knows I have. "Yeah," I admit.

"I want to talk about you and Harmony," he says. No point beating about the bush, might as well just dive right in and get it over with.

"Okay," I reply. It's not going to be a fun conversation for either of us judging by the look on his face.

"You two have been arguing a lot recently," Dad says linking his fingers together on the desk in front of him.

"We had one fight the other day but the rest of the time she's been ignoring me, nothing out of the ordinary," I correct. We weren't fighting before our new positions were announced—she didn't exactly seek out my company or talk to me a lot but it wasn't like we were at each other's throats.

"She came to see me after your fight the other day," Dad says fixing me with a look that tells me that I am in trouble.

"I figured," I reply. I mean why else would I be here if she hadn't?

"I did say the same to her before you jump down my throat but you can't speak to her like that kiddo," Dad says. "If it looks like there's hostility between the Head of the House and the Neo Warrior it could be used against you by any number of people. We need to keep the accord between us all in order to protect the House."

"It wasn't without good reason," I say. I can feel my temper beginning to flare but I try to hold it in. He says he's had this conversation with Harmony and I wonder if that went down as well as it had the other night. I can't ask that though because then I'll probably be in even more trouble than I already am when he finds out I eavesdropped.

"Please tell me your side of the story then."

Great…I really don't fancy reliving it but if he wants to know then he wants to know. Besides, Harmony could have told him all sorts of things so I might as well try and set things straight. "I was out back by the fountain with Trista, we were just messing around, having a water fight, and then Harmony came out and started shouting at us about how we don't know how to behave like we're kids again," I tell him.

"So you decided to shout back?" Dad asks.

"If it was just me that she had been insulting, then I wouldn't have bothered but she's angry at me, for whatever reason," (pretend I don't know exactly why), "and she took it out on Trista. That's not fair. No matter how she feels about me she shouldn't be taking it out on other people, it was out of order."

That seems to hang in the room for a while, Dad mulling over what I've just told him and me trying to steady the anger threatening to boil over at the memory. I still can't believe that Harmony would tell on me, aren't we supposed to be adults? She's older than me dammit and she's the one behaving like we're children. Dad sighs and pinches the bridge of his nose, that familiar 'I have two daughters and they're both driving me crazy' look that I haven't seen on his face in a while as he processes it.

Finally he looks up at me and I'm amazed to see that he's actually smiling somewhat. "You always were steadfastly loyal…that will serve you well when you get to the mainland and start training."

"What do you mean?" I ask.

"You stood up for Trista when she needed you to, even if it meant that you're now in trouble; there's not many people who can say that they would actually do that," he replies.

"*Am* I in trouble?" I ask, pushing ever so slightly.

"Both of you could stand to talk things over with each other but I don't know if that is such a good idea, given the circumstances," Dad replies.

"How so?"

"Harmony is very stubborn and it would probably be in your best interest to give her some time to cool off before you try talking to her again," he says.

"Great," I grumble.

Dad chuckles. "I know what you're thinking," he says. "You're thinking 'why do I always have to be the one to suck it up and go talk to her? Why can't she come to me for a change when she's got just as much to apologise for?'"

Is he psychic? The look on my face seems to tell him that he's hit the nail right on the head and he laughs, his usual smile splitting his face.

"Kiddo, I know it always seems like you have to be the one to swallow your pride but just hearing you out when she thinks that she's in the right is as hard for Harmony as it is for you to go and talk to her."

"It's still not fair," I mumble.

"It isn't, no," Dad says, "but she will change and develop when she begins her training for Head of the House. You're both so young but you'll grow very quickly as people when you begin your new positions. Harmony is going to have to change her attitude if she wants to succeed and have the people of the House respect and love her the way they do your grandfather."

After a long pause, I open my mouth again. "Harmony doesn't think I'm good enough to have been picked for the Neo Warrior."

"I know," Dad says.

"This is why we keep fighting," I say and I can feel hot tears beginning to prick the corners of my eyes.

"She has voiced these concerns to me, yes," Dad says and I really have to fight the urge to tell him that I heard her and that I already know. I'd really rather not get the disappointed face again when he finds out.

"I am though, aren't I?" I ask instead.

"What?"

"Suitable to do this?"

"Yes," Dad says.

"But isn't it usually the tradition to pass the torch to the next eldest family member?"

I can't not ask. Harmony, coupled with the whispering when I was picked and she wasn't and the clash with the man in the market all makes me wonder if it would have just been better if I hadn't been chosen at all. I know Trista is right, as is everyone who I've spoken to, and I should also respect the council's decision but it doesn't stop me from wondering.

Dad thinks about this for a moment before letting out a long, deep breath. "Sometimes," he says slowly, thinking over each word as he says it, "traditions should be broken. If it is in the interest of the House and the people."

"Okay."

"Have confidence in your abilities and our decision or do you *also* think that the High Council made a mistake?"

"No," I reply, despite how other people have been making me feel.

"Good," he says with a smile. "While Harmony may have been training for this longer and harder than you, that doesn't mean that you aren't capable of fulfilling the role."

"Okay." That's actually very comforting. It's not like I've ever slacked off in the training I've been given but I was never as serious as Harmony because I guess, deep down, I always thought that if I was ever in the running it would be because Harmony was too old. I need to be more confident in what I actually can do rather than worrying about how much better Harmony is. "Thanks Dad."

He smiles again but it's a little rueful as he shakes his head. "You two were so much easier when you were younger, there was none of this competition and you didn't want to kill each other all the time."

"I don't want to kill her *all* the time," I say and it's true: I really don't (you know, when she's not being a complete bitch to my friends). "She just rubs me up the wrong way sometimes."

"I know kiddo," Dad says with a sigh, "and I know that Harmony is being particularly difficult about this but please try not to rise to it. I understand that how she treated Trista the other day was awful and that she shouldn't be taking her frustration out on you in the first place that should have been our brunt to bear."

"Dad I've only got two more days left here," I say, "how much more time does she need?"

"It's Harmony so it's anyone's guess," he replies.

We fall back into silence for a long moment, both of us staring at each other like some kind of face off. There are so many questions that I want to ask him but while he's not as scary as some people's fathers (he's not like my uncle Keith who can level people with just a look) I've always been a lot closer to Mum. Dad's always been the one to teach us how to spar and teach us the ways and laws of the House whereas Mum has always been the one to read us stories before we go to bed, sit with us and listen to us talk.

"Hey Dad?" I begin after the silence has stretched on for way too long and I don't feel like I can take it anymore.

"Yes kiddo," he says. It's almost funny that even when he's supposed to be reprimanding me for arguing with Harmony he still can't shake the nickname. It's a bit like Mum still calling me 'baby' even though I'm eighteen.

"Do you think I should have been training harder all these years?" I ask. "That seems to be Harmony's biggest grievance, that I'm unprepared, and maybe she's right. I know you told me to trust your decision but I do wonder if I should have trained for this prospect more. Neo Warriors from other Houses do."

"Is this what you've been reading in the magazines or is this what Harmony has told you?" he asks, a small smile playing about his lips.

"Both," I reply.

"Well, your mother and I decided to take the more relaxed approach when it came to training you and Harmony. Harmony only trained as hard as she did because she felt that she needed to. She has always wanted to excel and that is an admirable quality."

"And me?" I ask.

"You understand the importance of stepping back, taking a break from the training and having some time to just be yourself," he tells me. "If you can't find joy within yourself and those around you then no matter how hard you train you'll always feel as if something is lacking. Do you understand where I'm coming from?"

"I think I do," I say. I do feel a lot more at ease now that he's pointed that out to me. It's something I never really realised about myself but it's true. I always wanted to train with Harmony and the older kids when we were younger but I also wanted to spend time having fun with Trista so I tried to balance both. So that means I may not be as skilled as Harmony is but, by the sound of what Granddad told me the other night, the fact that I know when to stop and have fun will help me to fit in a lot better.

"Good," Dad says and he smiles at me. It's the same smile I normally see and I'm pretty sure that all the seriousness is now over. "So with all that in mind do you feel more confident about being appointed?"

"I do yeah," I say.

"Good, then I think that's all we need to talk about."

We fall into silence again for a few moments before I finally open my mouth. "You got a lot of work still to do?"

Dad sighs. "Yes, unfortunately this is the part that comes with being the father of not only the new Head of the House but the new Neo Warrior as well: lots of paperwork."

"Would you like some company?" I ask.

"If you want to stay," he replies.

"Yeah sure." I relax into the chair a bit more and watch as Dad opens a drawer on his desk and pulls a book out of it.

"Here," he says, tossing it to me.

I catch it with ease and look down at the cover. It doesn't look like much to me: just a normal, old notebook with a slightly worn and battered cover. When I open it up and flick through the first few pages, I'm met with my grandmother's faded handwriting. I look up at Dad again. "Is this…?"

"That's your grandmother's diary from when she first became a Neo Warrior," Dad says, smiling. "She was the same age as you when she was selected and I thought that this might be helpful."

"Thank you," I gush as I turn back to the book.

"There's more where that came from, just let me know if you want the rest of them," Dad tells me.

"I will," I say. This is amazing! There must be so much in here that will help me when I get to the mainland. I hear the scratch of pen against paper and I know that Dad has already gone back to his work so I settle down and turn to the front of the book ready to read all about my grandmother's time as a Neo Warrior.

~ *** ~

I read in Dad's office until we both decide to head down for a very late breakfast. After another day with Trista, I take more of the journals to read down by the fountain. Grandmother's notebooks are fascinating! Filled with pages and pages of insight, magical techniques and fighting strategies and I need to know everything that they contain. Reading these is how I spend all of my free time over my last two days at home and it's a good way to avoid Harmony when I'm not out. It's not like she's actually spoken to me during meal times, when we have to be together, but that's fine. I don't have the energy to have it out at dinner in front of everyone. Tonight though, is the night before I leave so I feel like I should at least try and make amends with her otherwise who knows when I'll next get the chance to.

Trista and I got back from the beach late so I didn't really have much of a chance to wash up before dinner (which earned me a look of thunder from Harmony) and I don't want to leave it any longer so I don't bother going back to my room to shower after dinner. As soon as I'm sure she's in her room I quickly hurry down the corridor and knock before I can lose my nerve. As soon as I have I already wish that I hadn't as this is probably going to be awful but I've started this now so I have to go through with it.

It feels like an age before the door opens and as soon as Harmony sees me she scowls; clearly my appearance has ruined her night as much as it's going to ruin mine. "What do you want?" she snaps.

"Can we talk?" I ask and I'm happy to hear that my voice sounds surprisingly steady despite the fact that I feel like I'm going to be sick all over her.

"I don't think we have anything to talk about," she says, folding her arms across her chest.

"Well, I do," I say a little fiercely. I didn't quite mean it to come out like that but now it has I'm going to keep going.

"So talk," she says.

"Can I come in?" I ask, wondering if she really wants to have it out in the hallway.

"No," she says almost instantly.

"Okay…" I don't really know what I expected. "So you know I'm leaving for the mainland tomorrow morning?"

"As if it was hard to forget," she says. "It's all anyone has been talking about: Ariana Sirenia the great new Neo Warrior." The sarcasm stings but I swallow it down and hope that she doesn't see how much she's hurt me already.

"Yeah well I wanted to make things right between us before I left."

"So you leave it until the last night?" she scoffs derisively.

"Okay I deserve that, but you haven't exactly been approachable."

"Is that all you came here to tell me or is there something else?"

"I wanted to say I'm sorry for our fight the other day," I say. Just rip off the plaster and get on with it, don't prolong this conversation any more than need be. "I shouldn't have said the things that I did and I'm sorry."

"So you should be," she says.

What? Nothing in return for my trouble? I'm trying to be nice here and she's still being difficult. I take a deep breath and try again. "So nothing that you want to say to me at all?" I ask, hopefully.

"Aside from to tell you not to make our House look bad again I think I've said everything that needs to be said."

We're at a standoff: both of us glaring at each other and neither one of us wanting to budge because we both think the other is in the wrong. Finally the silence gets to me and I sigh, breaking eye contact with her and looking at the floor.

"I don't understand why you can't just be happy for me," I mumble but I know she's heard me. "Just tell me that it's all going to be okay and I'll be alright rather than getting on my back the whole time."

"Because I don't think it's all going to be okay," she replies as if that should be obvious. "I've watched you train over the years and yes you're good, there's no doubt about that, but you're lazy. You could be better and you should be if you're going to go off and train with Caspian Feioré."

"Stop throwing his name around like you know what he's expecting," I snap. It's getting irritating; every single time she wants to tell me that I'm not good enough or my abilities aren't at the right level she brings him up and I know that he's going to expect a lot from me but at the same time I'm only a new recruit. He can't really expect me to be at the same kind of level as the rest of them. Besides it's not like I'm completely clueless; I found one of my old magazines that had an interview with Caspian and he outlined his training regime so I at least know what I'm in for when I meet him.

"*This* is your problem," Harmony hisses, taking a step towards me. "You think that you know what's best and that you know what you're doing but you can't be like that as a Neo Warrior. You need to make sensible decisions and not let your emotions run what you do. You can't seem to do that otherwise you wouldn't be here yelling at me like a child."

"I'm not yelling!" I snap raising my voice slightly. I know I'm now proving her right but I can't seem to stop myself.

She smirks at me. "You're still such a child," she says. "This is why I knew that you weren't the right decision for this job."

"You think I don't know that? You think I haven't already had *your* supporters telling me that it should have been you?" I think back to that man in the market and the other whispers I've heard around: the traditionalists who think that it should have been her just because she's older. They don't know anything about what I can do and neither does she. She might have been watching me train but she's barely spent any real time with me over the last few years so she has no idea.

"And they're right," she says.

"Why?" I ask because I really don't understand. "Because you're older? Is that literally all it comes down to?"

"Because I knew years ago that it would come down to this one day and I started training," she replies. "I knew that I was going to have to be the best magic user on this island if I was going to join the ranks of the Neo Warriors and you…you have no idea."

"I'm not completely useless!" I tell her.

"But you're not competent," she immediately replies.

"How would you know?" I ask. I can feel angry tears welling up in my eyes but I'm determined that I'm not going to cry. Not in front of her. "I would have thought that if anyone was going to believe in me and support me through this it would be you. I know we're not exactly close but you're my sister. *I* think you're going to be a great Head of the House so why can't you just be there for me? I leave tomorrow and I don't know when I'm coming back."

"Because it should have been *me*!" Harmony yells at me. "*I've* been training for this. *I* gave up so much to train because I thought that, one day, I'd become the Neo Warrior! And then they chose you and all of those years have been wasted."

"Why do you think it was a waste? Surely if you're stronger now, then it wasn't for nothing in the end?"

"You wouldn't understand."

"But I'm trying to!" I yell, frustration building. So far she's not actually given me any real answers and I don't know how I can fix whatever it is that seems to be going on between us; I just seem to be making it worse.

"You know what, when I'm Head of the House if you don't come back to me within two weeks to say that you've passed your basic training then don't bother coming back at all!" she hisses glaring at me.

"Maybe I won't," I reply in kind. "Maybe I'll stay somewhere where people actually believe in me and that I'm not just a waste of everyone's time."

"Fine, stay on the mainland for all I care," she snaps. "It's not like we need you here. It's not like you could actually do anything to protect the island if you were needed to."

"I'll let my results do the talking for me," I say, fire fuelling me. I know I need to be careful because I might say something I regret but what does it matter in the long run? I leave tomorrow so we might as well air it all out tonight. "I'll pass in record time and then you'll realise that you were wrong."

"I very much doubt that."

"If you're going to be like this then don't come to see me off tomorrow!" The words are out of my mouth before I can stop them but once they are I realise that I don't actually want to take them back.

She looks shocked for a moment: I can see the hurt in her eyes but it's instantly replaced with fury and she recovers herself. She glares down at me again and whatever had been in her eyes before is replaced with contempt. "Fine," she says through gritted teeth before slamming the door in my face.

I don't even wait to see if she comes back out, storming down the corridor back to my room, filled with blind fury. Stupid Harmony! Why does she have to be like this? I don't understand why she just can't be happy and supportive. She's been cold in recent years but she's never been like this! We used to be so close but she's been putting this distance between us. Now it seems as if she doesn't care in the slightest that I'm going away tomorrow and I have no idea when I'm going to have the chance to come back.

The adrenaline suddenly disappears and I'm left with a hollow void in my chest. Despite everything I know, I'll miss her. All I wanted was the chance to make things right and I just made them worse. I can't go back and try again now; there's no way that she'll talk to me! My legs stop moving and I lean against the wall, the tears that I've been desperately trying to hold back beginning to spill down my cheeks. I slap a hand over my mouth to stifle the sob but it hurts my chest to do so. Sinking to my knees I start crying, leaning against the wall for support. I've ruined my chances to make up with her and now I don't know when I'll see her again to apologise.

~ *** ~

It's late in the evening: it must be getting on for ten or eleven now and I'm sitting on my bed staring out at the night sky with all the lights turned off. I tried not to spend too long crying in the corridor so, thankfully, no one found me and I managed to get myself back to my room unnoticed. I didn't fancy turning on the lights and this is probably the last time that I'm going to see the sky like this. From what I've been told from people who have been there, there are a lot of lights dotted around on the mainland, especially around the capital, so it's likely that there's going to be a lot of light pollution where I'm staying. A shame really: there's nothing like looking up at the stars when it's completely dark and just thinking.

The lights suddenly click on and I turn to see Mum standing in the doorway smiling at me. "You okay baby?" she asks.

I wipe a hand over my face to catch any lingering tears and swivel round so that I'm facing her. "Yeah I'm okay."

"You sure?"

"Yeah," I say again. If I say it enough, I might even start to believe it myself.

"Did you have a good last week?" she asks, coming to sit down beside me.

"I did yeah," I reply, giving her a small smile.

"Your hair's a state," Mum laughs as she runs her fingers through the untidy strands. It was windy today and I should have tied it up, especially as we were swimming in the ocean and it got wet, but I didn't. Twisting it around in my hands after fighting with Harmony didn't help either. I twiddle a lock of it around my finger and look sheepish.

"Yeah, sorry."

"Don't be sorry," she says, turning me so that my back is to her. "Give me your brush."

I lean over to my bedside table and grab my hairbrush, handing it to her before wriggling back into position. She begins to run the brush through my hair. It should hurt, considering how knotted my hair probably is, but it doesn't; it's relaxing and I close my eyes, breathing deeply.

"I heard you and Harmony still aren't talking to each other," she says, "and that you got into another fight."

"Not really," I mutter, biting my lip and playing with the hem of my shirt, "and yeah we did."

"Is this still the same argument?"

"Yeah…"

"What was it about?" she asks.

"Just stuff," I mumble. She probably knows. Probably the first thing Harmony did once we had finished screaming at each other was go and complain about me to the rest of the council, or at least to Mum and Dad again.

Mum chuckles. "This is me you're talking to," she says. "You know you can tell me anything."

"I know," I sigh.

"So what happened?"

"You know," I tell her.

"Indulge me," she says and I can hear the smile in her voice.

"I went to try and clear the air after the last few days and we just ended up shouting at each other again."

"Harmony's adjusting," Mum says. "That's not an excuse but she's never been very good at being overly gracious, especially when it comes to losing something she thinks she has already earned."

I stare at my hands for a moment, not wanting to voice what I'm thinking but I know I should. "She's not coming to see me off tomorrow, is she?" I ask. A tiny part of me had hoped that she wouldn't take it to heart but, realistically, I know she took me at my word.

"I'll see what I can do but I wouldn't count on it," Mum replies.

"Great," I mutter. "She hates me, I have no way to make this right and I don't know what I'm supposed to do about any of this."

"Oh baby, you're eighteen. You're not supposed to know what to do," Mum says and hugs me. I lean my head back and rest it against her shoulder. "Besides, despite what you think, Harmony doesn't hate you."

"Sure seems that way right now," I say.

"It might do but this isn't the first time the two of you have fought like this," Mum says. "Remember when you were nine and you got into that huge argument with her. I can't remember what it was about but I remember that neither of you spoke to each other for about three weeks until we locked you in a room together until you stopped being stubborn."

"I don't think you and Dad locking us up until we work it out is going to work this time," I say smiling wryly. "We're older and have better control of our magic—we might end up killing each other."

"Don't knock it 'til you've tried it," Mum says, laughing as she goes back to her brushing.

"I'm pretty sure if you do you're going to have to reselect a least one of us," I say with a chuckle.

"Fine," Mum says, sighing theatrically, "I'll come up with a better plan."

"Or I could just be an adult and go and try to apologise to her again," I say.

"You could," Mum says, "and it's very admirable that you would but, I think in this instance it might be better if you leave it for now. You've already tried and it didn't go to plan so give her some time. Once Harmony has had a moment to cool down, once you've been gone a month or two, she'll realise that she misses you and you'll get a letter of apology from her."

"You think?" I ask.

"I'm your mother," she replies, "I know."

I turn round and hug her. "Thanks Mum."

"You know I've always got your back baby," she says hugging me back. "If you ever need me while you're away just write and I'll send a letter straight back. If you need me to come out to the mainland, then I will be there faster than you can think."

"Thanks Mum," I say. I tighten my arms around her for a second before I pull away. "I think I'll be okay though: I should be able to make at least one friend…I hope."

"Yeah also it would be very uncool and not give you much of a rep if your mum turns up with you," she laughs and gently flicks my nose. I wriggle it and grin at her. "You'll do just fine, you know that."

"I hope so," I say.

"No matter what anyone says, you'll be fine because you, my darling, are a Sirenia and Sirenias always have a way of working things out."

"Really?" I ask, raising an eyebrow at her.

"Trust me," she says, dropping a kiss on my forehead. "You'll be just fine."

"Okay," I reply and in that moment I completely believe her. Who cares what anyone else says? My mum believes in me and my best friend believes in me. I can make my own way in the world and I'll come back the best damn Captain that the House of Neptune has ever seen.

Chapter 6

I take Mum's advice and don't try and talk to Harmony again. In the morning, I don't see her at breakfast (which is good as I don't have to avoid talking to her while I'm eating) and when I pass her in the corridor on my way to the bathroom I say nothing and don't make eye contact. It's been exhausting, sneaking around and feeling like I'm walking on eggshells around her, but I'm leaving today so I don't have to deal with her for much longer now.

Mum did say she was going to try to convince her to come and see me off, as no one really knowns when I'll be home again, but I'm not holding out much hope. To be honest I'm ready to go. I'm fed up of waiting and I just want to get to the mainland so I can start my training and meet the rest of the Neo Warriors. Not having to creep around Harmony all the time will be a bonus. Whatever doubts, I'd been feeling about the whole thing have been completely erased; my desire to get away from Harmony is stronger.

I stand on the dock in front of the ship that will be my home for the next two weeks while we sail over to the mainland. The House of Neptune is situated on the smallish island of Neyara about halfway between the mainland and the east coast of Cimmerian. With a population of only two hundred thousand, we are (what my dad likes to call) the first line of defence in the event of an invasion. Having said that there hasn't been an invasion from Cimmerian in a while, so we're now just a House of fisherman, sailors and river gypsies. We know these waters better than anyone else so we have the advantage over all enemies.

We're a simple House but we do still like to go in for ceremony when a new Neo Warrior or council official is chosen. I vaguely remember when Michael was sent off to the mainland as the new Neo Warrior—I was only about twelve at the time and I remember the docks being filled as people came to see him off and to wish him luck. It makes my heart swell with pride and excitement to see that today is no different for me.

The crowd fanned out in front of me is huge: so huge that I can barely see any space between everyone gathered here. For the most part, I think they're people from the surrounding villages and others who usually work down at the docks but it's still amazing. I don't think I've ever seen this many people in one tiny space before so there could be others here too. It's so cool! All these people, regardless of their reasons, have come to see me leave and are happy for me to represent them.

One of the ship's sailors comes up to me and salutes. A tall man with soft eyes, a winning smile, and hair the colour of sea-foam tied back into a low, sleek ponytail that sits in the middle of his shoulder blades. He's at least ten years older than me and he's got an impressive set of muscles on him, probably from working on a ship.

"We're nearly loaded and ready to go when you are, Ma'am," he says. "We're just waiting for the tide to turn. Say the word, and we'll set sail."

"Um, sure thing, thank you." I say and nod at him. I guess I'm going to have to get used to people asking me for orders and having my word be what makes the final decision...well, with my squad, not the other Neo Warriors. Not yet at least. I'll be taking over Michael's old squad so it's not as if they will require much training—they'll just have to get used to my way of leading them. *I'll* have to get used to my way of leading so it will be a learning curve for everyone involved.

I feel a gentle hand on my shoulder and turn to see Mum and Dad standing behind me. Trista and my granddad aren't far behind them and just in front of the crowd are the other members of the High Council. There is only one person that I can't see. That figures too; I didn't really expect Mum to be able to convince her to show up after everything that happened even if I hoped she would. She's probably still angry and I don't blame her. I try not to think about her as I let my dad pull me into a tight hug. He feels so solid and familiar that I feel my nerve slip a tiny bit.

"Give 'em hell, kiddo," he says as I hug him back.

"I will, Dad," I tell him.

"Just remember: stick to your training, listen to what your Commander has to tell you and, most importantly..."

"Always remember to duck in case of surprise attacks," I finish, grinning. He's been saying that to me ever since I was old enough to learn how to spar;

it's almost like his catchphrase now. He smiles and pulls me into another hug. "That's my girl."

"Love you Dad."

"Love you too kiddo," he says, "and don't forget, if you need anything just write to us—we're right here to help you. There's no shame in asking people for help if you need it."

"Thanks Dad."

"You're going to do fantastically so don't you worry about a thing," he says as he places his hands on my shoulders.

"I won't let any of you down," I say. "I've got this."

"I know you do," he says. He looks me up and down and smiles wistfully. "Every bit a Sirenia. Your grandmother would be so proud of you, you know. It's a shame she's no longer here to see you head off."

"I won't let you down, I promise," I say, swallowing the slight lump in my throat.

"I know you won't," he says. "You'll be fantastic."

He squeezes my shoulders and I grin at him before he steps to the side and allows Granddad to come forward while both Mum and Trista hang back. Granddad takes my hand and gives it a squeeze. Now that I'm standing with him in the sunlight, he still looks old but not as old as he did the other night.

"Ariana," he says, his voice low and gravelly, "I'm sure you will do a fine job and you will make us all very proud."

"Thanks Granddad," I say, practically beaming at him. I will, there is a reason I am here: the council wouldn't have picked me if they didn't think I could do it and I will hold onto that for as long as I need to.

"I took the liberty of bringing you a little something to celebrate," Granddad says. He slips his hand into the inside pocket of his jacket and pulls out a small silver hip flask and hands it to me. It's beautiful; an intricate pair of koi carp entwined together around the astrological symbol for Neptune engraved on the front—the crest of the House of Neptune—and our insignia 'Glory under the seas' engraved beneath it. It's so beautiful and thoughtful that I'm speechless. I stare at him wide-eyed and smile.

"Thank you Granddad!" I grin and throw my arms around his neck.

"That's not the only thing," he says and there is a twinkle in his eye.

I look at him questioningly and he nods at the hip flask. I take the top off and give it an experimental sniff. The smell hits me and I can already feel the burn in the back of my throat from a few nights ago. Grinning at him, I replace the top and he winks at me.

"Just a little token for your first night on the mainland," he says.

"Thank you Granddad," I say.

"That will help you keep up with the rest of them. Pass that around first night and you'll do just fine," he says.

"Thank you." I say again.

He takes my hand and gives it a squeeze. "Just be yourself and they'll love you."

"Promise?"

"Promise," he says.

I squeeze his hand back before he lets go and steps away. Almost as soon as he's gone Trista practically jumps on me, wrapping her arms around my neck and hugging me tightly. I hug her back just as tightly and I feel her shoulders shaking as she cries into my neck. Oh no, she'll set *me* off at this rate.

"Good luck," she says, sobbing quietly into my shoulder.

"You too," I say.

"You'd better write to me," she says. "Every single day."

"Of course I will," I chuckle.

"Good."

"Although you know after a while my letters will just be me saying the same thing over and over again," I say.

"I don't care," she says, tightening her hold on me. "I just want to hear from you and know that you're alright."

"You'll have to write to me too," I tell her.

"Every day, as soon as I have a return address," she says.

"Good because I want to hear all about Jackson."

"I promise," she says.

"Take care of yourself."

"Come back safe," she whispers and as she pulls away I can see the tracks on her face where tears have been making their way down her cheeks.

"Hey," I say, reaching over and wiping away a new tear that begins falling with my thumb, "please don't cry. I don't want you to be sad."

"I'm sorry," she says, wiping her face with the back of her hand. "I'm just going to miss you so much."

"I'll miss you too," I say and I feel a lump in my throat. This is harder than I thought it would be. I knew leaving the island would also involve leaving Trista but saying goodbye to my best friend is really difficult.

"You have to promise me that you'll take care of yourself and not run headlong into anything dangerous," she says.

"I promise I won't," I say.

"And don't eat any weird mainland food that you're not sure about and make sure that you make at least one new friend…but not a better friend than me, and if there is anything that you can't do then don't push yourself and get hurt just because the others are doing it."

"Okay, okay," I laugh, holding up my hands in defence. "I promise that I will keep safe and not over do it."

"Good," she sniffs, "because I know what you're like: you do too much just to prove that you can keep up."

"When have I ever done that?" I ask, grinning, knowing that she can give about nine examples.

"Just make sure that you come back alive," she says, hugging me again.

"I'll be fine," I say and hug her back. "Besides, I'll be back for the wedding so you'll see me again before you know it."

"Okay," she nods as she pulls away.

"Miss Sirenia," Jackson says, his huge frame suddenly appearing behind Trista's shoulder, placing his arm around her, "or should I say Captain Sirenia?"

"Captain Sirenia," I muse, grinning again, "I like the sound of that."

"Would you permit me to offer my congratulations to you as well?" he asks.

"Of course," I say. It would be rude not to.

Jackson turns to smile at me before he sinks down to one knee. He places one hand over his heart while he takes one of mine with the other. My face begins to heat up and I'm pretty sure I'm blushing. I can't look at him without feeling embarrassed but I can't look at anyone else either so I settle for staring up at the sky and pretending this isn't happening.

Please get up I am not comfortable with this!

Jackson softly kisses my hand before he gets to his feet again. He's at least a foot taller than me and twice as wide and I feel completely dwarfed in comparison. Are they all this tall from his House! He must be at least six foot five, if not taller.

"I promise on my honour, as a member of the House of Pluto, that I will do my best to keep Trista happy and safe while you are away," he says. "She will be my world, my queen and my everything. I make this oath to you now, and I will do the same in front of members of both our Houses when we are married. I know that Trista values your opinion over all others and so I will do the same. If there is anything that I do that either you or she are unhappy with, then I will lay down my life for either of you to do with as you wish." Wow! That's quite a speech.

Casting a glance over at Trista she's as stunned as I am, although she now seems to be crying tears of pure joy. I can't say that I wouldn't be doing the same if someone said something like that about me to someone that I cared about. Of course Jackson would make a speech like that. I pretend to study him for a moment, as if scrutinising his honesty. He seems like a nice enough guy so I'll give him a helping hand.

"She likes cake," I say suddenly, my expression never changing.

"Pardon?" he asks.

"I'm not saying it's the key to her heart or anything, and I'm not saying that you shouldn't also do all of those other things, but Trista likes cake," I say.

A huge smile spreads over his face and I can't help smiling back. Aside from the fact that he seems to just have a very infectious smile I can't pretend to be the stoic, over-protective best friend for much longer. My face won't stay that deadpan.

"So does Ellis," Jackson says. "He absolutely loves cake; you bring him cake and he will love you forever, especially if it's something with raspberries in it."

"Raspberry cake," I nod, committing it to memory. "Got it."

"You'll recognise him immediately as he looks like a larger version of me," Jackson says.

Larger? Beg pardon? This man is already the size of a barge and he's telling me that his brother is bigger than he is! I'm going to look like a fairy compared to him! I think I'm going to have to get a bit more buff if I want to be in either of their leagues.

"Don't look so worried," Jackson chuckles. "I know he sounds terrifying but, in reality, Ellis is a massive softie."

"As long as I don't forget the raspberry cake," I say, trying to relax my face.

"Exactly," he says.

"Thank you," I grin. That's a good start: cake and alcohol will make me friends.

"Good luck to you, Captain Sirenia," Jackson says, saluting me. "I have every faith that you will make a fine Neo Warrior and you'll do your House and your family proud."

"Thank you," I say saluting back. Just as he turns to go I hail his attention again, smiling sweetly. "Oh and Jackson…"

"Yes?"

"If you do anything to hurt Trista in any way, whatever contract there is between our Houses is moot. Never mind me, she will kill you herself," I say. I'm smiling but *I* can't even tell if I'm joking or not.

He seems to take it rather well and throws his head back, laughing. "I would expect nothing less from either of you."

He turns to Trista and wraps an arm around her shoulders, pulling her close to comfort her as I turn to my mum. She smiles at me and opens her arms wide. I practically fling myself into them, wrapping mine around her neck and hugging her tightly. She hugs me back just as tightly, gently stroking my hair. With her holding me like this, I almost don't want to let go. I can't imagine not seeing her every single day. Even when she's holed up all day with boring council stuff to do, she always makes sure that she comes and spends some time with me. It used to be the three of us—me, her and Harmony—but it's just been me and her in recent years. That lump is forming in my throat again and tears prick the corners of my eyes.

"You'll knock 'em dead, baby," she whispers as she strokes my hair.

"Mum," I whisper back, burrowing my head into the join between her neck and shoulder. The tears are pricking harder now and I don't want to cry in front of all of these people but, right now, there is a good chance that I might.

"Yeah?"

"I'm scared," I tell her. My voice is barely above a whisper and I'm amazed that she can even hear me at all. Under all this bravado that I've been shoving out at everyone I'm actually scared as all hell. What if I don't pass basic training? What if I fall flat on my arse and make a fool out of myself in front of everyone?

Mum laughs softly. She pulls back and presses her forehead to mine. "You are going to be one of the finest Neo Warriors we've ever had," she says. "It might not feel like it right now, but you've got twelve years to become the absolute best that you can be. You'll throw yourself into your training and I know that you won't let yourself fall behind. There will be eleven other people all pushing you to be the very best. You'll be fine. When you put your mind to something, there's nothing you can't do and if you need further proof: you're a Sirenia—you were born to do this."

"Thanks Mum," I say smiling at her. "I love you."

"I love you too."

"Um Mum…" I begin tentatively before I can stop myself. I don't know why I'm about to ask this but it seems to be coming out of my mouth before I can stop it.

"Yeah?"

"Where's Harmony?" I ask and as soon as the words are out of my mouth I regret them.

Mum's smile falters. "I'm sorry baby," she says. "I tried to talk her into coming but she wouldn't."

Ouch… That stings.

I expected as much; I didn't see her in the crowd and I know she's still angry, but it really hurts that my own sister wouldn't even come and see me off before I leave. Harmony and I haven't exactly been on the greatest of terms over the last few days but I thought she'd at least hang out in the back of the crowd with the other council members and scowl. Clearly she can hold a grudge for much longer than I had originally thought.

Taking a deep breath I push the pain down, plaster a smile on my face and pretend that I don't still want to burst into tears. Harmony aside, I want to cry because I'm going to miss everyone so much and it's weird going away and leaving behind my whole life for a brand new one, but Harmony not coming to see me off is the thing that hurts the most. I think Mum can tell but she doesn't say anything so I swallow it down.

"No matter," I say, rubbing the back of my hand quickly over my eyes as if I'm unaffected.

"I can just write to her when I get there."

"Make sure you write to all of us when you get there and when you get settled in," Dad says with a smile.

"At this rate, I'll spend my entire first week there writing home," I laugh.

"You'll do fine kiddo," Dad says, ruffling my hair.

"Excuse me sir," a gruff voice says from behind me. I turn to see a thickset man, only a little taller than I am, standing behind me. Dad smiles when he sees him and goes to clasp the man's hand, shaking it vigorously. The other man seems quite happy to see Dad too so I wonder if they're old sailing buddies.

"Adams," Dad says beaming. "Good to see you. How have you been?"

"Good to see you too sir," the man (presumably Adams) says. "I have been very well and yourself?"

"Good, good," Dad says. "How goes it?"

"We're ready to leave now sir," Adams says. "The ship is stocked and at the next turn of the tide, which should be within the next couple of minutes, we're looking to push off and set sail."

"Splendid," Dad says, rubbing his hands together. "Then there's really only one thing left to do." He puts his arm around my shoulder and pulls me forward so that I'm standing next to him in front of Adams. "Adams this is my daughter, Ariana Sirenia, our new representative Neo Warrior. Ariana, this is Captain James Adams, the finest Captain I have ever had the pleasure of serving under in my sailing days."

"Hi," I say and give him my best smile.

"Captain Sirenia," Adams says and salutes.

"You don't have to call me Captain, Captain," I say. I want to laugh at the absurdity of the situation—I don't really have a proper rank or title yet and people are already calling me Captain and speculating about Commander—but Adams looks so earnest that I can't.

It's so weird though: a fifty-something-year-old man is saluting *me*, calling *me* Captain and treating me with way more respect than is necessary. Is this what being a Neo Warrior feels like? Because if it is, it's cool! I can't wait to get to the mainland and join the rest of them.

"Begging your pardon, Captain," Adams says smiling, as he drops his salute and extends his hand to me instead, "but I have always been one to respect someone's rank regardless of how new to it they are."

"It's an admirable quality," I say as I shake his hand.

"One of my many," he chuckles. "So are you ready to set sail?"

"I am," I reply. "I must admit, I'm not much of a sailor but I'm willing to learn and I enjoy being out on the water."

"By the end of this trip, you'll be a skilled hand on deck," he says. "Me and my crew will turn you into the finest sailor there is."

"Thank you, it's an absolute pleasure to meet you, Captain Adams," I say.

"And an honour to meet you too Captain Sirenia," he says. "Now are you ready to see the ship?"

"Very much so," I say. I turn to the crowd behind me and salute them.

I've know the salute of the Braxian army ever since I was four years old: right hand over your heart in order to protect yourself from attack, left arm across the stomach in order to reach for a concealed weapon if need be. (…What? We're superstitious and lots of people have tried to kill us over the years.) Doing it now, in front of all these people, actually makes it feel as if it means something. It means that I'm ready to fight for them if the time comes. These people are my family, and not just the ones I'm blood related to, and I would do anything in order to protect them.

"Thank you everyone," I say loud enough so that the entire dock can hear me. "I will do my best to represent the House of Neptune for what we are—honest, hard-working individuals who carry their own weight in the world—and make each and every one of you proud. For the honour of Neptune: glory under the seas!"

"Glory under the seas!" the crowd cheers back.

That was cool. I've never led one of those before.

Applause strikes up and I feel my chest swelling with pride. Every single one of these people in front of me thinks that I can do this and that makes me think that I can as well. Mum's right: as long as I give it my all I should be fine. I'm willing to learn and as long as someone is willing to teach me then I can pass my basic training in no time at all. And if no one is willing to teach me, I'll just learn how to do it myself.

The applause doesn't die down as I follow Adams onto the ship; if anything it seems to get even louder. I can't keep the smile off my face. This is all for me—how cool is this?

"What's say we push off now?" Adams asks, a mischievous twinkling in his eye. "The tide is perfect, the wind is starting to pick up and it will make for an absolutely phenomenal exit after a speech like that."

"I like the sound of that," I say.

"You heard Captain Sirenia," Adams shouts to the crew members who have been milling around on deck. "Weigh anchor, set the sails and push off now."

Everyone on deck begins to scramble to what I assume are their designated positions as Adams barks orders at them. I watch for a moment, letting it all wash over me that this is really happening and I'm not just dreaming. After another moment or two, I make my way over to the edge of the ship and look down at my family and Trista, still smiling up at me from the dock. I feel a tightening in my chest and it all suddenly becomes very real again: I'm leaving and I have no idea when I'm going to be back, on top of the fact that I've never left the island before. It's a lot to swallow but the way they're all looking at me, filled with such pride and love, I know that I will do my best to make them all proud.

The ship begins to move away from the dock and I peer over the edge as much as possible without falling to see the gap between the ship and the dock getting wider. This is it: I'm really leaving and it's too late to turn back now. I look over at my mum and I feel those tears forming in the corners of my eyes again. She winks at me and blows me a kiss. I blow one back, swallowing the tears down and smiling.

"Bye everyone," I call, waving.

There is a cheer from the crowd and some of them, my family among them, stop clapping to wave back at me. The ship begins to pick up speed as the wind also starts to blow harder and then all of a sudden we're moving too fast. Before I know it, the people on the shore are fading into the distance. I keep waving, even though my arm is beginning to ache with tiredness, and don't stop until I can barely see them anymore.

Eventually I drop my hand and grip onto the edge of the ship's railing for support. I take a deep, shuddering breath to steady myself. Saying goodbye is hard. I know that I'm going on to better and more exciting things and when I come back and see everyone again it will be as a fully-fledged Neo Warrior Captain but it's still hard knowing that could be months from now.

After a moment or two, I feel a hand on my shoulder and I turn to see Adams standing behind me, smiling fondly. I wipe a quick hand over my face to get rid of the tears in my eyes; he probably noticed but he's nice enough not to say anything.

"So," he says, "would you like to see the ship and meet the rest of the crew?"

I take a deep breath and nod. "Yeah, I'd like that." My voice is a little thicker than normal and a lump has formed in my throat but I manage to swallow it. If I can put on a brave face now and get through the rest of the day, then if I still feel like crying when I go to bed I can.

Adams looks at me with kind eyes. I think he knows that I'm struggling and wants to distract me. It's definitely working; also I'm going to be spending about two weeks on this ship so I should probably get to know who everyone is, where everything is kept and how you're supposed to sail one of these things.

"Let's introduce you to the rest of the crew then."

~ *** ~

The tour of the ship is pretty much what I expected—what I imagine the tour of any ship would be. Let's face it, there's only so much you can get on a boat, regardless of size. It's still interesting and the crew members are all great: up for a laugh and ready to help me if I have any questions. Everyone always said that I make friends easily and the crew accept me as one of their own within hours. I think it helps my case that I'm all too willing to learn how to sail a proper ship and willing to help out on deck.

It's a full on day of learning new things and new faces, so much so that I haven't had any time to feel homesick at all. By the time evening rolls round, I'm exhausted and ready to flop down onto my bed in my quarters. I haven't seen my room yet; it was the only place Adams didn't show me on the tour. It's mostly because I asked him not to. Knowing what I'm like if I had seen my room and been given any time alone in there I might have let the pull of homesickness get the better of me. I would have stayed in there for the rest of the day—instead I've made a lot of great friends and become a proper member of the crew.

The sailor I met on the dock this morning shows me to my quarters. I ended up spending most of the day in the crow's nest with him and he showed me what was needed to be a good lookout. His name is Levi and he's quite the talker, which is nice—I can't imagine how boring it would have been sitting up in the crow's nest with someone who didn't want to say anything and just sat there quietly. Luckily for me this crew seems to be filled with talkers, or maybe that's just because they've got someone new to talk to. Either way I'm not complaining.

"You know, when my little brother found out that I was going to be sailing on the same ship to the mainland as you he completely flipped out," Levi says as we walk down a corridor that leads to the Captain's cabin (obviously belonging to Adams) and my quarters.

"Really?"

"Oh yeah," Levi says. "Aaron's been a fan of the Neo Warriors since he was old enough to recognise who they were and learn their names."

"How old is he?" I ask.

"He'll be six next month," Levi says. "He keeps saying that when he grows up he wants to be a Neo Warrior but he also says that he wants to do what I do and I keep telling him that he's going to have to pick one eventually. Then again he also says he wants to be a fish when he grows up so there you go."

"He can take a twelve year gap from sailing," I say.

"I suppose you're right," Levi says, scratching his chin absent-mindedly. "Though every time he mentions wanting to be a Neo Warrior mum always gives him a clip round the ear and tells him not to be so stupid."

"Why?"

"She thinks it's far too dangerous."

"Okay that's fair," I say. "I mean I don't think being a Neo Warrior is going to be dangerous but I haven't even had my basic training yet." I got this job about a week ago—what do I know?

"This is true," Levi chuckles. "I keep telling her that it's no more or less dangerous than being a sailor but she doesn't seem to listen. I think in her head Aaron's going to stay her baby boy forever because she can't imagine him as anything else at the moment."

"Mums are like that," I say, smiling fondly as I think of how my own has always called me 'baby' and will probably never stop either.

"I also tell her that I'll look after him if he does come on ship with me but she doesn't seem to be overly fond of that idea either."

Damn! Why can't Harmony be more like this guy? He's the perfect older sibling and he's not too hard on the eyes either (but that's just a bonus for me).

"So who are you replacing?" Levi asks. "I've been away on ship for a while and have no idea who's who anymore. Who are we getting back?"

"We're not getting anyone back," I reply. "My cousin Michael, the last Neo Warrior, died in service."

"I'm sorry," Levi says, "I didn't even think about that possibility."

"It's okay," I say. "Neither did I."

"No, I shouldn't have said anything," he says running a hand over his hair. "I haven't really been keeping that up to date with who is Neo Warrior while I haven't been on the island and I really should."

"It's okay," I say again. "I mean it's not okay what happened, but it's not like Michael and I were particularly close or anything. It's just kinda weird though."

"What do you mean?"

"Well…just that Michael was only the same age as my sister Harmony, so in theory he should still have had another five or so years of service left," I say. "I mean it's not like he could have been killed in action and I would have thought they would have sent him home if he was as sick as they say. It might simply be nothing and he just got ill really suddenly but something about the whole thing doesn't sit too well with me."

"I can understand why," Levi says. "He's your family."

"I just don't really get why we haven't been told anything about how he died or anything about what happened to him," I say. "I mean the council must know what happened to him so I don't know why they wouldn't say anything to me about it. Especially when I have to go out there and do the same thing."

"True," Levi says as he pulls a key out of his trouser pocket. "My advice would be to try not to worry too much about it for now and maybe ask someone when you get to the mainland, as hard as that may be."

"Yeah…"

"The council will have been told," he reassures me.

"I know my aunt must know," I say. "She would have demanded to be told and she's kind of a battle-axe when she wants to be."

"Ex-Neo Warrior?"

"Nope."

Levi whistles. "Well then… What about the rest of your family, any Neo Warriors?"

"Different aunt and grandmother," I reply.

"Nice."

"Yeah, she was my dad's mother, her husband was a soldier, Head of the House is my mother's father and his wife was an explorer," I say. "Looking at my grandparents and the kind of people they were and other members of my family I supposed I was born to fill a role like this. Like Michael…"

Suddenly the full weight of what I'm about to do hits me again and I fall silent. This is crazy! I'm old enough to do this and I know the dangers going in. Michael knew the dangers going in. Everyone knows the dangers when they go into this! I suppose I never thought of them in relation to *my* death because I was so excited. I'd rather not die before I finish service but there is a slim chance it could happen. No one knows where the dice are going to fall.

"Hey do you know how to surf?" Levi asks, changing the subject and bringing me out of my thoughts.

"Yeah why?" I ask.

"We've got a few boards knocking around down in the hull. If you want, tomorrow, I can throw a line over the side and you can go surfing," he says. I can see that he's trying to distract me and I'm not ashamed to admit that it works. That sounds amazing!

My smile practically rips my face in two. "Can I?"

"Sure thing," he says. "We do it all the time when we get bored. It's also really good for close range spear fishing, fixing problems and cleaning the outside of the ship."

"That sounds awesome!" I say. "I can't even remember the last time I went surfing on open water."

"We can definitely make it happen then," he says, grinning as we reach a door at the end of the corridor. He unlocks it and pushes it open before handing me the key. "And this is your room."

He stands aside so that I can go in first and my jaw drops open. The room is huge: ornate and decorative, filled mostly with dark wood furniture and with a large four-poster bed in the centre. There is a writing desk and a sofa in front of a small table and another plush chair opposite. This is the same size, if not bigger, than my room back home and, considering that we're on a boat, I wouldn't have thought that was even a possibility.

"Wow…" It comes out as more breath than word.

"Nice isn't it?" Levi chuckles as he follows me into the room.

"This is…it's wonderful." Even that doesn't feel as if it does the room enough justice but I can't think of a better way to describe it.

"And this is all yours until we get to the mainland."

"Wow…"

I'm completely bowled over. This room is absolutely beautiful! It has everything anyone could possibly need and more and I could quite happily just stay in here. I probably shouldn't, for need of fresh air and food if nothing else. In the corner of the room, I see my two suitcases and my small backpack ready and waiting for when we hit the mainland and I'm suddenly completely exhausted again, ready to get in bed.

"This over here," Levi says pointing to a receiver, "will get you down to the sailor's bunks. So if you need anything at all, doesn't matter when it is, just give me a shout."

"Thanks," I say, smiling at him. I'm overcome with the strongest urge to hug him but I think better of it as that might be a bit weird. It's just that everyone has been so nice to me and I don't feel like I can express my gratitude enough.

"No problem," he says, smiling back. "I'll let you get some sleep but if I could ask one thing before I go…"

"Um…sure…"

"Would you sign this for my brother?" he asks. He pulls a carefully folded up piece of paper and a pen out of his pocket, unfolds it and hands it to me. It's the poster that I saw plastered all over the docks market.

"Oh my god," I laugh.

"He'd kill me if he found out I had met you and didn't get your autograph for him."

"When's his birthday?" I ask as I go over to the writing desk, laying the poster out. This is the first time anyone has ever asked for my autograph so I'm going to do it properly.

"Next month," he replies.

In the neatest (and most legible) handwriting, I can manage I write 'To Aaron, Happy Birthday, love Ariana'. I put a kiss then sign my name in the usual squiggle it is before I hand the poster back to Levi.

"Thank you so much," he says, grinning at it. "He'll be chuffed to bits when he sees this."

"No problem," I smile.

"I'll leave you alone for the evening; any problems just give me a shout, and I'll see you in the morning," he says. "Good night."

Levi gives me a nod and another smile before he leaves the room, closing the door behind him. Part of me wants to stay up and have a nose around the room but the other part (a much larger part) is overcome with fatigue again. I just about have the energy to drag myself over to my suitcases and rummage around until I find my night clothes. Welling up a little bit again when I see that Mum slipped Ducky in when I wasn't looking, I get changed and slip into bed, falling asleep instantly.

~ *** ~

Most of my time sailing from Neyara to the mainland is spent either reading in the crow's nest or learning how to sail with Levi and the rest of the crew. I go surfing quite a few times and learn the ins and outs of life on a ship this size and what each member of the crew does. It's really interesting and something I might consider looking into once I've done my twelve years of service, that way I can still travel.

I've been sitting up in the crow's nest reading and being a look out for a while. I love the way the air feels up here, the smell of the salt on the wind and just how peaceful it is compared to the hustle and bustle of the deck. There's a small pile of books about military training and tactics (I've been trying) next to me but after a while there was only so much I could take in so I've moved on to a book Levi gave me about a guy who tried to bring his mother back from the dead. It's really cool but it's pretty gruesome and, even with access to powers like some of the other Houses have access to, isn't something anyone should attempt. I don't even think it can be done but I don't think I'd want to try.

"Hey Ari!" I hear someone call my name from down on the deck below.

I stick a bookmark in and close the book before I look over the edge of the crow's nest and see Levi grinning up at me.

"Hey Levi," I call down, "what's up?"

"Get down here," he tells me, "there's something I want to show you."

I grab hold of the rope I used to climb up, encase my hand in a film of water to avoid friction burn and slide down, landing on the deck a few seconds later. Levi regards me with a raised eyebrow as I grin at him.

"I would have waited until you climbed down, you know," he says.

"It was more fun and faster this way," I reply.

"If you say so," he chuckles.

"So what do you want to show me?" I ask.

"This..."

He places both his hands on my shoulders and steers me towards the very front of the ship and points out to the horizon in front of us. I don't know what I'm looking at, at first—it all looks like the ocean to me. Then he points to something right out in the distance, a huge landmass that is appearing on the horizon. It's just an outline but I can definitely see the silhouettes of buildings jutting out into the sky and, if I squint really hard, I can just about see the palace: the home of Brax's Royal family.

Oh my god! I'm finally here!

All I can do is stare, my mouth hanging open and my eyes wide as I drink in the sight of the mainland. This place looks amazing! There's going to be so much that I need to see and do and I'm so excited I don't really know what to do with myself.

"Wow!" I breathe.

"Thought you'd like that," Levi chuckles behind me.

"This is amazing…"

"If the wind stays as it is then we should be there tomorrow morning," he tells me.

"Really?"

"Yeah."

"I can't wait," I say and it's true: I can't. I'm so excited to get there and meet the rest of the Neo Warriors. I can also start my training. Nerves be damned, this is going to be brilliant! I really hope I have time to have a look around before I have to get started.

I hear the fierce beating of wings above us and look up, shielding my eyes against the sun and I'm both shocked and amazed once again. Above us are about seven or eight messengers from the House of Mercury heading for the coast, their wings strong and powerful as they fly through the air. I stare, open mouthed again, unable to stop myself. I wonder if Luciana is up there… Oh my god I'm actually going to meet her soon! This is the coolest thing!

Before I can even finish processing that thought, there's a crackle of electricity and I turn to see three members of the House of Jupiter riding their own lightning through the sky out to sea. I've heard about Jupiter Storm Chasers but never seen any in real life before and they look just as cool as the Mercurian messengers.

"You okay?" Levi asks and I can hear him trying to muffle his laughter at my star struck state.

"Yeah," I squeak. Way to go Ari…not very dignified for a Neo Warrior, is it? Pull it together!

"You excited?"

"So excited!" I reply.

"You're going to love it," he says.

"I know," I say.

"You're going to be just fine," Levi says.

"You think so?" I ask, looking round at him.

"I know so," he says, "because you, Ariana Sirenia, have a good heart. You're determined, you're passionate and you will stop at nothing until you are the best Neo Warrior you can be."

"Okay…" I turn away without saying anything else and look back out to the mainland. I've waited so long for this and now it's finally here I'm unable to keep the smile off my face. The mainland is so close I can practically taste it in the spray of the ocean. Brax here I come…

Chapter 7

The ship pulls into the dock, the anchor thrown overboard, and we finally come to a stop in the mainland port the following morning. As soon as we're at port I'm up on deck looking around, my eyes wide as I take everything in. There are hordes of people everywhere! People of all ages, Houses and sizes, more than I've ever seen before. They either all seem to be trading with the ships just coming in to port or helping to reload and restock the ships about to leave. The air is thick with people shouting and I can barely distinguish one voice from another. There are smells as well: the lingering smell of the sea on the air but also the smell of cooking food wafting over from the nearby buildings. I can smell animals and sweat from everyone running around. It's filthy, raw, and all I can do is stare in wonder, trying to take it all in.

This is incredible! The dock back home is quiet compared to this. Even on a particularly busy day it's nowhere near as crowded as this. There are literally bodies everywhere; I can barely see the pavement beneath their feet. It's such a confined space and I wonder if everywhere on the mainland is going to be as bustling as this. It stands as such a contrast to where I've come from where some parts of Neyara are completely deserted.

It takes me a while to get my bearings but I shake myself out of my stupor so I can help with unloading all the cargo for trade from the ship. I keep stopping to look around so I must be more of a hindrance than a help but everyone indulges me this moment to just stop and take it all in. Everything is so new and so big and I just can't believe it. All I can do is stand there and stare up at the buildings that surround us. Back on Neyara the biggest building is the old converted palace I live in but here everything is much larger. Most of the buildings surrounding the docks are huge—at least the same height as the House if not taller. I guess there are a lot more people living on the mainland so they would need to have larger buildings to accommodate. Everything here just seems to be bigger and more intense than anything I've ever seen or experienced.

It all feels like it's too much. There's too much going on and I don't know where I want to go and what I want to do first. Do I want to explore? Do I want to get off the dock? Do I want to go back to my quarters and take a minute? I probably should actually finish what I'm supposed to be doing and go find Katarina Navroe before I go off exploring on my own. Someone playfully bumps against my shoulder as I watch two men argue over the asking price of a barrel of fish. Glancing over my shoulder I see Levi standing in front of my suitcases, with my backpack slung over one of his shoulders.

"Trade you," he says, nodding to the crate in my hands.

"Sorry," I mumble, a little embarrassed that I said I would help and have so far been none whatsoever.

"Don't be," he chuckles. "I was like that the first time I came to the mainland too. It's a madhouse here and you never really get used to it, especially when you go back to Neyara and everything is so quiet. It never helps that as soon as you get used to one extreme it's time to go back to the other."

"I don't think I'm ever going to get used to this," I say as another huge ship, this one emblazoned with the crest of the House of the Sun on its sails, begins to move away from the dock, all those aboard frantically running to weigh the anchor as they move off. "Where do you suppose they're going?"

"No idea," Levi says as he takes the crate from me. "They could be going over to Neyara, they could be going out into open water to collect supplies or they could be on a diplomatic visit to another country. You can never tell here."

"Wow…"

This is all so new and exciting. I can't believe I'm finally here and I get to see what life is like on the mainland. If I'm lucky, I might get to visit some of the other Houses during my basic training. That would be cool—meeting new people, being a proper official. I know that the House of the Stars is located quite near the capital so that might be one of the first places I visit.

"The ship's all unloaded now," Levi says, breaking me out of my thoughts, "so this is where you and I go our separate ways."

"Oh…okay." I've been so distracted by everything around me that I almost forgot what I'm supposed to do now that I'm here. Come on Ari, you actually have to do things, not stand around looking surprised. People will eat you alive if they find out you've never been to the mainland before so act like you know what you're doing!

I turn back to Levi and he hands me my backpack, which I sling onto my shoulder. I'm a little sad; he's been like a big brother to me ever since my first day on the ship and I'm really going to miss him. I smile up at him.

"Thank you for everything Levi," I say, "you've been amazing."

"Thank *you* Ari," he says, smiling. "It's been fun having you on board. I've had a great time teaching you to sail and you've been an absolute joy to be around."

"Thanks."

"Good luck with your training and hopefully I'll be on the next ship you sail back to Neyara on."

He puts the crate down and opens his arms so I can hug him tightly and he hugs me back. I can't express in words just how brilliant he has been over the last fortnight and I really hope I do see him again as I most definitely won't forget him in a hurry.

"I hope I do see you again," I say.

"I think you will," he grins. "I don't think this is the last time our paths will cross and maybe, next time, I can introduce you to Aaron. He'd love to meet you."

"That sounds awesome," I say. I pull away from the hug and step back, hitching my backpack up higher on my shoulder. "So I guess this is goodbye then."

"See you around Ari," he says, ruffling my hair.

"Thanks again Levi," I say, smiling at him before I take the handles of both of my suitcases and turn to face the crowd in front of me.

For a few minutes, I look around, searching for anything that looks like it can be a customs office but everything all looks the same, built in the same style and I can't tell. Levi chuckles behind me and places his hand on my shoulder.

"Customs is that red brick place over there," he says, pointing to a small manned gap between two slim buildings.

"Thanks," I say, my face probably as red as those bricks. Smooth…

"No problem," Levi says. He gives me a clap on the shoulder which turns into a gentle shove in the right direction.

I let out a quick puff of breath to steady my nerves and make my way over to the gap. Even just navigating the dock is a minefield, especially with two huge suitcases. There are so many people shouting in so many different languages that it's hard to distinguish one voice from another but I don't think any of them are yelling at me specifically so I pay it no mind.

For the most part, people in Brax speak either Braxian or Universal (which is spoken by everyone throughout the Worldwide Kingdoms and makes things much easier at diplomatic meetings). However each of the twelve Houses of Brax has their own language (usually with some Braxian dialect thrown in there). I don't know about the other Houses, but for the most part, we just speak Universal on Neyara, mostly because we're the first port of call for the empire for someone heading east. As far as I'm aware people only speak their own House's language when they want to pass on secret information, want to insult someone so they don't understand or need to make themselves distinguishable over a sea of other voices—like here.

I have to jostle and weave my way through the crowd to avoid getting in anyone's way and that is a challenge in and of itself. Looking around I just can't believe how much there is going on here. Not that I thought it was going to be quiet—not in the slightest, but this is way more people in one small space than I thought—but I wasn't prepared for just how busy it would be.

Finally I make it to the gap and, sure enough, there is a sign that reads 'Customs' hanging between the two walls either side. There is a huge queue so I join the back and, while I wait, I watch all the people rushing by. It's fascinating because, unlike on Neyara, everyone looks so different. Aside from the fact that people from the mainland have a different look to them so do members of each of the Houses so it's kind of like looking in a pond with thousands of different kinds of fish. There's such a wide array of people it's genuinely quite hard for me to keep up with it all.

Slowly but surely the line moves while I'm too busy looking around in wonder at everything and before I know it I'm at the front of the queue. I can't stop myself from grinning; I'm way too excited and happy about this and probably should tone it down a little but I don't want to. This is it!

I'm finally on the mainland about to go to Brax's capital for the very first time!

"Next," the man behind the small desk calls.

I pick up my suitcases and step forward. He is a squat, chubby man, tiny circular glasses sitting on the bridge of his round nose with the grey eyes of people from the mainland and thinning magenta hair. Judging by the crow's feet around his eyes he's probably mid-fifties, early sixties, and most likely lost any interest he had in his job when he hit thirty-five.

"Good morning," I smile at him as I put my suitcases down but his expression doesn't change. He just looks up at me, bored and unimpressed.

"Name, House and state your business in Brax please," he says.

"I am Ariana Sirenia of the House of Neptune," I say, although I would have thought where I was from was kind of obvious—you don't get many people with blue hair and turquoise eyes who aren't from the House of Neptune…at least I don't think you do. Normally you can tell where a person is from by the colour of their eyes; hair colour does vary but everyone from each of the different Houses and the mainland have very specifically coloured eyes. "And I am the newly appointed Neo Warrior for my House."

That seems to get his attention. Looking up from his ledger he eyes me suspiciously. He's taking longer than necessary to process this as he studies my face. I can hear a few whispers of 'Neo Warrior' behind me but I try to ignore them.

"And the real reason why you're here please," he says finally.

"Pardon?" I ask. It feels a very stupid question but I'm a bit taken aback by the fact that he's questioning it in the first place.

"I need the reason for your visit to the mainland or I can't let you in," he says.

"I just told you," I reply. "I'm the new representative Neo Warrior for the House of Neptune."

"Of course you are," he scoffs.

"I am," I say. Why doesn't he believe me?

"To be a Neo Warrior you need to be over eighteen years of age," he says, "and you do not look eighteen."

"I can assure you I am," I say. I'm trying to be polite to this guy, really I am, but he's starting to piss me off a bit and the whispering from behind me is getting louder. So much for a warm welcome…

"Do you have any identification documents?" he asks.

"Um…yes, I think so," I say. Slipping off my backpack I begin rummaging inside it, trying to find my ID. I can feel everyone else in the queue staring at me as well as the whispering and a heat begins to creep up the back of my neck. After ransacking the back pocket of my bag, I still can't find it. Please let it be in the front… If it's not there then I have no idea where it is and I've probably lost it. Unless it's in one of my suitcases but I don't know any more. I'm getting more and more agitated by the second and I still can't find my bloody ID!

"Is there a problem here?" a woman's voice asks.

I immediately stop and look up to see a tall, willowy woman standing behind the man with a hand on her hip. My jaw drops as the first thing I notice about her is her eyes: bright yellow, like daffodils and even more piercing than in the posters. Her hair is a vibrant shade of burnt orange and kept in dreadlocks, pulled back from her face in a high ponytail. It's her!

It's Katarina Navroe of the House of Uranus!

The customs man gapes at her before jumping up from his seat and saluting her, his jaw slack and his eyes bulging. Oh man you are in so much trouble, I can't help thinking with brattish glee.

"Second Commander Navroe," he cries, "what can I do for you?"

"I just wondered what the hold-up was," she says and flashes a grin in my direction. "I've been waiting for the new Neo Warrior to arrive for a while now but she hasn't shown up. Has Ariana Sirenia come through here at all?"

The man looks from me to her and then back at me again. I do try not to look overly smug at his gaping expression as he realises what a monumental cock up he's just made. He hastily makes a note in his ledger.

"So Ariana Sirenia is it?" he asks me. "House of Neptune?"

"New representative Neo Warrior," I reply nodding. I shouldn't feel smug but I do: that timing was too perfect.

He stamps a card and hands it to me. It's a very simple white card that has my name and House, the date and a stamp that says 'Approved entrance to Mainland Brax' on it. He looks quite begrudging as he gives it to me so I make sure to give him my sweetest smile when I take it.

"On your way," he says and motions for me to go through.

"On *your* way," I say, nodding at him. I walk through the gap (finally on the mainland properly, yay!) and go to meet Katarina.

"Hey," she says, smiling at me, "you must be Ariana."

"Yes, hi," I say. I can't stop myself from staring up at her in awe. Now that I'm closer her eyes look even more vibrant than before and I can't help getting a little star struck. Hers are the kind that follow you on the posters and they're really something in real life. "Thank you for that."

"No problem," she says, waving me off, the movement looking so effortless and graceful. I am already amazed by this woman and I've been around her for all of three minutes. "Shall we head off? There's a carriage waiting to take us to the barracks and we can get you settled in."

"That sounds amazing."

"Did he give you too much trouble?" she asks.

"Nothing I couldn't handle," I lie.

"Oh I almost forgot," she says, clapping her hands together. "So formal introduction: I'm Katarina Navroe—but you can call me Kat. I'm second-in-command of the Neo Warriors and I'm from the House of Uranus."

She holds out her hand to me and I take it. "Ariana Sirenia," I say smiling, "of the House of Neptune."

"You got a nickname?" Kat asks.

"My friends call me Ari," I reply.

"Good enough for me," she says. She takes one of my suitcases and begins to walk away from the docks.

Picking up the other I follow. I still want to stare at everything but I keep my eyes forward to keep up with her. There will be time to stare at everything later, for now I'll just get to wherever she's going to take me.

"So is this your first time on the mainland?" she asks.

"Yeah," I reply, "first time I've left Neyara."

"How are you finding it?"

"It's very different," I reply, "but good different, if that makes sense."

"Yeah I get that," she says. "I remember my first time in the capital. I'd never been out of the Ureccan quarries before and I hadn't come into contact with that many people who weren't from my House so it was kind of daunting."

"Is that where you're originally from? Quarries?"

"Yeah," she replies. "About a two hour journey north from the capital you come to the Ureccan mountain range with a load of quarries at the bottom and that's where my House is."

"You guys are a mining House, right?" I ask.

"For the most part, yeah," she says. "I mean I liked living in Urecca, still do when I go back, but there's not a whole lot there so I was quite glad to get out when I hit eighteen."

"How old are you now?" I ask.

"Twenty-eight," she replies.

"What?" I squeak. No way! She can't be ten years older than me! She sure as hell doesn't look twenty-eight. Then again I guess Harmony doesn't exactly look twenty-five…how do you even look an age anyway? Really she doesn't look super old or super young (which apparently I do, thank you very much Mr Customs Man).

Kat laughs. "Believe it or not I am. How about you?"

"Just turned eighteen," I say.

"I figured as much but I thought I'd ask," she laughs. "So was that why you were having so much trouble with him?" She nods her head back in the direction of customs.

"Yeah," I say. "Wouldn't believe that I was eighteen or that I was the new Neo Warrior."

"I must admit that if I didn't know you were eighteen, I would have pegged you for younger as well," Kat says.

"Great," I mutter, pouting slightly. I'm supposed to appear older and more sophisticated now I'm a Neo Warrior, apparently I still look like a kid.

Kat laughs and ruffles my hair. "I wouldn't worry too much. Sammy still looks like he's about thirteen so you won't be the only one."

"Okay," I mumble. I'm guessing they call Samuel Yonglass 'Sammy' (bet he loves that) and I realise that in a short time I'm going to be enrolled as one of them. The thought of meeting the others immediately perks me up. I'm going to meet Luciana Van Garret soon! How am I going to act? What if I open my mouth and nothing but nonsense comes out? I think Kat has noticed that I've suddenly gone quite stiff because she gives my shoulder a playful bump with her fist.

"So you looking forward to starting your life as a Neo Warrior?" she asks.

"I am yeah," I reply, trying to sound nonchalant and not like too much of a fangirl. I'm supposed to *be* one of these guys now so I should try to be cool.

"Good," she says, "it's always better for you if you're excited to start."

"So when will my training start?" I ask.

"First thing tomorrow morning most likely, if Caspian has anything to say about it," she chuckles.

"I've heard a lot about him," I say, remembering what my grandfather told me about him, what I've read about him and what I've picked up from other people. He sounds like a terrifying man. I'm both apprehensive and excited to meet him. The guy sounds like an absolute hard-arse but at the same time like an absolute living legend so he has every right to be as hard on his troops as he sees fit.

"I'll bet," Kat says, rolling her eyes. "There are so many rumours that fly around about Caspian Feioré and only a handful of them are actually true."

"Really?"

"Caspian puts up this front but he's alright," she says. "He'll give you a hard time, no doubt about that, but he only does it because he sees potential in you and he knows that you can do better than you realise."

"Okay," I say, nodding. The guy still sounds kind of scary but at the same time I'm still getting those butterflies of anticipation and excitement fluttering to life in the pit of my stomach whenever anyone mentions his name. He's going to be the one who decides whether I make it or break it so I've got to make sure that I impress him right off the bat, no questions asked.

"But you'll find all this out when you meet everyone," Kat says.

"Okay," I say again. That makes sense.

Kat finally comes to a stop. We're quite far from the docks now, it's a lot calmer and there seem to be less people rushing around and shouting overhead. There are a few people here and there but it's mostly just the two of us. We're on a roadside and there's a sizeable carriage parked, two sleek grey horses attached to the front, ready to pull it. Powerful and tall, one of them snorts while the other picks up its feet impatiently. They're absolutely stunning! Sitting atop the carriage is a man with shaggy, moss green hair and also has the grey eyes of people who live on the mainland. He is drawing something in a sketch pad while he waits, casting glances every so often at the horses (so I assume he's drawing them).

"Hey Park'er," Kat calls as she leads me over to the carriage. "I found her. Sorry to keep you waiting."

"No trouble milady, no trouble at all," the driver, Park'er, says as he closes his sketch pad and sticks his pencil behind his ear. "If you don't mind my asking what was the cause of all the hold up?"

"Few issues at customs but it's all sorted now," Kat says. "Park'er this is Ariana Sirenia, Neo Warrior for the House of Neptune. Ariana this is our driver, Tatum Pankhurst but we call him Park'er because well…that's what he does; he parks the carriage, which he often refers to as his lady."

Park'er jumps down from the top of the carriage and gives me a small bow. "It is an honour and a privilege to meet you milady," he says with a slight farmer's drawl to his accent.

"Likewise," I say smiling at him. I hold out my hand and he shakes it. "I like your horses," I say and nod towards them.

"Thank you very much milady," Park'er says, beaming proudly. "Finest animals you could ask for on the mainland. This is Tornado," he indicates the one on the right, the larger of the two, "and this is Misty. Reared them from foal to now and they serve me well."

"They're absolutely beautiful," I say. We have a few horses on Neyara but they're usually kept by people as pets rather than used as working animals as everything is done out on the ocean so it's not very often that I get to see any.

"Well, thank you kindly, milady," Park'er smiles. "I'm sure they're glad to know you think so." He pats Tornado's flank fondly before he nods to the suitcase I'm still holding. "Shall we get your things loaded on the back and head off?"

"Yes please," I reply. I've stopped trying to hide my excitement. There's no point. It will come seeping out eventually or it will all come out in one big burst and I'll end up looking like a crazy person.

Park'er takes both of my suitcases and loads them on to the back of the carriage while Kat opens the door and gets in. I take one last look over my shoulder before getting in myself. After a few minutes, the carriage dips slightly and I assume that Park'er has gotten back on because the next thing I know we slowly begin to move.

"Oh by the way Ari," Kat says after a few minutes, "welcome to Brax."

~ *** ~

The ride from the docks to the barracks isn't a long journey at all, maybe twenty minutes in the carriage and we're not travelling all that fast. Most of my time is spent staring out of either of the windows at everything. I still can't get over how new and exciting it all is and I'm still incredibly surprised that I'm even here at all. Kat points out a few things and places of interest to me as we drive past and tells me a little bit about them. If she finds my constant questioning annoying she doesn't say so, she just continues to tell me more and I lap it up. She obviously knows what it's like to suddenly come to somewhere as busy as the capital after spending your entire life just in your House. It likely would have been different if my dad or someone else in the family was a trading sailor and I came here a lot; I might have come with them once I was old enough.

In between my questions, Kat asks me about myself and tells me a few things about herself too. She's from a small family from the Ureccan quarries who specialise in using the minerals in rocks to make a number of different things that people use every day, like parts for ships and carriages that people forget are needed. She joined the Neo Warriors at eighteen, served her time and became second-in-command about two years ago. Her life sounds really interesting (especially since joining the Neo Warriors) and so does her magic. I sort of understand when she explains it but, much like the magic of the other Houses, I'm not totally sure of the full ins and outs of it. I've heard and read about what they do but I've never seen it first-hand. People from the House of Uranus are earth movers and she shows me while we are waiting at a crossroads, making some of the pebbles by the roadside rattle and jump a few inches.

It's so cool watching other people use their magic. I've hardly seen anyone from other Houses do it and now I'm probably going to see every single other House's magic in one day. I'd love to see the magic of the royal family—I've heard that it's something to behold. There are some I know about more than others, the obvious ones like the House of Mars or the House of Jupiter but there are a lot I don't actually know what it is they do because there's been no written record that makes sense and they're quite vague in interviews. Better get used to it though. The rest of them might not all be as endeared with my wide-eyed wonder as Kat is.

Finally we pull up in front of what looks like an old castle. It's a little out in the sticks—we travelled through a wood to get here—so it's really quiet and, looking up at it, seems incredibly peaceful. We leave the carriage and Park'er gets my suitcases down for me.

"Thank you so much," I say just before he can climb back onto the carriage.

"It was my pleasure milady," he says, stopping to bow to me again. "I hope that your training goes well and I look forward to seeing you again soon."

"Likewise," I say and smile at him.

"And if you ever want to come to the stables, Tornado and Misty will be more than happy to see you," he says.

"Thank you," I beam at him.

He nods before he jumps up onto the carriage and with a small flick of the reigns is moving off. Kat and I watch as he leaves before she turns to me, placing a hand on my shoulder and grinning.

"So are you ready to go inside and meet everyone?" she asks.

"Oh my god yes," I say. My excitement still seems to be masking my nerves and I am very thankful for that. I don't want to get too star struck too early though.

"Then follow me," Kat says. Grabbing one of my suitcases she heads off in the direction of the huge wrought iron doors. She lifts one of the huge knockers and lets it fall back down, the sound resonating off the walls all around us. A moment later the door slowly swings open and a man of about forty, with a shaved head and dressed in the uniform of the Braxian army greets us. I look at his face a little closer and see that he has turquoise eyes like me. Holy crap…another Neptunian!

"Second Commander Navroe," he says saluting, "we have been awaiting your return."

"Lieutenant Springer," Kat says, nodding at him. "At ease." Springer drops his salute.

"Did you have a pleasant journey?" he asks.

"We did," Kat says, grinning at me. "It's the first time Ariana has been to the mainland before."

Springer seems to realise that I'm here as well and he salutes again, this time directing it at me with a huge grin on his face. Wow I still can't get used to that…

"Ariana Sirenia," he says, dropping his salute. "Why, the last time I saw you, you were only about this big." He holds his hand at about his mid-thigh. Oh wow! That was a long time ago, I'm about the same height as him now (we're not a tall House). "How does it feel to be on the mainland, Staff Captain?"

Staff Captain? I'll ask Kat when we're alone.

"It's fantastic," I say, grinning back at him.

"I hope that the journey to the mainland was pleasant," Springer says.

"It was, thank you," I reply. "How long have you lived on the mainland?"

"About thirteen, fourteen years now," he says. That explains why I was so tiny the last time he saw me.

"Do you like it?"

"I really do and it's wonderful to see you again." he says. "Sad about Michael but I'm glad we've got you representing us."

"Thank you," I say.

"Springer could you see to it that Ariana's cases are taken up to her quarters, please?" Kat cuts in, changing the subject. "I'm sure Commander Feioré will want to meet his newest recruit as soon as possible."

"Right away, Second Commander," Springer says. He salutes both of us again.

"Thank you Springer," Kat smiles at him. "Have a pleasant rest of the day."

"You too Second Commander, Staff Captain I hope we have a chance to talk about Neyara soon."

"I'll make sure we do Lieutenant," I say, smiling. I still can't get used to this; people so much older than me saluting me and calling me things like Captain and milady but I suppose I will in time. I mean being basically House royalty I'm used to the stares and people knowing my name but the titles are definitely something to get used to; I've never had an official one before.

Once Springer has my cases and backpack Kat heads off, me at her heels a few seconds later. I'm making sure that I look where I'm going but also staring all around me, drinking it all in. I don't know if everything is just more fancy on the mainland but this entire building seems to be made out of the finest polished stone and the attention to detail is insane! If I get a chance later I'm going to come back and have a look at all the paintings on the walls properly—they seem to be telling some kind of story but I can't tell what it is from the fleeting glances I'm giving it.

"This is the barracks specifically for the Neo Warriors and the high ranking members of the army," Kat explains as we pass under a huge marble archway. "All the training is done here: the grounds out back are more than large enough to accommodate and we have plenty of space for everyone to live here comfortably."

"This place is amazing!"

"Isn't it just?" she chuckles. "This used to be the summerhouse of the king of Brax before the Neo Warriors were founded. After the first war it was converted and used as a home for the Neo Warriors to use when they were in the capital."

"I'm going to need a map for this place," I say.

"You get used to it quick enough," Kat laughs. "If there's anything you need though, don't hesitate to ask. The staff here are great and the rest of us are here to help you as well."

"Oh that was a thing I wanted to ask," I say, suddenly remembering, "why did Springer call me Staff Captain?"

"Before you complete your basic training, you have the provisional rank of Staff Captain," Kat explains. "Once you pass you become a fully-fledged Captain and start moving up in the ranks from there."

"Okay," I say, nodding. That makes sense. I figured I would probably have to wait until I passed to become a proper Captain despite what other people keep calling me.

"So I can show you around and introduce you to everyone if you want," Kat says.

"Yes please."

"How much do you know about the rest of them?" she asks.

"All by name, a few by sight," I reply.

"The ones in the posters?"

"Yeah."

"Okay good. For the most part, everyone's quite social so they're always together but there are some people who have places they hang out in more than others. It'll probably be easier if I take you to them first."

"Okay."

We turn down a corridor with huge windows on one side, the sun streaming through and warming the place pleasantly. The first door on the right that we come to is ajar so I assume someone is in there but Kat still knocks.

"Come in," a voice says from inside. Kat pushes the door open and I follow her in.

The room is also quite well-lit but this is mostly from artificial lights hanging from the ceiling. The walls and all the furniture are brilliant white and, coupled with the lights, it almost hurts to look at them. In the very centre of the room is a huge table with what looks like a dead body laid out on it. My stomach lurches unpleasantly as Kat and I take a step closer and I see that it is definitely a body and it's open down the centre.

Sitting on a stool behind the body (presumably so that she can get a closer look at what she's studying), with her hands inside its open chest, is a woman with cropped golden hair and glasses. She doesn't seem to notice either Kat or I, her entire attention focused on whoever it is she has her hands in. She's wearing a white lab coat with the sleeves rolled up and I think there are gloves underneath the layer of blood that goes up to her wrists (god, I hope she's got gloves on).

Kat clears her throat. "Amara, company," she says.

The woman, Amara, looks up and peers at us through the glasses. "Oh…" She seems to realise that there are other people in the room (surprising as she was the one who told us to come in). She pulls the gloves off, dropping them into a small bowl next to the body and pushes her glasses up onto her head, pushing her fringe back with them.

Wow…

Without the glasses on the gold of her eyes really shines and I can't seem to look away. I've never seen anyone whose eyes look like that (then again I'd barely met anyone not from the House of Neptune until today, so everyone's eyes are dazzling to me). She stares at me, almost as if she's appraising me and I try not to shrink under her scrutiny.

"Amara, this is Ariana Sirenia, the new Neo Warrior for the House of Neptune," Kat says gesturing to me. "Ariana, this is Amara Solarium from the House of the Sun."

My breath stills. Of course it's her! That explains the eyes and, I suddenly realise, the artificial lights too—they're tiny balls of sunlight. It's amazing that she can do that with her magic and sustain it without even thinking about it. I want to get to that level of ability someday. I've never seen her before as she doesn't do many interviews and her sticker for the huge poster is one of the rarer ones.

Nervously I hold out my hand to her. She looks at it for a second before she gets to her feet. I'm surprised to notice that she only stands about half an inch or so taller than I do; we're practically eye-level. Rather than taking my hand and shaking it, like I expect, she takes hold of my wrist and holds my hand up to her face, examining it. I barely move but out of the corner of my eye I see Kat covering her eyes with her hand and shaking her head in despair. So apparently this happens a lot, not that that's overly comforting.

"You have water magic if you're from Neptune House right?" Amara asks suddenly.

"Um, yes," I reply.

"Can you run some water through your fingers?" she asks.

I obey, running a small rivulet of water through my fingers, twisting it round and sending it back over itself. She doesn't let go of my wrist the entire time, watching the water move through my fingers.

"Okay stop," she tells me after a minute or two. "You suffered a fracture to your right wrist when you were nine is that correct?"

"Yeah…" I reply, wondering how on earth she could have figured that out from just holding my wrist while I do a bit of simple magic. When I was nine years old, I was out in the grounds with Trista and I ended up falling out of a tree while trying to rescue an injured bird. My wrist does sometimes click as a result from the fracture but how on earth did she work out the exact age? That's insane!

"Can I?" she asks.

"Sure…" I reply, a little unsure. I'm not totally sure what she's asking that she can do because she's already randomly holding onto me.

She stares at my wrist intently and I suddenly feel the skin under her fingers heating up and a soft golden glow surrounding my hand. A second later the warmth stops and she lets go of me. I wiggle my fingers and rub the area with my other hand. It's still a little bit warm but it doesn't hurt or anything.

"Try it now," she tells me.

I run another rivulet through my finger and I'm amazed to see that it runs smoother and faster as well. I jump a little, catching the water in my palm before I accidentally spill it all over the floor and make it disappear.

"How did you…?" I begin, staring open mouthed firstly at my wrist, then at her and then back again.

"Amara is our resident doctor," Kat explains. "She knows everything there is to know about the human body."

"Wow…" I've read what I could find about Amara Solarium but never realised she was this impressive a physician.

"She can pretty much look at you and tell you what's wrong with you even if you don't know anything is," Kat continues.

I stare at Amara open mouthed again. "That's so cool!"

"The residual stress that resulted from the fracture was stunting your magic in that hand but only slightly," Amara tells me matter-of-factly, as if this was something I had actively come to ask her about. "It should be easier for you to do small intricate magic now."

"Thank you so much," I say, beaming at her. "That was amazing!"

"No problem," she says and smiles at me. "Happy I could help."

"And can you believe she's only twenty-three," Kat chuckles.

"What?"

That can't be right! How is she only five years older than me and can just diagnose something I didn't even realise was a problem by watching me do a bit of simple magic? I should have worked harder on my own magic when I was growing up—then maybe I'd be able to do something as cool as that without even thinking about it!

"I've been doing this for seventeen years so it figures that I'd be good at it by now," Amara says.

Seventeen years? So she started practising medicine when she was six? Holy crap!

"S...so are you the doctor for the whole army?" I ask, trying not to sound too bowled away by the fact that she is so far out of my league that we may as well be a different species.

Amara shakes her head. "Just the Neo Warriors. They have other people from the House of the Sun working with the other troops. I organise them but I wanted my primary focus to be on the Neo Warriors. Speaking of, I'll have to schedule you in for a full medical check-up and physical at some point."

"Medical check-up and physical?"

"Amara likes to make sure that we're all in our top physical peak every once in a while," Kat explains.

"Okay..."

"We can talk about it later, once you're settled in," Amara says. "It will just be an afternoon of your time. See when you have some time off training."

"Sure thing," I don't know how comforting it is to know that she wants to poke and prod at me for a full afternoon but it would be good to know if there is anything else wrong with me that I didn't know about.

"I should probably get back to work before he dries out," she says, nodding to the dead guy and I just about manage to suppress a shudder.

"Yeah, get back to your dead person," Kat chuckles. "We'll see you later at dinner."

"I'll be there once I've finished," Amara says as she pulls on a new pair of gloves and slips her glasses back onto her nose.

"See you later," I say and follow Kat out of the room and back down the corridor.

If there is a doctor as talented as Amara seems to be here then how did Michael get so sick so quickly and why wasn't she able to do anything about it? The more I think about Michael's death and the more I find out about the kind of place he was living in and with who the more questions I have. I want to ask but now doesn't really seem the time, especially as I still have loads to see and Kat pointedly changed the subject last time Michael came up. Probably best to leave it for now and ask later. One question I do have does seem rather pertinent to ask now though.

"So what was she doing with a dead guy?" I ask when I think we're far enough away so that she won't be able to hear us anymore.

"I have no idea," Kat replies, "and, to be perfectly honest with you I don't want to ask. I've known her for five years and occasionally she does things like this where she somehow acquires a body and spends the day poking around inside it."

"That's…" Oh god how do I even begin to describe how creepy that is? "…interesting."

"Disgusting is the word you're looking for," Kat says. "As far as I'm aware she just gets them from a local morgue so I'm not going to question it too much."

"Right…"

"So now you've met the weirdest one of us, still want to meet the rest of them?" she asks.

"Yes please."

"Good," she smiles. "Amara is an absolutely brilliant doctor and she's very easy to get on with but she does take some getting used to."

"She did seem quite intense," I say. That's putting it politely.

"Don't worry," she chuckles, "the rest of them are equally as bizarre in their own way."

"Oh…" Great.

Chapter 8

After we leave the corridor Amara's office is on, Kat takes me up a huge flight of spiral stairs that seems to keep going up and up forever. I keep one hand on the banister so I don't get dizzy and fall while I look around at the numerous paintings all over the walls. There are some that depict heroic battles, others are portraits of previous Neo Warriors (the one of my grandmother is really cool and I must admit I do look a lot like her when she was my age) and there are a few maps of Brax as well as a couple of world maps. When I get time I'm going to wander around and find out everything there is to know from the paintings and who all these people in the portraits are. I recognise the ones from my House, as they have been hanging on the walls for years now and I recognise the Neo Warriors from my life time but the rest of them (in particular the older ones) are all faces I've never seen before. Studying the maps would be a good idea as well—I'll know where we're going when we start heading off to new places.

Once we reach the very top of the stairs Kat takes me down another corridor. There is a lot less light up here and no windows at all; it's almost like an attic. Aside from the soft glow of the candles lining the walls it's pitch black. The atmosphere up here is weirdly relaxing and a little creepy at the same time.

"Up here is kind of like the chapel," Kat says, voice soft. "For the most part, people come up here to have somewhere quiet to chill out and just have a moment to themselves. No one really uses it to pray anymore because none of us come from overly religious families."

"Okay," I say quietly. I feel like I shouldn't be talking above a certain volume either, like in a library or at a formal ceremony, so I don't disturb anyone.

When we come to the heavy wooden door at the end of the corridor, Kat pushes it open and silently ushers me inside. The room is small but not cramped: there is enough space for a couple of people to be in here at the same time and still not disturb each other. There are two people already in here, a man and a woman. The man is sitting cross-legged and seems to be hovering a couple of inches above the floor and the woman, who has a sheet of long white hair, seems to be vaguely glowing in the dim light.

Kat gently knocks on the door to get their attention and they both look round and see us standing in the doorway. The woman's eyes hit me first: shining a soft silvery colour and, like her hair, almost glowing in the darkness. Illyria Lunest…oh my god! She's so ethereally beautiful I can't seem to look away from her and all I do is stare for a moment, utterly dumbfounded until I finally manage to close my mouth and tear my eyes away to look at the man. I say man, Samuel Yonglass looks younger than I do. He stands out much less in the darkness as he doesn't seem to have the same radiance she does but his hair is still quite light. I can't see what colour his eyes are from here but knowing he's from the House of Saturn they're probably pink.

"Ari this is Samuel Yonglass, House of Saturn, and Illyria Lunest, House of the Moon," Kat says, gesturing to each of them in turn before she gestures to me. "Guys this is Ariana Sirenia from the House of Neptune."

"H…hello," I stammer, still hardly daring to speak any louder, and give them both a small, awkward wave. Illyria gets to her feet and as she comes towards me I notice in the dim light that most of her exposed skin, aside from her face and neck, is covered in swirling tattoos that look like craters on the moon. They've always been there in the posters but seeing them in real life is even more spectacular. She stands a little taller than me, about the same height as Kat, and she hugs me as she reaches me.

"It's lovely to meet you Ariana," she says as she tangles a hand into my hair.

"It's nice to meet you too," I say, trying not to sound as confused as I feel. I'm not sure what's happening here. Is this a thing that people from the House of the Moon do or is she just very touchy feely? The hand in my hair suddenly tilts my head up so that she can look into my face, staring deeply into my eyes. Her eyes seem to glow brighter and I can't bring myself to look away again. The hand that's in my hair comes to rest against my temple, her palm warm against my skin and it feels kind of nice but still weird. "Um…can I help you?"

"Sorry," she chuckles, "probably should have given you some warning there." That's nice…she's still not letting go of me though.

"She's already had Amara grabbing her with no explanation whatsoever and she hasn't even met Remy yet," Kat says.

"Oh lord don't introduce her to Remy," Samuel says, "he'll be all over her."

"Lock up your daughters," Kat chuckles.

"You'll know him when you meet him," Illyria tells me, finally letting go.

"I've see the shoots," I say, thinking back to the day I opened a magazine to see Renton Remelston naked and immediately closed it again, face aflame.

"Oh, those…" Illyria giggles.

"The less said about those, the better," Samuel says with a roll of his eyes. He steps forward from behind Illyria and extends his hand to me. "See, in my House, we shake hands like normal people." He shoots a pointed look over at her but she just smiles at him, shrugging, and pays him no mind.

"Hi," I say, taking his hand, very *very* grateful that someone has given me a normal greeting. Now that he's closer I can see that his eyes are a light pastel pink colour (just as I expected) and his hair is a muted turquoise, very similar to my eyes. He only stands about as tall as I do, I think I might even be a little bit taller than he is.

"So you practise water magic, is that correct?" Samuel asks.

"Yes I do," I reply.

"So you can manipulate water that is already there and you can create your own from nothing as well?" he asks.

"Yeah," I reply. I'd never really thought about how my magic works before; I've always just done it without thinking. That must be the same for all magic users though: eventually it becomes muscle memory and requires no prior thought.

"Fascinating, you'll have to show me some time," he says. "I use air magic so I'm never without it, wouldn't know if I could create my own."

"Oh I don't know, you're full of hot air sometimes," Illyria chuckles.

Samuel shoots her a glare. "That was uncalled for, why would you say that?"

Illyria just shrugs at him and smirks.

"Um…so what kind of magic do you use?" I ask her tentatively, hoping she's not going to randomly start touching me again.

"I come from a House of Dream Walkers," Illyria replies.

"Pardon?" Is that as cool as it sounds because it sounds really cool but that is not an explanation?

"It's a lot of mind magic," Illyria explains. "Mostly telepathic connections with people so I can communicate with everyone if I need to but I can also enter a person's dreams while they're sleeping."

"That's incredible!" I say, admittedly a lot more enthusiastic about this than Samuel's magic but his is very similar to mine and this isn't. "How does that work?"

"I establish a telepathic connection with someone and, from then on, I can communicate with them," she replies.

"So will you need to establish one with me?" I ask.

"Already done sugar," she says but her lips don't move. I suddenly realise that she didn't actually speak and I just heard her voice inside my head. My jaw drops and I stare as she holds out her hand, the one that had been on my temple only moments ago, so that her palm is facing me and I see that the tattoos continue on her palms to. The one she is holding out to me is glowing the same faint silver as her eyes. Immediately I touch my temple, wondering if she put something on there, but my skin feels normal.

"Wha…"

"Great, now you've freaked her out," Samuel says.

"And I thought get Amara out the way first, that will be the worst bit," Kat sighs, shaking her head.

"Sorry," Illyria chuckles and smiles at me. "I know I should have asked first but, for some reason, it works better when the person isn't aware of it, then they don't try to subconsciously fight me, even if they're totally fine with me doing it."

"That…sort of makes sense," I say, my voice still coming out rather high and squeaky—very embarrassing.

"Or maybe it's just that you're inappropriate and like to touch people without asking," Samuel says, giving her a sideways glare.

"No," Illyria chuckles, "that's Remy."

"True."

"And I should probably go and introduce her to the infamous Remy," Kat says, "before she wants to run away all together."

"He'll probably be down in the parlour," Samuel says.

"Either that or trying to weasel his way into some unsuspecting girl's bed," Illyria says.

"Well, it is Remy, nothing would surprise me," Kat says with a roll of her eyes. "Shall we head off, Ari?"

"Okay," I nod. I turn to Samuel and Illyria. "It was nice to meet you both."

"You too, sweetheart," Illyria says, "and don't worry; I won't pop into your head unannounced without good reason."

"Thanks," I say. Oh god... Must remember to keep my thoughts in check when she's around, just in case.

"See you at dinner," Samuel says, "and prepare to get thoroughly grilled by everyone."

"Okay," I say a little nervously.

"See you later, guys," Kat says as she puts an arm around my shoulder and steers me out of the room. "So that was Sammy and Illyria," she says when we're outside.

"Is it rude to ask if he's really twenty-one?" I ask, nodding my head back in the direction of the door.

"Not with a face like his it isn't," Kat sniggers. "He is and Illyria is twenty-three, same as Amara."

"And does she always do that with people she meets?" I ask tentatively.

Kat rolls her eyes and shakes her head in exasperation. "Not usually, just with new Neo Warriors and members of her squad," she says. "Like I said, they're an eccentric bunch but you get used to them easily enough and they're all loyal as anything."

"Okay," I nod. That sounds kind of ominous but everyone has been very nice so far, if a little on the weird side.

"If we hit there next, as I'm sure there will be at least one person inside, do you want to see the library?"

My interest is piqued at the word 'library'. "Can I?"

"Of course you can," Kat smiles at my obvious excitement. "Everything inside this building and the grounds around it is for you to use if you want to or need to. If there's anything else you need that you can't find, just ask someone and we can probably get hold of it for you. It's one of the perks of being a Neo Warrior."

Kat takes me back down the corridor and back down a couple of flights of stairs before she steps out onto a new landing. I follow her over to another large set of ornate doors, these ones with intricate patterns carved into the wood, and pushes one of them open. My mouth hangs open as we enter this huge cavern of books that seems to stretch from floor to ceiling.

This place is beautiful! I could live in here for the entire thirteen years of my service and probably still not make a dent in all these books. Light pours in from the centre of the room and I look up to see a huge skylight filled with all kinds of different coloured glass creating a rainbow painted on the floor. Can this just be my room now? I think I could quite happily live here for the rest of my life, never mind my time here.

Kat leads me through the stacks until we reach a small open space with large plush chairs and curled up in one of them is a man, who doesn't look that much older than I am, his nose buried in the book he's reading. Much like everyone else I have seen I can't take my eyes away from his hair—it comes down to his ears and would be falling in front of his eyes if the fringe weren't clipped back. It's jet black at first glance but there seems to be flecks of colour in it. The more I look the more I notice and I realise that those little flecks seem to be shifting and changing without him turning his head making him look as if he's constantly in motion without moving a muscle. As we get a little closer I realise that the flecks actually *are* moving.

My jaw drops as I watch his hair for a moment. It looks just like the night sky when I used to gaze out of my window back home. The little flecks of colour, I notice upon closer inspection, look like constellations and tiny galaxies floating around in his hair—no prizes for guessing what House he's from. I could easily watch this guy's hair for hours if he'd let me.

"Orion," Kat whispers. Her voice, as quiet as it is, still seems to echo in the cavernous room and the man looks up from his book. I'm taken aback a second time because his eyes are exactly the same as his hair; jet black at first glance but they seem to hold the recesses of the entire cosmos. I feel my breath catch in my throat as he looks over at me. His eyes seem to be staring straight into my soul and I don't want to meet his gaze but I can't seem to look away.

"You must be the new one," he says, his voice also very quiet in the echoey room.

"Hi," I say, my own voice more breath than word.

"This is Ariana Sirenia of the House of Neptune," Kat says gesturing to me when it becomes apparent that I can't make my voice work on its own anymore. "This is Orion Esteria of the House of the Stars."

"Hi…" I say again. I feel a blush begin to creep across my cheeks but I can't take my eyes off him, he is literally the most beautiful person I have ever seen in my entire life—his eyes and hair alone have me completely spellbound. There's a reason why I've never seen him before: he is the rarest Neo Warrior to get a sticker of.

"Are you much of a reader Ariana?" Orion asks.

"Yes," I reply and have to force myself not to add 'sir' after. I mean, yeah, he's my superior but I doubt he's that much older than me and that's going a bit too far.

He puts his book down and gets to his feet, coming to stand in front of me. I'm surprised to notice that he's actually significantly shorter than I am and I'm not exactly what you would call tall. He must be about five foot three at most! As he slowly looks me up and down I watch him take in everything, and it would be uncomfortable but I'm starting to get used to people doing that when they meet me. Obviously they've all met Neptunians before but I suppose I'm still new and interesting enough that they want to appraise me. Orion seems to study me for longer than necessary before he holds out his hand.

"Maybe one afternoon you should join me up here," he says. "See if we can find you something to read."

"That would be lovely," I smile and take his hand. His skin is incredibly cold but he doesn't seem to notice or comment on how much warmer I am compared to him so I say nothing, I just continue to smile.

"If you ever want to find Orion and he's not it his room, he'll be up here," Kat says.

"Guilty," Orion says, with a shrug, not even remotely apologetic. He doesn't seem to smile much…he's obviously one of those people who keeps himself to himself and isn't super social. I'll have to find out once I get to know him a little better. I'd like to spend more time around him, just so I can watch his hair if nothing else. I know that's kind of weird and creepy but this guy is stunning to look at. I also really want to know what kind of magic he uses but I'm not quite sure if it's rude to ask. It probably is so I won't at the moment; I don't want to ruin the tiniest impression I've made by messing it up in the same conversation.

"Will you be down for dinner later?" Kat asks, thankfully saving me from whatever decision I had been about to make about breaking social norms.

"I can be," Orion says as he goes to settle himself back down in his chair.

"Please do," Kat says. "We'll be having a special one as it's Ariana's first night so if you're not down then I'll send someone to come up and get you."

"I'll be there, don't worry," he says, waving her off and picking his book up again.

"We should get on and finish this tour," Kat says placing her arm around my shoulder and beginning to steer me away, seeming to know that I'm quite clearly spellbound. I blink at her touch and feel as if I've come back to myself somewhat.

Orion gives me a small smile. "Nice to meet you Ariana."

"You too," I say, shyly. I still feel as if I can't quite look away from him but I don't want him looking at me with those intense eyes anymore.

Kat leads me out of the library and as soon as I'm no longer around Orion the spell seems to break. I shake my head, a shiver running down the entire length of my spine. Kat chuckles as she gently closes the door behind us.

"I know the feeling," she says. "I was like that the first time I met someone from the House of the Stars. You get used to it after a while, especially if you're around them a lot so you should be able to look directly at him after a week or so."

"That's good," I say. "I think I'd find it hard to concentrate if I felt like that every single time he walked into a room."

"Orion tends to keep himself to himself—he knows the effect he has on people so he steers clear—you'll have to actively seek him out if you want to spend time with him but he'll really appreciate it if you do," Kat says.

"Is that why he stays up in the library all the time?" I ask.

"Pretty much."

"That's fair."

"I'm pretty sure that the rest of them are going to be down in the parlour so I can take you down there and you can meet them all in one go," Kat says after a pause. "We can also get you something to eat; I'll bet you're hungry."

"I am actually, yeah," I say, suddenly realising that I haven't eaten anything since breakfast on the ship this morning and I'm ravenous. I can't believe that it's even the same day—so much has happened!

"Then let's go get you some food."

We head down the stairs, through a large hall and then down another set of stairs into a basement room. Much like upstairs there are no windows but this feels less creepy and more homey. The further down we go the more I can hear a number of raucous voices coming from below. The closer we get to the bottom, the louder the voices get and that's probably what makes it feel so homey—upstairs was too eerily quiet.

Finally we come to the bottom where there is a door that has been left ajar. Kat pushes it open and leads me into a well-lit room with a huge table in the centre. The walls are lined with various barrels of drink and shelves of every kind of food I could possibly dream up and I'm suddenly reminded again of how hungry I am. (Never leave me in this room alone when I'm hungry or stressed; I'll eat everything.)

Sitting around the table, each of them with a tankard in front of them are Ellis De'Latore, Renton Remelston, Dmitri Tavaron and Penelope Heitztaff. They all look older than the others I have previously met but not by a lot. Penelope has her back to me, her long hair the deep grey of a storm cloud is tied back in a high ponytail and Dmitri next to her has shaggy, earthy coloured hair. The huge bear of a man, with giant shoulders, brilliant purple eyes and a shaved head, looking exactly like Jackson but with less hair and bigger muscles, is obviously Ellis. Remy has bright orange eyes and deep crimson hair that flops in front of his eyes. He's quite a pretty guy—soft features but with a cheeky, boyish charm—but he's probably one of those guys who is very aware of just how attractive they are. They all look just like their poster but they're real and in front of me and it's brilliant.

Remy looks up and sees Kat standing in the doorway. He shoots her a slick grin.

"Hey Navroe, come for a drink?" he asks and his voice is deeper than his face would suggest.

"Have you already moved on to the hard stuff without me?" Kat counters with her own question, laughing as she makes her way further into the parlour.

"Depends what you call the hard stuff," Remy says. "That piss-water you drink is hardly what I would call hard."

"And that shit from your House is?" Penelope asks.

"Well, I'm sorry we don't all drink things that can kill us," Remy grumbles.

"Aww I thought your face matching the colour of your hair was wonderful," Penelope laughs a deep, throaty laugh.

"Hey Kat who's the new one?" Dmitri asks, turning to look at me and my heart stops.

Oh…my…god!

Forget what I said about Orion—this is the most beautiful man I have ever met! Rich, dark hair, the colour of freshly tilled, damp soil, and deep brown eyes; he is, without a shadow of a doubt, the hottest man I have ever laid eyes on. His chiselled jaw could cut glass, his smile makes my knees feel weak and the muscles under his shirt are quite obvious. Instantly I take back all my scepticism about Trista telling me that I'm going to meet the man of my dreams here because I think I just did. My face immediately begins to heat up and I shuffle nervously under his gaze even though he's smiling kindly at me. He's so much hotter in real life than the posters make him out to be.

"Oh yeah," Kat says as if she's only just remembering that I'm here (to be fair looking at this guy I'm only just remembering I'm here). "Guys this is Ariana Sirenia: newbie from the House of Neptune."

Everyone turns to stare at me and I suddenly feel very self-conscious again. Kat puts her arm around my shoulders and pushes me forward so that I'm closer for them all to inspect me. I feel a bit like a show horse but I'm hoping this is the last time people are going to be staring at me—for today at least.

"Hello," I mumble, shuffling my feet again. It's very daunting being surrounded by people who are not only older than me but, for the most part, taller, all much more competent at magic than I am (because they've had longer to practice) and are more experienced soldiers.

"Ah Jackson told me to expect you," Ellis says, smiling at me. He gets up and reaches across the table to shake my hand. "He said he's met you already."

"Ellis, hi," I say as I shake his hand. Goddamn his grip is strong. His hand dwarfs mine and I'm certain that my entire body is the same size of one of his arms.

"That's me," he says as he sits back down. "Ellis De'Latore of the House of Pluto."

"Hi." I say, smiling at him.

"This," Kat says, gesturing to Remy, who totally knows he's hot, sitting beside him, "is Renton Remelston from the House of Venus but we all call him Remy."

"The infamous," I say without thinking. Yep, I can see that. Everything everyone has said about him and everything I've read makes complete sense now.

"Oh, so you've heard about me then," Remy says, looking smug. "I mean with a reputation like mine, how could you not have." He gets to his feet, takes my hand across the table and presses a kiss to the back of it. I really don't like it when people do this—why do people keep doing this? It's weird, they've only just met me! "My dear Ariana, may I say that you have the most exquisite eyes I have ever seen. Would you perhaps like to accompany me on a walk of the grounds this evening?" he asks, slipping into perfect Neptunian.

"You speak Neptunian?" I ask, gaping at him.

"Remy speaks every language he can chat up a woman in," Ellis chuckles.

"What can I say?" Remy shrugs. "There's just something so ethereal about the Neptunian language. It's like water rolling off the tongue." He turns his attention back to me. "So what is it you've heard about me? My prowess on the battle field? My prowess as a lover?"

"I'd hold your horses if I were you," Kat says. "She's heard about you from Sammy, Illyria and me…and by the way, she's eighteen."

"Oh," Remy says immediately letting go of my hand as if he's about to be arrested if he stays in contact with me any longer and sits down. I'm legally an adult (everyone is as soon as they hit eighteen) if that's what's giving him pause but I don't mind him letting go.

"If I were you, I'd ignore everything he says," Penelope says, turning to face me and I'm a little bowled over by how green her eyes are. I really hope that this is something I eventually get used to. If I ever have kids, I'm going to make sure they meet people from other Houses at a young age so that they don't stare when they meet them. "He's an idiot and you seem like too smart a girl to let yourself get swept away by him."

"Thanks Heitztaff," Remy mutters darkly, pouting like a sullen teenager. "And maybe you want to watch what you say, I am your superior officer after all."

"Then act like it," Penelope says. She turns to me and holds out her hand. "Penelope Heitztaff but everyone calls me Penny. I'm from the House of Jupiter."

"Hi," I say, taking her hand and shaking it.

"And this," Kat says, indicating the beautiful man sitting next to Penny, "is Dmitri Tavaron from the House of Earth."

"Nice to meet you," Dmitri says, taking my hand and shaking it.

"N…nice to meet you," I stammer. Oh god! Why can't I keep it together? I must have met handsome guys like him before but this is ridiculous! First Orion and now him—but this man is insanely beautiful. It's an effortless, rugged beauty and I both want and don't want him to look at me. I look down, to take my eyes away from his face and notice that his left arm is entirely metal from the elbow down. My eyes widen involuntarily and I think he notices as he chuckles softly, lifting his left arm so I can see it properly.

"Lost it when I was twelve in an accident," he says.

"What happened?" I ask before I can stop myself.

"I was crafting and I wasn't paying enough attention to what I was doing," he says, "but because people from my House specialise in metal magic I managed to make myself a new arm."

"How does it work?" I ask. Probably a bit rude but it's yet another brand new thing that I've never seen before.

"Basically the same as a flesh arm does," Dmitri says, flexing his metal fingers. "It's connected to my nerves by magic so I can still move it exactly the same."

"That's so cool!"

"So Ariana is this your first time in the capital?" Penny asks.

"Yeah," I reply. "First time I've been off Neyara."

"So we've got a real newbie on our hands," Remy says. "Pull up a seat and join us."

"Yeah, we want to know everything about you," Ellis says.

"Um okay," I say and sit down gingerly on the bench between Dmitri and Penny. I can feel myself blushing slightly and I don't know if that's because everyone is about to start grilling me or because I'm sitting next to Dmitri.

"So you're only eighteen huh?" Remy asks.

"Yep," I nod. "Birthday was last month."

"And so pretty," he says, shaking his head.

"Remy…" Kat scolds as she sits down on the bench, next to Ellis.

"So how's that sister of yours?" Ellis asks.

"What, Harmony?" Ellis knows Harmony? "How do you know Harmony?"

"That's her name, Harmony," he says, clicking his fingers. "I met her once when she came with your dad to the House of Pluto. Before I became a Neo Warrior, there was the potential talk of her and I getting married rather than Jackson and Trista."

"Oh…" That's a surprise…I never knew that.

"Ah, I do love a good wedding," Remy muses.

"Only because there's unsuspecting girls you can hit on," Illyria says from the door. I turn to see her and Samuel come to join us. Now that she's out of the dark Illyria doesn't seem to be glowing as much as she was when I first met her. Maybe her hair and eyes just look brighter when it's dark, like some kind of moonlight channelling magic. If so, that's amazing!

"Guilty as charged," Remy grins.

"What a slut," Samuel says, rolling his eyes.

"Hey Sammy," Remy grins, "you jealous because you want a body like mine rather than looking like a scrawny teenager?"

"You're hilarious Remy," Samuel says as he sits down on Dmitri's other side.

"Has he already tried it on with you Ariana?" Illyria asks as she pours herself a drink before sitting down.

"Um…you guys can call me Ari if you like, I don't mind," I say, feeling a little nervous. "Everyone back home calls me Ari—and yes he has."

"Honestly Remy," Illyria chuckles, "you really are a piece of work."

"You say that like it's news Illyria," a bored voice says from the door as Remy shrugs. I cast a glance over my shoulder and my jaw hits the floor for the umpteenth time today (really need to get a handle on this).

Oh my god, it's her! It's Luciana Van Garret!

My breath catches in my throat again and I have absolutely no idea what to do with myself as she comes into the parlour and over to the table. God, she's even prettier in real life than she is in pictures: brilliant blue eyes and hair the colour of the sky on a sunny day. She's got sharp, fox-like features and looks completely badass with her figure hugging outfit, a pair of goggles hanging around her neck and her long leather trench coat. Oh god her wings will be under there! At some point I'll get to see her flying up close! She looks down at me and I can feel all the blood in my body come rushing up to my face.

"Who do we have here then?" she asks, surveying me.

"Luciana, this is Ariana Sirenia, she says you can call her Ari, our new Neo Warrior from the House of Neptune," Kat says. "Ari, this is Luciana Van Garret from the House of Mercury, our resident pilot."

"Hello," I say and I'm so embarrassed to hear that my voice comes out quite high and squeaky. Why can't I control myself and not freak out when I meet cool people? I should have asked if I could hold off meeting all of them in one go and taken it slowly.

"Nice to meet you Ari," Luciana says and I'm so glad I'm sitting down or my knees would probably have just given out.

"You too," I say. Now I've got to add another person to my list of people I'm going to have to get used to talking to. This list is already longer than it should be; what is wrong with me?

"You ever been flying Ari?" she asks.

"N…no," I stammer, shaking my head as quiet chatter picks up from some of the others behind. Thank god they're not paying attention to my wreckage of a response.

"I'll have to take you sometime," Luciana says, "it's a lot of fun and you get a huge adrenaline rush from it."

"That would be great," I say, unable to stop the smile spreading over my face.

Luciana chuckles. "When you've got a day off from training I'll take you."

"Thank you so much," I gush.

"Don't mention it," she says and sits down next to Illyria, who hands her a drink. "So Remy's already hit on you? You're a pig Remy."

"I was being friendly," Remy says, looking deeply offended but I don't think he is.

"If you fucking say so," Luciana says derisively.

"So Ari have you met everyone now?" Penny asks, changing the subject.

"I don't think so," I reply. As we've gone round I've been keeping a mental tally in my head of everyone and I think I'm still missing one House.

"She hasn't met the Commander," Kat says.

"And he's a barrel of laughs," Luciana mutters.

Kat raises a disapproving eyebrow at her but says nothing. Granddad told me that Caspian Feioré is super serious and also kind of a badass (not the words he used to describe him but the gist) and I'm actually quite nervous about meeting him. I was nervous about meeting everyone but him more so than any of the others, even Luciana. This man is literally going to decide if I make it as a Neo Warrior or if I go home in disgrace after a week.

"So you've met Orion then?" Dmitri asks.

"Yeah," I reply, "we saw him in the library."

"Did he show you any of his bullshit space magic?" Remy asks.

"No…" I say. Space magic? Like, producing stars and stuff?

"Shame," Ellis says. "It's so hard to describe what he does but when you see it it's the most fantastical thing you'll ever see."

"Bullshit is what it is," Remy says.

"Don't let him hear you say that," Kat chuckles.

"Yeah he won't come out of his cave for a week," Samuel says.

"So Ari, how are you finding your first time on the mainland?" Illyria asks.

"It's great," I say. "It's a little overwhelming because there's so much I've never seen before but what I have seen is really beautiful."

"We'll have to take you to some of our Houses some time," Luciana says.

"Really? Would I be able to?"

"After you pass basic training, I don't see why not," Kat shrugs. "They'll need to know who you are eventually."

"You'll pass basic training in no time," Remy says, waving her off. "It's a piece of piss, you'll breeze through it."

"Is that so Captain Remelston?" a deep voice asks from the door.

The entire room suddenly falls silent and I know exactly who is standing in the doorway behind me without having to turn to face them.

Oh no…I'm not ready for this.

"Commander Feioré," Remy squeaks as he suddenly jumps to his feet and salutes. Everyone else follows suit a little slower, myself included, and finally I turn to see the man I've heard so much about standing in the doorway.

Commander Caspian Feioré is exactly how I pictured he would be: tall, handsome and powerful with a jaw that can cut diamond and piercing eyes. It's quite daunting being in his presence but I just about manage to hold myself together as he comes to stand in front of me. He stares at me, his eyes a flaming red but with no warmth to them and his hair, slicked back and out of his face, is the colour of slowly burning wood.

"You may be seated," he tells everyone and they all go to sit down, myself included. "Not you," he tells me and I jump slightly, staying resolutely on my feet. I'm not shaking, at least I don't feel as if I am, and I'm going to take that as an accomplishment. "You must be the new replacement from the House of Neptune. What's your name?"

"A…Ariana Sirenia," I tell him, a little irritated with myself that I can't keep the stammer out of my voice. I can't help it though. He's actually terrifying—I just had no idea how terrifying until now—he must be nearly thirty as he's been Commander for a while now and you can tell he knows what he's doing.

"Have you had any military training before Sirenia?" he asks.

"No sir," I say shaking my head. "Have you had any training at all?"

"Minimal sir," I reply.

"We have a long way to go then," he says.

"Yes sir." God I feel pathetic. This guy probably spent his entire childhood training for this and is disgustingly disappointed with me that I didn't do the same. Maybe Harmony was right all along...

"Do you know how we operate in the Braxian army Sirenia?" he asks.

"Yes sir," I reply. That much I do know. I at least had the good sense to find that out before I arrived.

"Good," he says. "That's one less thing in the long list you need to be taught. I trust you have been introduced to your new comrades as well?"

"Yes sir," I say.

"It's taken care of Caspian," Kat says and there is a definite edge to her voice. Probably because she's second-in-command, she can get away with that but her tone is clearly telling him to lay off. His eyes flick over to her for a second (at least I think they do; they leave my face but I haven't dared to take mine off him) before he looks at me again.

"Then I would be remiss if I didn't introduce myself properly," he says. "I am Commander Caspian Feioré from the House of Mars. You will address me as Commander Feioré or simply Commander, is that clear?"

"Yes Commander," I say.

"I will oversee your basic training and mould you into the kind of soldier that will best serve the Braxian army," he says. "I will push you to your limits because I expect you to exceed them. I do not tolerate laziness or apathy. If you follow my orders, then you will do well. If you do not, then you and I are going to have a problem, understood?"

"Yes Commander."

"Your predecessor was talented but he was nothing special so the bar is set low," he says. "If you exceed my expectations, which believe me are not high, then you will earn my respect. Until then you are less than worthless to me."

"Yes Commander." I can feel myself blushing, angry tears of embarrassment pricking the corners of my eyes. It's the first night and I get a dressing down in front of everyone, one that I haven't even done anything to deserve.

"Be on the training ground first thing tomorrow morning and I will assess just how much work is to be done with you," he says. "Let's see what the water princess can do."

"Yes Commander."

He reaches over and flicks a lock of my loose hair over my shoulder, eyeing it disdainfully.

"You'll want to tie that back so it doesn't get in the way."

"Yes Commander."

"My opinion of your House is not high," he says. "I trust you will try to change that."

With that, he turns and stalks out of the room. I wait until I can no longer hear his footsteps before I finally let my knees give out and I sink back down onto the bench. I can feel myself shaking and I'm desperately trying not to cry. After a moment, I feel a gentle hand on my shoulder and I look up to see Dmitri smiling at me.

"You alright?" he asks.

I nod, blinking away the tears and not quite trusting myself to speak as I turn round to face the table again.

"You did well," Ellis says. "He does it to everyone when he first meets them."

"Yeah Sammy cried the first time Caspian spoke to him," Remy says, shooting a smirk Samuel's way.

"I did not!" Samuel snaps, his face turning scarlet.

"You did a little bit Sammy," Illyria says.

"Does he do that a lot?" I ask, finally able to talk without my voice trembling.

"Occasionally," Penny says.

"Everyone gets the Caspian treatment when they first arrive," Dmitri says. "I wouldn't take it personally."

"It's his way of asserting his dominance," Luciana snorts.

"He's a good Commander," Kat says, "but he does have a tendency towards being a little on the hard side. Having said that he does get results: we're the finest team there has been for a long while. Our physical fitness and endurance compared to that of previous teams from times of peace show that he gets results."

"I wouldn't worry too much about what he says to you," Dmitri says, giving my shoulder a gentle squeeze. "He means well, he's not angry with you, you'd know if he was."

"Okay," I nod and give him a small smile.

"So Ari," Ellis says, changing the subject, "you a drinker at all?"

"Hey look who finally came out of their caves," Remy laughs before I can answer. I turn and see Amara and Orion coming into the parlour.

As soon as the words are out of Remy's mouth Orion turns to leave but Amara grabs his collar and pulls him back. She drags him over to the bench and deposits him in the vacant space on the end next to Samuel and sits down opposite him.

"You're hilarious Remy," she says.

"Aren't I just," Remy grins.

"So Ari," Ellis says again, turning the focus back to me, "you have a drink?"

"Well," I say, suddenly remembering the flask Granddad had given me, which I had put in the inside pocket of my jacket for safe keeping, "I do have this." I pull it out and show it to everyone.

"What's in there?" Orion asks.

"Neptunian gin," I say.

"Someone get some glasses and pass it around then," Luciana says, clapping her hands and rubbing them together. Ellis gets to his feet and goes over to one of the shelves to get us all some shot glasses.

"So Ari," he says on his return, "tell us everything about yourself."

"Um...there's not that much to tell really," I say as I begin to pour some gin into each of the glasses.

"Oh come on," Penny says, "you've never been to the mainland before and it would be nice to hear your stories of your House."

"Okay," I say, "There's some really beautiful coastline and beaches around and the House is in this old converted palace in the middle."

"And you grew up in the House?" Illyria asks.

"Yeah, my granddad is currently Head of the House and my sister, Harmony is taking over after he retires," I say.

"So are you the youngest?" Dmitri asks.

"Yeah."

"And does your sister look anything like you?" Remy asks.

"Honestly Remy," Kat chuckles, shaking her head.

"You have a one track mind," Samuel chides.

"I was just asking!" Remy protests.

"So this gin," Luciana says, holding up her glass and inspecting it, "we all do a shot of it and then you have to tell us everything there is to know about you. Sound fair?"

"Okay," I nod. Oh man, where do I even begin? Thankfully whatever I tell them, I only have to tell it to them once.

"On three?" Kat says.

"One, two, three, drink!" everyone shouts in unison before taking their shot. This time I actually rather enjoy the burn of it hitting the back of my throat. I slam my glass down on the table. Here goes nothing.

"Okay," I say, "so I control all forms of water, I can create water from nothing and I can breathe underwater."

"You can what?" Penny asks.

"That's amazing!" Amara cries, her eyes lighting up.

"That's weird," Ellis chuckles.

"Can we see?" Remy asks, clearly just as fascinated as Amara at the prospect of that one. I must admit it's not one that usually comes up in conversation, mostly because I've only ever come into contact with people who can do it too.

"Um…I guess so, if you have a large bucket of water I can stick my head in," I say, now wishing I hadn't bought it up. Ellis is right, it's quite weird and my guess is that people who have never seen this before are going to be completely grossed out by it.

"There's an empty bucket in the corner," Illyria says. "Can you fill it and use that?"

"Sure." I say. I get up, go to the bucket she's pointing to and bring it back to the table. If I'm going to do this, I might as well do it so that they can all see. I place my hands over the rim, concentrating my magic, and it begins to fill. I can feel butterflies in my stomach; I've never shown this off before.

Once the bucket is as full as I can get it without making a complete mess I stick my head in it as far as it will go. It's a lot deeper than I thought and I can get right down to my neck. It takes a few moments but eventually I can feel the gills opening up. I can hear muffled shouts of encouragement and excitement through the water as I hold my head under longer, completely at ease with breathing through the sides of my neck. After a long time, I've lost track of how long, I feel a tug to the back of my shirt and I pull my head out of the water. Suddenly switching the way that I breathe makes me gasp loudly as I stand up, hair and face dripping, looking at the sea of fascinated and mildly disgusted faces in front of me.

"That's phenomenal!" Amara cries again, her eyes so bright they hurt to look at.

"That's disgusting!" Orion says, his gaze stuck on my neck.

"So you can't drown?" Luciana asks after a pause.

"No," I reply, voice slightly ragged as the gills on my neck begin to close. It's painful when they first open up and when they close and talking is quite difficult when I'm out of the water and they haven't closed properly.

"That's incredibly useful," she says, watching with rapt fascination as the skin smooths itself over to normal once more.

"You make it sound like you're *planning* on drowning her," Ellis says.

"I'm not, I'm just saying," Luciana says, putting her hands up in defence. "Just think about how useful it would be to have someone who can breathe underwater."

"Did Michael never tell you that we could do that?" I ask, wringing the water out of my hair over the bucket in an attempt to make as little mess as possible.

Penny laughs softly. "We all have our secrets Ari, even from each other."

"What do you mean?" I ask. Houses keep secrets from each other, that much I know, because I have no idea how some of their magic works (and I'm very excited to see it for myself first hand). I would have thought that it was impossible for the Neo Warriors to keep secrets from each other though, given that we're all working in such close proximity.

"There are things some of us choose to keep to ourselves," Samuel says. "When we need to tell people we do but it's always good to keep some things to yourself."

"Oh…" Maybe I shouldn't have told them about breathing under water if it's not widely known.

"We have an agreement though," Remy says, leaning back in his chair. "Everything that we learn about each other and our magic is strictly between us. None of it gets back to the media or gets to be public knowledge."

"So no one else will know about this?" I ask, gesturing to my neck where the gills have now completely closed.

"No," Dmitri says with a smile. "Your secret's safe with us."

I feel my heart skip as I look at him and I just about manage to smile my thanks. Oh god, why did he have to be so much sexier than his posters?

"Thank you." It comes out a lot more breathy than I'd like but, hopefully, everyone will think it's some embarrassment about what I just revealed and actually having done it. It would be even better if they thought it was still from changing the way I breathe.

"So now the serious stuff is over," Kat says, cutting through the silence that fell, "let's get down to the fun stuff and more drinks."

There is a chorus of agreement and I relax as I put the bucket on the floor and sit down again.

Chapter 9

We spend the rest of the night drinking and the others thoroughly interrogate me about my life, taking great delight in sharing information about each other that is way too personal for a first night. It gets especially worse when everyone starts getting a little bit tipsy—I now know things about Remy that I wish I didn't. I make sure I sneak a glass of water for each alcoholic drink I have (as Granddad taught me) and I feel a little cheeky as I can basically make my own hangover cure. Dmitri notices me discreetly using magic to fill my glass with water when Luciana is passing round the Mercurian vodka and is nice enough not to point it out to the others, simply giving me a conspiratorial wink and asking if I can do his glass too.

After everyone's gotten to know me, I feel like I know them all and Orion's passed out after yelling at Remy, Kat shows me to my bedroom. It's another huge, fancy room but I'm too tired to properly explore it. Instead I fish out my sleeping clothes and Ducky (deciding to unpack another time) and fall face first onto my huge four-poster bed.

In the morning, I feel pretty good—not hungover and relatively well rested—and I take some time to have a proper look around the huge room that is apparently all mine. It's only half past five so I've got stacks of time before I'm supposed to be down on the training ground and who knows when I'll next have this kind of opportunity.

There is a window stretching from the floor to the ceiling that overlooks the training ground, the bed that I had fallen into is another beautiful four-poster, like I had on the ship, and so comfy—no wonder I fell asleep straight away. There is also an adjacent bathroom with a huge bath and shower as well as a writing desk, chairs and a sofa. I'm amazed that they have the space for twelve rooms like this plus everyone else that lives here but then again I probably only saw about a fifth of the place yesterday and even that was huger than I could have imagined.

Looking out of the window the sun is only just peeking over the tops of the surrounding trees. There's no one out on the training ground so I sit down at my desk and write a couple of letters—one to Mum and Dad and one to Trista to tell them that I'm safe and settled. I could talk about the mainland for pages and pages and pages but I reign it in for now, although I do gush a bit more in Trista's letter. Once I'm done I get dressed; later on I'll ask Kat where I can take the letters to get them sent over to Neyara but for now I do not want to be late for my first day of training (regardless of whether Caspian is outside or not) so I head for the door.

Just as I'm about to open it someone knocks on it. Surprised, I open the door and see a man in his late thirties, possibly early forties, with slicked back deep blue hair and turquoise eyes: another Neptunian.

"Morning…" I say staring at him, unsure of who he is, how he managed to find my room or why he's here in the first place.

"Staff Captain Sirenia," he says, saluting me.

"That's me, yeah," I say and salute him back.

"Forgive me for the less than formal introduction, I am First Officer Jenkins," he says, "leader of the Sirenia Squad."

"The Sirenia Squad?" I ask. I have a squad? I assume that's what he means by the Sirenia Squad. Cool, I have a squad. How awesome is that?

"Yes Ma'am," Jenkins says.

Yep, I guess that's my squad.

"I'm sorry to disturb you so early," he continues. I guess it *is* still early although I feel like I've been up for ages.

"That's okay," I say, waving him off, "I was just on my way down to the training ground anyway."

"Wonderful," Jenkins says, smiling at me. "Commander Feioré sent me up to collect you and show you how to get down to the grounds."

"Thank you so much," I say, closing my bedroom door behind me and smiling at him. "It would have probably taken me ages to get down there on my own without giving up and climbing out the window."

"The hallways are a little maze-like if you're not used to them," Jenkins says as we head off down the corridor. "It doesn't help that there are so many stairs and so many doors that lead to different places."

"Hopefully I'll get used to them eventually," I say.

"You will," he chuckles. "Once you've been here for a week or so you'll know your way around and even have found a few of your own secret short cuts."

"Most of those will probably be to the kitchen," I laugh although I highly doubt it will only take me a week. "I tend to gravitate towards kitchens whenever I'm somewhere for longer than a few days."

"A girl after my own heart," Jenkins grins and I return the gesture.

After a pause, I open my mouth again. "Just out of interest…"

"Yes Staff Captain?"

"What exactly do I do with my squad?" I ask. That feels like such a stupid question. I wish I wasn't such a newbie at this and had actually bothered to ask my aunt more questions before just thinking 'yeah I can totally do this' and being excited. Oh well, you live and learn…

"For the moment, you personally don't have to do anything," Jenkins says. "I'll be taking care of everything in terms of the actual leading of the squad and for the most part that will remain true during your time as a Neo Warrior. The squad leader takes care of the day to day duties but ultimately we all answer to you."

"Okay."

"The squad is there as an emissary of you," he explains. "Say, for argument's sake you are detained with an appointment and are needed elsewhere then the rest of the squad will act on your behalf following your previously given orders."

"How big is my squad?"

"Thirty of the finest Neptunian men and women the Braxian army has to offer," he says. "They are trained as rigorously as you will be in order to make sure that they are at their top physical peak. The squad reflects the Neo Warrior and the House they come from."

"Okay," I nod. I might ask Dmitri or Kat about their squads later although I'll probably learn the most from Jenkins on this one. It would be handy to get another Neo Warrior's perspective though. Everyone seems so willing to answer any questions I have so I can ask any of them and they'll tell me but if Jenkins is happy for me to leave him to it until training is over I can watch him and learn that way. "Will I learn about squad leading during my training?"

"That will come later," he says. "Commander Feioré will want you to be up to his standard as a soldier before you are given full charge of the squad."

"Does Commander Feioré have really high standards even for basic training?" I ask.

"Commander Feioré is one of the best commanders we have had for a very long time and he does push people to their limits but he gets results," Jenkins says. "If he pushes you then he knows that you can do better, regardless of whether you know it yourself."

"So people keep telling me," I say. "And if I don't meet his expectations?"

"He will train you so that you do," Jenkins says which is sort of comforting. "He's never let a soldier fail before and he won't start with you."

"So he's going to beat me into submission?"

"If you like."

"Fantastic…"

I'll just have to do what he says and go from there. I'd really prefer it if I didn't get a dressing down in front of my squad as well—getting one in front of everyone else was embarrassing enough. They were all very nice about it though and by the sounds of it he does it all the time so I guess that's just one of his motivational techniques.

"How long does basic training usually last?" I ask.

"As long as it takes until Commander Feioré deems you are ready to progress," Jenkins replies, "but usually it's about two months." Again oddly comforting but at the same time really not. I hope it doesn't take me more than two months. How embarrassing would that be? I guess Jenkins can already read me like a book as he laughs and claps me on the shoulder. "I wouldn't worry too much though—no granddaughter of Charlotte Sirenia will take that long to finish her basic training."

"I do have some shoes to fill," I grin.

"But you also have good family traits," Jenkins says as he pushes a door open and we step out into the morning air. It's a little chilly and I can see my breath as I exhale but I'm probably going to be running around soon so I'll warm up in plenty of time and it will get warmer as the day goes on.

"So when did you join the army?" I ask as we make our way out into the open grounds.

"I joined when I was nineteen and slowly made my way up to First Officer of a squad by sheer force of will," he replies.

"How long did that take you?" I ask.

"About eleven years," he says.

"And how have the rest of your squad leaders fared in that time?" I ask.

"I've only ever had two and both of them fared well."

"One of them was my cousin, Michael."

Jenkins sighs, sadly. "Michael was a fine Neo Warrior. I am very sad that he was taken from us so soon but, at the same time, I am very excited to be working with you."

"Thank you," I say. "I hope I can live up to the expectation."

"I'm sure you will," Jenkins says.

I toy with the idea of asking him what happened to Michael but something is holding me back. It's the same thing that has been holding me back from asking anyone who might actually know—I'm scared because I don't want to find out that it wasn't an illness and something worse happened to him. If I do, then that means admitting that something might happen to me as well so I stay quiet.

We finally reach the edge of the training ground and there is a lone, solitary figure (that I assume is Caspian) standing in the centre. As we get closer I see that I was right. Caspian acknowledges my arrival with a curt nod (nice friendly greeting) and both Jenkins and I stop to salute him.

"Staff Captain Ariana Sirenia," Jenkins announces my arrival. It feels as if it should be moot—Caspian can quite clearly see that I'm standing beside him—but I suppose that is just how introductions have always been done so I'm not going to question it.

"Thank you Jenkins," Caspian says nodding at him. "You are dismissed."

"Thank you sir," he says before turning and leaving.

I, on the other hand, am still holding my stance and feeling decidedly nervous now it's just me and Caspian. This man could literally kill me with one hand if he wanted to and not use much power to do it. Caspian begins to slowly circle me, like a shark in deep water, looking me up and down as if appraising me. The clothes I'm wearing for training are very different to the ones I was wearing yesterday—these are a little more fitted and show just how scrawny and physically unfit I am. I really should have trained more...

He finally returns to stand in my line of vision, which is a little more comforting than having him where I can't see him. "I see you took my advice about your hair," he says suddenly. I tied my hair back in a high ponytail this morning (and felt like I was staring at Harmony at my age when I looked in the mirror). It's a weird feeling having it all scraped back as I'm so used to it just being free about my shoulders.

"Begging your pardon Commander," I say tentatively, hoping that I don't get yelled at, "I assumed it was an order so I followed it."

Caspian says nothing for a moment, simply raises an eyebrow and surveys me. "It seems we'll make a soldier out of you yet," he says finally. "Now to begin your basic training, what are your current levels of physical fitness?"

"I don't know sir," I admit. "I've never measured them but I have previously been able to hold my own while sparring with others older than myself."

"That is something, at least," he says. "I will test you now and see what needs improvement, although I'm not holding out too much hope."

"Yes sir." Well, that's comforting…

"First, a question."

"Yes sir?"

"Do you know what it means to use the Braxian salute?" he asks.

"I do sir," I reply, pressing my hand a little harder to my chest and staring directly into his eyes.

"And do you know why?"

"Because we are to be ready for if we are ever betrayed, sir," I reply. "It also shows the dedication and resolve that we as Braxians have within us to stand against those that may try to oppress us."

He studies me for a moment before nodding. "Good," he says. "At ease."

I drop my salute but certainly don't feel at ease as he begins to circle me once again. I want to follow his eyeline but that would end up with me trying to impersonate an owl. Despite the chill of the morning air, I can feel a heat creeping up the back of my neck. I don't like being silently stared at for too long and this would definitely constitute as too long.

"Your frame suggests you were built for speed," he comments. I suppose so: I am quite lithe and skinny and if I could run for long periods without dying then I suppose I would have the perfect build for it. I've been told I'm like a torpedo in water "I'd like to test this."

"Yes sir."

"If you can keep pace with me, then I will consider that impressive," he says.

"Pardon…sir," I hastily add.

"You and I are going to run a lap of the training ground," he says. "If you can keep up with me, then I will consider that impressive."

"Yes sir," I say trying to keep my voice steady. The training ground is huge! I'm not going to have a fun time with this.

"Are you ready?" Caspian asks.

"Yes sir," I say, bracing myself against the ground.

"Try to keep up," he says. And with that he's off. A second later I'm behind him.

Oh man this guy is fast! It doesn't help that his legs are longer, he's taller and that I haven't really done any heavy duty running for a long time.

As we run round the training ground I just about manage to stay relatively close behind him. There is a substantial gap that I never really manage to close and I don't have a hope in hell of out running him but I manage to not make the gap any bigger. By the time we're halfway round the grounds, my lungs are burning and my legs feel as if they're going to give out at any second. The chill of the air is no longer noticeable—all I can focus on is the sweat beading on my forehead and the dull ache in my legs. I can barely draw breath and I'm not going to be able to continue standing once we're done. It feels like I'm going to pass out, vomit or both. No wonder Harmony was so angry about me getting chosen when I can barely run around a training ground without feeling like I'm going to die. Everything hurts and how am I still managing to follow him?

We're getting near to where we started and the gap between us has grown more than I would have liked it to. I can't give up! Despite how much everything hurts and I know I'm going to regret this later I push myself, forcing all the energy I have into my legs and running as fast as I possibly can to catch up. With a final burst of speed, I manage to close the distance ever so slightly, skidding to a halt when Caspian finally stops.

Almost as soon as we're done I drop to my knees, my legs giving out completely, bracing my hands against the floor and fighting to pull air into my lungs. Before I can properly catch my breath though, there's a boot pushing into my chest from below.

"On your feet," Caspian orders.

I can't! I can't move.

Closing my eyes doesn't help as the boot is suddenly pushing harder, making it even more difficult for me to breathe. I arch my back away from it to relieve the pressure somewhat but that only seems to make it harder to catch my breath. There's nothing for it—I'm going to have to stand up. It takes every last ounce of energy that I have to push myself from the ground to my feet, heaving Caspian off as I do. I'm shaking as I stand and it feels as if I might pass out at any given second but I manage to stand, looking him in the eye as I wobble slightly.

"Impressive," he says, "I thought that was you for the day. Seems you're made sterner stuff than I give you credit for."

"Thank you sir," I pant, my voice more breath than word.

"We need to build on your endurance but for a first try that wasn't too bad."

I nod, unable to speak as I force myself to try and breathe normally. I can feel a stitch stabbing my side, biting into my skin and making me ache. My head begins to spin. Shit…I'm going to pass out! I need to do something…

With shaking hands, I cup them in front of my face and, through sheer force of will alone, manage to conjure up some water. I splash it over my face and the cold hits me again. The need to pass out seems to have subsided for now and I shake the little droplets out of my fringe.

"For a first time that wasn't bad but you will need to do much better to become a good soldier," Caspian says. "Yes sir."

"We are in a time of peace at the moment but it will not always be like this. One day you may see action and on that day you will have to be ready to fight," he says.

"Yes Commander."

"People say that there are no winners in a war. They are wrong; there are," he says. "You win if you are still alive at the end. If not, you are either ill prepared or unlucky and if you were to die on the battlefield it would serve you better if you are unlucky. It would give your family greater comfort knowing that you were equipped to win but the circumstances weren't in your favour rather than you were not trained properly."

"Yes sir," I say. Whether that's true or not I don't know. I can't imagine it is a comfort to any grieving family to know that their loved one was just in the wrong place at the wrong time but I suppose that would be better than knowing they were sent into a fight unprepared. Right now I feel unprepared; there is so much more to being a Neo Warrior than I would have ever thought possible but I will learn how to do this properly.

"Now can you breathe again?" he asks.

"Yes sir," I reply. I still feel like a jellyfish but I did manage to catch my breath while he was talking so I don't feel as much like I'm going to keel over.

"Good," he says, "then let's go again."

My eyes widen to the size of saucers. Again!

Before I can say anything, he's already off and I wonder how on earth he has the endurance for it but I ignore the burning in my legs and follow him. God, I hope this gets easier…

When Caspian has deemed that my training for the day is finished, he dismisses me to Amara's office for my physical examination. I don't know how I feel about a physical exam right after running drills all day; I want to go and shower but Caspian said immediately so I head over without hesitation. Even though I'm sticky, sweaty and really want to go and change my clothes I don't want to disobey one of Caspian's first orders. Of course I get lost and a highly amused Ellis finds me and shows me the right way to go. Eventually I'll get used to this place but right now every corridor looks the same.

I knock on the door of Amara's office once we arrive and hear her call me in from inside. I turn to Ellis and smile at him. "Thank you for helping me," I say. "I'd probably still be wandering around in the halls if you hadn't found me."

"No problem," he says, giving me a pat on the shoulder, "and good luck." The pat turns into a gentle shove through the door but gentle for Ellis is not quite so gentle for me as I'm about half the size of him and I stumble into Amara's office.

It's still as bright as outside in here and this time I notice the artificial suns spaced out around the room. Amara is sitting at a desk, scribbling something down on a notepad and I have to clear my throat quite loudly in order to get her to notice that I'm here. She looks up, surprised even though she told me to come in, and pushes her glasses up so that they're holding her fringe back.

She smiles at me.

"Afternoon Ari," she says brightly. "How was your first morning of training?"

"Tiring," I reply, taking a few steps towards her, finally working up the courage to leave the safety of the door. "Sorry I haven't had time to shower or get changed at all, the Commander told me to come straight here and I got a bit lost. Ellis had to bring me."

"Quite alright," Amara says waving me off. "Come in and have a seat."

She gestures to the empty chair in front of her desk and I feel like I'm about to have some kind of interview, or I'm in trouble and it's incredibly daunting, especially considering how crazy smart I know she is. I perch on the edge of the seat rather than relax into it as I'm pretty sure that I'm going to have to get up again in a few minutes.

"So," Amara, says breaking me out of my thoughts, "let's start with the easy stuff and then we can get down to something a little more fun."

"Okay…" I say, drawing the word out as I try to guess what part of a physical can be considered fun. I guess to her it's all fun as she seems to really enjoy poking and prodding around with people.

"Just a few questions to start off," she says. "Firstly, are you allergic to anything?"

"Cats," I reply.

She scribbles something down in her notes. "Well, you're unlikely to come into contact with any of those here," she says, not taking her eyes off the paper in front of her. "Any medication allergies or anything I should know about? Are you currently taking any medication for anything?"

"Not that I'm aware of," I reply. As far as I'm aware cats are the only thing that I've ever had an allergic reaction to. I found this out after a stray cat wandered into the grounds of the House (but that could have been because it had fleas). I've sort of kept away from them since then and I've never had anything that could be considered an allergic reaction to medication. "Although a lot of our medicines are herbs and stuff from the sea," I tell her just in case there's some weird and wonderful stuff that she uses that I've never been exposed to before.

"So typical Neptunian medication then?" she asks.

"I guess so yeah. We had a family doctor and nothing he ever gave me made me go funny so I should be fine with that."

"Okay…" She scribbles something else down and I can't help but lean forward and try to peek at what she's writing but I can't read a word of it. I know that people joke about doctors having bad handwriting but hers just looks like squiggles. I couldn't read that if I tried! She may be writing in Sunese but, even then, I still wouldn't be able to read it. "I have medicines catered to each and every House here for what everyone is used to and some stronger things for if they need something extra."

"Cool," I say. I'm not sure what else I can say. That's an incredibly clever way of doing things; to have medication that we're all used to so that no one suddenly develops a strange reaction is genius. The more time I spend around Amara the more in awe I am of her and her skills—she is probably, save Caspian, the most incredible person here. She's so smart and I would love to just sit and listen to her talk for hours, which (by the sound of things) she would probably do if I gave her the opportunity.

"Most Houses tend to use herbs and concoctions of their own but with trade down at the markets I can easily get my hands on those in order to make something you're more comfortable or familiar with," she says, looking up at me and smiling. Her eyes are so bright they almost hurt to look at for too long and, I could just be imagining this, but they seem to get brighter the more animated she becomes. "Next question," she continues, "are you sexually active?"

"Um..." That's quite a jump; to go from allergies to whether I'm shacked up with someone but I suppose these are things she needs to know. "Define active," I settle on in the end. It's not exactly helpful but I don't really know how to describe my brief fumble with Marco two years ago and my lack of contact with men ever since then. She looks up at me and I can tell that she's unimpressed so I just grin sheepishly at her. "Sorry," I mumble.

"Awkward question I know, but I like to get that one over and out the way with early," she sighs. "You wouldn't believe the answer I had from Remy when I asked him."

"I can imagine," I chuckle, unable to stop myself.

"I nearly threw him out of my office right there and then," she replies.

"Wow."

"So proper answer or shall I simply take that as a no?" she asks.

"It's a no," I tell her.

"So no partner back home or anything like that?" she asks.

"No," I reply shaking my head. "Don't really have any desire to find one while I'm here either. I just want to get on with my training."

"Sensible," she says smiling at me. "Not all of us are like Remy and try to sleep with everything that moves."

"Really?" I ask.

"You sound surprised," Amara chuckles.

"I'm not surprised," I say hurriedly, putting my hands up in defence. "Sorry that must have come out sounding really judgemental."

She laughs again. "You're fine."

"Engage brain then speak?" I ask, embarrassed.

"Probably a good idea," she says, giving me a smile. "Remy is the only one of us who is actively trying to seek sexual partners. Everyone else is more concerned with other things or already have partners back home."

"Okay," I say, nodding. "Do you have a partner?" I ask before I can stop myself. So much for engaging my brain...

"No," she replies as she goes back to writing something in her notes. "I'm not interested in people as anything other than biological beings that I can study or fix if they are broken. I prefer to interact with the bleeding or dead."

"Fair enough."

"Actually Michael used to go out with Remy a bit but I think that was to keep an eye on him more than anything else," she mutters before looking back up at me. "Now, every girl's favourite subject: periods."

"Regular," I reply with shrug. "They usually last like five days or so and they're kind of a pain."

"You may be interested to know that people from the House of the Sun have developed a drug that will take care of those if you want to take it," she tells me.

"Really?" I ask sceptically. Sounds too good to be true to me, but then again, if people from the House of the Sun are all as clever as her then anything is possible.

"In the simplest way I can put it, it is a drug that will effectively sterilise you for as long as you want to take it," she replies. "So far most of the others have decided to take it."

"How does it work?" I ask: the sound of it is kind of scary but on the other hand it would be great not to have to deal with periods during training as the first day usually knocks me out.

"It's one injection, if you want it, that works instantly and is a combination of various hormones and House of the Sun magic that will stop your periods until you get an injection of the re-starting agent, which is made of pretty much the same thing," she says, leaning forward on the desk and linking her fingers together in front of her face. "If you don't want to have the re-starting agent, that's absolutely fine too. I've had the first injection and I know that I won't be having the restart because my life is easier without having to deal with periods and I know that I don't ever want to have children."

Silence falls as I think this over. "So let me get this straight," I begin, "I can have this injection, no periods, no nothing for the next twelve years—I don't need to remember to take anything daily and I don't need to get any kind of top up during that time—and then at the end of my service I have this re-starting injection and everything is all back to normal?"

"Like you never had it done in the first place," Amara replies.

"Then sign me up," I tell her. It's a no-brainer! It's not as if when I get periods I'm completely out of commission for three days like Trista but to not have to think about them during training and anything else I might have to do would be amazing.

A smile spreads over Amara's face. "Okay then, I can administer that at the end of the exam and you should be good to go."

"Awesome," I say. Yes! No more blood and pain for the next twelve years! "So how did this come about?" I ask.

"What do you mean?"

"Has this always been available to Neo Warriors or is this something recent?" I ask.

"Fairly recent," she replies as she delves into one of the drawers in her desk for something, "I developed it not long after I was made Neo Warrior. It was partly because I could see how much the others were suffering with periods during training. It seemed to be as much I was with them and it was also partly because I caught Remy making a horrendous joke leading to Luciana threatening that he would end the day how she began it: lying in a pool of blood."

"Understandable." She concocted that all by herself? Just how intelligent is she?

"She still threatens to do that to him every so often but that's because he seems to delight in rubbing her in particular up the wrong way," Amara says as she pulls out a small rectangular box that probably contains this wonder injection if I'm having it at the end of this exam.

"Does he have a death wish?" I ask.

"I think he gets bored," she replies.

"Right…" He must just be crazy then.

"Okay and last question before we move on to the actual physical part of the exam," she continues, "have you had any major medical experiences like operations, going under general anaesthetic etcetera that I should know about as your primary physician?"

"Just the wrist and you fixed that," I reply.

She makes another note on her sheet of paper and looks up at me with a smile. "Excellent," she says. Going back into her drawer for a moment she pulls out a pair of gloves. As she pulls them on there is a glint in her eye, a brightness like the sun that makes her eyes hard to look at again. That I don't know if it's excitement at the prospect of what she's about to find out about me or she just enjoys giving physicals look. She gets to her feet and I'm suddenly filled with a strange sense of dread. I don't think I actually want to do this now. "Now if you just want to take your clothes off I can begin the exam." Did she just…?

Is that necessary?

"What?" I ask after that request has sunk in.

"Strip down to your underwear and we can start the exam," she says again.

"O…okay," I mumble. I've never had a proper physical from a doctor before. Sure, there were physicians I went to see on Neyara when I was sick but never anything more than them looking in my mouth, ears or eyes. I know she has to make sure I'm completely fit and healthy so I can actually do this job properly but it's still kind of daunting as her grin has started to turn a little manic.

Trying not to make eye contact, I get to my feet and swiftly rid myself of my training gear, once again aware that I didn't actually have time to shower before coming over here. I strip down to my underwear as instructed and stand in front of her, waiting. She makes a few quick notes on her pad, eyes darting over every inch of me that she can see.

"Okay, what now?" I ask, feeling decidedly awkward. Heat fans over my face, I can't look at her directly because of both her eyes and embarrassment and I fight the urge to cover myself up. I'm in pretty good shape because I do a lot of swimming but it's still very daunting standing almost naked in front of someone I barely know, even if they are a doctor.

Amara gets up from behind her desk and comes round to join me on my side. Her eyes are so bright now they could probably light up the entire room by themselves. Even though she's shorter than me, she's incredibly intimidating because I know how talented she is. I watch as her eyes trail over my neck for a second and I think I know where this is going before she even opens her mouth.

She finally looks up at me and her eyes are wild with excitement and fascination.

"Can you show me those gills again?" she asks.

Chapter 10

Trista,

I hope everything is going well with you and Jackson. I loved reading your last letter about the House of Pluto and I can't wait to come and see you there. To be honest I'm looking forward to going somewhere other than the training ground as it's the only place I've been in the last couple of weeks! Caspian's working me ridiculously hard but he said (rather begrudgingly I thought) that I'm improving so I can rub that in Harmony's face when I next see her! ...I'm not petty, I promise.

Thank you for the picture of you and Jackson. You two look so cute together and I'm so happy that you're enjoying your time with him. Ellis is hilarious and I'm sure you'll love him when you finally get to meet him too. He's so much fun and so are the others. I can't wait 'til we come to the House of Pluto on official business then you can meet them all too.

I should be done with my basic training soon as Caspian has been pushing me so hard. I feel like I'm getting stronger and that I can take on the world now, completely different to how I felt just before I left. Having said that, Caspian now wants me to take on some of the others so I might be singing a different tune after fighting one of them!

I'll let you know how it goes when I write next time and how many of them I've faced off against. I'm really hoping that it won't be that many of them cause they're all still so much stronger than I am. Don't get me wrong, I'm good and getting better but I'm still not at the same level as people like Dmitri or Kat.

Speaking of Dmitri...oh my god he's so hot! I know we saw the pictures and said that he was a honey but he really is! He's so freaking gorgeous and I get all blushy and nervous when I'm around him, it's so embarrassing! It's really stupid and I never thought I would be like this but apparently I am. I don't want to tell you this and inflate the ego but you were totally right! He is quite possibly the man of my dreams! I just need to get him to actually see me as potential and not just the kid he has to train.

Sorry! This letter has basically been all about me! Send me one all about you and don't ask me any questions just tell me what's happening with wedding plans. I miss you so much and I can't wait to see you again, hopefully it won't be too long before I do.

All my love, you beautiful ray of sunshine.

Ari

Dear Mum and Dad,

Hope everything is going well at home. Just to let you know that my training is coming on and I should be finished with my basic soon. I'm very excited as I think I'm going to be meeting the king once I've finished but I need Caspian to confirm that before I get too excited. When I get the Captain's patches on my uniform, I'll send you a picture.

Hope everything is going well with Harmony learning the Head of the House position. I know I haven't written to her and I will but I'll do it when I have something concrete that I can show her. I miss you all so much and I can't wait to come back home and see you when I'm a proper Captain!

Love to you both and everyone else back home!

Ari

I try to keep up with writing to Trista and my parents, making sure that they're up to date with my progress and everything going on in my world. The pages and pages that I get from Trista and Mum in return are great. It's nice to hear about what's going on with them and I know that every letter that I send to my parents will filter back down to Harmony. Eventually I'll get around to writing to her myself, partially because I know that I should. I'm still a little nervous because of how we left things but at this rate I'll see her before I write to her again. There is a pile of half-finished letters to her strewn over my desk that I've started writing and then stopped halfway through because I either don't know how to finish them or I have to go to training and then can't find the nerve to pick them up again when I'm free.

It feels as if I've been training forever now (even though it isn't) so I should finally be able to send one to her saying that I'm a proper Captain. We need to make things up at some point but I know that I've gotten better over the last few weeks and will continue to get better so I can tell her that. I have no idea if Caspian has written to anyone back home but no one has said anything in their letters to me so I'm assuming not. Maybe he's waiting too…

After that first day of training, Caspian told me that he would be putting me through the same kind of treatment every day—he's not wrong. Caspian has me running physical drills all day, every day for a week and by the time it's over I think I've done more exercise than I've ever done in my life. I'm still not as good as he is but I'm definitely improving. My strength, endurance and stamina have grown and I can now keep up with him when he makes me run alongside him. My training often has an audience, the others wanting to watch me if they have nothing better to do, so I'm not surprised to see Penny, Kat, Remy, Dmitri and Ellis sitting at the edge of the grounds when I arrive back after lunch one day.

I try to ignore them, focussing on Caspian as I make my way over to him. Samuel is standing next to him and I wonder if he's been drafted into drills as well. Most of the time Caspian ignores our audience but occasionally he will make them join in if he thinks they're taking a little too much leisure time to watch me. They're all supposed to have their own training regime that they stick to but I very rarely see any of them down here with me unless it's to watch. I never really train with anyone other than Caspian but sometimes I do get to go swimming with some of the other girls. It's mostly Kat or Illyria as Luciana's wings get in the way, Amara doesn't swim and (in Luciana's words) it's all fun and games until Penny sneezes in the pool and we all die.

I salute as I stop in front of both Caspian and Samuel. "Staff Captain Sirenia reporting for training," I say. It has become my formal greeting every time I meet Caspian out here. He seems happy with it so I'm not going to change it just because someone else is joining us.

"At ease," he tells me. "Are you ready to continue your training?"

"Yes sir," I reply. He had me running drills again all morning but I feel pretty ready for whatever he's going to throw at me next. One of the wonderful things about building up my strength for an entire week is I've started to come back from the short break I get for lunch and don't still feel like I want to die.

"Wonderful," he says. "This afternoon I have something different for you."

"Sir?" I guess it has something to do with why Samuel's with him and I can only assume that it's time for me to start sparring with the others.

"Sirenia, Yonglass, the two of you are going to spar," Caspian says. I look over at Samuel and, despite my week's worth of training, neither of us looks as if we can throw a punch that will do any damage.

"With fists?" I ask before I can stop myself.

"With magic," Caspian says, as if that should have been obvious. Oh…that makes a bit more sense. "The two of you will spar until one of you is the clear victor."

It's probably going to be Samuel. Let's face it: I've only ever sparred against people who use the same kind of magic as I do and the last time I did that I was about sixteen. Caspian has had me doing physical drills for so long I've barely used any magic at all apart from random little bits to stop myself from becoming too rusty. Still, if I can at least hold my own then that might give me a few more points from Caspian.

"I won't go easy on you just because you're a newbie," Samuel says, grinning at me.

"I won't go easy on you just because you're old," I shoot back.

"Cheeky little shit," Samuel says, ignoring Caspian's reproachful look.

"What can I say?" I shrug and give him a mischievous grin.

"I'll make you pay for that 'old' comment," he says.

"I'd like to see you try," I say.

"Your smack talk sucks!" Remy shouts from the stands.

"Do you want to join them Captain Remelston?" Caspian asks. "You can spar against me."

"No sir!" Remy calls back.

"Then keep your opinions to yourself unless someone asks you for them."

"Remy aside, I'm going to make you pay for calling me old," Samuel says again.

"Bring it," I say, hoping that I look vaguely confident rather than how nervous I actually feel.

Oh dear god I may actually die here! What the hell am I supposed to do in a fight where I've never seen what he can do with his powers? I know bits and pieces but I don't know the full extent of it because I've never had time to observe him while he's training.

"Have you quite finished?" Caspian asks.

"Yes Commander," we both say in unison.

"Good. Sirenia take your place over this side," Caspian says, signalling to his left hand side. "Yonglass, you're over here."

Both Samuel and I take our respective position and ready ourselves for a fight. He flexes his fingers and I crack my knuckles for good measure. It doesn't do anything but it makes me feel as if I can give the illusion of being intimidating.

"Are you both ready?" he asks.

"Yes," Samuel says.

"Yeah," I reply but it comes out as more of a squeak than the confidence I want to sound like I have.

"Spar on three, two, one, begin," Caspian says.

I hold my ground, waiting for Samuel to make the first move. This is a mistake on my part as, before I realise what's happening, I'm lifted up into the air with a very loud, very undignified squeak. I twist, trying to look down, and just about see Samuel smirking up at me.

That rat bastard!

Well, two can play at this game. He thinks he's won since he's already got me up in the air like this but he hasn't. He may have more experience and his forte may be all around him but I won't go down that easily, not with both Dmitri and Caspian watching (the others as well but those two especially). I can't embarrass myself in front of either of them again. If I lose this without even putting up a real fight Caspian is never going to see me as anything but useless and I can't prove to Dmitri that I'm on the same level as girls his age.

With a clap of my hands, I spread my arms wide, conjuring about six water spears in the air to then throw my arms in Samuel's direction making the spears shoot down towards him. He puts his arms up to shield himself and the vortex of air he is holding me up with disappears. I fall to the floor but just about manage to catch myself on a column of water from my right hand to stop myself face planting the ground and breaking my nose.

Samuel, now looking decidedly damp and unimpressed, sends a boom of air my way. It hits me square in the chest and the breath is knocked out of me, sending me crashing to the floor again. Before I can get to my feet, he sends another blast of air down on top of me. Managing to roll over onto my front makes it a little easier to breathe and I look up to see him take a step towards me, his eyes cold and focused. It hits me at that second that he could actually kill me if he wanted to. He controls the air around us…

Suddenly it begins to get harder to breathe. I keep trying to pull air into my lungs but it's almost as if there's nothing around me and I'm stuck in a complete vacuum. Samuel is holding his hand out, palm towards me, and I know that this is his doing. I've seen enough people do magic to know when it's being used even if I can't see it.

"Struggling there Sirenia?" he asks.

I try to choke out a response but that's a bad idea as it gets harder and harder to breathe normally.

"See this is something fun that I can do," Samuel says. "I can disrupt the air flow around a single person if I want to. I can draw all the air away from their lungs and make it so that there is none left for them to breathe."

I can tell that he's not wrong: the corners of my vision are starting to go black and it feels as if I might pass out at any given moment.

"Caspian…" I hear Kat say and briefly (possibly stupidly) take my eyes off Samuel for a second to look over at them. Kat looks as if she's about to jump in and stop the fight but Caspian holds a hand up.

"Wait," he says.

He's waiting for me to pull out some spectacular escape but I don't know what I can do and the lack of oxygen is making things so much harder. If only I could catch my breath for a second, then I'd be able to maybe get back at Samuel. A small blast of water shoots out from between my fingers, something that can happen when I'm under stress and it suddenly hits me.

Water! Of course, I'm an idiot!

Bringing both my hands up to either side of my head, I swiftly create a bubble of water around my head that goes down to my shoulders. It takes a few seconds but the gills on the side of my neck open up and I take a deep gulping breath. It feels so good to breathe again!

Samuel drops his hand, looking confused, and I cast a quick glance over at Caspian to see a small smile playing about his lips. Clearly, this is what he was waiting for. I turn my attention back to Samuel and yes, he has the power to kill me, but I can do the same.

The water splashes over me as I let my hands fall, ending the effect. The fact that I'm soaked doesn't bother me in the slightest; I can breathe again so it no longer matters. Placing my hand on the ground causes a stream of water to trickle his way, saturating the ground beneath us and making it difficult for him to stand. One step wrong and Samuel slips on the wet ground, falling backwards. He's stunned and I take that as my opportunity to conjure heavy water manacles that pin both his hands and his feet to the ground with an extra one around his neck for good measure. With his hands bound, he can't use his magic, I can actually win this. I push myself to my feet, holding him down as he struggles for a second or two before he realises that he isn't going to be able to get out of the manacles and lets his head drop to the floor.

"Okay, I give," he says.

As I let go of the pressure the water falls away from him, sinking into the ground. The adrenaline that had been coursing through me just seconds before is gone in an instant and I fall to my knees, breathing heavily and staring at my hands as they sink into the mud. An equally muddy hand appears in front of my face and I look up to see Samuel smiling at me. I take his hand and let him pull me to my feet.

"Good fight," he says.

"Right back at you," I reply. "I really thought you had me there for a second."

"Just a second?" he asks, grinning at me.

"Well…a bit more than that," I admit, chuckling. "You're amazing."

"You're not too bad yourself," he says.

"Well done, Sirenia," Caspian says from behind us, "you won more with luck than skill but that will suffice for now. That was an impressive move though; activating your gills in order to counter his breath attack."

"Thank you Commander," I say.

"You will need to do much better if you are going to make it as a Neo Warrior though," he says.

"I'll do my best sir," I say and salute him.

"You had better," he says before he turns to Samuel. "Yonglass you need to improve your technique as well. Now that you are no longer the youngest you will need to up your game or she will start to catch up to you."

"Yes Commander," Samuel says and he also salutes.

"Both of you go and get yourselves cleaned up, you're filthy," Caspian tells us. I cast a look first at Samuel and then at myself. We're both covered in mud and I have to bite the inside of my cheek to stop myself from laughing. Hopefully Caspian doesn't notice. "Sirenia."

"Yes sir?"

"We shall call it for today," he says. Thank god for that, I thought I was about to get in trouble. "Tomorrow we shall start again, building on your magical skills in relation to your physical skills."

"Yes sir."

"You're dismissed," Caspian says and leaves the training ground.

We watch him go and as soon as he is out of sight Samuel and I turn to each other and dissolve into giggles. We laugh until we can barely breathe anymore, at just how absurd and filthy we both look. The others come over from the stands to join us, save Penny who heads back towards the castle. I wipe the sweat and mud off my forehead with my arm; I feel disgusting and am in desperate need of a bath.

"So Sammy, how does it feel to be beaten by a baby?" Remy asks, giving Samuel's shoulder a playful bump with his fist.

"I wouldn't know, you've never managed to beat me," Samuel says, throwing Remy a sideways smirk.

"I think I need to teach you to respect your commanding officers," Remy chuckles and moves to get Samuel in a headlock. Samuel jumps away but Remy gives chase.

"Stop it, leave me alone!" Samuel growls at him.

"Never!" Remy laughs.

"You'll get dirty too and then we'll both be in trouble," Samuel cries as Remy continues to chase him.

I choose to watch and laugh; neither Kat or Ellis seems as if they are going to stop this so I won't either. In the commotion, I don't notice Dmitri until he's holding out a small bottle of water to me.

"Thanks," I say, taking it and having a long drink.

"Thought you might need it after that," he says. "Although you could just drink your own I suppose."

"It's not as satisfying," I say, which is true. Drinking conjured water is fine if you don't need it for more than a pick-me-up to keep going but if you're genuinely thirsty it won't be enough to satisfy you.

"You did really well today," Dmitri says and gives my hair a ruffle. I feel my heart speed up and I'm blushing but thankfully I can pass it off as just being hot after the fight.

"Thanks," I mumble. "I still need to do better though."

"That will come in time," he says. "You can't expect to be perfect right away." He moves to give me a supportive hug but I back away slightly.

"I'll get you covered in mud," I mumble. "I need to go shower."

"Want to hit the bath house?" Dmitri asks. "It's great for relaxing and working out the tension in your muscles and is fun because you can talk to people."

"That would be great," I say as I down the rest of the water. I need a wash desperately and if Dmitri is going to be in there without many clothes on I'm okay with that.

"The rest of you coming," he asks.

"For a bath? Hell yeah!" Remy cries happily as we begin to head off the training ground.

"Just what you need after a hard day's work."

"What do you need a bath for?" Samuel asks. "You haven't done anything all morning."

"Just watching you two working up a sweat was enough exercise for me," Remy grins.

"And this is why everyone always beats you," Samuel says.

"No they don't!" Remy cries.

"He's not wrong Remy," Ellis chuckles. He wraps a huge arm around Remy's neck, pulls him into a headlock and grinds his knuckles into the top of his head.

"Wow rude!"

~ *** ~

The rest of my training seems to fly by. Caspian has me running drills practically every day but there are days where I'm training with other people if he's busy. I have training with practically everyone else, save Amara whose 'training' (if you can even consider it that) consisted of giving me *very* thorough medical examinations before sending me on my way feeling exhausted and ever so slightly violated. When he's not doing my training, Caspian makes sure to check on my progress and at the end of every session he always says that I'm doing well, which is really encouraging as I feel as if I'm actually achieving something. But then this is always immediately followed with that I can do better, so it has it's good and bad parts.

Thankfully everyone is really supportive, especially Dmitri and Kat. They are also around for a lot of my training and after a week or so I can be around Dmitri without blushing (even if every time he smiles at me he does make my heart do little flips). Training with everyone is fun and it gives me a chance to get to know them all better. I now know who likes to keep themselves to themselves and who wants to socialise and have a laugh. As it turns out I fall into the category of both, depending on my mood, but for the most part I'm happy to hang out with whoever is around. The great thing is that they've accepted me as one of their own so quickly that they all know this.

I can feel myself getting stronger and the more I push myself the better I get at the physical training (which Caspian pushes me to complete first) until I can run around the training grounds without even thinking about it. By the time I reach the end of the two weeks, I've got some serious muscle definition going on; I no longer look like a scrawny teenager and I can handle myself better when I spar with the others.

On my final day of training (or what everyone has told me is going to be my final day of training) it is me, Caspian and an audience of all the other Neo Warriors, Jenkins and a few other high ranking members of my squad. Just like my very first day, Caspian makes me run around the training ground with him and I can now keep up with him. I've been running around the damn ground about three times a day for the last fortnight so I no longer feel like I'm dying each time. I'm nowhere near as fast as he is but I manage to stay level with him— I don't outrun him but I hold my own. He pushes me and tests me to the best of my skills and once we're done he dismisses me for a shower and tells me to come to the main hall in my uniform.

My formal uniform is laid out on my bed for me. It's surprisingly comfy for something that looks quite tight when it's on and it's really easy to move in despite the fact that it is very figure hugging—it makes my arse look phenomenal. It's just a pair of simple black trousers and a black short sleeved shirt. Over the shirt is supposed to be a jacket with the insignia of the Braxian army on the front of my left hand side and the crest of the House of Neptune on my right. When it's on, it looks incredibly smart but for some reason I can't find the jacket. In the end, I just leave it and go down in my shirt.

I push open the door of the main hall and am met with the applause of all of the other Neo Warriors as well as the people from my squad. At the end of the room stands Caspian and Kat, both waiting for me. Kat appears to be holding something black and I realise it's my jacket (which would be why I couldn't find it upstairs). I walk up to stand in front of them and as I reach them the applause stops. I salute.

"At ease," Caspian says and I drop my stance. "Ariana Sirenia of the House of Neptune, you have completed your basic training and have earned yourself the rank of Captain."

"Thank you Commander," I say, practically beaming at him. I figured that when he told me to come here in my uniform that this was what he wanted me for but it's still amazing to hear. Caspian's praise is rare and when it is doled out I'll store it like food for a long hibernation of him being his usual stoic self.

"You are now considered one of the best of the best of the Braxian army and will behave as such," he says.

"Yes Commander," I say.

"You are now in charge of your own squad, working closely with First Officer Jenkins," Caspian says and I shoot Jenkins a smile. He has been an absolute saving grace the last few weeks as well. If he hadn't been around to help me through certain aspects of being able to lead a squad, then I would be going in totally blind. "You will be introduced to His Majesty King Elric IV tomorrow before we begin your second phase of training."

"Yes Commander," I say again.

"All that remains now is for you to be given your jacket," Caspian says. "It has your new patch attached, so that everyone will know your rank upon looking, and for you to receive your initiation tattoo."

"Thank you Commander."

Without another word Kat comes forward and holds the jacket out to me. I take it from her and put it on, noticing the new patch—a single sword behind a shield with the royal Braxian crest on it—on my left sleeve with pride. I beam up at her and she winks at me.

"Well done," she whispers before saluting me and going back to stand next to Caspian.

"Welcome to the Neo Warriors Captain Sirenia," Caspian says.

I salute him again and there is another round of applause. Trista and Mum are going to be so proud when I tell them about this! *I'm* so proud of myself. My chest swells and I can't contain it so I end up beaming at everyone. A small smile plays about Caspian's lips and that fills me with more pride than I could have thought possible. I made him smile! It doesn't happen very often and I managed to do it! As I turn and salute the rest of the room all of them returning the gesture.

"You are all dismissed," Caspian says. "We will be leaving for the royal palace tomorrow afternoon so I suggest that you celebrate tonight if you so desire but refrain from drinking too much alcohol. It would not do to turn up for an audience with the king hungover."

He leaves the hall and within seconds I'm surrounded, everyone clapping me on the back or hugging me. I can barely even distinguish the voices between them before a hand comes down on my shoulder and I turn to see Ellis grinning at me. The look on his face is anything but comforting and I'm pretty sure I know what's about to happen: booze.

"So are you ready to get your initiation tattoo?" he asks.

Ah... That...

"Initiation tattoo?" I ask, suddenly feeling a little sick. The rest of them all pull up their right hand sleeves to reveal tattoos, about the same length as an index finger and of their Houses planetary symbol, on their wrists. I've seen them all before but I paid them no mind. Now that I'm about to get one myself my stomach drops. "Right..."

"So, you ready to get yours Ari?" Luciana asks. "Be one of us for real?"

"Y...yeah," I stammer. I'm not totally sure if I am ready for this—tattoos take ages to do and they're really painful.

"Relax," Orion says, "you'll be fine."

"Yeah," Illyria adds, "it only hurts for a second."

"Just like a conversation with Remy," Samuel says, smirking. Remy says nothing but gives him a sideways glare.

"You ready Ari?" Dmitri asks.

"Yeah," I say. As soon as it's him asking me I'm instantly more willing to do it and less nervous. He winks at me encouragingly.

"Penny would you like to do the honours?" Kat asks.

"Okay Ari, come sit over here and stick your right arm on my lap with your wrist up," Penny says, smiling kindly at me.

"Okay..." I say, trying not to show my nerves. My voice sticks in my throat and my tongue feels like it's too big for my mouth but I follow her to a couple of chairs that line the edge of the room. We both sit down and I dutifully place my right arm across her lap.

"Can you make a fist for me," she tells me as Amara hands her this weird looking stamp with a bottle of turquoise ink attached to the bottom. I do as she says and clench my fist as she places the stamp lightly on top of my skin. "You ready?"

"As I'll ever be," I reply. I'm incredibly unsure about this but the rest of them have all got it done and they've all been fine.

"Okay, it will hurt but it won't be for long," she says. "Count back from three for me."

"Three, two, one…"

As I reach one she presses the stamp down onto my skin and it feels as if thousands of tiny needles are stabbing me all at once. I purse my lips but I can't stop the tiny whimper of pain as I squeeze my eyes shut, letting my head hang forward, waiting for the sensation to pass. After a couple of seconds, Penny removes the stamp, the pain stops and I open my eyes.

On my wrist, the wet ink still glistening, is the planetary symbol for Neptune, exactly the same size as everyone else's. I stare at it with wide eyes. This is so cool! Penny hands the stamp back to Amara before Luciana hands her a clear bandage which she wraps tightly around my wrist over the tattoo.

"This will stop the bleeding for tonight and you need to wash it first thing in the morning so that you don't get any infections," Penny tells me.

"Sure," I say, still marvelling at the tattoo, the pain of getting it all but forgotten.

"I'm impressed," Illyria says. "You did very well."

"Yeah when Amara got hers done she cried, if you can believe it," Ellis says and seems to take great delight in telling everyone.

"It was a reaction of the tear ducts to the sudden pain stimulus with very little warning," Amara says flatly. "I did not cry."

"Amara, you cried," Luciana says, "just admit it."

"It was a reaction to the sudden pain," Amara squeaks. "It was a perfectly normal reaction, we are not talking about this anymore!"

"If you say so," Luciana smirks at her. "Keep telling yourself that if it will make you feel better."

"So Ari," Dmitri says, placing a hand on my shoulder and turning the focus back to me, "you're a fully-fledged Neo Warrior now, how does it feel?"

"It feels absolutely fantastic," I say.

"Now, I know we have to be at the palace tomorrow for a formal function," Kat says, "but we have cause to celebrate tonight, even though we can't raid the larder for all the alcohol we have. Caspian's orders," she adds as some of the others groan.

"Yes, we do," Remy says, throwing his arm around my shoulders and pulling me close. "Our little Ari is officially one of us."

"So it's completely up to you—this is your night to celebrate—what do you want to do first Ari?" Kat asks.

Oh my god! I have no idea. My stomach growls and I realise that, in all the excitement, I haven't eaten anything since lunch time. "Maybe get some food?"

"Spoken like a true Neo Warrior," Kat chuckles.

Mum,

I'm going to make this a short one, mostly because you'll all find out soon and I've got to be ready to be at the palace first thing tomorrow.

In this envelope, I've enclosed two photos of myself; one is of me in my brand new uniform—both patches and everything—and the other is of my brand new Neo Warrior tattoo.

There will be an official statement that goes around everywhere and it may even reach Neyara before this letter does but at the moment there isn't a faster way for me to tell you. I just wanted you to be the first person I properly told.

I did it Mum!

I'm a proper Neo Warrior now!

I hope you and Dad are proud of me and I hope that I can continue to make you all proud of me as I move on to the next phase of my training.

By the sounds of it, as soon as the next bit is over, I might be able to come home and see you all but I'll know more after tomorrow. I'll let you know as soon as I do.

I hope you like the pictures and I hope I see you soon.

I love you

Ari

Chapter 11

I don't drink all that much. Not that I'm a massive drinker anyway but the idea of meeting the king hungover is not a very pleasant one. For one thing, I want to keep my wits about me in case I get called on to speak and I want make sure that I'm not too drunk to properly take care of my new tattoo. Also I know that there's a slight chance that I might run into Harmony and she'd probably murder me if I show up at the palace hungover. Occasionally the skin on and around the tattoo stings but for the most part I forget about it. It's still a night of high celebration and by the time I finally get to bed I'm exhausted but happy, falling asleep almost instantly and ready to start my first day as a proper Neo Warrior.

The following morning I wake early and write two quick letters; one to Trista and another to my parents to tell them the good news before dressing in my uniform. I look at the patch on my arm with pride, grinning at myself in the mirror before trying to tame my furious bed head. It takes a lot longer than I thought and I'm still fiddling with it by the time there is a knock at the door. Damn! That probably means I'm now running late because I've been preening. I dart to the door and pull it open, finding Penny smiling at me.

"Bad morning?" she asks, nodding at my still untamed hair.

"I don't know what's wrong with it," I groan, "it's just not doing what I want it to."

Penny laughs softly, takes the brush from me and steers me to my dressing table, sitting me down in front of it. "Let me sort it."

She begins to brush out the tangles. I don't know how she does it but it seems to work much better than my attempt.

"Aren't we going to be late?" I ask.

"No we're fine," Penny replies as she parts my hair into sections. "I was up early and thought I'd pop in just to make sure you were doing okay after last night."

"Yeah I didn't drink all that much in the end," I say, watching her in the mirror as she begins to intricately twist and braid my hair.

"You nervous?" she asks.

"A little," I reply. "I mean that's normal right? We're going to meet the king."

"You'll get used to it," Penny laughs. "It's scary at first because, like you say, he's the king but that goes away after a while."

"Okay." She's right, I'll get used to the idea of being in the presence of the king like I got used to the idea of training with Caspian and being around Dmitri all the time.

A few moments later she ties off my hair and puts down my brush. "There," she says, smiling at me, "all done."

I try to look in the mirror at the braid but the angle is wrong so I give up. I just about see most of it and it looks amazing. "Wow!"

"Like it?" she asks, chuckling.

"It's beautiful, thank you so much." I turn to smile at her and she reaches over, giving a slightly longer bit of my fringe a gentle tug.

"Shall we go?" she asks.

"Yes." I reply and follow her down to the front gates where there is a large fancy carriage waiting for all of us.

I'm amazed that the carriage can fit twelve adults but it's clearly much bigger on the inside than it is at first glance. Everyone else is in full dress uniform, just as they were last night, with the crests of their Houses in exactly the same place as mine and their rank patches emblazoned on the front. Both Kat's and Caspian's are slightly different—fancier for one thing. I'll get one of those one day if I work hard enough. I'm not the last person to arrive thankfully and once everyone is present the carriage sets off. I spend most of the ride looking out of the window at the passing country. I've been at headquarters for so long and I want to see more of Brax so while the others chat away I watch the countryside.

About three hours later the carriage pulls up out in front of the palace and, hell, if I thought the place I'm staying in is huge this place is like double the size! It's insane! You could quite literally fit the House back home in here three times and still have space left over and there are only a few members of the royal family! What do they do with all the extra space?

We are met by a herald and shown inside. As we're led through the corridors I can't stop myself from staring around me in absolute amazement and adoration.

I want to go and look in every room and see what this entire palace houses but Samuel gives my sleeve a tug when I stop for a second too long and I dutifully continue to follow Caspian and the others until we come to a huge, ornately carved set of mahogany doors. The doors slowly swing open from the inside to reveal a beautiful throne room filled with people, all awaiting our arrival.

"Commander Caspian Feioré and the Neo Warriors," another herald announces as we walk in. All eyes are on us as we make our way through the centre of the room to stand in front of the king's throne. He is flanked on both sides by who I assume are the Heads of the Houses as I see Harmony among them. I hadn't expected to see her so soon; I thought there was a chance that she might have been here but I'm still not ready. Her gaze catches mine and I instantly look away. No, I can't let her being here bother me. I'm a Neo Warrior now: I've passed my training and that's something that I can feel proud about.

As we reach the throne Caspian sinks down to one knee and the rest of us follow suit. I'm really nervous—why wouldn't I be? I'm in front of the king and most of the royal family, not to mention all the Heads of the Houses as well as unexpected Harmony. I don't want to make a fool of myself and I want to show Harmony that I've done much better than she expected me to. Hopefully Caspian will say something nice about me that she will hear.

I cast a sneaky glance up at King Elric. I've seen his portrait in quite a few places and his face is printed on all of our money so I know what he looks like but somehow seeing him in person is very different. His eyes—the black rimmed white of the royal family—stand out with his deep black hair. Even though he looks as if he is getting on a bit, his hair is still as jet black as some of his children. His face is neutral, unreadable, with lines around his eyes and mouth that paint a wealth of experience and a life well lived.

He looks at all of us and my eyes snap to the floor just as his gaze falls on me, not quite up to making eye contact yet. Once I think he's stopped looking at me and moved on to someone else I look up again to see him gesture for Caspian to stand.

"Commander Feioré," he says warmly as Caspian stands, the rest of us remaining kneeling, "how wonderful to see you. I trust you had a pleasant journey."

"Thank you, Your Majesty, it was most agreeable," Caspian replies.

"I have been informed that your new Neo Warrior has finished her basic training and earned her stripes—is that correct?" the king asks. Oh god, we're jumping right in with me then! Okay, direct and to the point.

"It is sire," Caspian says and turns to me. With a small nod of his head, I realise he is telling me that I need to stand and go join him. I push myself up on shaking legs and very carefully, so I don't stack it in my new uniform in front of all these people (Harmony included), make my way over to stand next to him and salute. "Your Majesty, this is Captain Ariana Sirenia of the House of Neptune."

King Elric looks me up and down and I hold my salute. "Captain Sirenia," he says, talking directly to me and my heart just about stops, "related to our new Neptunian Head of House I presume." He smiles over at Harmony but I don't dare look at her. I'm not taking my eyes off his face until he's finished speaking to me.

"Yes sire," I say. "I'm her sister."

"Is this your first time in the capital?"

"This is my first time away from my home island sire," I reply. I'm not totally sure how I'm supposed to behave in front of a member of the royal family so I'll just sort of copy what Caspian does until I get the hang of it (although he can probably get away with more than me because he's the Commander). As long as I'm not overly familiar with him or anyone else from the royal family then I'll be fine.

"And how are you finding it?" he asks.

"I haven't seen much of it sire," I say, "having been concentrating on my training, but what I have seen is very beautiful." Not bad on reining in the excitement—gush about your time here to someone who maybe isn't the king.

"Splendid," King Elric says, smiling at me before he turns to Caspian. "And how is her progress in training Commander Feioré?"

"If she continues to build on the skill, she has shown during her basic training I would say that she will pass her second phase of training within a month at the longest," Caspian replies. Was that a compliment? It felt like a compliment and, coming from Caspian, that might be one of the only times I'll receive one in public so I'm going to take it as one and be thankful. I almost want to take a glance over and see the look on Harmony's face (for entirely petty reasons, of course) but I won't; I keep my eyes on the king. I can feel smug about proving her wrong later—this is my moment to shine.

"Perfect," King Elric says, smiling at me. "She has completed her basic training just in time for her first diplomatic mission."

"Diplomatic mission sire?" Caspian asks.

I suppose we do go on diplomatic missions—we must be here for something when there isn't a war. We must have something to do other than just train on the off chance that we do suddenly get thrown into battle aside from magazine interviews.

"The king of Cimmerian will be celebrating his Golden Jubilee next week and he has invited a few representatives from neighbouring countries, Brax included, to the celebrations," King Elric replies. "I would like the Neo Warriors to go and represent our great country."

"We would be honoured to represent both you and Brax sire," Caspian says.

"Good," King Elric says, smiling before turning serious. "I trust you understand the weight of this visit, Commander Feioré. We have enjoyed peace with the Cimmerians for so long that we cannot afford for it to be broken now."

"We will act accordingly and do nothing that may incur the beginning of a war between our countries," Caspian says.

"Very good," King Elric nods at him. "I have every faith that you will not let your country down."

"You have my honour and my word," Caspian says.

"Both of those I hold in very high regard Commander Feioré," King Elric says. "You are the pinnacle of our army as well as individuals held highly among our citizens so, if the Cimmerian king is as agreeable as he has always seemed, he should stay a friend to us. And now to other business…"

I just about manage to keep up with the rest of the conversation but it's a lot of names that I don't know and a lot of places I've never heard of so I don't have much input but, then again, none of the others really do either, save Caspian. With the introductions over and the announcement that we are going to Cimmerian for their king's Jubilee we are moved to the side, more of a backdrop than anything else. I try to diligently listen but every so often I find myself catching Harmony's eye and instantly look away from her. She may try to talk to me afterwards…I wonder why she's here on her own as well because I don't see Granddad anywhere.

When King Elric calls his council to an end, people begin to mingle and I see Harmony making a beeline for us. Oh no! I don't want to talk to her—it's going to be awkward and tense and the others will be watching as well, not to mention a load of people that I don't know will be listening in too. If she causes a scene, that's on her head and not mine. She smiles at Caspian as she reaches him and I realise that this is happening; she's doing that smile when she wants something. I'm already uncomfortable—this is going to be so awful—I really hope that this doesn't take too long.

"Commander Feioré," Harmony says in her most saccharine voice, making me feel ill, "can I have a quick word with my sister before you leave, please?"

"Of course, Lady Sirenia," Caspian says, inclining his head. He turns to me. "Return to the carriage as soon as you're ready."

"Yes Commander," I say and salute him. I watch as he and the others leave, wishing I was going with them before turning to smile at Harmony. It's a forced smile and she knows it too; she doesn't even bother to try.

"So you passed your basic training then?" she asks.

"I did," I reply, "and in record time too."

"You've exceeded my expectations," she says. "I didn't expect you to pass at all."

"It's nice to know you think so highly of me."

"Just make sure you behave yourself in Cimmerian," she tells me.

"Don't worry, I intend to," I say. We stand there and stare at each other for a moment. I want to say something but I don't know what won't make her go off on one. She looks just as she always has and I suddenly realise how much I've missed her, even if she has been kind of a bitch recently. "You here alone?" I finally ask, to make conversation as she won't be happy if I just walk away now.

"I am yes," she admits. "Granddad thought that I should come alone in order to debut myself as the next Head of the House."

"That makes sense…"

"I was expecting you to write," she says.

"Didn't think you'd want to hear from me unless I had passed," I admit. "I wasn't expecting to see you here today otherwise I would have sent you a letter before now."

"It was a last minute decision that I was to come unaccompanied," Harmony says. "Any message you would have sent would be waiting for me on my return."

"Oh…" I don't know what else to say to her. There's nothing much I *can* say to her as neither of us is willing to talk about the argument we had before I left. I worry my lip with my teeth, we've covered everything and I shouldn't hold up the others. "I should probably go," I say finally.

"Yes, don't keep Feioré waiting," she says.

"I believe you'll find there's a Commander on there," I tell her, irritated that she's still throwing his name around like she knows him when I'm the one who's been training under him for the past few weeks.

A snort of derisive laughter meets my ears. "Caspian's girl already," she says.

"So what if I am?"

"Honestly," Harmony says with a nasty smirk, "I can't say I'm surprised."

I turn, not wanting to listen to anything else she might have to say if she's going to continue being like this, but just before I leave I cast a glance over my shoulder at her. "For what it's worth, it's good to see you." I don't wait for a response so I don't hear if she gives one. I just head outside to join the others.

It's dark out, making everything seem very solemn as I make my way back over to the carriage. I don't know whether I'm imagining it but everyone seems to have gone suddenly quiet and I would hazard a guess that it has something to do with the fact that we're being shipped off to Cimmerian. I must admit, I'm a little on the anxious side too. Mostly because I have literally just got to the mainland and now I'm supposed to be jetting off somewhere else I've never been to before, it's all a bit daunting.

"Ready to go Ari?" Kat asks.

"Yeah," I say, ready to go home and get in bed, preferably after some food. It's been a long day and there was a break in proceedings but not long enough to get a proper meal. Just as I'm about to get into the carriage I see Luciana hanging back out of the corner of my eye. Kat turns to her as she notices too.

"I think I'm going to fly back," Luciana says.

"Okay," Kat says, "do you want any company?"

"Nah, I'll be fine," Luciana says waving her off. "I'll see you when I get back. Can you take my coat for me though?"

"Sure thing," Kat says.

Luciana slips off the long leather coat she wears and hands it to Kat before unfurling her wings. I stare in absolute wonder, having not actually had the chance to see them aside from in pictures before. They are amazing! Strong and powerful and a smoky grey in colour they are at least as large as I am tall. She must have a wing span of at least seven foot or so altogether and seeing them in real life is something else! I watch intently as she puts her goggles on before pushing herself off the ground and into the air.

Kat sees me staring after her, open mouthed, as she disappears into the sky and chuckles. She hands me Luciana's coat and I instantly feel as if I've been given something precious to hold on to. I'm a little bit dizzy about the fact that it's still warm.

"Do you want to keep hold of that?" she asks. "I think it will be safer with you than it will with me."

"Okay," I say, nodding.

"Good," Kat smiles. "Shall we go?"

"Okay," I say again and slip into the carriage.

Kat climbs in behind me and, once we're both sitting, she slams her fist twice on the roof and Park'er pulls away. It feels as if there is more room in the carriage now and I look around, noticing that Remy isn't here either. I hear him laugh from outside and I realise that he's talking to Park'er, sitting outside with him while the inside of the carriage is completely silent. After seeing how talkative everyone usually is, having them all go sombre on me is really disconcerting.

Should I say something to lighten the mood?

I could tell them about my tense conversation with Harmony, that might amuse someone at the very least. I'm afraid to ask the one question I want to ask as it might make me feel worse if my suspicions are correct. Thing is I'm going to have to ask if at some point though otherwise I'm going in blind once again.

As we move away from the palace the silence seems to stretch on longer and longer. I need to say something; this is really starting to get to me now. I've never been great with silences—you'd think I would be after getting the silent treatment from Harmony for so long. I like noise, it lets me know that something's going on. There's always noise in the House from people pottering around and I always think even if you're angry and screaming at each other it's better than stewing in silence.

Okay, I'm doing it.

"So what's Cimmerian like?" I ask, finally breaking the silence. "I don't know much about it so will I need to take warm clothes or anything?" It seems like a silly question to ask but I have no idea anyway and I need someone to be saying something.

"I wouldn't say so," Kat says, shrugging. "Not at this time of year anyway. Place's weather is pretty much like Brax, especially the southern part we're going to."

"Okay," I say, nodding. That sort of answers my question but hasn't sparked any great debate as no one jumps to add to the conversation. Okay, regroup and try again. "So what are the Cimmerians like?" This time I sort of direct the question at Samuel who is sitting beside me, desperate to get someone else to say something.

"Wouldn't know," he says, "never met any; this will be my first time."

"For the most part, they tend to give us a wide berth," Ellis says after a short pause. Oh good, people are weighing in now.

"Yeah," Penny agrees. "I know the one and only time I ever went there most people used to give me an awkward sideways glance before walking away but it really depends what part you go to. They're not used to seeing people who look like we do and there's a lot less diversity over there than there is here so of course they're going to stare. Some of the people are really friendly but some are less so. It's like going anywhere new."

"The people who live in the cities aren't too bad," Dmitri says, "and the people that live on the coast closer to Brax are used to us because of all the trade that goes through there but once you get further out—like going really far inland—they tend to get a bit intimidating and don't really like non-Cimmerians."

There is a derisive snort from Orion in the corner. "Fucking sand rats!"

"Esteria," Caspian's voice cuts through the surprised silence that falls. "I will not tolerate that kind of language from any of my subordinates. If I hear you talk like that again, I will have you court marshalled. Do I make myself clear?"

Orion looks embarrassed and turns to glare out of the window. "Yes Commander Feioré," he mumbles.

Even I know a racial slur when I hear one, especially when said with that much venom but I didn't expect it to come from Orion; I didn't think he had it in him. He must really have a reason to hate the Cimmerians that must stem from more than just previous animosity between the two countries but there is no way I'm going to be the one that asks.

"And what about you Sirenia?" Caspian asks, turning to me. "What do you know of the Cimmerians?"

"Um..." Oh no, that's put me on the spot. There would be no point in me lying. It's obvious I don't know nothing from the pure and simple fact that I asked in the first place. "I don't really know anything much," I admit. "I know things I've read in history books and I've been told things but I've never met any Cimmerians so I can't comment. I'm going there with an open mind."

Caspian studies me for a second. After a good few weeks of this, I'm used to his scrutiny and just about manage to hold his gaze. The longer he stares the more I start to worry that I've said something wrong though.

"Very admirable," he says finally and I feel my grip on Luciana's coat relax—I hadn't realised that I was clutching it as tightly as I was. I let out the breath I've been holding as he continues. "If you only listen to the opinions of those who already have an in built prejudice, then you will never be able to make up your own mind."

Another silence falls as everyone seems content to leave it at that. It answers my question well enough and Caspian isn't wrong in the slightest. All I had ever heard about people from the House of Mars was that they were ruthless warmongers but I haven't seen anything that would suggest that from Caspian. He's a hard-arse on the whole soldiering thing and during training but he gets results. It's obvious that he doesn't want us charging into a war—he wants to keep the peace as much as anyone. He's a good man and a good Commander so I'll follow his orders and won't question him. That actually sounded a little like praise though, and it's not the first time, so maybe he's not such a hard-arse after all...

"I for one find them fascinating," Amara says after a pause. "Never actually met one but there is a lot less diversity among them than there is among the Braxian Houses. I'd love to have a look at the genetic make-up of one just to see how much it differs from our own. Who knows, their lack of magic may make them a different species to us all together. I'd love to know."

"You sound like you want to dissect one," Penny says.

"If I could get my hands on a recently deceased body, I would not be totally adverse to that," Amara says, "but I imagine there are quite a few people who would take offence to it."

"And this is why we don't leave you alone around people," Ellis laughs and gives her a nudge in the ribs with his elbow.

"So, is Ari going to complete her second phase of training before we go or after we come back?" Illyria asks before Amara can rise to his good-natured ribbing.

"Afterwards," Caspian replies. "We fly out for Cimmerian in three days and that is not enough time to complete her full training."

"So I'll start when I get back?" I ask.

"Yes," Caspian says. "This may be a break but this does not give you the excuse to get lazy. I want you on top form to get back on the training ground as soon as we return."

"Yes Commander," I say and suddenly we're right back in hard-arse mode. Oh well, I'm getting used to it.

~ *** ~

The next two days before our trip to Cimmerian are relatively uneventful, mostly spent packing. I send more letters to my mum and to Trista (telling them that I saw Harmony but only telling Trista how I felt about it) and I try to get a bit of exercise in each day. Taking Caspian's words to heart, I want to be ready to launch back into training as soon as we're done in Cimmerian. The night before we're due to leave I go to bed before it's even dark but I don't get a whole lot of sleep being too excited and apprehensive about leaving.

On the third morning after our meeting with the king, as instructed, I go down to the training ground and find that a huge, streamlined airship with huge wings that must span at least forty feet, has taken up most of it. I stare up at the sheer size of it in astonishment. It's not the first time I've seen one but it's still crazy. One flew over Neyara years ago and I remember asking Dad about them: an invention of the Mercurians and Saturnians for large numbers of people who can't fly but need to travel at speed.

Dawn is only just starting to break and I'm quite glad that I'm not the last person here when I reach the small group already there. No one is particularly talkative first thing in the morning and I'm practically asleep standing up but by the time everyone has arrived I'm more awake and the sun is creeping higher in the sky.

With everyone present, Luciana ushers us onto the airship, talking animatedly about what everything does as she goes. I barely understand any of it, having most of my knowledge about Mercurian flight technology being that they have wings, but I listen dutifully as she seems excited to be showing someone and no one else seems to be awake enough to pay attention. All of us take a seat (I strap myself in with the belts as tightly as possible as this is the first time I have been on a craft like this and the description she gave me of how we are to take off wasn't exactly comforting) and Luciana takes her own seat in the cockpit at the front.

"Good morning everyone, this is your Flight Captain speaking," she says, her voice amplified by speakers all around us. "We will be taking off very shortly so can you please ensure that you are strapped in comfortably and that all personal belongings are stored under your seats? There are emergency exits on the craft at the very front, the very back and in the centre but as most of you are unable to fly they will be pointless while in mid-air. If we're required to make a landing on water, then please turn to the water magic user and hope that Penny doesn't sneeze while you're in the ocean. It will take us approximately seven hours to reach Cimmerian from here so sit back, enjoy the ride and are you motherfuckers ready to fly?"

"Less of the theatrics please Luciana," Caspian says from his seat just behind the entrance to the cockpit.

Luciana sighs. "Aye Commander," she says, her voice still amplified. "Preparing for take-off, brace yourselves if you're unused to flying."

Taking off from the ground might actually be the worst thing ever. I'm already nervous as we start to move and as the airship builds up enough speed to get us into the air my stomach lurches horribly. To suppress the overwhelming urge to be sick I have to bite by lips together, clutching the sides of the seat for support. I keep gripping the seat until we're steady in the air before I can look around at everyone else. Judging by the way most of the rest of them look there aren't that many of us who are comfortable with flying. Orion's face is almost grey and he looks as if he's a second away from vomiting; Ellis's jaw is tight, eyes focussing on the back of the seat in front of him and Remy has stopped talking. Sweat is pricking on the back of my neck; I feel like I'm going to be sick if I move too much and I just want to lie down but I don't seem to be able to have the option to do so here.

"You alright Ari?" Penny asks, voice annoyingly chipper while I feel like I'm dying. I just about have the energy to prise a hand of the seat and wave her off.

"Just not used to flying," I mumble.

"Try this," Amara says as she tosses a small vial of clear liquid into my lap. She also seems to be faring fine. Her, Penny, Samuel, Illyria and Luciana seem to be the only ones not desperately suppressing the urge to be sick (even Caspian looks a little green around the gills). I'm quite thankful that Luciana isn't sick because she's the one flying this thing and I would really like to not plummet thirty thousand feet back to earth, especially if we land on the water as apparently I'm supposed to be the one who is in charge if that happens. That thought makes my stomach lurch again—I can't be trusted with people in this state!

"What is it?" I ask when I've managed to swallow the need to vomit again.

"Just a little something I've been working on; should combat the sickness while we're flying," Amara says.

With a shaking hand, I open the vial and take a sniff. Really I should have learnt with the Neptunian gin not to do that but this one smells rather nice—sweet and sugary but with a hint of peppermint. Without asking any more question I down the whole thing. It doesn't taste terrible; in fact it tastes exactly how it smells, and I do feel my stomach begin to settle somewhat. Okay this I can just about handle for the rest of the journey.

"So what does it do?" I ask, sinking back into my seat and feeling more at ease.

"Combats motion sickness," Amara replies. "It gets to work immediately and makes you less susceptible to vomiting."

"That's good," I mumble.

"I haven't got it quite right though."

"What do you mean?" I ask, blinking slowly at her. Suddenly I feel very heavy, like my limbs are weighing me down and like my neck is too fragile to support my head.

"I'm still working on the side effects."

"And I'm what, the guinea-pig?" I ask, my voice beginning to slur and I can't quite seem to keep my eyes open all the way for more than a few seconds.

"If you like," Amara grins.

"Yeah, the rest of us have learnt not to take anything from her unless we've seen the side effects on someone else first," Remy chuckles derisively even though he looks about as awful as I imagine I do.

"Swell…"

"You'll be fine in a few hours," Amara reassures me. "It's just made you a little drowsy—you'll sleep it right off and be fine when you wake up."

"How long'm I gonna sleep for?" I ask.

"Five, six hours tops," Amara says. Oh that's comforting…

"Solarium, stop testing your latest drugs on the unsuspecting," Caspian says. "I would like to not have to take her home in a coma."

"She'll be fine," Amara says.

"You say so," I mumble as I lean back in my seat and pass out.

~ *** ~

I wake up to Luciana's voice announcing that we will be landing in Cimmerian shortly. I have no idea how long I slept for but, by the sounds of it, it was basically the whole flight. On the one hand, I'm a little disappointed as I would have liked to watch the world go past beneath me but at the same time I don't think I'd have been able to do that without throwing up. I'm still not overly happy about being Amara's guinea-pig but I must admit I feel better and I slept through most of what would have been a very unpleasant trip.

"Feeling better?" Penny asks as I rub a hand over my face.

"Yeah actually."

"Good, because we'll be landing soon," she says.

"Oh great…" I sort of forgot that since we had gotten up here we have to get back down again and that is even less appealing.

"Yeah you woke up for the worst bit," Ellis says, sounding a little jealous that I managed to sleep at all.

"Fantastic…" I mumble closing my eyes, my stomach turning as we begin our decent. Just my luck…

Going down is even less pleasant than getting up and I feel awful as every time I think we're getting close to the ground everything lurches horribly. I grip the edges of my seat, cold sweat prickling my skin and I want more than anything to be able to get out of this stupid airship and into fresh air again. I will begrudgingly admit this is much faster than going by boat but get me out on the waves any day—none of this airborne crap.

After what seems to take much longer than it should, we finally touch down on the ground and stop moving. There's a collective sigh of relief from everyone who was suffering from the flight and, along with everyone else, I push myself up on shaking legs and leave the airship, thankful to finally be on solid ground again.

When I step outside, I'm met with brilliant midday sunlight and once my eyes have adjusted enough to see there is a thriving world in front of me. It's just like when I first arrived on the mainland: I wasn't sure what was going to greet me but now I'm here it's nothing like I imagined but then again I don't really know what I imagined.

There are people everywhere, mostly falling into two camps—either starting to unload the airship or staring at us in awe. Looking around, there does seem to be a lot less diversity in terms of colour like people have told me. Everyone here seems to look the same: they don't have distinguishing features like hair or eye colour that immediately stands out, unlike us. No wonder people are staring.

A young boy of maybe five or six in the crowd stares over at us with wide eyes so I give him a friendly smile but he hides his face in his mother's skirt. I can't say I blame him, if the most interesting hair colour I had ever seen at that age was light brown and someone with blue hair turned up I'd think they were weird and scary too.

"So Ari," Luciana says, clapping me on the shoulder, "how was your first time flying?"

"Unpleasant," I reply through my hand, covering my mouth as her jolting me brings on another wave of nausea.

Luciana snorts. "It's not for everyone. Personally I much prefer flying out in the open air than I do in an airship."

"Captain Van Garret," a man in overalls says as he approaches the two of us, "we're ready to move your airship to our airfield for cleaning and refuelling if you're happy for us to do so."

"Sure thing," Luciana says. "I'll come with you; she's a bit temperamental if she's been on a long haul flight."

"Thank you Captain," the man says and bows.

"See you later Ari," Luciana says and gives my hair a ruffle. I don't mind that from the others as much as I thought I would. It doesn't help that I am one of the shortest Neo Warriors (only standing taller than Orion and on par with Samuel and Amara) but it's a nice gesture that makes me feel like their younger sister.

With Luciana gone, I turn my attention to Caspian as he is met by another man, this one in a uniform. It is a browny-beige colour with an intricately embroidered red sash across his front and what I assume is the crest of the Cimmerian royal family on his left breast pocket. He salutes Caspian, one much different from our own—his left hand at his temple—which is a little strange to see, and Caspian returns the gesture using our own salute.

"Commander Caspian Feioré and the Neo Warriors on behalf of His Majesty King Elric IV of Brax," Caspian announces.

"Commander Feioré," the man says, acknowledging the greeting. "General Masterson of the Royal Cimmerian Guard. I have been sent by His Majesty, King Zircon, to escort you to the royal palace where you will be staying during the Jubilee celebrations."

"Thank you General Masterson," Caspian says, nodding at him. "If you lead the way, we shall follow."

"Of course Commander," Masterson says. "We have provided carriages to take you all to the palace."

"That won't be necessary, thank you," Caspian says, holding up his hand. "Myself and my comrades have been travelling for a very long time and would appreciate the chance to stretch our legs."

"As you wish sir," Masterson says.

He turns and the rest of us follow him, apart from Luciana (who is animatedly talking to the men on the airfield). I can still feel eyes on me and it's a little disconcerting—I can't quite tell if they're staring because they hardly ever see people like us or because there's an underlying hostility—but I try to ignore it. I'm with the others so it's not as if anything is going to happen if the locals *are* hostile.

I'm very glad for the walk to the palace: it isn't all that long and it's nice to be out in the fresh air. I feel a lot less sick after a few big gulps of air and the walk helps my legs to feel less rubbery. It's only a twenty minute to half an hour walk to the palace and before I know it we're there. If I thought the palaces back in Brax were crazy huge, this place could probably fit the entirety of Neyara inside it!

Everything about the palace is ostentatious, with everything made out of some kind of precious stone rather than just brick and there are portraits and tapestries everywhere. Even the sinks in the bathroom we use for washing up after the walk have gilded taps. It feels a bit like overkill but, then again, I'm still new to all this so who knows if this is just the norm in Cimmerian houses.

A herald tells us that there is a banquet being held tonight as the start of the Jubilee and that we will be considered the king's guests of honour. I'm still getting used to this whole 'guest of honour' thing (especially in a country that is supposed to hate us but so far everyone has been pretty nice). I'm glad I had the forethought to pack a nice dress for the evening otherwise I would be screwed.

Caspian gives us the afternoon to do as we wish and I toy with the idea of going into the town we passed on the way to the palace. The thought of going on my own is a little daunting as I don't want to get lost (and the possibility of running into open hostility hangs heavy in my mind) so when Dmitri, Remy and Illyria ask if I want to go with them I jump at the chance. I'm rather looking forward to exploring this place and spending the afternoon with Dmitri will be an added bonus.

"So what do you think of Cimmerian so far Ari?" Dmitri asks as we walk through the town's crowded market.

"It's totally not what I expected," I reply truthfully.

Dmitri laughs. "That was the same thing I thought when I first came here. I wasn't sure what to make of this place I had only heard very biased things about it and the way they received Braxians. There will always be a bias, and the same with them and Brax, but from what I've seen it's not like how it's described."

"The people aren't either," I say. I look over at Illyria, who is proudly showing off her tattoos to a market stall owner, while Remy seems to be chatting up a very pretty girl a few feet away. She seems very taken by him and he seems to love the fact that someone is finally paying attention to his flirtations as he's always met with stone faces from all of us. "I expected...I don't know, more hostility."

"There will always be a bit of underlying hostility," Dmitri says. "You get the radical groups on both sides, which you'll come across if you hang around here and places away from the docks on the mainland but for the most part you only receive stares."

"I've noticed," I say as another small child stops to stare, open mouthed, at my hair and Dmitri's arm (what little he has of it on show) before being dragged away by her mother.

"I'd try not to use magic here though," Dmitri says. "Just in case."

"Sure," I reply. Not that I would but it's a sensible thing to do. The lower a profile we keep (you know, as best we can considering how much we stand out) the better for us.

We stop in front of a stall offering various fabrics and while Dmitri is talking to the stall owner I feel a small tug on the back of my shirt and turn to see two children: a girl and a boy, who look as if they are probably twins, both with the same curly copper coloured hair, and are probably only about ten at most staring up at us. The girl shuffles awkwardly and opens her mouth but before she can say anything her face goes bright red and she closes it. The boy gives her a nudge in the back and she tries again.

"E...excuse me," she begins timidly, "are you two from Brax?"

I look up at Dmitri. No point denying it—we stand out even without our uniforms (which I changed out of and was probably a sensible thing to do so). Even so I don't know what I'm supposed to say to them 'yes, we're the scary magic users people tell you to worry about'. I think not somehow...Dmitri seems to know what to do though. He smiles at the children and kneels down so that he is eye-level with them.

"We are, yes," he says.

"So do you know how to do magic?" the boy asks.

"We do," Dmitri says. The boy looks at him in wide-eyed adoration, as if this is the best thing he has ever heard.

"Is your arm magic?" he asks, nodding towards Dmitri's metal hand.

"It is," Dmitri says, pushing the sleeve of his jacket up higher to give the boy a better look.

"I made it myself."

"That's so cool!" the boy cries, staring in wonder at the intricate metal work. The girl tugs on my shirt again as her brother begins to grill Dmitri about how his arm works. I kneel down as well so that we're face to face.

"Can you do magic too?" she asks me, her voice barely above a whisper.

"I can, yeah."

"Can you show me?" she asks.

I think for a second. Dmitri literally just told me not to do this but no one seems to be looking at us that closely so I can probably get away with it and she seems so curious about it so what's the harm. "Hold your hands out like this for me," I tell her and cup my hands together in between the two of us.

She copies me and I place my hands around hers, holding mine a little above hers. Both of us stare at her hands, her in awe and me in concentration as I conjure up a tiny water butterfly in the middle of her palms. She stares in amazement as the butterfly flaps its wings a few times before it melts into her hands, the water running through the tiny gaps in her fingers to drip onto the ground. When she looks up at me, her eyes are bright and her face splits into a grin.

"That's amazing!" she says, her voice still quiet and breathy. She's so excited. I just grin at her. What a cutie!

"Elsie!" a harsh voice cuts over the moment from the other side of the market. "Joshua! Get over here *now*!"

Both children suddenly stiffen and turn to see an angry, imposing woman standing a few feet away. I assume that's their mother as they both look very similar to her and the pair of them scuttle over to her when they realise that it's her who's calling. The boy, Joshua, tosses a thanks over his shoulder as he goes.

"I've told you so many times not to talk to strangers," their mother snaps as they reach her, "and you're certainly not to approach people like *them*."

As soon as she says it, I suddenly become hyper aware of the subtle whispers of 'Brax', 'Braxian', 'magic users' and other comments aimed at Dmitri and I saturating through the crowd. I suddenly feel even more exposed than I did before and I don't know if I'm only just noticing this or if people have been making comments all day and I just hadn't heard. Unconsciously, I take a step towards Dmitri and he puts a protective hand on my shoulder.

"Do you want to carry on?" he asks. He seems completely nonplussed by the racial slurs filtering into the conversations around us. Maybe I'm just paranoid and hearing things…

"Sure," I say, even though I don't sound it, and we carry on walking through the market. One thing Dad always used to say to when I was little was not to listen to what other people said, especially if they said it loud enough for you to hear: hold your head high—they win if they know that they're getting to you.

"You okay?" Dmitri asks when I don't say anything for a moment.

"Yeah," I say, giving myself a shake. "Sorry, still getting used to things."

"Understandable," he says. "That's the first time I've had that in a while." He nods his head back in the direction of the woman. He can see something written all over my face because he chuckles. "She's just worried about her kids, don't take it personally."

"Okay," I say and give him a small smile. He smiles back and my heart flutters. I wonder if I'd be in with a shot with him? Maybe when I'm older and look less like a kid, maybe he might be interested in me and see me as something more than just another comrade. "I guess we're still kind of scary to some people."

"We do have the power to wipe out entire countries," he says. "When you think about it from the perspective of someone who can't use magic that alone is terrifying."

"I'd never thought of it like that before."

"There will always be people that are unsure about other cultures but everyone tends to have the same mind set—let's be happy with the peace we have while we have it and pray that it lasts as long as possible."

"Yeah," I say. I open my mouth to change the subject and ask him another question but I'm suddenly distracted by a familiar smell. I turn, following my nose, until I find a stall covered in flowers and there, right in the centre of the display is a bunch of Neptunian water lilies. I haven't seen these since I left Neyara! They don't grow in other soil, how on earth did this guy get his hands on some?

"Um, excuse me…" I hail the seller's attention. An old man, probably in his sixties or seventies, turns to smile at me.

"And what can I do for you, young lady?" he asks. His voice is gravelly and he reminds me a bit of Granddad.

"Those flowers," I say and point to the water lilies, "where did you get them from?"

"Sometimes when I head over Brax way I stop off at the House of Neptune and trade with the sellers at the docks," he says. "You look like a native Neptunian."

"I am," I say. It's kind of obvious—we all look the same to people not from our House.

"Your homeland is lovely and your people so friendly," he says. "The last time I was there I discovered a bunch of these flowers and I found myself quite taken with them. Traded some of my best silk for them."

"How much for one?" I ask.

"Normally I would charge ten censa, these flowers are very rare outside the House of Neptune, as I'm sure you know, and they are very beautiful, but for a genuine native Neptunian asking: six," he replies.

"Really?" I ask a little surprised. I would have thought that, considering he traded his best silk for them he would want more than that.

"What can I say," he says with a smile, shrugging, "I just love your homeland."

"Okay then," I say and begin rummaging in my pockets for some change. I'm not going to sniff at a deal and this is the first reminder I've had of home since I left. I pull out some change and as soon as I look at it I realise it's all Braxian.

"Ah…"

"It's fine," the man says. "I'll happily take Braxian."

"Don't worry, I'll get this," Dmitri says and hands the seller some coins, "and keep the change."

"Thank you kindly young sir," the seller says and pockets the money. He picks the flower from the centre of the bunch with the largest and bluest petals and hands it to Dmitri. "For your young lady."

"Thanks," Dmitri says and my face catches fire. Hopefully he didn't notice but the seller makes it sound like we're a couple. He smiles at the seller before he turns to me and places the stem behind my ear so the flower is keeping my hair out of my face. My heart is pounding and I can feel a faint blush creeping across my cheeks as he turns that smile on me and everything gets a hundred times worse. Oh god! I am literally struggling to hold it together with him being this close. I know I've gotten much better at being a normal person around him but I'm still quite shaky, especially when something like this happens. I'm just not used to this kind of attention from men, and definitely not from ones I like.

"Thank you," I say, my voice barely above a whisper but he seems to still hear me over the noise of the crowd.

"Despite prejudices, despite the bias you hear from everyone about each other, sometimes people will surprise you for the better. You just have to find those moments and enjoy them," he says. "Now shall we get you some Cimmerian money?"

"That would be great," I say. He offers me his arm and I take it. We must look like a couple walking down the street arm in arm. I try not to think about that too much because that will just result in an even redder face and I must match Remy's hair as it is. Think about nice safe subjects, like this banquet thing tonight.

Oh crap…am I going to have to dance tonight? Oh god that's not a nice safe subject! Not a safe subject at all! I hate dancing, especially in front of other people. Can we go back to talking about racial slurs?

Chapter 12

Being out with Dmitri is wonderful. He's funny, he listens to me and he doesn't just treat me like a kid because I'm nine years younger than he is. He's a really nice guy and I can't help from smiling the entire time we're together. I manage to keep myself from blushing the whole time as well but that's more to do with the fact that I'm also very aware that we're not in our own country. People do continue to stare at us but, for the most part, everyone is friendly and happy to have the extra trade so no one gives us any trouble.

I'm still grinning like crazy by the time we get back to the palace. We lost Remy and Illyria somewhere in the crowd but Dmitri assured me that they could make their own way back. He leaves me at the bottom of the stairs in order to go and find a library somewhere so I make my way back up to our rooms alone. As I'm about to turn the corner to the corridor our rooms are on I hear raised voices. I hang back for a second and listen, it sounds like Caspian and Luciana and Luciana does not sound happy.

"You can't make me do this," she hisses.

"I can," Caspian replies, "I'm your commanding officer."

"That's not fair!"

"No it isn't," Caspian agrees, "but I have *asked* you to be sensible and if you continue to seem to want to go along with this ill-advised venture then I will be forced to *order* you."

I should leave, I know I should but like with Harmony and Dad, I can't seem to make my legs work *to* leave. Curiosity is outweighing the sensible part of my brain that knows if I get caught I'm dead; not only will Caspian kill me Luciana probably will as well. I continue to hang back and listen: probably the worst idea in the world but I do need to get to the room eventually so I might as well wait until they're done.

"You can't order me to cover myself up," Luciana says, "my wings are part of me! Just like Dmitri's arm is part of him."

"I have asked Tavaron to do the same and he is more than willing to keep his arm covered while we are here," Caspian says.

Ah so that's it…Luciana and Dmitri are the only ones out of all of us whose magic is visible for all the world to see. I can understand where Caspian is coming from saying that they need to cover up because we've all been told it's not advisable for us to use magic while we're over here but at the same time it's not fair to ask someone to hide a part of themselves just because of where we are.

"Well, maybe he is but *I'm* not," Luciana snaps.

"Van Garret I understand your frustration, I really do," Caspian tells her, "but I'm trying to keep all of us as safe as possible while we're here. No, it's not fair that either of you have to hide any part of yourselves but the fact of the matter is that while we are in Cimmerian we need to stay as out of trouble as possible. Surely you can see the sense in that."

"This isn't over," Luciana hisses. "You don't want to piss off the people that want to kill us but have you actually considered how *we* feel in all of this? Magic is part of us, it's who we are and we can't always hide it."

"Van Garret can you at least give me your word that you will for tonight?" Caspian asks, still sounding surprisingly calm considering the way Luciana is talking to him, probably because he doesn't actually like this any more than she does. "You know I wouldn't ask this of you unless it was necessary."

"I'll think about it," Luciana spits angrily and slams the door in his face.

I can't stop myself from gasping at that—she actually slammed the door in our commanding officer's face! She could be in so much trouble and I'm genuinely amazed that Caspian hasn't flown off the handle and burnt the door down. What he does do, however, is turn to look in my direction. Oh crap! I didn't realise the gasp was that loud but it must have been as he comes down the corridor towards me. I want to run, knowing that he's probably going to chew me out and let out the frustration he kept in during that conversation on me.

"How much of that did you hear Sirenia?" he asks smoothly as he reaches me.

"From when you said you'd be forced to order her," I reply, deciding it's better not to lie. I just about manage to keep my voice steady so he doesn't know how afraid of him I am.

"Maybe you can talk some sense into her then," he says and I can't help but be shocked. That is not what I had expected at all.

"What?"

"Talk to Van Garret," he tells me, "see if you can succeed where I have failed."

"I… Is that an order?" I ask, not sure what to make of this. Is he crazy? He must be if he thinks that *I* can persuade Luciana to do something that she doesn't want to and that I don't believe she should have to.

He looks me up and down for the briefest of moments and I feel like I'm back in the parlour on my first night again. No matter how much time I spend around Caspian Feioré he still has the ability to make me feel like a child again.

"It's a request," he says finally and pats my shoulder once as he leaves.

I turn to stare after him for a moment, utterly confused but if he seems to think this is something I can do then I might as well try. Shaking my head I make my way over to the door. If I'm going to actually do this, then I need to do it quickly otherwise I'll lose my nerve and Luciana will have had time to get even angrier. Hurrying to the door I let myself in—she's sitting on her bed and no one else seems to be in. Her hair, which I've noticed seems to change with her mood like the sky changes with the weather, is a stormy grey so I know I'm in for a rough time.

"Hi," I say brightly, trying to pretend that I didn't just overhear her yelling at Caspian. When she doesn't turn around, I try again. "You okay?"

"When did you get back?" she asks, voice harsh.

"Not that long ago," I reply, trying not to stammer. If I'm going to be convincing and do what Caspian wants, I have to keep her from knowing just how nervous I am about having this conversation in the first place.

"Right." Monosyllabic replies are never a good sign when someone's angry but I'm not supposed to know that she's angry.

"I ran into the Commander on my way up here," I say trying to sound nonchalant but I don't know if she believes me. She just huffs in response so I take a deep breath and decide to try again.

"Are you sure you're okay?"

"My god what the fuck is it you want?" she snaps, turning to face me.

The ferocity hits me like a slap in the face and renders me speechless so I simply stare at her. Fear stricken I swallow the instant lump in my throat and try to hold it together. I've idolised her for years now, I finally get to meet her in person and would even be lucky enough to think we were friends then I mess it up by pushing her when she's angry. My eyes instantly start to fill with tears and at the same time it pisses me off how easy it is to make me cry sometimes.

"I'm sorry," I say hurriedly. I want to turn and run away, leave her until she's calmed down but I can't seem to get my legs to move.

She lets out a long sigh and lets her head fall forward. "No I'm sorry, that was uncalled for," she says, sounding as if all the fight has left her.

"It's fine," I say, "I'll leave."

"No stay," she says and she sounds so defeated that I don't immediately try to run away again. She pats the space on the mattress next to her. "Come, sit."

I do as I'm told and go to sit down on the bed next to her. I'm practically perching on the edge I'm so nervous—being this close to her while she's this furious—but I suddenly feel an arm around my shoulder and she pulls me into her side. "Um…Luciana?" I mumble, not sure what's happening.

"Sorry for being a dick," she tells me, hugging me tightly to her side.

"It's okay," I mumble, sniffing.

"No it's not," she sighs. "I was angry and I shouldn't have taken it out on you."

"Wanna talk about it?" I ask.

"How much of my argument with Caspian did you hear?" she asks in return.

"Most of it," I admit. "He then asked me to talk to you."

"That figures," she snorts softly.

"Can I ask," I begin tentatively, "if you don't want to cover your wings up why do you wear your trench coat so much when we're at home?"

"It seems stupid, doesn't it?" she laughs softly. "Me not wanting to hide here where it's actually dangerous to be out with our magic whereas at home I'm more than happy to keep them out sight." She sighs again. "I have a seven foot wingspan and, as much as they're part of me, they do get in the way, like how you Penny and Kat all tie your hair up. It's like that."

"Makes sense."

"So it's something I do because I want to, not because I'm supposed to do it," she says. "We shouldn't have to feel like we can't be ourselves. It's like asking us to cover our hair or hide our eyes when we go outside."

"Some people were muttering about us being Braxian while I was out with Dmitri and the others," I say. "It wasn't anything much but it was enough to make me feel a bit uneasy."

"You were safe with Dmitri though right?"

"Yeah I was fine but I could still hear it."

"See, we shouldn't have to feel this way!" she says. "There hasn't been any kind of war for years and we're still tiptoeing around them like we're not welcome here. It's fucking frustrating! The king has invited us so there's no reason why we shouldn't be here and no reason why we should have to keep ourselves hidden."

I let that hang in the air for a moment before speaking again. "Can I ask you something else?"

"Fire away."

"If it's more practical to keep them out of the way for certain things, wouldn't it just be easier *to* do what you do at home?" I ask, hoping that she won't fly off the handle again. "I mean just for dinner tonight."

"Trench coat doesn't exactly go with an evening dress," she chuckles, "but I do see where you're coming from."

"Yeah but you're Luciana Van Garret," I say, smiling up at her, "you can wear anything and it will still look cool."

She laughs and pulls me close. "You're a good kid," she tells me and kisses my forehead. "Sorry I snapped at you."

"It's okay," I mumble. "You were pissed off, I understand." And I do. I'd hate to be told to cover up a part of myself when I shouldn't have to. I understand where Caspian is coming from on this one but at the same time there are better ways to go about it.

"Thank you for this," she tells me. She pulls back so she can look me over and reaches up to brush her fingers near the flower still in my hair. "This is pretty, where did you get this?"

Instantly heat is rising up the back of my neck. "Oh!" I squeak, suddenly remembering my afternoon with Dmitri. "Just from the market, nothing special really."

Her raised eyebrow says she doesn't believe me but she's good enough to let the subject drop for now.

~ *** ~

"I'm actually quite looking forward to tonight," Amara says as she adjusts the collar of the dress shirt she's wearing.

"You're excited about something that isn't a dead body—that's novel," Illyria teases as she puts on a pair of silver crescent moon shaped earrings, looking in one of the mirrors of our huge suite. We were given two on arrival at the palace: one for us girls and the other for all the guys. I don't know how their suite looks but if it's anything like ours it's huge, grand and over the top (like most other things in the palace).

There are six double beds as well as an adjoining bathroom that contains a bath big enough for at least three of us and three separate showers. We also have enough room for all our luggage (which on my part wasn't that much) as well as two huge dressing tables and loads of light streaming in through the wall length windows. Clearly the Cimmerian king is either really happy to have us as guests of honour or he's showing off just how wealthy he is. I'll probably find out one way or the other when I meet him.

"I'll have you know I'm excited by live ones too," Amara says, shooting her a sideways glare.

"I have never seen you express excitement about living bodies unless they're bleeding," Illyria says.

"That's not true either," Amara huffs.

"I can actually attest to that," Luciana says as she smooths her long black coat over the top of her dress, keeping her wings folded underneath. "She was very excited when she saw my wings. Spent the best part of my medical exam on them, didn't you Doc?"

"Can you blame me? I'd never seen a Mercurian's wings up close before," Amara says. "Not living ones anyway."

"Are dead people easy to come by in the House of the Sun?" I ask, a little unsettled.

"You'd think so the way Amara goes on about them," Penny teases. "You understand most people find that creepy, right?"

"I understand people on a biological level," Amara says. "I do not understand them on a personal level."

"How do you mean?" I ask.

"If someone is dead I can study them, find out how they died," Amara explains. "If someone is bleeding or injured, I can fix them but I have no idea how to talk to them."

"I've noticed," I say. Amara can be a little unorthodox at times but I'm not going to say that outright—she does my medical exams and has access to anaesthetics.

"You know what—I'm actually quite excited about tonight as well," Kat says. "We're at a party, there's going to be good food, dancing and I've heard Prince Onyx is quite the looker."

"And I've heard he's a colossal dick," Luciana says as she runs a brush through her hair, which is the same light blue it always is when she's in a good mood. The movement is so elegant and graceful that I can't help but stop and stare for a second. I hope I'm that graceful when I get older and less a baby deer struggling to walk when I'm in heels.

"Shame," Kat sighs theatrically as she pulls her dreadlocks back into their usual high ponytail.

"You banking on hooking a prince Kat?" Penny asks.

"Not particularly," Kat replies. "I have more important things to be doing with my time than chasing after men, despite what my grandmother says."

"She does realise you're second-in-command of the Braxian Neo Warriors, right?" Luciana asks incredulously.

"But *I* haven't produced any heirs yet," Kat says with a wry smile. "My sister has."

"Speaking of chasing after men," Illyria says, turning to me and smirking, "our little Ari was stepping out with Dmitri this afternoon."

All eyes turn to me, and my face bursts into flame. Thanks Illyria! There is no way I'm going to get out of this without an explanation so I might as well just bite the bullet.

"He took me to get some Cimmerian money," I say, a little defensively.

"That all?" Penny asks raising an eyebrow and smirking at me.

"Yes," I say finally.

"Sure it was," Illyria teases.

"Dmitri's not a bad choice though," Luciana says taking some of the heat off me before I can retaliate. "You could do a lot worse than Dmitri Tavaron."

"Like?" Kat asks.

"Remy for a start," Luciana says. "I bet he's already rated us in order of appearance."

"He has," Amara says. "I heard him."

"For fuck's sake," Luciana sighs.

"You'd be surprised to know that you ranked quite highly Luciana," Amara smirks.

"That's nice, I don't give a shit," Luciana says. "Remy's a pig."

"You know it's only good-natured ribbing. He only does it cause he gets a reaction out of you," Kat says. "You enjoy his company really."

"If you fucking say so," Luciana grumbles. "I can safely say that I wouldn't ever consider *him* as potential husband material."

"I don't think I would consider *any* of the guys potential husband material," Kat says. "I've known them too long."

"Neither would I," Illyria says.

"Yeah but you've been with Serenity since you were fourteen," Luciana says.

"Who's Serenity?" I ask.

"Basically Illyria's wife," Kat says. "When are you finally going to put a ring on it girl?"

"We've said we'll get married once I've finished my service," Illyria says.

"Some of the guys aren't too bad," Penny says.

"Oh yeah?" Luciana snorts.

"Ellis and Dimitri aren't too bad," Penny says. "Orion and Sammy are a bit young for my taste but Caspian's very attractive."

"He is a honey," Kat agrees.

"No denying he is very aesthetically pleasing," Amara says. "He has a symmetrical face and is in exceptionally good physical condition."

"Just a shame about the rod he keeps up his arse," Luciana says with a roll of her eyes.

"So what are men like on your island Ari?" Illyria asks, changing the subject and shifting the focus back onto me.

"They're okay, I guess," I reply as I readjust the front of my dress for probably the hundredth time. "I didn't really spend any significant amount of time with ones that weren't related to me if I'm honest."

"As long as none of them were like Remy then I imagine they were quite nice," Luciana says.

"There were probably a few like Remy," Illyria laughs.

"There was a guy on the ship that I came to the mainland on who was quite nice," I say. "He taught me how to tie a sailor's knot." Luciana, Penny and Illyria all dissolve into giggles. "Did I say something funny?"

"Oh my sweet little Ari," Penny wheezes as she tries to catch her breath.

"What? I don't get it," I say, looking between the three of them as they continue to laugh.

"Just ignore them," Amara tells me. "They're being childish." This only seems to make them giggle harder.

"Okay," I say and pick up my hairbrush. Clearly I have missed the joke so I'm not going to ask. I begin to brush out my hair but I hit a knot I didn't know I had and the brush ends up getting snagged. After a harder tug, it comes free, ripping out a few hairs in the process. Looking at my reflection in the mirror, studying myself, I hadn't realised just how long it had gotten. I've been wearing it tied back pretty much since Caspian told me to and I can't even remember the last time I had it cut.

"You've got such lovely hair Ari," Penny says, appearing behind me and running her fingers through it. "Do you mind if I do something fancy with it?"

"Not at all," I say as she takes my hairbrush and begins to brush it again. It's so comforting and it reminds me of home and of Mum. I feel a slight catch in my throat. It's been so long since I've seen her...Penny's fingers through my hair are comforting though.

"I always wanted a cute little sister who would let me do fancy things with her hair," she sighs as she puts down the brush and begins to separate my hair into sections.

"Does she not let you?" I ask.

"I'm the oldest of four, I have three brothers and no they don't," she replies.

"Not even the one who looks like a sheepdog?" Kat asks.

"Nope," Penny replies.

"Shame," I chuckle. "You can play with my hair any time you want though."

"Thanks," Penny says, grinning; she seems to be enjoying this a lot and there is a tiny part of me that doesn't know if I should be worried or not. I mean, it feels really good so I'm not going to complain and I would have gotten into a complete mess on my own. "Trust me, when I'm done with you, you'll be fighting them off tonight."

~ *** ~

The banquet hall in the Cimmerian palace is quite possibly the most ostentatious and grand room in the entire building (and I didn't think that was possible considering the other rooms I've seen) with walls that seem to go on forever and a ceiling I can barely see it's so high up. There are portraits along the walls and grand tapestries hanging from the ceiling. I have no idea what half of them are of but they are intricate and stunning, with gold edged frames that are perfectly polished. The solid wooden floor is also polished and so clean I can practically see my face in it when I look down. It's a little over the top and more than a little intimidating. And I had thought the Braxian royal palace was crazy!

Five room length tables are placed in rows and filled with people, all in beautifully elegant outfits, not to mention the tables are also covered with some of the most delicious food I've ever seen in my life. Huge joints of meat, whole fish that look closer to sharks in size and plates piled high with potatoes and vegetables that smell delicious. I don't think I've eaten more than a sandwich since Brax and I'm suddenly aware of just how hungry I am. There are a number of empty seats in the centre table, near the head, which I assume are reserved for us.

A few seats away, at the very head, sits a man who I assume is the Cimmerian king. Sitting on his right hand side is a man of about thirty or so (I guess that must be his son; he looks like a younger version of the king) and on his left are four woman, all different ages, who must be his daughters. They all have the same dark hair as him.

"Presenting Commander Caspian Feioré and the Neo Warriors of Brax," a herald announces as we make our way over to the empty seats. The king stands as we approach and beams as we stop in front of him.

"Friends," he says, throwing his huge arms wide to us, "greetings and welcome to Cimmerian."

"It is a pleasure, as always, to see you again King Zircon," Caspian says and kneels before him. The rest of us follow suit.

"Oh don't worry about the formalities," Zircon says. He seems a very jolly sort of man, not at all how I expected but then again I am pleasantly surprised by most people in this country and their hospitality. Caspian gets to his feet, the rest of us following. "How long has it been since we last had the pleasure?"

"Too long Your Highness," Caspian says.

"Clearly," Zircon says, "you're Commander now."

"Yes and I have acquired three new Neo Warriors since our last meeting," Caspian says.

"Have you now?" Zircon asks, his eyes flitting to those of us he doesn't recognise.

"Allow me to introduce Captain Orion Esteria of the House of the Stars, Captain Samuel Yonglass of the House of Saturn, and Captain Ariana Sirenia of the House of Neptune."

Samuel, Orion and I step forward for Zircon's inspection and he beams at us as if we were long lost family members returning home. What I imagined when I thought of the king of Cimmerian was someone a lot scarier but this man seems incredibly welcoming. Even Orion seems more at ease after actually seeing him.

"Welcome to my court all of you," he says. "I am Zircon, king of Cimmerian. This is my son Onyx," he says, indicating the man on his right. Onyx barely gives any of us a passing glance, his unfriendly gaze fixed entirely on Caspian. So Luciana's right, the guy's probably a dick. "And these are my lovely daughters: Emerald, Sapphire, Ruby and Diamond." The girls seem a lot more friendly, all smiling at us, apart from the one named Sapphire who, like her brother, chooses not to acknowledge us either.

"We are honoured to meet you," Samuel, Orion and I all say in unison, kneeling before him again which Zircon seems to find very amusing.

"Enough of all that, we are among friends." He laughs a great, booming, infectious laugh as the three of us stand again. "Come: sit, eat and we shall all get to know each other." Well, with an offer like that…I'm never one to turn down free food.

I end up sitting next to Zircon's daughter Diamond who has rather dark hair for someone called Diamond. Her eyes must be what defines her name as they do, quite literally, shine like the light catching the edge of a diamond. During the first course neither of us really say much to each other—I don't really know what to say and I don't think she does either; she's probably never been this close to a Braxian before—so I mostly eat and listen. The food is amazing and the conversation is pleasant, even though I'm not keeping up with all of it. That is until I hear Zircon mention Luciana and I suddenly pay a lot more attention.

"I hear tell that Captain Van Garret has a wingspan of seven feet," Zircon says offhandedly to Caspian. "Is this true or just a rumour?"

"Captain Van Garret?" Caspian offers turning to Luciana with a small smile.

She looks at him cautiously for a moment, like she's not sure if he's messing with her or not after their conversation earlier, before she turns to Zircon and smiles. "It is yes," she replies. "My wingspan is longer than I am tall."

"How tall are you?" Zircon asks.

"About five foot nine," Luciana replies.

"Would you permit me to ask to see them?" Zircon asks.

Luciana's gaze darts back to Caspian for the briefest of seconds, almost looking for confirmation, before she turns back to Zircon again and smiles. "Of course."

She gets to her feet and goes to stand in an empty space a little way away from the huge tables. Effortlessly she slips the trench coat from her shoulders, revealing her wings. She drops the coat to the floor and there is a second's pause before her wings suddenly unfurl with a force that could break someone's arm and the sound of rushing feathers. An audible gasp fills the room as everyone stops what they were doing to stare at her. There is a moment of silence before Zircon begins to clap.

"Those are wonderful," he says, clearly enraptured.

"Thank you sire," Luciana says. "Everyone from the House of Mercury is born with wings, they're normally longer than our height and they tend to stop growing around the same time that we do." She turns so that everyone can have a good view of the wings protruding from between her shoulder blades.

"And do all people from your House keep them underneath clothing?" Zircon asks and, as I'm quite close, I can see colour flash to life on Luciana's cheeks.

"I keep mine under the coat for practicality," she replies, obviously choosing her words carefully. "I'm often in rooms that aren't large enough to properly accommodate them and sharing that space with other people so I wear a trench coat to keep them out of the way. When I'm at home, I don't bother."

"And how do you sleep?"

"On my front for the most part, occasionally inside them if it's cold."

"They are absolutely fascinating," Zircon says as Luciana bends down to retrieve her coat. "I would be honoured if you would allow me to see you fly at some point during your stay."

"Take you with me if you like," she replies, clearly without thinking as she suddenly seems to stop and realise what she's just said.

Zircon throws his head back and laughs loudly. "That would be wonderful, thank you very much."

"Thank you," Luciana says before returning to her seat. I'm turn back to my food, barely listening now that the conversation has turned away from Luciana when I suddenly hear my name cut through the chatter.

"So Captain Sirenia, I have heard that the Neptunians are the best musicians in all of Brax," Zircon says, suddenly turning to me. "Is this true or is this just a rumour as well?"

"No, it is true sire," I say and I can feel myself starting to blush. As well as being renowned for our skills on the water we are also known for our musical prowess as well. I had no idea that the reputation had stretched to Cimmerian though.

"And what about you Captain?" Zircon asks. "Do you sing?"

"I've been told I sing very well sire," I reply. I think I know where this is about to go and I know I won't be able to refuse but this is going to be so embarrassing.

"Would you be so kind as to regale us with a song?" he asks.

"If you so desire me to sire," I say.

"Please," he says. "I have always loved music and I would very much like to hear just how good the Neptunians are."

"I certainly hope I live up to your expectations," I chuckle a little nervously and get to my feet. The room suddenly falls silent and all eyes turn to stare at me. I take a deep steadying breath and open my mouth to sing. My mind goes completely blank of anything that I could possibly sing here. The only two things leaping to mind are the Braxian National Anthem (which probably won't go down too well) or one of the rhymes Mum used to sing to me when I was little. That's probably a better bet so I decide to go with that.

Sleep little siren, safe in the ocean
Let the waters guide you home
Fill your dreams with happiness
Find in your heart no sadness
Sleep little siren, home on the ocean
Let the waters bring you home

I sing, almost on autopilot, not daring to look at all the faces around me (just knowing that they're watching me is bad enough). As I finish I'm met with rapturous applause and I can feel my face turning red. This is too embarrassing for words! Then again, while I feel like I want the ground to open up and swallow me whole, everyone else seems to have enjoyed the song so I guess that's something. I hurriedly sit down, hoping that this spotlight will be turned off me and move on to someone else soon.

"That was wonderful," Zircon says. "Thank you very much for indulging me; you have a beautiful voice Captain."

"Thank you, Your Majesty," I reply. "My mother used to sing that to me when I was a child."

"It's a very beautiful song," Zircon says. "Fit for a voice like that."

"Thank you sire."

"And I had thought I had heard the most beautiful voice from my daughter, Sapphire, here but I think I may have been proven wrong," he says.

"Oh I doubt that," I say suddenly clocking the glare Sapphire is shooting my way.

"She's certainly got some good competition," Zircon laughs heartily. "Wouldn't you agree Sapphire?"

"Yes father," she says, her tone clipped but he doesn't seem to notice.

I open my mouth to say something but Zircon has already moved on, changing the subject and discussing military tactics with Caspian. Before I turn my attention back to my plate, I accidentally lock eyes with Sapphire, sitting beside him. The look she gives me could have reduced me to a pile of smouldering ash on the floor. I want to look away but I can't—I'm completely held in place by her glare.

A gentle touch on the back of my hand breaks me out of the stare and back to the real world once again. I turn my attention to Diamond who is smiling shyly at me.

"That was beautiful," she says, her voice quiet over the chatter that has started up again.

"Thanks," I say and I know I'm blushing again but I can't help it. I never really have been good at taking compliments and singing in front of rooms filled with people isn't something I'm all that used to.

"I'm Diamond," she says and holds out her hand, "but I guess you know that already so officially, Diamond."

"Officially Ariana," I say taking her hand and shaking it. "Although most people call me Ari so feel free."

"Okay Ari," she says, smiling. "Ruby and Emerald call me Diaya so you can as well if you like."

"Hi," I say, returning her smile.

"So you're a Neo Warrior?" she asks.

I nod. "Yep, passed my basic training earlier this month."

"And you're how old?"

"Eighteen."

"That's incredible," she says. "I can't believe you can do that at eighteen."

"I don't know," I shrug. "I'd say being princess of Cimmerian is pretty incredible too."

"I suppose it is yes," she says. "I'm the youngest of all the king's children."

"How old are you?"

"I'm seventeen," she says. "Onyx is the oldest, and the only male heir to the throne, then Emerald, Sapphire, Ruby and me."

"And does Sapphire always look like she wants to stab people?" I ask, casting another sideways glance at her. She's looked away from me for now but I imagine that if we made eye contact again she would have that same murderous expression on her face.

"She's not overly fond of Braxians," Diaya says.

"Ah...right..." That would explain why she looks like she's ready to snap at a moment's notice.

"Onyx isn't really either. He thinks father's 'little fascination' is going to get us all killed one day," Diaya says. "Emerald and Ruby don't appear to have any thoughts one way or the other."

"And what about you?" I ask, suddenly feeling a little on edge and more than a little uncomfortable. I forgot for a moment that I'm surrounded by people who could very well hate me and want me dead.

"I like the ones I've met," she says. "I don't believe what some people say about everyone from Brax being evil and out to kill us. The impression that I have gotten from the people that I've met was good enough to make me ignore people like Onyx trying to tell me that you're all heathens."

"That's comforting," I say with an awkward grimace.

Diaya laughs. "Don't look so nervous," she says. "As long as father is on the throne, you'll be safe here."

"That's good," I say, relaxing. "Just out of interest how does your father take to Onyx talking like that?" I ask. It suddenly occurs to me that Onyx has yet to say all that much this evening, probably because he's surround by Braxians (and those who are supposed to be the strongest to boot). If Onyx is going around saying things like that though and Zircon does seem to like Braxians, I imagine that there will be more than a few arguments about his choice of language.

"Mostly he doesn't do it when father is around," Diaya says. "He used to and he used to get into a lot of trouble for it so he stopped. If someone asks his opinion in public, then he will voice his concerns but he's very controlled about it. If you ask him in private though, when father's not around, he'll say what he really thinks."

"How does that not get back to your father?" I ask.

"Most people who go to ask Onyx his opinions already hate the Braxians anyway," Diaya replies.

"That makes sense."

"Change of subject," she says suddenly (god, yes please), "who is that talking to Ruby? Onyx looks like he's going to murder him." I look over to the woman she's gesturing to and see Remy talking to her, fiddling with a lock of her hair. She's smiling at him so he at least picked a good one to try it on with. Oh Remy…don't ever change.

"That's Remy," I laugh. "He does this with pretty much every girl he meets so I'd watch out for when he introduces himself to you. He did the same thing to me when we first met."

"He's quite good looking," Diaya giggles. "Must be nice to have someone paying that kind of attention to you."

"Yeah but after you've seen him hit on about eight different women in a row you realise you're better off not going there," I say. "Once he realises he's not getting anywhere he calms down and you can have an actual conversation with him."

Diaya giggles. "I'll bear that in mind. So how long have you been a Neo Warrior?"

"Couple of months now… Wow."

"What?"

"Nothing," I say, shaking my head. "I'd just never thought about it before. I've been doing this for longer than I realised. What with training I never really noticed."

"Time flies?"

"Something like that," I say. "More than anything I don't think I'd noticed because I always feel like I'm doing something."

"Must be nice to have something to occupy your time with," she says, smiling a little sadly.

"You not got much to do most of the time?" I ask.

"Not really," Diaya says. "I very rarely even leave the palace. I spend a lot of time up in the library."

"How come you don't go out much?" I ask and suddenly realise that it's probably incredibly rude of me to just ask that—I mean this girl is a princess after all and that is kind of a prying question. "I'm sorry," I say hurriedly, "we can talk about something else if you want. That was kind of rude and nosey."

Diaya laughs a soft musical laugh. "It's alright," she says. "My father is rather over-protective of me as I'm the youngest and doesn't really like me venturing out of the palace on my own and most of the time there's no one to accompany me."

"Don't you have bodyguards or minders or something?" I ask.

"Sort of," Diaya says, "but father's still weary so even then I don't really get to go out all that much."

"That's a shame, I'm sorry," I say.

"It's fine," she says but I can tell that it's not.

A sudden thought comes to me and this may be a really bad idea but it might make her happy. "Hey, why don't I go out with you into town one day?"

"Really? Are you sure?"

"Yeah, why not?" I grin. "I went out into town earlier today and people gave me quite a wide berth so we won't be disturbed either."

Diaya laughs again. "As long as you're sure and you don't mind."

"I wouldn't say it if I wasn't."

"Is that where you got the flower?" she asks nodding to the lily Penny tucked into one of the braids in my hair.

"Yeah there was a guy who was selling flowers from my home island so I bought one," I say. "It's been a long time since I've been home and I never expected to see something from home here of all places."

"It's beautiful."

"Thank you," I say, my hand touching the end of the stem.

"You know, I've never left Cimmerian," Diaya says suddenly.

"I was the same," I say. "Up until a few months ago I'd never even left my home island and now I've been to both Mainland Brax and here."

"Is your home island nice?"

"It's beautiful," I say. "You should come and visit sometime, maybe when I've finished my service and have time to show you around properly."

"That would be lovely," she says. "I've always wanted to travel but never really had an excuse."

"Call it a royal visit and we'll go the whole nine yards for you," I grin. She returns my smile. "Fantastic."

~ *** ~

I spend the rest of dinner chatting with Diaya. She's very easy to talk to and we get on quite well. As we're about the same age, we have a lot in common. She tells me all about the history of the Cimmerian palace and I show her a bit of under the table magic when no one is looking. I cast a quick glance in Sapphire's direction before I do this but she seems to be doing everything in her power to pointedly ignore all of us. The banquet wears on and after the plates are cleared away Zircon calls for music. Thankfully not from me this time as a huge set of doors are opened to reveal an adjacent ballroom that is just as big and just as beautiful as the banquet hall.

As people are beginning to move from the tables into the ballroom, Onyx finally speaks up and a tense hush falls over the banquet hall.

"Commander Feioré, is it true that your Neo Warriors are the best of the best of the Braxian army?" he asks, his eyes fixed on Caspian. There is a strange smirk playing about Onyx's lips and for a moment I wonder if Caspian is going to say anything at all in response but he simply smiles and inclines his head.

"It is Your Highness," he says. "We are the strongest members the Braxian army has to offer, trained to release our full potential on any enemy when necessary."

"And is what I have heard also true that your current team is the strongest that there has been for a good few generations?" Onyx asks, still fixing Caspian with that odd smirk as he swirls the remaining wine in his glass.

The entire room seems to have stopped, everyone listening to the exchange between two very powerful men. I can't tear my eyes away—it's like watching two lions snarling, about to go for each other. I'm half expecting one of them to suddenly blow up at the other but it all seems to be very civil for the most part, mostly because Caspian isn't biting at Onyx's bait.

"It is yes," he replies. "I have trained my team to be the best and I will accept nothing less than perfection from them along with myself."

"Admirable," Onyx says before draining his glass.

"Thank you Your Highness."

"So what would you say to a little friendly match tomorrow?" Onyx asks, still with that smirk. "Your five best against my five best in tests of stamina, accuracy, speed, dexterity and strength. Then we will see just who has the stronger team."

"If it pleases the king, then I don't see any reason why not," Caspian says nodding in Zircon's direction.

"I think a friendly match is a splendid idea," Zircon says jovially, clearly not noticing that Onyx is trying to engage Caspian in a giant pissing contest. "I would very much like to see the skills of the famed Neo Warriors of Brax as I have only heard tell of Caspian Feioré and his exceptional team."

"Then I accept your challenge," Caspian says, turning to Onyx. That smirk remains on Onyx's face and it is deeply unsettling.

"Of course you understand that this is a contest of abilities on a level playing field," Onyx says. "Any use of your magic and you will be immediately disqualified."

"I would accept nothing less," Caspian says. "If this is to be a *true* contest, then it goes without saying that magic will not be used."

"Splendid," Zircon says before Onyx can make any kind of snide remark, still completely oblivious to the rising tension. "We shall commence the competition tomorrow at midday down on the training ground and we will see which leader has taught his troops better." He claps his hands in delight. "Oh what fun this will be!"

Fun isn't exactly the word I would use to describe what's likely to happen judging by the look on Onyx's face. He seems as if he's out to prove something. I have no idea what but I doubt it will place us in a favourable light.

"I hope that we provide ample entertainment," Caspian says, smiling at Zircon.

"I trust that you will honour our terms of a fair fight," Onyx says coolly as he gets to his feet.

"I trust that you will too," Caspian replies, his tone still as polite and as courteous as ever but the small smirk gracing his lips speaking volumes.

Oh my god! That was brutal.

Onyx's jaw tightens and he shoots Caspian a glare before he turns and heads to the ballroom, Sapphire at his heels. Zircon laughs and claps Caspian on the shoulder.

"You do know the perfect ways to rile my son up, don't you my boy?"

"Just a little friendly ribbing before a *friendly* competition," Caspian says, emphasising the 'friendly' part, almost like he knows that it's going to turn ugly.

Zircon laughs and heads off towards the ballroom. I hang back with Diaya, opting to wait and try to watch from the sidelines for a while and pray that no one asks me to dance. As the two of them pass me I see Kat grab Caspian's wrist out of the corner of my eye.

"Are you insane?" she hisses and I just about hear her over the chatter of the crowd. "Why on earth would you accept a contest like that?"

"Because he would have persisted until I did," Caspian replies matter-of-factly.

"And what if we win?" Kat asks. "You know that he'll accuse us of cheating so what is your solution then?"

"Then we will have to make sure that there is no way he will be able to," Caspian says.

"But—"

"There is no cause for concern, I know what I'm doing," Caspian says. He takes her wrist and pulls her hand off him before making his way into the ballroom. Kat shakes her head and sighs, following him. "I hope you do." I'd never thought of it like that.

Obviously this is Onyx's way of trying to assert his dominance over Caspian and Caspian actually rising to the challenge (which I hadn't expected him to do). In theory, everything will go smoothly because none of us are going to use magic but if Onyx loses then there is no way that he is going to accept that we won on skill alone. Maybe Kat's right: maybe this isn't such a good idea after all.

"Hey," Daiya says from beside me, bringing me back to the real world again, "shall we go dance?"

"Um…okay," I say nervously.

She giggles. "Come on, it will be fun."

"Okay," I say. "You're going to have to teach me Cimmerian dances, I'm not very fast at picking up steps."

Diaya laughs again. "Stick with me, I've got you covered."

"Sure," I say, smiling. I follow her into the ballroom where people are already beginning to pair up for the first dance. A man in his mid-twenties in a grey suit approaches Diaya.

"Would you care to dance with me, Princess?" he asks.

Diaya looks at me and opens her mouth to refuse when I feel a hand on my shoulder. I turn to see Caspian standing behind me.

"May I have this dance?" he asks.

I glance at Diaya and she grins at me. I turn back to Caspian and smile nervously. "Sure thing." It's probably obvious just how weirded out I am by this request but I'm not going to turn down my CO, that would be insane. Caspian produces his arm for me and I take it. He leads me to the dance floor, placing his arm around my waist and pulling me close. I try not to blush and concentrate on not standing on his toes.

"I see you succeeded where I failed," he says as the music begins.

"Pardon?" I ask, looking up from our feet.

"Van Garret," he clarifies. "You managed to persuade her to continue as she normally would and keep her wings out of the way."

"She shouldn't have to," I reply and it's the only time I think I've ever spoken back to Caspian.

"You're right," he replies without seeming to notice the fact that I'm probably being insolent. "If it weren't for the friendship and protection of King Zircon, we would not be welcome here and neither of you would be safe." He leans closer so that only I will be able to hear him. "I never heard Michael sing, or anyone else from your House for that matter, I assume that there was no magic involved?"

"No sir," I reply. "Some of us can use magic to enchant people while they sing—my sister Harmony can—but I've never been able to do it myself and I wouldn't here."

"Probably wise," Caspian says, still close enough so that only I can hear him. "I don't imagine you would have been stupid enough to try even if you could but I just wanted to make sure. There are still many things about your House that I can only guess at."

"I could say the same about your House too sir," I say.

He chuckles softly. "I think you'll find that most people from the House of Mars are surprisingly uncomplicated Sirenia." His hand feels warm against the small of my back and I don't know if the heat creeping up the back of my neck is because of that or the close proximity.

"Sir, can I ask you something?" I begin tentatively.

"You may."

"Why go ahead with this competition?" I ask.

"Are you questioning my decision?" he counters with a question of his own.

"No sir," I say hurriedly. "It's just that…how do you know that this is going to be a fair fight?"

"It won't be," Caspian replies. "Each of my soldiers, including you, have more skill than his entire army."

"Really?" I find that hard to believe; I've only just started my training, how can I be better than Onyx's soldiers who have been training for years?

"I'm going to let you in on a secret Sirenia but don't let it go to your head," he says. "Every single Neo Warrior candidate is approved by the reigning Commander before the announcement is even made to the rest of their House. You came highly recommended and I gave my approval so here you are. If you need any more encouragement than that, then you are beyond my help."

My cheeks must be like a beacon by now and he must know just how much of a bomb he's dropped on me. There was never any doubt of my skills—Caspian always thought I'd be a good Neo Warrior from the start… Harmony was wrong when she said that he'd think I was a joke because of my lack of skills—he already knew exactly what I could do before I even started my training. This is done with everyone so we really are the best of the best.

"It may not feel like it at the moment because you're still only halfway through your training but, believe me, you have the skills to take on any one of these soldiers," he tells me.

"Thank you sir," I say, unsure what else I can say to praise like that. He's never normally this chatty, maybe it's the wine we had with dinner.

"But you don't have to so try not to worry so much and just enjoy the celebrations while we're here," he finishes. "We have a lot of work to do for your second round of training when we get back to Brax."

"Yes sir," I say and try to put all thoughts of the competition tomorrow out of my mind. All I really need to do for now is concentrate on not stepping on him.

The rest of the evening flashes by in a surreal blur of dancing with each of the other Neo Warriors (even the other girls) and random members of the

Cimmerian court. By the time I get back to our room, I'm exhausted and just about have the energy to change into my sleep clothes. I listen to Penny, Kat and Luciana discussing tomorrow's contest for a few minutes before I close my eyes. Thankfully they don't ask me my opinion or about the few times I danced with Dmitri as I danced with everyone and let their voices wash over me and lull me to sleep.

Chapter 13

The sun beats down on the Cimmerian army's training ground as we assemble along with the royal family and a large section of Onyx's army. Looking over to where the king and his family is sat I catch Diaya's eye and she gives me a smile and a wave, which I return before I head to the stands with the rest of the Neo Warriors. I feel quite anxious—much too anxious considering that I'm not actively taking part in this ill-advised competition—I just can't shake the feeling that something is going to go horribly wrong in all of this.

It's all I've heard people talking about: everyone has been gossiping about a contest between the best of Onyx's army and the best of the Neo Warriors, resulting in quite a few sideways glances in our direction when people realise just who it is that can hear them. I try to ignore the stares and listen to what they're saying, which is mostly spreading the word; I wouldn't be surprised if the whole of Cimmerian didn't know by now. They've sure as hell built it up to be the fight of the century and, really, I can't blame people for talking it up so much.

They're all excited for a clash of the titans fight and, considering that this is supposed to be a contest of skill, that probably isn't way off the mark meaning the crowd might end up baying for blood if they don't get a fight. I must admit the atmosphere is electric—two groups of the best of the best going toe to toe—but the crowd is a lot bigger than I expected it to be. The stands are full of people who have come to watch and maybe I would be excited too if there wasn't this underlying worry in the pit of my stomach.

After overhearing Penny, Kat and Luciana talking this morning before dawn, when they thought the rest of us were still asleep was enough to make me worry and the build-up is only making it worse.

"Do you think Caspian knows what he's doing?" Luciana asked Kat.
"Not really," she replied.

"He must know the risks otherwise why would he have agreed to this in the first place?" Penny asked. "He never does anything without good reason."

"I know but if this goes wrong..." Kat said.

"What do you mean if it goes wrong?" Luciana asked.

"I don't know," Kat said and I heard the tired exasperation in her voice. "I just don't think this was a good idea."

"Couldn't exactly refuse a prince though," Penny said, rational as ever.

"No," Luciana agreed, "and it wasn't as if that fucker gave him much choice."

"Luciana..." Kat chided.

"I'm just saying," Luciana hissed. "This isn't going to be a fair fight: no matter how much he dresses it up we are not going to come out of this winning."

Kat had sighed deeply. "You're right, I know you are," she said. "I just hope Caspian knows what he's doing."

I don't think any of them knew I was awake and I haven't mentioned overhearing it so none of them have said anything. The more I think about it, the more I wonder if Kat is right and that Caspian is insane but then again he seems to know what he's doing so I'm trying to trust him. He is my Commander after all, who am I to question his decisions when I literally know nothing about Onyx or Cimmerian politics and customs?

Caspian must know what he's doing—why would he have agreed to it in the first place? He's not the kind of man to put the rest of us in unnecessary danger so I don't think he would have agreed if he thought there was a chance something was going to go wrong. As long as there is no possible way for us to be accused of cheating by using magic then I think we'll be alright. I'm still sceptical but I'm only watching so I'll try and enjoy it.

I take my place in the front of the stands with the others, sitting in between Dmitri and Luciana (very glad that I have been around the both of them long enough to not have a fit about this) with Remy, Amara and Illyria behind us. In the centre of the training ground, standing before Zircon's makeshift throne (erected for occasions such as this I suppose), are Caspian and Onyx. Behind Caspian are Samuel, Penny, Orion, Kat and Ellis, all standing to attention, while Onyx has five of his own soldiers—also three men and two women—standing behind him.

I'm so glad that Caspian didn't pick me for this. I know that this is supposed to just be a friendly match but it feels as if there is way too much at stake and two of the guys on Onyx's side are huge—like Ellis huge. I wouldn't fancy going up against either one of them, no matter what the contest was. One of them looks like if he flexed the wrong way his shirt would just burst off into tatters! And I thought the largest people I was ever going to meet were people from the De'Latore family!

A hush falls over the grounds as Zircon raises his hand and stands. "Welcome one and all, to this fine day's match," he says, beaming at the crowd.

A herald sporting the colours of the Cimmerian royal guard steps forward. "A test of skill between the five strongest members of the Cimmerian army, trained by Prince Onyx, first son of the crown, against five of the Neo Warriors of the Braxian army, trained by Commander Caspian Feioré," he says. As if anyone doesn't know why they're here.

There is raucous applause and cheering from the crowd, their excitement obvious. I must admit the atmosphere is contagious but at the same time I think we all have just cause to be apprehensive. The herald waits for the cheering and applause to die down before he speaks again.

"Commander Feioré," he says, turning to Caspian, "if you would like to introduce your five Neo Warriors."

Caspian steps forward. "I present to you Samuel Yonglass, Penelope Heitztaff, Orion Esteria, Katarina Navroe and Ellis De'Latore," he says. Each of them looks as fierce and formidable as he has made them sound. Having sparred against most of them I know what they're capable of and, even without magic, it's bloody impressive.

"Prince Onyx," the herald says, "if you would like to introduce your five soldiers."

Onyx is about to speak but before he can Caspian raises his hand. "If I may," he says, still sounding as polite as ever, "I would firstly like my Neo Warriors to demonstrate their magical abilities, to showcase what they can do."

Onyx snorts derisively. "And what good will a demonstration do you Commander Feioré?" he asks.

"Braxian magic is very distinctive," Caspian replies, "especially if one knows what they are looking for. I believe it will be good for those moderating the proceedings to know what they should be observing in order to prevent any unwarranted accusations. If it pleases the king of course."

Caspian is basically calling Onyx out on accusing us of cheating if he loses already. I'm almost amazed Caspian hasn't been taken somewhere and shot but Zircon likes him so I'm guessing it's that. Onyx gives him a cold stare.

"Please yourself," he says.

"I will allow this," Zircon says and there is a glimmer in his eyes. Even the king of Cimmerian is fascinated by our magic. I suppose it's one of those things that if you don't get to see it very often then of course it's going to be interesting. I'm actually a little excited for this as I've never seen Orion or Ellis use their magic before so I have no idea what it is they do. They don't tend to use it so it must be something spectacular.

"Thank you sire," Caspian smiles, nodding. "Second Commander Navroe if you would like to begin."

Kat steps forward. She seems a little reluctant at first and I can understand why—doing the one thing we shouldn't while surrounded by Cimmerian soldiers is not the smartest idea but we do have the king's protection and permission. She casts a glance at Caspian, who nods, before she raises her hands, pulling up two huge columns of earth and rock, both at least ten foot tall and as wide as a carriage, from the ground behind her as she does.

I can't take my eyes off her. Even having been around them all for as long as I have I'm still blown away with just how impressive their abilities are. Kat has just pulled rock from the ground as if it was nothing. There is a ripple of applause with a few fascinated gasps from the crowd as she lets the columns sink back into the earth, smoothing the ground over as if nothing had been disturbed. Doing it like that was probably sensible on her part: she could have caused an earthquake or something equally as devastating; then we would have really been in trouble if collateral damage had occurred.

She steps back into line with the others and is replaced by Penny who takes her place and lifts an arm up. Above us the sky begins to cloud over, thick black storm clouds blocking out the sun, before a fork of lightening cracks down from the heavens into the palm of her outstretched hand. She grabs the bolt and throws it back skyward, the clouds disappearing once it's burst through them, returning the sky to the clear blue it had been moments before. I'm amazed that she managed to do that without injuring anyone nearby (or herself for that matter) but, having seen her do stuff like that with her magic before, she is just *that* good. She steps back into line and is replaced by Samuel.

I've been on the receiving end of Samuel's magic quite a few times during sparring and it's not fun. He's powerful and probably could kill people if he decided to take the air out of any given room. I watch, transfixed, as he closes his eyes and seems to take a deep breath. A fierce wind begins to whip all around the grounds, making flags flap and the people in the stands hold onto their hats and coats. It stops just as soon as it begins as Samuel opens his eyes again and people begin fixing their rumpled clothes and hair. He goes back to stand with the others and is replaced with Orion.

"Watch his hair," Dmitri whispers from beside me.

"What?" I whisper back but as soon as Orion raises a hand out to his side I see exactly what he means.

All the colour seems to drain out of Orion's hair, leaving it a gleaming, brilliant white that shines like starlight even in the middle of the day. The black that had been in his hair seems to be travelling along his skin. I watch as it passes over his face, down his neck and across his arm to his outstretched palm. The others were fascinating but I physically can't take my eyes off Orion's hand as a black hole begins to form just a few inches away from it, seeming to be drawn from the black that had originally been in his hair. He literally has a black hole coming out of his skin!

He steps into the black hole and disappears, taking it with him, only to suddenly reappear at the very edge of the training ground. There is a gasp from the crowd as he steps back into the black hole only to reappear where he had been standing a few seconds ago. The black hole disappears and travels up across his skin again to seep back into his hair, returning him to how he looks the rest of the time.

That is incredible!

I'd never actually found out what Orion does until now. Remy calls it 'bullshit space magic' (and to be fair 'bullshit space magic' is actually pretty accurate) but never gave me a proper explanation. That was the most fascinating thing I have ever seen! I think the hair changing colour only makes it cooler too. I really should have asked Orion about his magic before now…not that he would necessarily have told me. Seeing something like that makes me realise why Houses keep things like that from each other, having an ace in the hole like that would be amazing.

Finally, Ellis steps forward and Caspian goes over to stand next to him. Again I don't dare take my eyes away from the scene in front of me as Ellis places his hand over Caspian's chest, right above his heart. A soft purple glow begins to emanate from Ellis' hand as he draws it back and pulls a sphere of glimmering gold out of Caspian's chest along with it. He holds it in his palm for a moment and I turn my attention to Caspian. He doesn't seem to be moving or breathing…I look up at first to Dmitri and then Luciana and neither of them seems to be worried but I feel as if someone should be.

Ellis gently pushes the sphere back into Caspian's chest and as soon as it has disappeared inside him again Caspian seems to come back to life. He smiles at Ellis and the two of them clasp hands before Ellis goes back to stand with the others.

"What was that?" I whisper to Dmitri, still unable to take my eyes off Caspian. What the hell just happened to him?

"Plutonians deal in soul magic," he replies.

"Sorry, what?" I ask, dumbstruck. "Are you saying that was Caspian's soul?"

"Yeah he does have one," Remy sniggers from behind.

"Are you kidding, that's amazing!" I whisper more to myself than either Remy or Dmitri. I can't believe Caspian was okay with that. That level of trust! I don't know if I'd be happy being used for a demonstration where someone took my soul out of my chest, just in case anything went wrong, but clearly Caspian has that much faith in Ellis' abilities.

"Do you see why Caspian picked those five?" Dmitri asks.

I think about it for a second before the penny finally drops. "Because they're distinctive," I reply.

He nods. "While all of our powers are distinctive, some are harder to trace than others and their powers are easy to spot."

"So Onyx can't accuse us of cheating," I say. That makes sense. So Caspian does know what he's doing…

"In theory," Luciana says from beside me. I open my mouth to ask her what she means by that (although I think I know) but Caspian starts talking again.

"You have seen what my Neo Warriors can do," he says and he sure as hell doesn't sound as if he just had his soul pulled out of his chest a few seconds ago and then put back in. "As you can see, their powers are easily recognisable. If they use them, you will know."

"That was a fascinating display Commander Feioré," Onyx says and he sure as hell doesn't sound fascinated, sounds more smug and smarmy than anything else. "Now if we can proceed with the competition."

"Of course, Your Highness," Caspian says. "I merely wanted to showcase their skills to prove that they do not need to use their magic in a test of physical ability."

"Then they will have met their match in my soldiers," Onyx says. "I present Christopher Armstrong, Robin Kensington, Chantelle Corrasa, Michelle Delano and Harrison Flaightly of the Cimmerian army."

Caspian makes no reply but I can see the doubt evident on his face. He doesn't think that Onyx's five will be any match for the guys he has chosen. The attitude that Caspian is flinging around like there's no tomorrow without even saying a damn word is astounding! No wonder Onyx already looks furious.

"Splendid," Zircon says, clapping. "Now that everyone has had a just introduction we shall proceed."

"The first will be a test of stamina," the herald announces from the sidelines. "If all those not participating would please make your way to the edge of the grounds."

Everyone apart from Samuel and a thickset man with huge muscles and cropped blonde hair, who stands about a foot or so taller than him, make their way to the edge of the training ground and out of the way. The thickset man squares up to Samuel, looking down at him and smirking (clearly thinking he's won already) but Samuel just looks calmly ahead as if he is sparring against Remy or Ellis.

On first glance, I know which one I would rather put my money on to win but I've been sparring with Samuel for quite some time now and I know that if you don't beat him early you're screwed because he can just keep going and going. He has stamina I can only dream of and there's no way that he'll lose unless this guy stores all his energy in his huge muscles.

"The first event is a test of stamina between Samuel Yonglass of Brax and Christopher Armstrong of Cimmerian," the herald announces. "It will consist of three laps of the training ground followed by a series of muscular exercises. Gentlemen, take your places to begin."

Again, just based on looks alone, I wouldn't be putting money on Samuel (which is probably why Onyx looks so smug) but knowing him the way I do and having seen him sparring so many times, I don't think he's going to lose, despite being so much smaller. Both Samuel and Christopher make their way over to the herald and take up a stance to begin running. The herald raises a starting pistol into the air.

"On your marks, get set, go!" he calls out and fires the pistol.

The stamina test looks brutal; it's making me tired just watching it! After three laps of the training ground (which is nothing to sneeze at) Christopher already looks as if he's starting to flag a bit. No sooner have they finished the laps, and it's quite a close finish too, then they are given fifty sit-ups to complete followed by fifty push-ups and then fifty pull-ups on a bar, one after the other with no breaks. By the time they are on to the push-ups, Christopher is definitely beginning to struggle but Samuel still looks as cool as ever, like he could go on for the rest of the day if he wanted to.

By the time they are completing the last of the pull-ups, Christopher looks as if he can barely pull himself up from fatigue while Samuel only seems to have broken a marginal sweat. They're just beginning to finish the last ten when Christopher loses his grip on the bar and drops to the floor, unable to push himself back up onto his tired legs. Onyx doesn't look happy as Samuel finishes his last few pull-ups and drops gracefully to the floor, still as calm as anything.

"The winner," the herald announces, "Samuel Yonglass of Brax." There is a round of applause from the crowd (and a few cheers from us) as Samuel and Christopher shake hands before they both bow to Zircon and make their way over to the edge of the training ground with their respective COs. Samuel looks incredibly pleased with himself (can't say I blame him) and Caspian gives him a small smile filled with pride.

"Boy did good," Luciana says.

"Yeah, looks like our little Sammy has more stamina than we thought," Remy chuckles.

"Speak for yourself," I say. "I know he could have carried on all day if he wanted."

"Oh really?" Remy asks, his tone suggestive. "And how would our sweet little Ari know that? I do hope you haven't been up to no good out of training hours."

"Maybe because she's been sparring with him unlike you, who seems content to spend most of your time slacking off you lazy twat," Luciana says with ill-disguised contempt.

"Always such a kind word for me Luciana," Remy grins, placing a hand over his heart. "If I didn't know any better, I'd think that you actually rather like me."

Luciana's face contorts into one of abject disgust and she opens her mouth to berate him but is cut off by the herald.

"The second test will be a test of aim," he announces, "between Penelope Heitztaff of Brax and Robin Kensington of Cimmerian. Those participating, please step forward."

Penny pushes herself off the wall and makes her way over to stand in front of Zircon. As she passes him I notice that Caspian places his hand on her shoulder and she gives him a small smile. Neither of them seems to say anything but there seems to definitely be something passing between them. I don't know if anyone else notices (no one says anything so I'd assume not) so I don't draw attention to it.

Whatever passed between them is over before it begins and Penny takes her place next to Robin, a small wiry boy (probably not that much older than I am, or maybe even younger), in front of Zircon. Two soldiers bring each of them a box and open them to reveal two identical long bows and three arrows. Both Penny and Robin take the bow and arrows and the soldiers leave, taking the empty boxes away with them.

"You will be presented with three moving targets, the shot closest to the centre on each of them wins," the herald says. Both Penny and Robin ready the bows and the herald raises his starting pistol. "Begin!" he shouts before firing it.

A target is suddenly fired at high speed over both of their heads. Robin seems to react slightly quicker than Penny does and fires his arrow but he doesn't quite hit the middle of the target. Penny, however does. She takes her time, notches an arrow, takes a deep breath and releases it all in the matter of a few seconds. It hits the centre of the target and I can't stop the involuntary gasp I let out.

"Looks like Penny's been practising," Illyria says.

"Good for long range combat," Dmitri says.

"What do you mean?" I ask.

"With power like Penny's, that can cause huge amounts of collateral damage, it is quite hard to hit a single target," Amara says. "She took up archery so she can hit her target without killing everyone else in the process. She has perfect vision and now near perfect aim."

"She's amazing!" I gasp more to myself than anyone else and Luciana chuckles beside me, clearly amused.

Penny hits both her other targets, missing the dead centre on the second by only a few inches, and beating Robin by miles. Maybe the pressure got to him or maybe Onyx didn't pick quite as well as he thought for this one; either way he's starting to look furious. I wouldn't want to be in Orion, Kat or Ellis' shoes for the world. Penny makes her way back over to Caspian and the smile on his face is one I've never seen before.

"The third test is a test of speed between Orion Esteria of Brax and Chantelle Corrasa of Cimmerian," the herald announces and I turn my attention to him rather than Caspian and Penny. "Both participants please step forward."

Orion steps into the centre of the grounds in front of Zircon while a tall, spindly woman with a shaved head from the other side joins him.

"Oh this is going to be good," Remy says as Orion and Chantelle square off against one another. She stands a head and shoulders taller than him and looks down at him, smirking. She mutters something that is loud enough for him to hear (probably because it was supposed to be) and Orion suddenly looks about ready to kill.

"Oh she's insulted his height," Illyria chuckles.

"How can you tell?" I ask. I can't hear what's being said between them from that far away but she might have some kind of super hearing with her magic.

"Just look at the way he's glaring up at her," Luciana says. "It's a good thing there isn't anything sharp to hand otherwise it would be going in her face."

"Let's just say Orion has a few issues about his height and people passing comment on it," Illyria says.

"Right…"

"Have you ever seen Orion run?" Dmitri asks, changing the subject from Orion's diminutive stature back to the competition.

"No," I reply.

"Then you are in for a treat."

"What do you mean?"

"Just watch," Dmitri says with a grin.

"This race will consist of a sprint from one side of the training ground to the other," the herald says. "Please take your positions."

Orion and Chantelle make their way over to one side of the training ground. Orion looks a little stiff as Chantelle says something else to him. He's already irritated and probably wants to just use his magic to get there so that he doesn't have to talk to her but dutifully doesn't. She probably wants to get a rise out of him, trying to make him mess up out of anger. Hopefully he won't, not when we're doing this well.

The herald raises his starting pistol again. "On your marks, get set, go!"

The shot rings out around the grounds and it's almost a case of blink and you'll miss it. Both Orion and Chantelle are ridiculously fast, like nothing I've ever seen before—it probably helps her being so tall and him being so wiry. They're both running neck and neck from one end of the ground to the other and I've never seen anyone move that fast. Chantelle seems to have a bit of an advantage being that much taller than him but Orion is holding his own quite nicely. Clearly he makes up for his short stature with speed. It's probably also the short comment—he's determined to beat her after that.

The race is practically over before it even starts and, while it's an incredibly close call with barely any time between them, Orion's hand slams against the wall at the other end of the grounds a few seconds before Chantelle's. Both of them are fighting for breath but she seems to be snarling something at him, the look on her face is out to kill. Orion glares at her and makes his way over to Caspian and the others.

Chantelle doesn't seem to be done though as she follows him, still looking murderous, before she is stopped by Onyx. Orion gives her nothing more than a look of contempt before going to stand beside Caspian, who gives him a clap on the shoulder. Orion flushes and hides behind his hair but seems to appreciate the gesture all the same. Chantelle is still fuming at her marginal loss but, after a look from Onyx, backs off.

"Clearly they're not all gracious losers," Remy says.

"You really think Onyx is going to be?" Luciana asks.

"He's not going to take this well," Illyria agrees. "Is Caspian trying to prove a point by beating him on his home turf?"

"Who knows," Luciana says.

"We'll just have to hope that Onyx is more gracious than we expect," Dmitri says. That's comforting…

"The next test will be dexterity," the herald says, quietening the crowd again, "between Katarina Navroe of Brax and Michelle Delano of Cimmerian. Will both participants please step forward."

Kat makes her way over to stand in front of Zircon and the others. She is joined by another woman of a similar height and build. The two of them shake hands before turning to Zircon. He seems very excited by the prospect of whatever these two are about to do. Occasionally I've looked over at him, watching him as he surveys what's going on and he seems to be enjoying himself as much as the rest of the crowd. The only one not enjoying himself is Onyx, especially now that he's been completely schooled by Caspian. Even if his two remaining people win their respective rounds we'll still win overall.

Four soldiers come forward carrying two tables between them. They place them down one in front of Kat and one in front of Michelle before another two bring over pieces of what look like dismantled rifles. All the parts are spread out on the tables before all the soldiers step away, leaving Kat and Michelle with them.

"This is a test of dexterity," the herald says. "The one to assemble their rifle the fastest will be declared the winner."

"Before you begin," Zircon says, suddenly putting up his hand, "just to make things a little more interesting, you will each have your dominant hand tied behind your back. Let's see how you do with only one hand at your disposal."

Now that does make things more interesting.

Both women present their right hand to be tied behind their backs, Michelle casts a nervous glance in Onyx's direction while Kat looks completely at ease. Two of the soldiers return, each with a length of rope and secure the proffered hand behind each woman's back. Once they both have their hand secured the herald raises his starting pistol.

"On your marks, get set, go!" The pistol is fired and both Kat and Michelle set to work assembling. It's fascinating to watch, especially Kat who seems to be having no problem at all even with only one hand.

"How is she doing that?" I ask, gazing at her open mouthed as she uses her elbow to secure one part of the rifle while she slots another in to place.

"You know how most people only use their dominant hand to do literally everything while the other is just kind of useless?" Dmitri asks.

"Yeah…"

"Kat's ambidextrous. She uses both hands for almost everything."

"Wow!"

"For the most part, she's right-handed," Amara weighs in, "but when she was twelve, she taught herself how to use both of her hands to their full potential. A very smart move on her part, I've done the same."

"Does it take long to do?" I ask. It might be a good thing for me to do.

"Not really," Amara says. "If you want to learn, I'm sure, between us, Kat and I can help you."

"That's amazing!" Every new thing I learn about these people blows me away every single time. Their skill is unbridled and I want to catch up to them one day. If I train hard enough, then I actually could.

"See, Caspian knew what he was doing when he picked this team," Illyria chuckles.

"True that," Luciana agrees. "They all excel in the skill they've been chosen for so there's no way that they would lose, with or without magic."

"Not to mention that their magic is easy to spot," Illyria says.

"No chance of accusing us of cheating," Luciana says, an underlying sarcasm in her voice.

"Orion's magic isn't exactly subtle is it?" Amara says.

"Not really," I mutter although I'm only half listening. All I can do is sit there and watch in awe as Kat finishes assembling a rifle one handed. Watching her work is fascinating and knowing that *she* was the one who taught herself how to do that is just astonishing.

After a few minutes, Kat seems to have the rifle assembled and she places it down on the table in front of her. One of the soldiers comes over to inspect it. He picks up the rifle, cocks it and fires it into the air (probably a test to see that she actually managed to do it correctly and hasn't missed something). It goes off and Kat is declared the winner. Both her and Michelle are untied and they shake hands, Michelle just as impressed with Kat's efforts as I am.

There seems to be no animosity from the Cimmerians against us (well apart from Chantelle with Orion and the look on Onyx's face could probably reduce someone to a pile of rubble right about now). Everyone just seems to accept that we are better skilled. Probably because they didn't realise that we were until we proved it. It's quite satisfying really, knowing that we can hold our own is comforting.

"The final test," the herald announces once Kat and Michelle have moved back to the sidelines, "is a test of strength between Ellis De'Latore of Brax and Harrison Flaightly of Cimmerian. Will those participating please step forward?"

I watch as Ellis goes to stand in front of Zircon. He is joined by Harrison who is equally as big and beefy. Standing next to each other both of them are matched in height and size so this is going to be a total clash of the titans if they can both hold their own in whatever it is they're going to be doing.

"This test will be measured in hand to hand combat," the herald says. "The first to knock their opponent to the floor will be declared the winner."

"Bonus points if Ellis actually knocks him unconscious," Remy mutters with undisguised glee in his voice.

Oh my god this is actually going to be phenomenal! A guy like Ellis going up against a guy like Harrison, both of whom look like tree trunks, matched in muscles and weight, is going to be something truly spectacular to watch. Both men remove their shirts (hello boys…) and I'm blown away by just how much muscle there is on display right now. I sort of forget, when I only ever see Ellis clothed, that you could probably wash clothes on his abs and Harrison is exactly the same.

"Fighters, take your positions," the herald says, raising his pistol again and both men take up a stance ready to fight. "Three, two, one, fight!"

He fires the pistol, the sound ringing out, and Harrison lunges for Ellis. Ellis catches him almost immediately, holding him back and occupying both of Harrison's hands so that he can't throw a punch his way. Ellis uses that hold to then gain the upper hand and catch Harrison completely off guard with a sweep of his leg, getting him on his knees. It seems as if Harrison was expecting something like that though as he pulls Ellis down with him and they are scrambling around together, both trying to gain the upper hand over the other.

Watching Ellis fight like this, a no-holds-barred grudge match of brute strength—well, watching them all really—makes me realise that there's so much I still need to learn. One day I want to be someone Caspian (or whoever is Commander at the time) calls upon to showcase the skill of the Braxian army. One day I want to be someone hard to take down in a fight. As soon as we get home I'm going to make sure I train every single day so I can be this good!

Ellis eventually gains the upper hand and makes it impossible for Harrison to take it back from him. I have no idea how he did that but I watch as he heaves himself to his feet, dragging Harrison with him before flipping him over his enormous shoulders, arms around his neck in a choke hold. Harrison struggles as the herald begins a countdown (the crowd joining in the lower it gets) but he is unable to break free of Ellis' grip by the time the shouts reach zero, declaring Ellis the victor.

The crowd erupts into applause and cheers, all completely enthralled by that performance. Clearly they all came to see a fight and a fight was what they eventually got; it doesn't seem to matter to them who won or lost.

"And that, ladies and gentlemen," Remy says, talking exclusively to us, "is the power of the Neo Warriors of Brax."

"We are rather impressive, aren't we?" Amara observes.

Caspian looks incredibly proud of everyone and he claps Ellis on the shoulder as he hands him his shirt back. Zircon looks thrilled with what he's just seen and his daughters look rather impressed (save Sapphire). The one not looking so happy right now is Onyx. He looks ready to murder as he stalks over to Caspian and roughly grabs him by the collar, yanking him round so that they are facing each other. The sounds from the crowd immediately die, the entire ground falling silent as everyone stops to hear this exchange.

"I don't know how you did it but I know you cheated," Onyx snarls.

"How could we have possibly cheated?" Caspian asks, still as calm as anything despite Onyx's white knuckle grip on his collar. "You saw the kind of magic each of them uses. Did you see any of that during the contest?"

"That's not the point," Onyx says. "You…"

"Did you see any of them using their magic?"

Onyx growls, glaring at Caspian like he's going to rip his throat out. "I don't know how you did it but I will find out," he snarls. "There is no way you can be that good without using any magic."

"That's enough Onyx," Zircon says but Onyx doesn't seem to be paying him any attention. He's on a roll and he's not stopping.

"Maybe my men won because *I* actually know how to train my soldiers," Caspian says with a smirk.

Onyx splutters with rage before he violently lets go of Caspian's collar, shoving him backwards, and reaches for the sword at his side. In one swift motion he draws it, pointing it at Caspian's throat. "You've overstepped the mark, Feioré! How dare you insult me in my own arena! I'll make you pay for your insolence today."

"I said that's enough Onyx!" Zircon shouts, getting to his feet, and this is the first time I've seen him look anything other than warm and welcoming. There is a fury in his eyes that has never been there before and it's aimed solely at Onyx. "Commander Feioré and his team won fairly, on terms *you* set out. There were no signs of cheating anywhere, none of them used their magical abilities, they won on their skills alone. If you want to beat them next time, then you should rethink your training methods rather than accusing your competition of underhanded tactics."

"But father…" Onyx begins.

"I said enough!" Zircon shouts. "My word is final! You can either be a gracious loser and accept that Commander Feioré beat you or not, but I will *not* have my guests falsely accused. Now enough of this foolishness, do I make myself clear?"

"Yes father," Onyx growls, thoroughly cowed.

"Now put away your sword," Zircon orders.

Onyx glares up at his father for a moment before he does. He turns and stalks away, seething as he leaves the training ground. I watch him go, my eyes following him the entire time. He's not going to forget this in a hurry… Hopefully, if he has time to calm down, he won't use this as an excuse to start something. A silence hangs heavy over the grounds as Onyx leaves but once he has gone, a murmur ripples through the crowd. Ellis steps forward to stand in front of Zircon.

"I'm terribly sorry if I have caused any offence at all, Your Majesty," he says. "That wasn't my intention."

Zircon turns to him and smiles, back to his usual self once again. "Think nothing of it, my boy," he says. "Onyx has always been a very poor loser when it comes to competition. He will get over it once his pride has recovered. As for you all, that was a splendid match and I thoroughly look forward to seeing your powers again someday."

Seeing Onyx reacting like that makes me very glad that Zircon is so calm about the whole Braxian-Cimmerian back and forth because I don't imagine Onyx would have stopped if his father wasn't there to chastise him. Wars have been started over less and that makes me uneasy. Having said that, Zircon doesn't seem to be going anywhere any time soon so we can be thankful for that at the very least.

Chapter 14

The rest of our stay in Cimmerian passes by relatively uneventfully. There are lots of huge feasts, always followed by dancing, music and lots of speeches about Zircon and his reign as king. I didn't have any expectations about what a Jubilee ceremony would be like but the whole affair (particularly the speeches) seems to go on forever. Not that I mind: it's nice to be somewhere new, meeting new people and the food here is amazing—there's no way I'm going to be complaining about good food.

The celebrations are mostly reserved to the evenings so I have the days to myself and I spend the majority of them with Diaya. She shows me around the palace (which takes at least two days to see almost everything) and I take her into town. Being with her in the town is even stranger than going with Dmitri—everyone is staring, some clearly amazed at the princess and the Braxian spending time together but, for the most part, they're just so amazed to see her out in public when normally she doesn't get out much. To be honest if you live in a huge palace, with everything at your fingertips, you don't really need to.

I like Diaya: she's really friendly and easy to talk to. We have a lot in common (probably helps that we're around the same age too) and I like spending time with her. I also don't feel as if I've spent my entire time bugging Dmitri, Luciana or the others. Diaya introduces me to both Ruby and Emerald, who are very nice and seem happy that she's found a friend. She tries to introduce me to Sapphire but she doesn't seem interested in talking to either of us.

Time here goes by too quickly and before I know it two weeks have flown by and I'm waking up to our last breakfast. It's another grand affair, Zircon beaming at us all, thanking us for coming, and Caspian thanking him for his hospitality. I half listen to what's being said and simply enjoy my last meal here. If I eat lots now, then I won't have to think about food until we get back to Brax and, if the flight back is anything like the flight here, eating is going to be the last thing on my mind when we first land.

Once breakfast is over and everyone is getting up to leave the banquet hall, I push myself to my feet joining them. I've got some time to kill as I made sure that all my stuff was packed last night and I did an extra check before breakfast. I'm about to leave the hall along with everyone else, trying to think of something I can do where I won't be in the way, when Diaya comes over and takes my hand.

"Morning," I say, smiling at her, giving her hand a squeeze.

"Morning," she says, smiling back. "Have you got time to go for a walk around the grounds before you leave?"

"Yeah sure," I reply, thankful for the offer.

"Great," she beams and her smile lights up her entire face. "I wanted to be able to talk to you one last time before you left."

"Plus it looks like it's a nice day for it," I say, nodding towards one of the huge stained glass windows.

"Shall we go then?"

"Let's."

We make our way through the corridors until we reach a door and step out into the midmorning sun. I take a deep breath, relishing the fresh air before I spend my day stuck in a airship for hours on end. I'm ready to go home and start my next lot of training; despite the mandatory daily morning run with Caspian, the break from routine has been good. It's a beautiful day and I don't want to waste any more of it being inside than I have to.

"So is everything going to go back to normal for you now that the Jubilee celebrations are over?" I ask as we begin a leisurely walk.

"As normal as my life can ever be," Diaya giggles.

"This is true," I laugh. "Being a princess sounds exhausting."

"So does being a soldier."

"If I actually felt like a soldier, then I imagine it would," I say. "So far I haven't done that much other than my first stage of training and then come over here to represent."

"But training must have been quite gruelling," she says.

"Under Commander Feioré it is," I say. "He's a perfectionist."

"I noticed," she laughs but it is a laugh that dies away quite quickly. "Seems Onyx has taken it upon himself to try and outmatch him."

"I didn't realise it was a competition," I mutter.

"No, neither did I," Diaya agrees, "but that's my brother for you: always trying to prove that he is the best and is deserving of the throne."

As she says this, we reach the training ground and see a large chunk of Onyx's army running drills. I thought my training with Caspian was brutal: half of these men look like they can barely stand. How long they've been going for and how much more is Onyx going to push them before he lets them take a break? He doesn't seem to be there, the training being overseen by one of his generals, and I wonder how much of what he puts his army through he also puts himself through. One thing that can be said for Caspian: he may be hard but he will go through every brutal training regime he thinks up along with us. Onyx, however, doesn't seem to share that philosophy.

"How has Onyx been after losing?" I ask. I've barely seen him apart from at meals (during which he doesn't say anything) and he may not even have been entertaining his sisters, never mind anyone else.

"Unbearable," she replies with a sigh. "I think his pride was really damaged by Commander Feioré and by father shouting at him in front of everyone so he's been holed up in his room. The only people he seems at all willing to talk to are his generals, about training the troops harder, and Sapphire."

"I'm sorry," I say. I'm not really sure what I'm sorry about—Onyx's defeat, his humiliation, having us still here—but having her older brother suddenly behaving like a child can't be easy to witness.

"Don't be," she says, shaking her head. "I thought that he would have been better at taking the loss but, seeing as no one has even come close to challenging him like that he's obviously not. It's just one of those things."

"Losing in front of the home crowd can't have been easy."

"Yeah, that won't have helped," Diaya says, sighing again. She seems to deflate, like she's disappointed more than anything and I can't say I blame her. She looks at me again and plasters a smile on her face. "Change of subject," she says suddenly, "so what are you going to be doing when you get back to Brax?"

I let out a long breath. "Going to start my second lot of training, I suppose. I've done my basic fitness and now I'm going to have to prove that I have the magical skill to back it up; show I can handle my own on both accounts."

"Sounds intense," she says.

"Knowing Commander Feioré it probably will be."

"Promise me you'll write to me," she says. "I want to know about it all and I want to know how you're getting on."

"Of course I will," I say giving her shoulder a playful bump with mine. "I write to all my friends that I don't see every day, I can add an extra letter in there."

"Good because I want to know how your training is going and I want to know all about life in Brax—it sounds so exciting."

"Hopefully you can come over one day and I can give you a proper tour," I say. "Or better yet, come to Neyara and I can show you real Neptunian hospitality."

"Sounds wonderful," she says with a wistful smile.

"Then we'll do it," I grin.

"Good, I need to do more than just stay in this palace my entire life," she says.

"Being a princess not all it's cracked up to be?" I tease. I've spent enough time around her to know that it's not exactly the life she would have chosen for herself, given the option.

"I know I'm somewhere in line for the throne but I don't really have any desire to be queen. I'd rather just spend my time travelling and seeing the world. There's so much out there and there's only so much you can get from books and what people tell you," she says. "Also, being the youngest, it's highly unlikely that I'll actually become queen before I have to pass on the succession to someone younger."

That's why I like her so much—we both want the same thing: to see the world and meet interesting people, not sit in stuffy rooms listening to stuffier people.

"That's not necessarily a bad thing though," I say. "Gives you more freedom to do what you want to."

"This is true," she says. "Can you imagine though, Onyx letting me go over to Brax to visit you if he were king?"

"Highly unlikely," I chuckle. She'd probably be killed as a traitor for even mentioning Brax, Sister to the king or not.

"Exactly," she chuckles, "so you'd better hurry up and finish your next lot of training so I can come over and see you before that happens."

"I'll do my best."

There is a pause, the two of us just standing there staring at these poor soldiers still being made to run, before, apropos of nothing, she turns and hugs me tightly.

"I'm going to miss you so much," she whispers, voice thick with emotion. "You're the first proper friend I've ever had."

"I'm going to miss you too," I say, hugging her back. "I'll see you again though, I'll make sure that I do."

It's been really nice spending time with her on our own, away from everyone else, because we managed to forget that our countries' relationship is so volatile for the most part, not to mention that we're both from totally different worlds, her being a princess and all. We stay like that for a moment, hugging and just enjoying being in each other's company. I almost don't want to let her go, just stay like this forever. Being with her has reminded me so much of Trista and how much I miss her. Hopefully I can introduce the two of them. Diaya would love Trista and Trista always relishes meeting new people.

"Hey Ari," a voice calls, breaking us out of our moment. I turn and see Penny walking across the ground towards us. Diaya and I de-tangle ourselves from one another before we both turn to Penny. "You alright?" she asks as she reaches us.

"Is it time to go already?" I ask, knowing that's the only reason she's looking for me but it feels too soon. I thought I had more time than this.

"'Fraid so, honey," she says. "Carriages are ready to take us back to the airfield and then we're heading off."

"Okay," I sigh. It's weird: I was so nervous about coming here in the first place and now that I have a Cimmerian friend I want to stay longer.

"I'll come out to the carriages with you," Diaya says, smiling. "I have to come see my first proper friend off before she goes back home."

My heart tugs at her words and her smile and I'm filled with the similar desire to stay as when I first left the island. However I can't stay, not really. I don't think Onyx would take too well to me staying (he might try and have me arrested for one thing) and I do need to get on with my next phase of training.

We make our way round the edge of the grounds to the front of the palace, opting for staying out in the sunshine rather than going back inside. Penny and I are going to spend the rest of the day inside; I'd like to stay out for as long as possible. Caspian and the rest of the others are waiting next to two carriages, obviously meant to take us back to the airfield. The only people I can't see are Dmitri and Amara.

"Nice of you to join us Captain Sirenia," Caspian says, a chiding note to his voice and my face heats up.

"Sorry," I mumble, more than a little embarrassed.

"It's my fault," Diaya says, jumping to my rescue. "I wanted to say goodbye properly and kept her talking."

"Not a problem, Your Highness," Caspian says, nodding his head in a bow and giving her a small smile. I still can't get used to him smiling—it's not like it never happens but I'm so used to him being stoic it still hasn't registered as being normal. "Please take your time, we're still waiting on our final members to arrive."

"Thank you Commander," she says. "And once again may I say thank you so much for coming, on behalf of my father and the rest of my family."

"The honour was all ours," Caspian says.

"I'm sorry there aren't more of us to see you off," Diaya says.

"We have said our goodbyes to King Zircon and we get the pleasure of having you here," Caspian says. "There is nothing more we could ask for than that. If you would excuse me though, I must have a quick word with the driver."

"Of course," Diaya says and Caspian leaves us.

"I'll write to you as soon as I get back," I tell Diaya as we turn to one another.

"You'd better," she says before giving me another quick hug. "I'm going to miss you."

"I'll miss you too," I say and hug her tighter.

"Have a good flight back," she says as she releases me.

"I'll try," I reply, thinking about how unpleasant the flight over was.

I turn and am just about to get into the carriage when some sort of commotion can be heard coming from inside the palace. There seems to be a lot of shouting and, when I turn to look back, I can see people running past the windows through the corridors. Something major is happing inside and everyone seems to have noticed.

"What on earth…" Kat says, appearing behind me to look up at the palace as well.

We continue watching people run around inside for a moment before the front doors suddenly burst open and Dmitri hurries down the stairs to join us. He's frowning, looking more serious than I've ever seen him, and he seems to be in a great hurry to get away from the palace, needing to put as much distance between it and himself as possible.

"We need to leave now," he tells Caspian as he reaches the carriage.

"Why?" Caspian asks. "What's happening?"

Before Dmitri can respond, a pair of huge glass doors on one of the top most balconies are thrown open and a herald steps out. All eyes are on him as he raises a horn and gives it three sharp blasts.

"King Zircon is dead," he shouts and Onyx steps out onto the balcony to stand with him. "Long live King Onyx." What?

No!

This can't be happening.

I look over at Diaya to see her staring up at her brother in a gruesome mixture of horror and amazement. The colour begins to drain from her face and it looks as if she might faint as tears begin to brim in her eyes. What the hell happened? He wasn't even ill! Not that any of us knew about anyway, and I'm sure Diaya would have told me if he was (she told me everything else about her family), and he wasn't exactly old either. People don't just drop dead like that! How could this have happened?

I rush to Diaya's side. "Are you alright?" I ask. What a way to find out that your dad has died and your brother is now king. I place a hand on her shoulder and she seems to remember that I'm there.

She turns to me in a daze, eyes hazy and unfocused. "I don't know…"

"Sirenia come on," Caspian tells me, "we need to go now. Where in the fuck is Solarium?"

"Here," Amara says appearing at his side.

"Good we're leaving."

He's right. With Onyx now king it's not exactly safe for us to stay here for much longer, but I don't want to just leave Diaya like this. She looks as if a light breeze might blow her over, or that she might shatter into thousands of tiny pieces at any second. I take hold of her hands and give them both a squeeze. That seems to make her finally able to focus on me, really see me standing in front of her.

"Write to me," I tell her. "Let me know what's happened and I'll write back, I promise."

"Okay…" she says, still sounding as if she's in a daze.

"I'll listen if you need to talk," I tell her. I give her hands another squeeze before I jump into the carriage along with the rest of them and we head off, building up as much speed as fast as we possibly can.

Leaning out of the window I stare at Diaya until I can no longer see her before Kat coaxes me back inside. I sit and watch as the landscape flies by although I'm not paying that much attention. Nothing makes sense anymore. All I know is that Caspian wants us to get the hell out of here as fast as possible. Onyx obviously wanted us to know that he rules Cimmerian now and all of us are in very real danger if we stay. How on earth did Zircon even die though? When we saw him at dinner last night he was fine and this morning at breakfast he was as cheerful as ever so what happened between then and now?

It's going to look incredibly suspicious that we're suddenly disappearing after his death and, no doubt, Onyx will use that to his advantage to poison the Cimmerian citizens against us but it isn't safe here, not for a Braxian. I appreciate Caspian's need to get away as fast as possible before something even worse happens.

No one says anything the entire ride back to the airfield and before I know it we're back, Luciana's huge airship casting a shadow over the ground. She gives a quick thanks to the people of the airfield as the rest of us all file in. Having to be quick is quite good in this instance otherwise I may have ended up talking myself out of getting back on and I probably wouldn't have been the only one. As it is by the time Luciana is in the cockpit and revving the engine we're all strapped in and ready.

There's no typical Luciana excitement at the prospect of flying and no one seems willing to say anything (although that might be the result of take-off). The nausea hits me and I clench my lips together to keep myself from throwing up, closing my eyes as well. Eventually I feel a hand on my arm after a few minutes and I open my eyes to see Amara holding out another vial of that liquid to me.

"Want something to ease the sickness?" she asks.

"God yes," I say and I don't even think. I reach for it but before my fingers close around it Caspian's hand comes down, hard on Amara's shoulder.

"Solarium, a word please," he growls, and it is clearly an order not a request.

"Yes Commander," Amara says and I can tell from the look in her eyes she knows that she's in trouble.

Caspian gestures for her to follow him and they go to stand towards the back of the plane where they're less likely to be heard but it's a small space; from where I'm sitting I can hear every word and I'm sure everyone else can as well.

"Would you like to tell me what the hell you think you're playing at?" Caspian asks.

"I heard someone say that the king was dead—I went to investigate because something didn't sit right with me," Amara replies.

"Do you have *any* idea how dangerous that was?" Caspian asks and I can hear the fury in his voice. If I were Amara, I'd be quaking in front of him but when she speaks she still sounds as calm as ever.

"Of course I do," she replies "but I needed to know. You know what Onyx is like, this won't reflect well on us regardless so I decided to find out exactly how he died before we had to leave and I lost my chance."

"And?" Caspian asks. "I gather if it was worth risking your life for you at least got some interesting information out of it."

"I took sketches," Amara says.

I hear a rustling and I turn to see her pull a small notebook out of her pocket. I'm not the only one listening now, most of the others have also turned in their seats in order to watch the unfolding conversation. As soon as she begins flipping through the notebook I hear Remy whisper 'fuck me' to himself followed by a swift thud as Ellis hits him to get him to shut up. The only person not on the edge of their seat is Luciana but I imagine that she's listening as well if she can hear what's being said.

"This is detailed," Caspian says, taking the notebook from her and studying the drawing.

"This is a rough sketch," she replies. "Had I had more time I would have done better but I heard guards and thought it was a good idea to get out."

"Sensible," Caspian says. "So what can you tell me?"

"From the state that the body was in, it looks like he's just been burnt to death but this isn't the same as a fire burn," Amara replies.

"No I see that from the drawing," Caspian says.

"No it was definitely an electrical burn," Amara says. "On closer inspection, it looks like he was struck by lightning."

Everyone aside from Amara and Caspian turn to look at Penny. She stares around, wide-eyed, at all of us. "No…" she cries. "You can't seriously think…"

"There's more," Amara says bringing our attention back to her. "If you look at this mark around the chest, near where the heart is."

"It looks like a hand print," Caspian says bringing the sketch closer to his face so that he can have a proper look.

"Now obviously not how that works in the slightest but to the casual observer who has seen someone pull somebody's soul out of their chest once…" She leaves that statement hanging in the air as everyone turns to look at Ellis this time.

"No, you've seen me do it," Ellis says, holding up his hands in defence. "You know it doesn't leave a mark."

"But that's not what ultimately killed him," Amara continues.

"So this was all done after death?" Caspian asks, still looking at her sketch with a raised eyebrow.

"Yes," Amara replies. "Probably staged to make it look like we killed him."

"Well…" Caspian says and he sounds surprisingly calm about all of this. "So what *did* kill him if it wasn't any of this?"

"I didn't have time to get much more information before Onyx showed up with his guards but my best guess is that he was suffocated, but as I say I didn't have enough time to get a proper look for that."

Everyone turns round to look at Samuel who, unlike Penny and Ellis, continues to look as deadpan as ever. "You all know full well I was with Orion this morning."

"How long had he been dead when you looked at him?" Caspian asks Amara.

"Hard to say in the time I had with him but not long," she replies. "My best guess is that he was killed almost immediately after breakfast."

No one says anything. No one knows what *to* say. A heavy silence falls over all of us in the wake of this information and I don't think anyone wants to be the one to break it. I don't understand how this happened. None of us would be stupid enough to kill Zircon, we all know what it would start if we did but whoever did kill him has done their research. They knew the perfect time so that his death would leave the biggest impact.

"Caspian…" Kat begins finally.

"We wait," he says, handing the notebook back to Amara.

"What?" Kat asks.

"There's nothing else we can do other than wait to see the fallout of this," Caspian says coming back to take his seat again. "On our return, I will request an audience with King Elric and inform him of what has happened but as it stands there is nothing else we can do as we've now left Cimmerian."

"If you're sure," Kat says.

"Van Garret," Caspian calls to the front of the plane.

"Aye," Luciana calls back, clearly she has been keeping half an ear on this conversation and I don't blame her.

"How long until we touch down in Brax?"

"Six hours tops," Luciana replies.

"Get us there in five," Caspian tells her.

Luciana seems to think about this for a moment before there is the sound of whirring from the engines "Aye Commander." I watch her through the very small opening into the cockpit as she flips some switches. "Everyone fasten your seatbelts, this is going to be an unpleasant ride for all of us."

I can already feel myself starting to get nauseous again and swallow down the bile threatening the back of my throat. Reeling from all this new information plus flying isn't a good combination for me and there is a good chance I might be sick on this ride home. I close my eyes and lean my head back in my seat, trying not to think about the unpleasant sloshing of my stomach when I feel a gentle hand on my shoulder. I open my eyes and see Amara standing above me.

"Still want this?" she asks and holds out the vial of clear liquid.

"Yes please," I say and take it without hesitation, draining the whole thing in one go.

"You alright?" Amara asks once I'm done.

"Yeah," I reply even though I'm not. There's nothing I can do and I don't try to fight it—I just let it pull me into the confines of sleep. There really is nothing I can do at the moment except try to get through the flight and wait for the fallout when we get back home.

~ *** ~

Thanks to the drug I fall asleep incredibly swiftly and before I know it Illyria is shaking me gently, rousing me from my slumber.

"Ari," she says.

"Wha…?" I ask, still groggy from the drug.

"We're home," she tells me.

I blink a few times, rubbing a hand over my face and looking out of the window closest to me. We are home—not only that we're back on solid ground too, in the middle of the training ground.

"Oh…" I say. I slept the entire way back, I even missed the landing. Really not complaining on that front actually.

"Come on," Illyria says, helping me to my feet, "let's go inside and get some food in you."

"Okay," I nod and follow her and the rest of them back to the castle.

As soon as we reach the nearest doors Springer runs up to us and salutes. "Commander Feioré I trust you had a pleasant trip."

"Send a message to the king, telling him of our return and that we need an audience with him first thing tomorrow morning," Caspian tells him.

"Yes sir," Springer says and darts off.

I watch him go but I'm still not altogether there. The last couple of minutes in Cimmerian don't seem real. I suppose once it's sunk in and we start to see some kind of consequence of this it will all feel a lot more tangible.

Caspian turns to us. "We need to be prepared for the worst," he says. "After an event like that, we have no idea how Onyx is going to react or how long it will take him to do so. Get yourselves fed and rested and be ready to leave for King Elric's palace first thing tomorrow morning. Anyone who arrives out the front later than half past six is going to be running drills all day, every day, for the next month. Do I make myself clear?" There is a chorus of 'Yes Commander', from us all. "You are dismissed."

Caspian leaves, Kat at his heels, and an uneasy silence falls over us. No one seems to know what to say before Remy finally breaks the silence.

"Shall we go get some food?" he asks. "I've been craving some good, old fashioned Braxian grub since we left."

"That is the first sensible thing you've said in all the years I've know you," Luciana says.

The tension seems to dissipate somewhat but it's not entirely gone. We all still feel it, lingering under the surface, but no one is going to talk about it, not yet anyway. If I'm honest I'm worried because, from what I saw, Onyx isn't the sanest of men but there's not a whole lot that can be done yet. Now it's just a waiting game so I might as well eat, get some sleep that isn't drug induced and make sure I'm down out the front before half six.

~ *** ~

As it turns out I'm ready and waiting outside even before Caspian…two whole hours before Caspian in fact. What little sleep I get is uneasy and I finally give up trying at around half past three. I write three letters—one to my parents, one to Trista and one to Diaya, telling them all that I'm back in Brax and telling my parents and Trista about what happened while we were in Cimmerian (leaving out the part about Zircon's death). I put a detailed description about

Neyara in Diaya's letter in the hope that it might take her mind off what happened with her father. Even that takes less time than I thought it would so I head downstairs at about quarter to five and chat with Springer, who is on duty, until the others begin to arrive.

Clearly Caspian's threat carried weight because everyone is there well before half past six. Not everyone is fully awake but they're there. We head off swiftly and before I know it we're pulling up in front of the palace. We're led to the throne room and it's a much more sombre atmosphere than the last time I was here.

"Commander Caspian Feioré and the Neo Warriors," a herald announces as he pushes the door open. We stride to the throne and kneel before the king.

"Commander Feioré," King Elric says, his voice echoing in the hall around us, "it appears that you are the bearers of some rather distressing news."

"My humblest apologies sire but we are," Caspian says, getting to his feet.

"Please tell me," King Elric says.

"At the very end of our stay in Cimmerian, we were made aware that King Zircon had died and his son Onyx has been crowned in his place," Caspian says.

King Elric furrows his brow. "This is not good news at all," he says, shaking his head. "This is very distressing news indeed."

"The rest of our visit was very successful up until that. King Zircon and his family enjoyed our company as did a great number of the locals. However I must admit, I am rather anxious about the outcome," Caspian says. "And why is that?"

"Aside from the fact that the king was pronounced dead, it was made to look like a death by Braxian magic and we left, making it look very suspicious to the casual observer…"

"It does look as if we may have had a hand in his death," King Elric agrees.

"Indeed and I imagine Onyx will use this to his advantage in order to turn those who may have an affiliation with Brax against us," Caspian says. "It is Onyx being crowned specifically that gives me cause to worry."

"Yes?"

"On our first night in Cimmerian, Onyx challenged us to a test of skill," Caspian explains. "The conditions were that we did not use our magic—it was based on our skills as soldiers alone—and those conditions were met by all participants. Onyx was still outmatched though and he did not take his defeat particularly well."

King Elric says nothing for a moment. He seems to be thinking over this new piece of information and he looks incredibly uneasy. After a long pause, he sighs and shakes his head, his face grave.

"This is most definitely distressing news Commander," he says. "Onyx has always been rather volatile at the best of times but now I fear that he is in a position of power he has the opportunity to abuse that for his own ends. If he chooses to gather his forces and march on Brax, then we may be looking at another war."

"This was my concern as well sire," Caspian says. "What seemed to King Zircon as an amusing lesson in defeat was taken as a great insult by Onyx and I would not put it past him to take out his revenge on Brax as punishment."

"Was there any chance to reconcile with him and correct this misunderstanding before you returned?"

"Not for lack of trying on my part," Caspian replies. "While I did try to right the wrong while we were there Onyx seemed unwilling to listen to me or even converse with me. Then, by the time we were informed of the late king's death I thought that our best course of action would be to leave. I had to put the safety of my team over anything else."

"Very wise," King Elric says. "There's no telling what Onyx would have done if you had stayed. We will just have to wait for now and see what course of action he takes. What are your plans now that you are back in Brax?"

"We will begin Captain Sirenia's next course of training," Caspian replies. "Make sure that she has the magical prowess to handle herself in battle if need be."

"Very good," King Elric says. "I would like a full report on how she is doing. This may need to be a swifter training course than normal."

"Of course sire."

Okay, so I'm going to have to step up my game if I'm going to pass this training quickly; maybe it's a good thing Caspian made me go running with him while we were in Cimmerian. Knowing Caspian, this is going to be tough and it's probably going to be even more intense now the threat of Onyx is hanging over our heads. It's fine, I can do this—I know I can. I'll just have to push myself a little harder than I normally would.

"Now," King Elric says, "if there is no other business then—"

The doors to the throne room suddenly burst open, cutting him off mid-sentence as they crash against the walls. A messenger from the House of Mercury stands there, face red, panting and sweating, clutching the door as if it is the only thing keeping him on his feet. He tries to catch his breath, his harsh gasps the only sound in the otherwise silent hall. It takes a few minutes but he finally seems to compose himself. He pushes himself off the door and hurries over to the throne, kneeling at King Elric's feet.

"Your Majesty, I bring the most terrible news from the coast," he says. He still sounds breathless but he seems as if he's forcing himself to speak. This needs to be said and he needs to say it now.

"What news?" King Elric asks, sounding remarkably calm under the circumstances.

"It has reached our ear that King Onyx of Cimmerian has declared war on Brax and means to begin advancing on our land as soon as he has his army together," the messenger says. "How long is that?"

"It may only be a matter of weeks sire."

"And how have you come by this information?"

"A select number of Braxians stationed undercover in Cimmerian," the messenger says. "The new king gave a speech to one of the towns near the palace they were stationed in that we were responsible of the death of King Zircon and called for soldiers to join his army." No…this can't be happening.

This cannot be happening!

I'm not ready for this…I can't fight in a war, I don't know how to!

Cold sweat begins to prick the back of my neck and I feel as if the room is spinning. I try to keep breathing but it's getting harder and harder, as if there is a hand squeezing my lungs. The room is too warm, I can't breathe…

"It seems your plan may need to move slightly swifter Commander Feioré," King Elric says, turning his attention from the messenger to Caspian.

"Permission to return to our headquarters to begin Captain Sirenia's training, sire," Caspian says.

"Permission granted," King Elric says. "You have an exceptional team Commander Feioré, they will not let down their country."

"No sire," Caspian says. "We will lay down our lives to protect Brax if we have to."

"Let us hope that it doesn't come to that," King Elric says. "We will try for a negotiation for peace with Onyx but it is highly unlikely that he will be interested."

"I will send you a report of Captain Sirenia's progress by the end of the week."

"Thank you Commander," King Elric says. "Hopefully Onyx will need more time to assemble his army than it will for Captain Sirenia to be ready, giving us time to formulate some kind of plan."

"We will be as swift as we can Your Majesty," Caspian says, bowing again.

"That is all I ask for," King Elric says with a small smile. "You are dismissed."

Caspian turns and leaves the throne room, the rest of us at his heels. I can feel my legs shaking as I walk but it doesn't seem to show as I manage to make my way to the carriage without crumbling. As we reach the carriage Remy hops up to sit with Park'er and Luciana opts for flying back. Before she leaves, she gives me her coat to hold and I clutch it to my chest like a lifeline, hoping that it will give me some of the strength and confidence I'm going to need to pass this training quickly. I don't even know if I'm going to be able to make it back to headquarters without falling apart.

The silence that has been hanging in the carriage is suddenly broken, Caspian's voice cutting through the settled tension. "Sirenia…"

I jump at the sound of my name and clutch Luciana's coat tighter. "Yes Commander?"

"Now that we are at war your training will have to be swift and precise, do you understand?"

"Yes Commander."

"You will train day and night if you have to. I will turn you into a soldier in as little time as possible."

"Yes Commander." I have no idea what else to say. It's either I agree and do my best to meet his standards or I get sent home and they send someone else in my place.

"Good," Caspian says. "We will all need to be at our full potential. If Onyx can't be reasoned with, then this is going to be a war like we haven't seen in a long time." I can't help feeling that he's right about that.

The rest of the ride back to headquarters seems to take no time at all and as soon as we're back Caspian is barking orders at us.

"I want you all down on the training ground for drills," he tells us as we file out of the carriage and through the gates. "Tell your squads to be ready for battle at a moment's notice and someone find Van Garret."

"I'll go," Samuel says.

"Thank you," Caspian says before Samuel darts off. "We will try for a negotiation of peace first but it is unlikely that Onyx will accept that and will go ahead with the invasion anyway. We need to be ready to defend our land and our people. As of this moment we are at war."

"I'll go and inform the squad leaders that they are required," Kat says.

"Thank you," Caspian says and Kat runs off down another corridor. "The rest of you get down to the training ground as soon as you are changed into your combat gear."

I can feel my heart pounding in my ears and I can barely register anything as everyone begins to go to their separate rooms. It's like I'm in a daze, just letting my feet do the work and holding on to Luciana's coat for support. I don't even think about going to my room to change: I just start walking in the direction of the training ground before a hand on my collar suddenly stops me, snapping me out of my own head. I turn to see Caspian staring down at me, his face an unreadable mask like always.

"Not you," he says. "Tonight I want you up in that library reading up on everything there is to know about battle techniques and previous wars with the Cimmerians as I imagine your history is limited. I need you on your best form, knowing everything you possibly can learn in a short space of time, otherwise this will not go well for you."

"Yes Commander," I say. I feel sick and the words stick in my throat, choking me. There's a good chance I may even go and be sick and all that is going through my head is that I am so woefully unprepared for this. If something goes wrong, then I might never see my family again, never see Trista or Diaya…I might be getting sent home in a coffin…

"Sirenia," Caspian says suddenly, his voice ringing out through the darkness in my head, "I need you to remain calm." I think he can tell that I'm going crazy as he lets go of my collar and places his hand gently on my shoulder. I look up at him, really looking at him this time and he doesn't look as stern as normal. "I will not let anything happen to you, do you understand? I will make sure that you're ready by the time we have to face Onyx and his army. You won't be going in unprepared. Michael was the first soldier I have ever lost under my command and I will not let that happen again."

"Thank you sir," I say, my voice barely above a whisper and tears threatening to spill. "I'll do my best."

"I'll come and find you in a few hours, see how far you've gotten," he says. He turns to leave, heading for the training ground but I'm not ready to be alone yet.

No! Please don't leave me like this!

I feel like I'm staring my own mortality in the face and the slightest thing is going to shatter me into thousands of tiny pieces as if I'm made of the frailest glass. There's so much I need to ask him. Where should I start? What am I supposed to be looking for? What if I don't match up? What if I don't make it?

"Commander!" I call after him suddenly, letting my nerves get the better of me. He turns to me and if he is at all surprised by the cold sweat obviously forming on my forehead and the colour draining from my face he doesn't show it. "Commander I…I need to ask you something," I blurt out before I lose my nerve completely.

"Yes?"

"What happened to Michael?" I ask. I swallow the lump in my throat, clutching Luciana's coat even tighter like it has the answers or can at least give me the courage to hear the answer to the question I'm about to ask. "He was my cousin and I know that he died, I just don't know how. No one has told me."

Caspian doesn't say anything for a moment but I think I know what he's going to say. Michael wasn't ill and I think, deep down, I knew that all along. He was killed and none of us were told about it. Caspian comes back over to stand in front of me. I look up at him and tears begin to slowly make their way down my face; I can't stop them and I don't even try. He places his hand on my shoulder again.

"Michael was a good soldier," he says. "He was courageous and he knew the risks that this position entails. He was sent on a reconnaissance mission and during that mission he was captured, tortured and killed by a few rouge members of the Cimmerian army…or we thought that they were rouge members. After recent developments, they may *not* have been."

Tears are pouring down my face now and it is taking everything I have to keep my eyes on his. My head begins to spin while it begins to get harder and harder to breathe. I'm going to be sick.

I'm going to pass out. I'm going to die.

"Thank you," I finally manage to whisper.

"For what?" he asks. I'm surprised he even heard me. I can't actually get my voice any louder than this. If I do try to speak at a normal volume, I might just break down, start crying and never stop.

"For telling me the truth," I say.

I can feel myself getting light headed, my vision starting to fade, and I think I'm holding my breath just waiting for something to happen. I'm trying to process all of this but there's just too much. We're at war, Michael was killed in action and I don't even have the proper training to be able to keep myself alive, never mind anyone else.

My entire body shakes and I clutch Luciana's coat even harder. I shouldn't be—I don't want to damage it but I can't let go of it; that's the only thing keeping me together. I can't break. Not now, not in front of Caspian, otherwise he'll probably send me home and tell them to send someone better.

His hand leaves my shoulder and he places it on the top of my head, bringing me back to myself. I look up and see him looking down at me with blazing red eyes. He removes his hand and sinks down to one knee, placing his left hand over his heart. Half a salute.

"Believe me when I say this, I will not let you die," he says quietly, as if this is a secret between the two of us.

"Yes Commander," I say, my voice a little stronger now.

Caspian gets to his feet. "Go and get yourself cleaned up and head to the library. I'll be up to test you on how much you've learnt in a few hours."

"Yes Commander," I say again.

He turns and leaves and this time I don't say anything to stop him. I watch him disappear before I let myself go in a moment of utter weakness, sinking to my knees and sobbing into Luciana's coat. I don't know what I'm crying about or who for but if I don't let it out now then I won't make it through this and I promised Trista that I would come back alive. I can't break that promise: not now, not ever.

Part Two

Chapter 1

"Captain Sirenia?" Jenkins' voice says through my bedroom door.

Blearily, I open my eyes, expecting to see bright sunlight coming in through the windows but there isn't any. Am I late? I must be if Jenkins has come to get me but when I finally manage to crack my eyes fully open, I realise I can't be. It's only just beginning to get light so there's no way I can be late. No… No I don't want to get up! What even is the time and why is he knocking on my door? He knocks again when I don't respond, a little louder this time.

"Captain Sirenia, are you awake? I've been instructed by Commander Feioré to collect you for your training."

I blindly grope around for the clock. Seriously, what the hell? The sun hasn't even risen properly! Caspian can't seriously expect me to go out and train before it's actually light, can he? Finally my hand manages to find the clock (exactly where I left it on top of the bedside cabinet…I don't know what I expected). Pulling it close to my face so I can read the numbers I blink at it, still unable to focus properly. I have to stare at it for a good couple of minutes before I register what the time actually is. My eyes widen. What the hell?

Jenkins knocks again. "Captain Sirenia?"

"It's four-thirty!" I shout before I bury my face back into the pillows, still clutching the clock. Piss off, training at this hour! I'm barely going to be able to see a foot in front of my own face when the sun starts breaking and Caspian seriously wants me to train? I need to see if I'm going to be using magic and I can't do that if I'm squinting in the light. "Come back and get me when it's a reasonable hour."

Groaning I pull the covers back over my head, pretending to be asleep and hoping that I might actually be able to go back to sleep. If I ignore him, he'll go away, right? Wrong…

"I understand that Captain," Jenkins says, "but Commander Feioré said that if you aren't on the training ground in the next five minutes then he will send you home with a dishonourable discharge."

"I'm up!" I shout, instantly throwing my covers off and scrambling around for my clothes. If there is anything I do not need right now, it's that! "Give me ten seconds."

"Of course Captain," Jenkins says.

On no!

Oh bugger! Bugger! Bugger!

Where the bloody hell did I put my training gear?

Finally I find it (underneath a pile of clothes that need a clean; thankfully it doesn't smell too bad), pull it on and dart to the door. Clearly after yesterday's breakdown Caspian is back to treating me the way he always has. I think I'm thankful for that: I don't think I'd want him to give me special treatment because he didn't think I could handle myself.

Thankfully Caspian was the only one to see my complete lapse of mental strength and no one else has mentioned it so I'm guessing that it's something that's going to stay between the two of us. Once I had stopped crying and had a moment to gather myself it was almost embarrassing how much of a child I must have looked to him. I knew that going to war was going to be a possibility when I joined the Neo Warriors. There was always a chance that things were going to go badly with the Cimmerians and if the peace negotiations break down then we were going to be flung into the grips of a full blown bloodbath.

But I know what I'm doing now.

I spent all of last night in the library reading and now I know everything there is to know about the previous Cimmerian wars. Caspian eventually found me face down in a book and, once he'd woken me up, decided to test me on what I had learnt. I think he was impressed with how much I'd retained in so short a time because he left me to it, not coming back to check on me until it was nearly midnight when he sent me to bed. It took me most of the day but I do know what I'm doing now—all I have to do is complete his training.

Once I've finished hurriedly pulling on my clothes, I head to the door, yanking it open before I struggle to tie my hair back. Jenkins gives me a smile and I kind of want to punch him, but only because it's so early in the morning and he's woken me up. I finish with my hair and close my bedroom door.

"Okay, I'm ready," I say.

"Good morning Captain," he says.

"If you say so," I mumble. "How long do I have before Caspian tries to send me home?"

Jenkins chuckles. "You still have time, don't worry."

"Good."

We begin to make our way down to the training ground. I stifle a yawn and rub a hand over my face. Jenkins has learnt over the last few months that I am not a morning person so I probably won't be awake until the outside air hits me. Having said that, I should probably try and make some kind of conversation.

"How are you?" I ask.

"I'm fine Captain, and yourself?"

"Not terrible," I reply.

"I trust you had a pleasant night's sleep," he says.

"I slept," I reply. Restless as it was for the most part, I did actually manage to get some sleep that wasn't on top of a pile of books, which is an achievement.

"Are you ready for your next round of training?" he asks.

"I'm going to have to be," I say. In the long run, it doesn't matter if I am ready or not, not really. Either way I'm going to have to step up and make sure that I am, otherwise people (myself included in that one) might die. What happens will happen, I just have to try and be ready for it when it comes.

"I've seen you in your previous training Captain," Jenkins says, "you'll do just fine. You have nothing to worry about."

"Thanks," I reply and give him a small smile. "I don't really feel like it right now. I mean I know I *can*, I passed the first one, but I just don't really feel like it at the moment."

"That's because it's four-thirty in the morning," Jenkins says, smiling kindly.

"This is very true."

"So don't worry too much," he says. "Commander Feioré won't let you fail."

"No, I guess he won't." I hadn't thought about it that way but Caspian promised last night that he wouldn't let me die so he's going to make sure that I pass and that he trains me to be a proper soldier no matter what.

By the time we reach the training ground, Caspian is already there. Kat is with him and both of them look a lot more alert than I do. As soon as we step outside the cold early morning air hits me like a slap in the face and I am instantly much more awake. This is going to be intense and I need to have my wits about me so I'm quite glad that it's cold today. The cold will keep me awake until I have been up long enough to be alert on my own. As we reach Caspian and Kat both Jenkins and I salute.

"Captain Ariana Sirenia reporting for training," Jenkins says.

"Thank you Jenkins," Caspian says. "You may take your leave now."

"If I may, sir, I would very much like to stay and watch Captain Sirenia's progress," Jenkins says. "As her squad leader it will be pertinent for me to be able to take information about her training back to the rest of the squad."

"I see no reason why not," Caspian says, "as long as that is alright with Captain Sirenia."

"Yeah…sure," I reply. I'm not sure why they're asking me (I suppose in a way it kind of is up to me) but I'm not overly fussed. I suppose it would be good for the squad to know how I'm doing and that I can actually be a competent leader for them.

"Very well then," Caspian says, nodding at Jenkins. He turns to me and my stomach instantly feels as if someone has dropped a dozen snakes into it. "Now Sirenia are you ready to start your proper training?"

"Yes Commander," I say and I'm quite thankful that my voice doesn't come out as a high-pitched squeak. That would be too embarrassing for words. I have to prove to him that last night was just a momentary blip and I'm not completely terrified.

"Good," he says. "Firstly I will put you through drills, both physical and magical but I will save the magical drills for once it is lighter." Thank god for small mercies. "Once you have shown me what kind of skills you possess, you and I will spar using only magic. If you can hold your own against me, then I will class that as impressive."

"Yes sir," I say. Is he serious? He's the strongest Neo Warrior there is, I've literally been doing this for a matter of months and he expects me to be able to hold my own against him. Forget Onyx or the Cimmerians, this is how I'm going to die!

"Prove to me that I have something to work with and that I can turn you into a competent soldier in a matter of weeks," he says.

"Yes sir." Guess I'm going to have to…

"Then let's get started."

Caspian's training technique is very much the 'throwing the fledgling out of the nest and seeing if it flies', which is quite good considering how long I actually have to learn this stuff. He has me running the length of the training ground until the sun properly comes up as a 'warm up' (which thankfully is only about half an hour) before making me do simple conjuring while running to prove that I can do both at the same time. For the most part, I feel clumsy and uncoordinated, especially when he has me doing more complicated movement and magic together.

I just about manage to complete all the tasks he sets for me adequately enough. The worst one is dodging enemy and friendly fire as both he and Kat begin sparring with me caught in the middle. All I had to do was make sure that I didn't get hit and, thankfully, I didn't. I think both of them were holding back during their match but they would be against each other. This is supposed to be about me getting stronger at the moment.

During the entire morning Caspian doesn't really say all that much about my progress, just tells me to do things again every so often (mostly when even *I* know I didn't get it right). It's like that first morning all over again but a lot more intense because I've got to concentrate on both my physical and magical skills. A lot of the time I feel like I'm floundering but by the time he finally lets me take a break to get some food he tells me that I'm doing well. That's something at least—I'm not completely messing it up.

At breakfast, I eat like I haven't seen food for days. This is the most magic I've ever used in one day and it's taken its toll on me. By the time everyone else is up, finished their own morning preparations and come down to watch I'm already exhausted, by the time I get to lunch I'm ready to collapse. The rest is short lived though, as Caspian has me back running drills again as soon as my food has settled.

I collapse to my knees, panting and sweating, having just proven my skills at sending quickfire rivulets of water out in an attack. Back home, when I was just using little bits of magic for fun and the occasional spar against a family member, I had never thought that it would be this tiring to use it but it drains your energy (especially as I didn't have much for breakfast). If you're already quite emotionally charged, magic really wears you down fast, so I'm going to have to learn how to control my emotions a bit better. I'm also going to have to build up my stamina if I want to be able to do this without getting tired; I'll ask Samuel how he does it.

There are a few shouts from the stands and I turn to see Remy and Illyria cheering. Dmitri gives me a wave and I just about manage to smile at him. It's quite nice having the others there watching—even Orion and Amara have come out to watch. Knowing that they're all behind me is a great comfort; still can't help me get up faster though.

"On your feet," Caspian says, his voice resonating all around me.

I clench my jaw and push myself to stand up. My legs are protesting, trembling and desperate to give out again, but I can't exactly refuse him right now. More than anything I don't want him to think I'm too weak to do this. I've proven myself time and time again and I need him to know that I'm strong enough. I can feel myself shaking as all my muscles contract from overuse but I finally stand up straight, pull myself into a salute and meet his steely gaze. I can do this…I have to do this.

"Well done," he says. "Your skills are more advanced than I thought."

"Thank you, Commander." Not really a compliment but I'll take it.

"Next we'll see how well you fare when the enemy is firing at you," he says. "It's time the two of us spar."

"Yes Commander," I pant, still fighting to catch my breath as the whoops and cries from the stands get louder. Clearly everyone is excited at the prospect of watching me getting my arse handed to me by him. Fantastic…

I watch as Caspian removes his coat and throws it over to Penny in the stands. She catches it with ease and I turn back to him. Caspian is impressively built. He's not like Ellis, built like a brick shit-house, but he's still pretty buff. I look like a child compared to him and I'm very glad that this is not a test of strength. Slowly he rolls up the sleeves of his shirt and I can feel the bottom drop out of my stomach. He's serious about this. I can't hold anything back because he sure as hell isn't going to and he'll probably kill me if I do.

"When you are up against the enemy, they will be shooting to kill so I won't hold back and I don't expect you to either, understand?" he says.

Oh god! This is how I die!

"Yes Commander."

"Good."

My entire body beings to shake with fear. I am literally up against the strongest of the Neo Warriors and I am woefully underprepared. I'll just have to try and dodge until I can find an opening, that will have to be the plan if he's going to attack me with everything he's got. If I can get in a few lucky hits, then that will be enough for now. I may not have the kind of strength that he does or even the skill but I at least have agility on my side, for what that's worth. I watch as he raises his hand, fingers poised.

Here we go...

I dig the balls of my feet into the ground, ready to push myself off and jump out of the way at the last second. If I can see what he does first, I might be able to start a counter attack...then again... He smirks and my stomach lurches. This is it...

With no other warning, he clicks his fingers, sending a tongue of fire careening my way. I jump out of the way, spinning as I do to send some water in his direction but another tongue of fire joins the first almost instantly and I only just manage to avoid that one as well. I dig my heels into the floor again and send a jet of water his way.

He barely even flinches, clicking his fingers when the water is mere inches from his face and a small flame from his fingertips reduces my water to steam. And there goes the only advantage that I might have had against him. This is going to be way more difficult than I thought if his fire has the ability to reduce my water to vapour in seconds. He's barely giving me time to collect my thoughts, never mind think about any kind of counter attack as he sends wave after wave of flames hurtling towards me.

Tripping in my haste, I lose my footing while trying to avoid more flames and fall to the floor. I try to get up but Caspian sends an inferno my way and I flatten myself into the dirt to avoid singeing my hair or my face. This is what it's going to be like when we're up against the Cimmerian army—an unrelenting stream of people out to kill and all that is to be done is hope that you can get in a lucky shot before they get the chance. I should try for another counter attack but Caspian's too quick with sending fire at me that all I can think about is trying not to get burnt.

Rolling out of the way as another burst of flames scorch the ground where I just was I look back at him. His eyes are hard and I think he's beginning to get angry that I'm not fighting back but I can barely get my bearings. When he said he wasn't going to hold back, I figured this was probably what he meant but I had no idea he was *this* strong. I've never seen him in action before and this is just another in a long list of things that I wasn't prepared for.

Sweat pours down my face from both the heat and the exertion of not getting barbecued and I have no idea what I can do to fight back. I've been on my knees for the last couple of minutes with very little opening for me to be able to get back on my feet. I can't use the same tricks I've used on the others—he'll expect that—so I'll just have to try and fight him head on. I jolt up into a sitting position and send another jet of water his way.

He sends flames to meet it head on and it turns to steam again almost as soon as it makes contact. The fires cuts straight through the steam and towards my outstretched palm. I jerk my hand away at the last second but it's a little too late. The flames shoot past my shoulder and it takes me a second to register that they've actually made contact.

The pain is awful. It feels as if my skin is being clawed off by a red hot knife. I bite my lips together to muffle my scream of pain as I clutch my shoulder. The best I can do is conjure a bit of water to relieve some of the heat but as I let go I can feel water and something I don't want to think about slowly trickling down my arm. I breathe through the pain trying to ignore it and carry on with fighting Caspian but I'm starting to feel dizzy.

"I thought Neptunians were supposed to be adept at water magic," he says. "And yet you can't even stand up to someone with powers that should be weak to your own. How very disappointing."

Another flurry of flames roars above me but all I can manage is a small trickle of water to run over my fresh burn again.

There's no way I can win against him—not like this! I need more power but I'm already exhausted from having been doing this all morning that all my energy is gone. What little strength I do have left is reserved for keeping me from getting burnt to a crisp. He sends another jet my way and I just about manage to roll out of its path before I push myself to my hands and knees panting, desperately trying to catch my breath. I need to do something or I'm going to pass out from exhaustion and pain before I can even get a hit in.

"Caspian!" Kat shouts over the next lot of flames that roar all around me. "Stop! You're going to kill her."

"Then she dies here," Caspian says once the inferno has subsided and he sounds completely calm.

He's right. If I can't even face off against one of my comrades (who shouldn't be aiming to kill me), then how on earth am I going to be able to face off against someone who *does* want to kill me?

Caspian raises his hand again and I know what's about to happen.

I can't move my legs, I can't move my arms. I can't even begin to think about pushing myself to my feet. I have no strength left. This is it. If I can't dodge them, I can't get away. His flames will get me and that will be the end of it. They'll send someone else from the House and I'll be sent home in a matchbox.

No this can't be it…

I refuse to die here like this!

If I'm going down, it will be on the battlefield and I'll make sure that I'm taking the other person with me. There's so much I need and want to do that I can't just give up here. I promised Trista I would come back alive, I need to show Harmony that I am a soldier, I've got to know that Diaya is okay and I want to see my family and my home again. No, I need to stay alive. There is too much I have to live for!

Caspian clicks his fingers and another jet of flames comes hurtling towards me. Come on, now is the time for me to prove myself!

Pulling deep down, from the very depths of a resolve I didn't even know I had until now I raise my hands just before the flames hit me and a huge shield of water forms in front of me. It's like a giant wave holding back his fire and I can hear the hiss of steam from the contact but I don't let it up. If I do, then that's it. Using every ounce of strength I possess I push myself to my feet, my entire body shaking from the force of holding up this geyser. I can't even tell if he's still sending fire my way or not, I just keep holding the shield up.

"Ari!" Dmitri shouts over the rushing water in front of me. "Ari you can stop now, it's okay."

Instantly, as if his words broke something inside me, I drop my arms and the water crashes to the floor over me, saturating the ground and pooling at my feet. A few seconds later I join it, sinking to my knees and panting furiously.

Oh my god, I never would have thought that I had that in me. I fall forwards, my hands catching on the wet ground before I have the chance to smash my face into the mud. The pain in my arm doesn't even register anymore, there's so much adrenaline coursing through me. My fists clench as I shake from the effort of what I've just done and holding myself up. I'm exhausted and I can barely catch my breath. Can I pass out forever now?

Suddenly boots appear in my line of vision and I just about manage to look up into Caspian's face. There is a small smirk playing about his lips and a fire in his eyes that I've never seen before. I stare up at him for a moment, still panting furiously, before I manage to push myself back so that I'm sitting on my thighs. Even that takes the very last of my strength and I don't think I'm going to be able to move for a while after this.

"Well done, Sirenia," he says. "That was impressive."

"Thank you, sir," I pant.

"You've proved that there is some power hiding in there after all."

"Thank you, sir."

"On your feet," he says as he turns away, putting some distance between us again. "Solarium, can you come here, please?" he says looking over to the stands.

"Yes Commander," Amara says.

He turns to me again. "We'll get your arm cleaned up and then we'll go again."

"Yes sir."

"And Sirenia?"

"Yes sir?"

"See if you can hit me this time."

~ *** ~

I spar with Caspian for what feels like hours until I physically can't stand any longer and I feel like I'm going to pass out. By the end of the day, there's nothing left in my reserves and I'm on the floor unable to get back up again. It takes Ellis picking me up and princess carrying me for me to get to Amara's office some hours later so that she can patch me up properly. It takes a while for me to actually be able to think clearly as fatigue and pain have taken their toll and I think I did briefly pass out in Ellis' arms as he carried me there. I can hear Amara and Ellis talking as Amara begins to patch me up but I'm not quite ready to join in the conversation yet (I'm not even ready to open my eyes yet).

"So what's the prognosis, Doc?" Ellis asks. "She going to live?"

"Not if the Commander keeps on at her like this she won't," Amara replies.

"Shit, really?"

"You saw him out there today, he could have killed her," Amara says. I can feel the heat of her magic flowing through me and that same calming sensation I feel whenever she fixes me up. I still don't want to open my eyes yet and the feeling of her magic only makes me more sleepy.

Ellis sighs. "Better him than the Cimmerians."

"If he pushes her too much, then she won't be any use to anyone."

"Give her some credit," Ellis says "she held her own again her Commanding Officer and Caspian Feioré at that. Not many of us could say that at eighteen, hell I don't think many of us could even do much better now."

"Not many of us had to," Amara mutters, more to herself than to Ellis but I still hear her as she's standing close to my head. "We didn't have to fight him all out. No one else is going to go as hard on her as he did today and nobody else should."

"If he says it's part of her training…"

"So you agree with him?" Amara asks and I can tell from the tone of her voice she's probably glaring at him.

"I'm just saying she can take it," he replies and a tiny part of me wants to laugh as they begin to argue above me.

"She shouldn't have to!"

"We're preparing for war here," Ellis says. "All of us are."

"I know but—"

"So give her some more credit."

"Fine," Amara sighs. "I'll admit that she was able to hold her own today and that she is much more powerful than I would expect for an eighteen-year-old with no training."

"This is my point," Ellis says. "She's strong, they all are in that family."

"Weren't you supposed to marry her sister?"

"At one point, yeah."

Amara sighs. "If Caspian could just give her one day to properly recover, then she'll be fine but I know he plans on doing the exact same thing tomorrow and every day until he deems that she's a worthy soldier."

"And you think she can't handle much more?"

"She's unconscious Ellis! What do you think?" Amara exclaims and I just about manage to open my eyes so that I can finally be part of the conversation too. Is it because she thinks I'm weak? I need to show them all that I can keep up. I might be the youngest by a few years but I can be just as good as the rest of them are.

"I'm okay," I mumble, looking up at the both of them. It's bright in here, it always is, and the light hurts my eyes so I end up squinting at them but I've proven that I'm awake at least.

Ellis grins. "There's our fierce warrior," he says. "How you feeling?"

"I'm fine," I say and try to push myself up so that I'm sitting but Amara's hand on my shoulder immediately pushes me back down so that I'm lying again.

"No you're not," she says "and if you try to get up again there'll be trouble."

"Okay," I say and let her push me back down. Lying is much better than sitting at the moment, I have to admit that, as my head started to spin as soon as I sat up.

"Shall I go get Caspian so he can have a chat with you?" Ellis asks Amara.

"Please," she replies curtly as she gently begins pushing up the sleeve of my shirt to get another look at the first burn I sustained.

Ellis takes my hand and gives it a squeeze, throwing me a wink before he leaves. I watch Amara silently, feeling the heat of her hands as she passes them over my skin, a soft glow emitting from her palms. I suppose in circumstances like this it's easier for her to heal me with magic than it is for me to heal on my own. God only knows how long that would take for all this to get better on its own and we don't have the time if the Cimmerian army are going to be knocking on our door any day now.

"Amara…" I begin tentatively.

"Don't," she says sharply, looking up at me. "Don't tell me that you're fine because this is not fine!"

"We don't have time for me to be fine," I mumble.

Amara sighs and pinches the bridge of her nose. "No we don't and that's the problem," she groans. "I can't send you back onto a training ground like this but there is no way that I can say that to Caspian. He'll flip his shit if I tell him that you can't train even if I don't think that you're fit for it after what you went through today."

"I'll be okay, I promise." I think she can tell that I'm putting on a front because I feel like I need to—I have to make them think that I'm fine otherwise Caspian will probably send me home and get someone who can complete the training fast enough.

"Ari this is me you're talking to," Amara says. "If it's going to affect your health, I want to know."

"Okay," I say with a deep sigh, "I'm scared." I admit. I let that hang in the air for a moment and continue when Amara doesn't say anything. "I'm scared and everything hurts. I know I need to complete this training and I need to do it quickly but after that I actually might have to go and fight people—real people—who are trying to kill me. I'd never even left home until a few months ago and now I'm on the edge of a war that I don't think I have any hope of surviving unless I push myself through Caspian's training. How do I deal with that?"

"I'm not sure how to answer that," Amara replies "because I'm not sure how to deal with it myself."

"How do you mean?"

"It's strange for me," Amara begins. "I've never really gone in for large displays of emotion, you've probably noticed by now, unless it's something I'm particularly interested in. I come from a very clinical House and I've never had any cause for any kind of uncertainty in what I do. I've never worried about death—my own or the people that I care about—but now that it is actually a possibility and I realise I'm not actually prepared to deal with my feelings towards it."

"So we're both a bit screwed then," I chuckle weakly.

"I suppose you could say that, yes," Amara replies before she sighs again. "I don't want to see you get hurt, or any of the others, but I don't imagine that all of us are going to come out of this unscathed if we do end up in a war."

"No we probably won't," I reply. That was something I hadn't thought about the possibility of until now. Whenever I've allowed myself to think about a war with the Cimmerians I've only ever thought about *my* death and what that means, I didn't think about the possibility that some of the others could die as well.

"I suppose the only thing we can do is try to concentrate on the task at hand," Amara says, gently lifting up my shirt to look at the scrapes and burns on my stomach before using her magic on them.

"Yeah," I say and turn my attention up to the ceiling, letting the warmth of her hands wash over me. "Mind if I fall asleep?" I ask.

"Please do," she says. "You'll heal faster."

"Okay." It's barely out of my mouth before I can feel myself drifting off again. I don't think I'm even asleep for five minutes before I hear Caspian's voice as he enters the room and I fight off the sleep and open my eyes again.

"How is she?" Caspian asks Amara.

"Ask her yourself, she's awake," Amara tells him, her tone clipped. She's probably one of the only people who could get away with speaking to Caspian like that and not end up with a court martial.

"Sirenia?" Caspian asks and I force myself to smile at him.

"I'm fine," I reply.

"So you're perfectly capable of doing the same thing again tomorrow?" he asks with a raised eyebrow.

"Sure," I reply but it turns into a wince of pain as Amara prods something that hurts like hell.

"No she's not," Amara says firmly.

"But I know I need to train so I can handle it," I tell Caspian as I try to sit up and it would have been convincing but Amara prods me once more and I'm back to lying down again, stifling a cry of pain.

"If she ends up in here again tomorrow, then she'll continue to get worse," Amara says. "There's only so much my magic can fix in a short space of time and with her pushing her limits she'll deteriorate faster."

Caspian thinks this over for a brief moment until he finally speaks again. "Weapons training with Tavaron," he tells me. "That will give you a day to recover from your injuries but still allow you to train if that is what you want."

"It is," I say.

"Good," he says. "I'll tell Tavaron."

"Thank you sir," I say, giving him a small smile. I can't bear the thought of feeling useless, especially at a time like this so knowing that there is still something I can do while I wait to get back to full strength is good enough for me.

"Now get some rest," he tells me. "You start again first thing tomorrow morning."

"Yes sir."

Both Amara and I are silent until he has left the room and closed the door behind himself, then she turns to me. "Don't end up back in here tomorrow alright?"

"I won't, I promise."

Chapter 2

I still feel a little on the groggy side as I make my way down to the training ground the next morning but it's later than I started yesterday so that is at least something. Obviously after yesterday everyone thinks I've earned the right to have a bit of a lie in so I get to sleep until seven instead of being dragged out of bed at four-thirty. Dmitri decided to let me sleep, give me more time to rest and recover I suppose and I'm grateful as I must admit my muscles are still protesting as I head outside. I didn't have the courage to look in the mirror before I left my room but I must look an absolute state as I'm covered in either bandages or bruises but he smiles all the same when he sees me.

"Have you ever fired a gun before?" he asks, after we've finishes with the pleasantries.

"Can't say I have, no," I reply. "Not sure if that's a good thing or a bad thing at this point."

"Good to know," Dmitri says with a chuckle, "and no, it's not a bad thing. I had only fired a gun before I came here because we make them in my House and we have to test them before we're able to trade them."

"Hardly anyone who lives on Neyara has guns," I tell him. "Sometimes they end up coming through as trade but, as far as I'm aware, it's not something anyone has any need for. You don't exactly use guns for fishing."

"No I suppose not," Dmitri laughs. "So have you handled any kind of weapon before?"

"Not really," I admit. Again I'm not sure if this is a good thing or a bad thing at this point. It probably means my training is going to take longer because I haven't and I need to learn how to use one quickly.

"That's fine," Dmitri says. "Not all of us actually plan on using weapons to fight, it just helps with some of our powers."

"How so?"

"Remember what we said in Cimmerian about Penny and the archery?"

"Yeah, she took it up because it was safer than the crazy destruction she can cause if she uses her magic too much at long range," I reply. It feels a bit like I'm back at school and answering a teacher's questions.

"Exactly," Dmitri says, "same with Luciana." "Close range isn't her forte when she's flying so long range weapons are great for her."

"That makes sense."

"But as I say, not all of us use weapons in the same way," he says. "Mine are built into my arm so I don't have to carry anything, Ellis prefers hand to hand combat if he *can't* use his powers and then some of us don't use any weapons because they're unlikely to end up on a battlefield anyway."

"Like who?" I ask. I had thought the whole point of the Neo Warriors is that we *are* the battlefield for when war comes knocking but I guess that's another thing that has been retold by the media to make us more heroic.

"Amara's not a fighter," Dmitri replies, "she fixes what happens afterwards. Illyria's more like our communication station outside of the battle but probably would go out and fight if she was needed to. The rest of us are more suited to it, save perhaps Orion but there's still a lot about his powers that even we don't know because he's never told us and trying to get information out of him is like trying to get blood out of a stone."

"But everyone else would be out there fighting?" I ask.

"Yeah," Dmitri replies, "either our magic is more physical or we have more physical strength to hold our own."

"And then there's the Commander," I say.

"And then there's the Commander," Dmitri agrees.

"I've heard he's like an entire battalion just on his own," I say.

"Pretty much yes," Dmitri chuckles. "You know when you were sparring against him yesterday?"

"How could I forget?" I reply as I feel a twinge in the burn on my shoulder.

"That was him holding back."

"What?" He said he wasn't going to; that he was going to come at me with everything he had and I *still* ended up in the hospital at the end of the day! How am I supposed to prove myself to him if he doesn't trust me enough to not hold something back? I put everything I had into that fight and I still barely made a dent in his powers.

Dmitri must see something on my face as he laughs and ruffles my hair, the only part of me that doesn't hurt after physical contact. "Don't worry so much," he says. "None of us can stand up against Caspian when he uses his full power. In fact, I don't think I know *anyone* that could so don't let it get you down."

"So how am I supposed to impress him with my skills as a soldier if I can't face him at full power?" I ask.

"The fact that he went as hard on you as he did and you're still standing is enough to impress him," Dmitri tells me.

"You sure?" I ask. I wouldn't have thought that Caspian would have been very impressed by that. I feel like it was a poor show on my part as it took me so long to get a hit on him.

"You worry too much," Dmitri chuckles softly. "Training is meant to be hard, that's why it helps you to get stronger, so just keep going as you are and you'll be fine. Caspian hasn't tried to send you home yet so there must be something that he sees in you, even if you don't see it in yourself yet."

"Okay," I mumble. He's right, I know he is. The whole point of training is to help me to get stronger, but it also takes time: time that I feel I have less and less of at the moment, but that just means I'll have to make sure that I use what I do have to the best of my ability and get as strong as I can as quickly as I can.

"So," Dmitri begins, "do you want to try firing a gun?"

"Sure," I reply with a shrug. I don't know exactly how excited I am to hold a gun but since this is part of my training then I'll try it. I'd probably fare better with something sharp and pointy because I know that my aim isn't the best and I don't want to accidentally shoot someone I'm not supposed to, but hopefully the aim will get better the more I do it.

Dmitri goes over to a table lined with a number of different weapons and picks up a small pistol from it. For a moment, I think he's going to toss it to me and see if I can catch it but thankfully he doesn't. He comes back to me and places the gun in the palm of my hand. It's a lot heavier than I thought it would be and I don't know if that's because it's so small but it doesn't look like it should weigh all that much on its own.

"We'll start with this," he says. "Hold it in both hands, stabilise your shoulders for the recoil after you fire and make sure you've got a firm grip on it."

"Okay…" I can feel the nerves bubbling up inside me and I'm hit with the urge to be sick. I'm holding something made specifically for killing people. If I misfire this thing, then I could actually end someone's life. Honestly I don't know how comfortable I am with that.

"So we're going to try and hit that target over there," Dmitri tells me, coming to stand behind me and nodding at a row of large leafy balls hanging from a rope. "Remy made us those, specifically for this, and they're filled with water."

"Okay." My heart begins to race; he's standing too close and I don't know what to do about it.

"Now hold the gun in both hands to keep it nice and stable," he continues and I do as I'm told. He reaches round and places his metal hand underneath the butt of the gun, keeping it steady. I feel the chill of his fingers against the back of my hand and try to stop myself from blushing too much. "You okay?" he asks, his voice frighteningly close to my ear.

"Yeah," I reply but it comes out a lot squeakier than I would have liked. Just great Ari, way to look like a complete loser.

"You sure?" he asks, sounding concerned.

"Yep," I reassure him, "bit nervous, never held a gun before." That is at least half true. I think my nerves are half from actually holding the gun and the other half trying to figure out how to fire it and that's without his close proximity.

"Now fix your eyes on the target," he tells me, "and when you're ready, just gently squeeze the trigger to fire. It's going to be quite strange when you do and it will probably make you lose your balance first time around but I'm here and I'll catch you if you do stumble."

"Okay." Oh god, as if I couldn't be any more nervous than I already am!

I look over at the target and take a deep breath. It seems like it should be easy—there isn't really much more to it—but now it actually comes to it I don't know if I can do this. I swallow my nerves, slip my finger over the trigger and pull it.

The thing that hits me first is the noise and being propelled backwards from the force of it. If I'd known it was going to be that strong, I would have planted my feet on the floor better but I do land against Dmitri's solid chest and, as promised, he is there to catch me. Breathing heavily and heart pounding in my ears, I look over to see leaves hanging limply from the rope and a small puddle of water on the floor. Holy crap, I actually did it!

"Well done," Dmitri says, giving my shoulders a squeeze. "You hit the target."

"I probably just grazed it rather than *hit it* hit it," I say panting. I feel like I've just gone a round against Caspian and all I've done is move one finger.

"Still, that's very good for a first try, considering that you've never even held a gun before," Dmitri says. "Do you want to try again?"

"I'm not sure," I reply. I know if I were to do it again, I would probably get used to the feeling of holding and shooting it but there's something about guns that unsettles me. I can't quite put my finger on what it is but I think I'd rather stick to other weapons. "I don't know if guns are really for me."

"That's fine," Dmitri says. "If you want to have more of a go another time, you can. The first time is always the worst but you do eventually get used to it, I promise. Luciana uses guns and I have one built into my arm but they're not for everyone."

"What have you got in the close range weapon line?" I ask.

"Take your pick," Dmitri says, leading me over to his table. "I've got blades, blunt and heavy things, and I have a substantial number of things that are both."

"Where do you find all of this?" I ask, looking at everything laid out on the table in front of me.

"I make it," he replies.

"What?"

"Because we do a lot of metal work, people from the House of the Earth often make a lot of weapons for the Braxian armies," he replies.

"That's really cool," I say, reaching out and running my fingers over the flat side of the blade of a very sharp looking dagger.

"In fact, that's how I ended up losing my arm," Dmitri says. "I was messing around when I shouldn't have been. My arm ended up getting crushed and I learnt my lesson to always be careful around weapons when they're being made."

"And you made your new arm yourself?" I ask.

"Everything down to the last tiny details on the inside."

"That's astounding," I say, shaking my head in disbelief. "Everyone here is so amazing in different ways and I just don't feel as if I can measure up."

"You will," he says. "It doesn't feel like it now because you have to get through your training so quickly but you've got a long time to be as good as people like Caspian or Kat. You'll be fine, I promise."

"Okay."

I like talking to Dmitri (aside from the fact that I do really fancy him) he's always so encouraging.

"So any of these take your fancy?" he asks, gesturing to the table.

I look at the array again. There's so much to choose from that I'm not even sure where to start but as I take another look at the dagger the sun shines off it, making it look as if the blade flashes blue—the same blue as my hair. It's almost like it's begging me to pick it up and hold it. Without thinking, I wrap my fingers around the handle and I can feel an intricate design on the hilt pressing into my palm. I pick it up and look at it properly, it's covered in an ornate pattern of sea shells and it looks absolutely beautiful.

"This one," I say gripping it again and looking up at Dmitri with a grin.

He smiles. "Good choice," he says. "That used to belong to Michael."

"Really?" I look back at the dagger, opening my palm so that I can inspect the design a little more closely. This used to be Michael's…

"Not many people put stock in the heart of a weapon," Dmitri tells me "but there is always a reason that people pick what they do. This belonged to Michael and now it will serve you just as well."

"If you're happy for me to take it," I say. I've never really thought about fighting with a weapon before but at close range combat it will be good to have something else in my arsenal that can cause damage.

"Of course," Dmitri says with a grin. "It belonged to a member of your family after all."

"Wow…" I say softly, holding the knife up and admiring it again. "Would you like to try fighting with it?"

"Um…" I say, startled. "I've never used something like this before."

"Close your eyes for a second," he tells me and, without hesitation, I obey. Almost instantly I can feel the knife in my hand vibrating. It's not strong but it's strong enough and it feels as if something is flowing into me—this life force held within the blade that connects me to it. It doesn't make sense but I don't try to fight it; there must be a reason this is happening and Dmitri wouldn't tell me to do it if it wasn't safe.

I stand there, letting this force flow through my entire body until it seems to stop and I open my eyes. Looking down at the handle the shells seem to have changed colour—the same colour as my hair and eyes along with other blue and green combinations that makes it look absolutely beautiful. I shift my hold on it slightly and it moves with ease, as if I've been using this exact dagger my entire life. I look up at Dmitri in astonishment.

"And that's my magic," he says.

"What the…?"

"Magically manipulated metal takes on a life of its own so that it is intrinsically linked with the wielder," he replies. "It will be like an extension of your hand now. You'll still have to get used to fighting with it but it won't take you as long as it would if that wasn't made by a metal magic user."

"Thank you so much," I say, looking from him to the blade and back again. I can't believe that House of the Earth magic is this impressive. No wonder they keep things like this to themselves.

"Now," Dmitri says, pulling a similarly sized knife out of a holster at his hip, "how about you try and hit me with that?"

"Okay," I reply. I shift my grip and the dagger shifts with me. This is going to take some getting used to.

~ *** ~

Training feels as if it goes quite slowly. Mostly because I seem to pick up new injuries every day (which Amara is not happy about) and I end up having to halt certain aspects and move onto something different in order to recover. I start to get into a rhythm though and I can feel myself getting stronger. Caspian seems happy with my progress so I'm going to class that as good enough. I still can't beat him and every time he and I spar I end up in Amara's office again but he still seems to think I'm progressing.

One morning (thankfully on one of the ones where I'm not training at the arse-crack of dawn with Caspian) someone knocks on my door. I groggily sit up in bed and rub my eyes, turning to the clock. It's about quarter past seven so not too horrifically early but I'm still not totally ready to get up just yet. "Come in," I call, the sleepiness in my voice evident.

The door opens and Jenkins is standing there smiling at me. "Good morning Captain, I trust you had a pleasant night's rest."

"Yeah," I mumble and rub a hand over my eyes to try to rid them of the accumulated sleep. "Am I late for training?" I ask.

"Not this morning Captain but I was instructed that today would be the day I properly introduce you to your squad."

"Okay, I'm up," I say and heave myself out of bed. Despite what my body language probably says, I'm very excited for this and have been looking forward to it for a long time. I've wanted to meet my squad pretty much since I found out that I had one but so far haven't exactly had the time with all the other training that I've been put through.

"How are you feeling this morning?" Jenkins asks; obviously I didn't hide the wince of pain as I step down onto the floor well enough.

"Sore," I reply. "I'm okay though, this should go in a couple of days."

"I can imagine that Dr Solarium is displeased that you keep ending up in her office," Jenkins says with a chuckle.

"She'll get over it," I reply as I grab my training clothes. Not everything hurts as much as it has done after previous days, just a few muscles here and there, but I would like to stay out of Amara's office today if I can help it. She is getting more and more annoyed with every passing visit but it's never really directed at me, just the situation.

"I'm sure she will," Jenkins says before closing the door behind himself, giving me some privacy so that I can change.

I dress quickly and ready myself for the day before I grab the dagger I got from Dmitri and we leave my room. I no longer bother to lock the door anymore—there was never any need to in the first place but it sort of became a habit after the first few days.

"Commander Feioré seems to think that your training is going well," Jenkins says as we head out to the training ground.

"Well, that's something at least," I say with a grin. Considering that Caspian is usually the reason I end up going to see Amara I'm glad he thinks that I'm actually making some progress through it all.

"Thank you for permitting me to watch some of your training sessions," Jenkins says.

"No problem," I say. "I'm happy for people to see how I'm getting on, that way they can also tell me if I'm doing something glaringly wrong."

"It certainly looks like you're doing fine to me," he says with a smile.

I like Jenkins: he's straightforward and easy to talk to. I suppose that you'd have to be in order to be the second-in-command of a squad. When I haven't been on the training ground all hours, he and I have been talking tactics for leading the squad. I've never been in charge of people before and it's quite a daunting experience, considering that most of these people are a lot older than me as well—Jenkins said the youngest member of the squad is twenty-three and that's already five years older than I am. However they train, I'll put myself through the same because I think that's the mark of a good leader, like Caspian.

"So how many people are in the squad again?" I ask as we head down the staircase.

"Thirty of the strongest Neptunian soldiers the Braxian army has to offer," Jenkins replies. "All hand-picked by myself as second-in-command and I can vouch for the credentials of every single one of them."

"Brilliant," I say, "they must be good then."

"They are the very best that Neyara has to offer."

"And they have no problem being led by an eighteen-year-old?" I ask. In truth, it is something I've been worrying about a little. I'm the youngest of the Neo Warriors, I've only just started my training and I don't feel as if I have any right to be ordering people to do anything. I know my rank means that I am entitled to, but it's still rather daunting. Some of them I may have even met back home and all of them will know who I am already (from being a Sirenia never mind being their Neo Warrior).

"No one has voiced any objections to it so I doubt that they will, especially once they see what you're capable of. I'm sure they will accept you without question," he says.

"That's good."

My confidence in my own abilities has come on in leaps and bounds since I began my training (only helped by the fact that Caspian hasn't managed to kill me yet) but there are still a few things I worry about. If Jenkins thinks I'll be fine however, then I probably will be and that's enough for me, plus he can tell the rest of them that I've gone a few rounds against Caspian…I haven't managed to win any yet but it's still something and by the sound of it none of the others have ever succeeded in beating him either.

Walking down to the training ground is easy: I remember the route by heart now and I no longer get lost on the ground floor of the base. Upstairs is a little different as I don't go up there as much. There have been a few times when I've ended up going up one flight too high while looking for the library and ended up at the top of the staircase wondering how on earth I managed to do that. Things are starting to get easier but it's still all very new and terrifying, especially with this threat from Onyx hanging over all of us.

There's hasn't been any new information reach us since he declared war nearly a week ago and I can tell that everyone's on edge. No one really says anything—they're all their usual selves—and no one seems willing to talk about it, but there is definitely a tension in the air. We're waiting for news and it's not going to be good news whenever we receive it. The only person who has said anything to me or responded to my questions is, surprisingly, Caspian (and that one moment with Amara the first time I ended up having to be fixed) and he just told me to concentrate on my training and not worry too much until the time came.

When we reach the training ground off to one side, there are thirty people, in five rows of six, all standing at ease. They're all clearly from the House of Neptune, each of them with either blue or sea green in their hair. I haven't seen this many people from the House of Neptune in one place since I left Neyara so it's a little surreal at first but then it reminds me of home. Jenkins leads me to stand in front of them and, in unison, they all snap to attention.

"Introducing Captain Ariana Sirenia of the House of Neptune, your new leader," Jenkins says and in that moment I actually feel ready to *be* their leader.

There is a reason that I was picked for this and I know that I can do what I'm needed to. There is a good possibility that we will soon be at war and I'd like to keep all of these people alive if I can. Each of them is ready to follow me and I will make sure that I shape up. I look around at all of them, taking in each face so that I can commit them to memory as quickly as possible and I'll learn their names to go along as well.

"At ease," I tell them and they all follow the order without question. Okay, let's start this.

~ *** ~

Caspian continues to train me just like that first day, pushing me to my absolute limit, for the next two days. I train from the moment the sun comes up in the morning until nightfall and I can feel myself getting stronger. My limit seems to be increasing until I can stand against Caspian without ending up on my arse. I still don't manage to get anything more than a lucky hit on him but he pushes me until I can at least hold my own against everyone individually (and a few of them against me at once).

My training has pushed me harder than I would have ever thought possible, Caspian and the others knowing how to unlock power I wouldn't have even thought myself capable of. Determined to meet each challenge he sets for me, I make sure that I can make him look at me like he did on that first day—smile filed with pride and that fire in his eyes—after every single session. I tell my parents and Trista about my progress as well as send another letter to Diaya. I'm still waiting to hear back from her but I hope that the letters I've sent so far have at least given her something to take her mind off what's going on in Cimmerian.

By the time my training is up, we are sent word from the palace that Onyx and his army would like a parley in the middle of the ocean, halfway between Cimmerian and the very edge of Brax. That makes me a little nervous: an angry king and his army who are baying for our blood being so close to *my* homeland in particular but if this parley goes well then there may be no need for them to advance at all. There will be no need for a war and there will be no need for me to panic.

I finish the day's training panting, sweaty and exhausted. I've been sparring with Samuel and his stamina always gives me a run for my money. He reaches a hand out and pulls me up from the floor. He got me good and knocked me on my arse right at the last second. I always enjoy sparring with Samuel: it's such a good work out, especially now that we're nearly on the same level.

"You okay?" he asks.

"Yeah," I reply. "Nice shot at the end there."

"Thanks," he grins. "You got a few good hits in there too, you're way better than the first time we did this."

"Thanks."

"Let's go get showered."

"Please," I laugh.

We begin to head across the training ground. The prospect of a shower and food is very attractive right now but as we get closer to the back entrance I see Remy and Ellis coming towards us.

"Hey Ari, Sammy," Remy calls, waving. "How's training?"

"We're done for the day," I say.

"Looks like you two had a lot of fun," Remy chuckles, wiggling his eyebrows suggestively. "Getting all sweaty together?"

"Do you have to lower the tone for everything Remy?" Samuel asks.

"You won't give me anything about your personal life so I have to draw my own conclusions," Remy says, grinning at Samuel.

"So are you guys out here for training?" I ask Ellis, trying to steer the conversation away from Remy teasing Samuel for the rest of the evening.

"Nah, Caspian wants us all out here," Ellis says. "He wants to talk to us now that your training is officially up and we're supposed to be having this parley with Onyx soon."

"Right," I nod. I'd sort of forgotten about that ('forgotten' reading I haven't been thinking about it because I don't want to).

"I wouldn't worry," Ellis says placing a hand on my shoulder. "Everything will work out alright in the end."

"Sure."

Whether he's right or wrong about that is anyone's guess but I don't have time to answer as everyone else begins to file out as well, along with some of the squad leaders. We file up to the centre of the training ground, Caspian at the head, and line up in front of him. I really hope this isn't going to take too long because I really want to go shower and then flop onto my bed. This has been the longest week of my life.

Once we're all assembled, Caspian salutes and the rest of us return the salute. "At ease," he says and the rest of us drop our stances. "I know the past week has been difficult for all of us but you have all improved greatly and I'm very proud of each and every one of you. Tomorrow we will begin our sail out to parley with Onyx and no matter how it goes tomorrow I am confident that all of you will be able to hold your own on the battlefield, including our newest recruits." He looks over at me and Samuel and I give him a small smile in return.

"What would you like us to do during this parley?" Kat asks.

"We will meet Onyx in a manner as non-threatening as possible and we will try to resolve this without a war," Caspian says. "If we are successful, then you won't have to do anything but be there as back up."

"And if Onyx wants a war?" Remy asks.

"Then we will give him one," Caspian replies. "If Onyx wants a war, then we will throw everything that we have at him and we will make sure that every Braxian casualty is met with three Cimmerian ones. Onyx will rue the day that he ever declared war on the Braxian Neo Warriors. Each of you, along with your squad, is strong enough to take on his soldiers and we have already proven that they are outmatched even without our magic."

"Do you want the squad leaders to be at the parley as well?" Ellis asks.

"No," Caspian says. "If Onyx thinks that we are marching to war before we have spoken, then he will end up taking it out on our citizens. If we have to go to war, I would like to do this with as few casualties as possible."

That's sensible. If Onyx thinks that we're prepared for war before talking things through, then he will probably take it out on our civilians as punishment. Onyx is petty and this only seems to have proved it. I still haven't heard back from Diaya since I sent her quite a few letters and I'm beginning to wonder if there is a good chance that Onyx hasn't let her send one back. I hope she's okay and that she doesn't get dragged into all of this.

"We will leave for the harbour first thing tomorrow morning so rest up tonight and prepare for the worst tomorrow," Caspian tells us. "No matter what happens I have every faith that you will all be able to handle yourselves. If Onyx will not accept peace, then we will come at him with all the force of the Braxian Neo Warriors and their armies. For the glory of Brax and the honour of the empire!"

He salutes and, as one, we return the gesture.

"For the glory of Brax and the honour of the empire!" we all echo in unison.

"You are all dismissed for the day," Caspian tells us. "I suggest that you get some rest tonight for tomorrow we will be walking into what may be the start of a war." He drops his salute and the rest of us do as well.

I can't believe this is it!

If the bags under my eyes from the lack of sleep over the last week tell me anything, then this training will hopefully have paid off. I won't think about what might happen tomorrow; if I do then I'll spend the entire night awake and worrying. For now, I'll just be proud of how far I've come, be ready for what may come my way and get a good shower and a hot meal.

I follow the others as we leave the training ground, still a little lost in my own thoughts (how could I not be after everything) when I feel a hand come down on my shoulder. I turn to see Caspian standing behind me.

"Don't look so serious Sirenia," he says.

"Sorry Commander."

"No need to apologise," he says.

"Commander?" I began tentatively. Can I actually say what I'm about to or will it just make me look like a total failure as a soldier? All that pride, all the opinion of me that I have worked so hard to build up could just as easily be shattered in a matter of seconds by my next words. I take a deep breath.

"Yes?"

"Do you really think I'm ready for this?" I ask.

"I wouldn't have pushed you as hard as I did if I didn't think you were capable of it," he replies.

I let out the breath I've been holding and I feel weirdly, completely at ease. Caspian believes in me! He believes that I can do it so I should believe that I can too. "Thank you Commander, I won't let you down."

"Good," he says. "Now get showered."

"I will."

He gives me another one of those small, rare smiles before he carries on ahead to talk to Illyria and I allow myself to smile. I feel another hand on my shoulder and I turn to see Dmitri. He smiles down at me and I feel my heart skip. As well as proving myself to Caspian and to myself to boot, I didn't mess up in front of him and it was nice being able to be trained by him occasionally as well.

"Well done," he says. "You've come so far in such a short time."

"Thanks," I say, pulling my hair out of its ponytail and shaking it out with my fingers. "I never thought I would have been able to do that in my entire life."

"You have now," he says, "and you've done an amazing job."

"I'm still nervous about tomorrow," I admit.

"I think we all are," he says. "There's no shame in admitting that. I know I am and I'm sure Caspian is as well."

"Really?" That surprises me. I wouldn't have thought someone as strong as Dmitri or Caspian would be worried of something as simple as a parley. Then again this is Onyx we're dealing with.

"Onyx isn't a stable man; he wasn't even before his father died and now his insanity is only going to grow and get worse," Dmitri says. "This isn't something he is going to let drop, especially after what happened at the Jubilee, so we will just have to see how tomorrow plays out and take it from there."

"I suppose so," I say, that cold fear is creeping up my spine again. It's been a while since I've felt like this. Now that I've had this weeks' intense training I feel more confident, but the prospect of actually going into a war I don't feel ready for is terrifying. I made a promise that I would make it through and I need to keep it.

"Don't be so nervous," Dmitri says, putting an arm around my shoulder and pulling me close. My heart starts to beat faster and my face heats up (hopefully I still look sweaty from sparring with Samuel). "Caspian has trained you well, you have the skill to handle yourself on your own and the rest of us will all be right beside you if you need us. You'll be fine."

"Thank you," I say and smile.

"You need to believe in yourself a little more," he chuckles. "You're a good soldier and you'll make it through."

And I believe him, not just because he's Dmitri and he knows the right things to say but because he's right. I can do this and I will face everything thrown at me. I have to; I have too many people that I need to protect.

Chapter 3

Another early start sees the twelve of us filing into a carriage to travel to the docks the following morning. The meeting with Onyx is to be held off shore and I'm much more comfortable with the idea of sailing than I am with any other kind of transportation so I feel a little less nervous than I thought I would, though still not very talkative at this time in the morning. With a week's worth of intense training behind me not even a decent sleep last night can keep me from nodding off as soon as the carriage starts moving. The plan was to close my eyes for a few minutes but the next thing I know Illyria is shaking my shoulder to wake me.

"Ari, we're here," she says.

I rub my hand over my face. "Okay," I mumble, trying to pull myself out of the fuzzy confines of sleep, blearily looking out of the carriage window at the docks.

Even though it's still quite early in the morning, the sun only just beginning to brighten the place, there are people everywhere and all of them look busy. I watch them for a moment, all going about their daily lives, and I wonder if they know that we're sailing out to meet the Cimmerians in order to stop a war. Looking at the docks now, I would have guessed they didn't but, then again, maybe the docks never stop like at home.

I climb out of the carriage and follow the others through the throngs of people. Thankfully there is no problem with customs this time (which is something I can *definitely* do without) and that's probably because everyone recognises us. There are a few cheers when people realise that we're walking among them but I let most of the noise wash over me. That is until I hear someone calling my name.

"Ari!" a familiar voice shouts.

I turn and see Levi weaving through the crowd to get to me. I smile when I see him. "Hey Levi."

"I thought that must be you," he says, grinning from ear to ear. "Look at you, a proper Neo Warrior now."

"Yeah Captain and everything," I reply, smiling back and showing him the patch on my jacket. "It's so good to see you."

"You too," he says. "So what are you guys doing out here?" So they don't know…

"Heading out to the ocean," I reply, trying to be as vague as possible. If no one knows that we're going to meet Onyx or that we're on the brink of war then I don't want to be responsible for causing a panic by letting it slip.

"Sounds exciting," Levi says. "I bet it's been a while since you've been sailing."

"Yeah but I remember everything you taught me," I grin.

"Good."

"You over from Neyara?" I ask, trying to steer the conversation away from what *I'm* doing here.

"Yeah," he says. "Dropped in with some supplies day before yesterday. Heading back once the ship is loaded with new things to take back and trade."

"How is everything back home?" I ask. I know I get news from my parents when they write to me but it will be good to get a different perspective on what's happening outside of life in the House.

"Pretty good," Levi says. "Hey, Aaron was really chuffed with that poster of you. I am officially the best."

"I should hope so," I chuckle. "That was my first ever autograph."

"He's now even more determined that he's going to be a Neo Warrior when he gets older," Levi says. "Mum is already despairing."

"You can tell him from me it's a lot of hard work," I say.

"I can imagine," Levi says.

I want to tell him to watch out in case anything happens but I don't know how to do that without letting him know that something is wrong. If civilians don't know about the possibility of a Cimmerian invasion, it's clearly because the king doesn't want to raise a panic. If I do anything to mess with that, then I'll be in so much trouble with Caspian it's not worth it.

I cast a glance over my shoulder to see Caspian and the rest of them standing by one of the ships a few feet away. "Listen I've got to go," I say, "but look after yourself, okay?"

"You too sweetheart," he says. He pulls me into a quick hug and he smells just like I remember: sea air and the ocean.

"See you," I say before I dart off to Caspian and the others while Levi disappears into the crowd. It was nice to see him even if it was only a fleeting conversation. Seeing him makes me miss home just that little bit more and reminds me of just how many people I'm doing this for. I don't want war to end up on our shores.

"You alright Ari?" Kat asks as I join them.

"Yeah, sorry," I say hurriedly. "Just saw an old friend from the island."

"You ready to get on the ship?" she asks.

"Yeah."

"Then let's go," Kat says. She heads up the gangplank and I follow after her. "Hey Kat?" I ask, falling into step with her.

"Yeah?"

"Why does no one know about what we're going out to do?" I ask, hedging around the subject just in case the sailors on deck have no idea what's going on either.

Kat sighs. "I don't know," she says. "I guess the king doesn't want to cause alarm so nothing has been announced yet."

"That's what I thought," I say.

I know it's the right thing to do: if we can talk Onyx out of this war then undue panic will have been caused if everyone finds out that he wants to start something. At the same time, it feels wrong knowing that no one else knows that we could be on the brink of something huge. "Don't question it too much," Kat says after a moment.

"What?"

"I know what you're thinking," she says. "I was too but don't overthink it otherwise you'll go crazy."

"I suppose," I say.

"Just do what I've been doing," she says. "Keep busy and don't spend too long inside your own head."

"Okay," I say. I open my mouth to say something else but before I can a man, who I assume is the ship's Captain, comes over to us and salutes. He looks like he might be from the House of Jupiter, with his shaggy storm cloud hair, but his eyes are Neptunian. He must be someone born of two Houses. I haven't met many people who are born of two Houses but Trista's kids are going to be half Neptunian and half Plutonian so I'll know a substantial number eventually.

"Second Commander Navroe," he says. "Captain Austin," he introduces himself.

"Captain Austin," Kat nods.

"I have some distressing news, Ma'am. One of our sailors has been taken ill and won't be able to sail," he says.

"What does that mean?" Kat asks.

"I need to find another look out for the crow's nest before we can push off," he says.

"And how long will that take?" Kat asks.

He shrugs. "I don't know, Ma'am," Austin says. "Finding a sailor who is currently not otherwise occupied could take hours."

"We don't have hours," Kat says. "If you can do it in less than one, the Neo Warriors will make it worth your while."

"With all due respect Second Commander," he says, "finding a *skilled* sailor in that short a time is not possible."

I might not be the kind of skilled he's looking for but I know enough to help out and the faster we get out on the water the better. Kat already seems stressed, this is only going to stress her out even more and there's no telling how angry Caspian is going to be if he finds out so I can at least offer. I clear my throat and the both of them turn to look at me.

"I know how to sail," I say, raising my hand slightly awkwardly. "I'm not overly experienced but when I came over from Neyara the sailors on the boat I was on taught me everything they know."

"Have you spent time in a crow's nest Captain Sirenia?" Austin asks.

"Yes," I reply. "Most of the time I spent on that ship was up in the crow's nest. I know what I'm looking for if I'm up there and if I'm needed then there are plenty of other things I can do as well." Kat and Austin share a look. "I mean if Second Commander Navroe is happy for me to of course."

Kat and Austin share another look.

"You're hired," Kat says. She turns to Austin. "Looks like you've found yourself a sailor."

"Thank you, Ma'am," Austin says, looking relieved.

"I'll go tell Commander Feioré that we're ready to push off," Kat says, "I'll leave you with Captain Sirenia." She heads off back onto the dock leaving me standing with Austin in tense silence.

"Sorry for just jumping in like that," I say. "I thought it would help rather than getting Commander Feioré involved."

"Thank you so much," Austin says. "I have no idea what would have happened if he found out we were down a man."

"Now you don't have to worry," I say, smiling.

"Thank you Captain," he says smiling. He's not much taller than I am (and he really doesn't look that much older that Kat or Dmitri) but he seems as if he has the weight of the world on his shoulders, although some of that seems to have been lifted now. I'm glad I was able to help with that. I might not be able to do much, but what I can, I will.

"Shall I show you the crow's nest?" he asks. "Please."

~ *** ~

I'm so happy to be out on the ocean again—it's like being back home, where I know what I'm doing and everything makes sense. All of this stuff with Onyx and the Cimmerians has me so uneasy and being able to feel the waves helps. Aside from a 'what the hell is Sirenia doing up there?' from Caspian, no one questions me staying up in the crow's nest for most of the week and a half we're out on the water. In order to make the journey to the meeting point as swift as possible, a lot of the sailors are using their magic to make the waves carry us faster and I help from time to time. I prefer to have my hands and my mind busy.

Thankfully this time I seem to be one of the few people who isn't a sailor who isn't suffering from our method of transportation, probably because I've spent my entire life on the ocean. Being up in the crow's nest is great because I can see everything; sometimes people come up to join me and I even get to see the outline of the coast of Neyara as we pass. If things go well and we don't end up going to war, I might ask if I can stop off and say hello to my parents. I'm sure they'd be happy to see everyone and it would be better than being on the water for however long it takes to get home with no breaks.

We're closing in on the meeting point, only a day away now, and I'm up in the crow's nest as normal. I take a quick look over the side. I'm not expecting to see anything as both the sky and the waves were clear this morning so I'm a little surprised to see a looming presence on the horizon. Squinting against the sun I try to make out what it is that's coming towards us. It looks like storm clouds but there's something about them that isn't quite right. I pull a telescope out of my pocket and open it out before placing it to my eye.

It takes a while for me to focus but when I finally manage my blood runs cold. Coming towards us on the water are about forty or fifty ships, all bearing the crest of the Cimmerian royal family on the sails. What the hell is Onyx doing bringing an armada with him? This is supposed to be a peace negotiation!

Swallowing down my fear and anger, I close the telescope and pocket it before I climb down to the deck. I don't know if anyone will have seen this from down here but I need to warn Caspian about this. I could be wrong and it could just be back up or trade but we can't take that chance. If the Cimmerians are preparing for a fight now, then we are woefully outnumbered. How are we supposed to fight an entire armada with just twelve of us? None of the rest of the people on this ship are soldiers—they wouldn't be able to fight so it would literally be us against however many of them there are.

As I hit the deck I make a beeline for the entrance to the cabins below. Wrenching the door open I come face to face with Ellis. He grins at me. "Hey Ari," he says, "you alright?"

"You seen Caspian?" I ask.

"Yeah he's in his cabin," Ellis replies. "Are you okay?"

"I'm fine," I toss over my shoulder as I stride past him. I want Caspian to be the first to know. Darting down the corridors until I reach Caspian's cabin I pound on the door, breathing heavily when I arrive. A moment later the door opens and Kat blinks at me in surprise.

"Ari..." she says, staring at me, "are you okay?"

"I need to see Commander Feioré," I say, panting slightly. "Is he here?"

"What is it?" Caspian asks, coming into the doorway.

"Commander," I say, "I was just up in the crow's nest and I saw about fifty ships coming towards us all bearing the crest of the Cimmerian royal family. Onyx is bringing an armada with him!"

Silence.

Caspian stares at me for a moment, taking in my flushed face and weighing up how to respond to this piece of information. "Show me," he says.

"Yes sir," I say. He closes the door behind him and the three of us begin to make our way up to the deck. Without any instruction from Caspian I shimmy up into the crow's nest. I can hear him climbing behind me but I don't wait. As soon as I'm up there I pull my telescope out of my pocket and open it out. Before he arrives, I need to make sure that I didn't mess this up completely and that I did actually see what I thought. Sure enough though, the ships are still there and they seem even closer now. Caspian jumps in behind me and I hand him the telescope.

"Over there," I say, pointing. Looking up I watch as he places the telescope to his eye and looks out over the horizon to where I indicated. He stays like that for a moment before he solemnly lowers the telescope and hands it back to me.

"That's unfortunate," he says. He sounds surprisingly calm all things considered and he looks as cool as ever as he climbs out of the crow's nest and back down. I follow him back down and as soon as my feet hit the deck there seems to be a flurry of activity as Caspian calls us all to him.

"Navroe, head down to the armoury see how much artillery we have if we have to fight," Caspian says.

Kat nods. "Will do."

"Van Garret," Caspian says turning to Luciana as Kat leaves.

"Yes sir," Luciana says, saluting.

"Fly back to the mainland, assemble our fleet as quickly as possible and send them our way as soon as they're ready. If you can rally some troops by air that would be better."

"Can do," Luciana says.

"I know we're a good day's flight away so make sure that you take enough time to rest properly before returning," Caspian says.

"Sure thing," Luciana says. She strips off her coat and places the goggles she wears around her neck over her eyes before she folds her coat over her arm. Tossing a wink my way she take off, running the length of the ship, her huge wings beating as she jumps off the end and rises up into the sky, as magnificent as an eagle.

"The rest of you—I want you to be ready," Caspian says. "If Onyx tries to fight us out here when we are outmatched, it is going to be difficult for us to overpower him without losing too many lives. We will ready ourselves for the peace negotiation but, after seeing this, I would say that peace is the last thing on his mind."

"Yes Commander," we all say in unison.

"That was a good spot Sirenia," Caspian tells me as everyone else disperses to ready themselves to meet this armada. "Well done."

"Thank you sir."

"Ready yourself," Caspian says. "If it is a fight Onyx wants, then it is a fight he is going to get. We're in your forte here and you may be needed more than the others. Stay in the crow's nest and let me know of any and all developments."

"Yes sir," I reply before darting back up into the crow's nest. My head is spinning but I just about manage to make it up there without getting too dizzy. This is it. This is what my training has been about and this will prove if I am ready or not to fight in this war, although really if we could avoid one I'd much prefer it.

Taking my telescope out again I look out at the looming armada. Looking at it for as long as I can stomach I eventually lower the telescope again and put it back in my pocket. Soon I won't need it, I can already see the outline of the ships without it. I hope to god that Caspian can come up with a plan before it's too late.

~ *** ~

The following morning, everyone is assembled out on the deck. The ship's sailors are going about their daily business but there is an underlying tension that everyone seems to be carrying. I'm tense but I try not to let it show too much. The last thing I want is for anyone to think that I'm nervous and start coddling me. I'm a soldier now, so I'll damn well act like it.

We face off against Onyx's armada. To be just one ship in front of an army of this many is quite daunting. If Caspian is bothered by Onyx suddenly showing up with about fifty other ships, he doesn't show it. He looks as calm and collected as ever as one of the ships, the one at the head, breaks off from the rest and crosses the small distance to meet us.

"All of you stay silent," Caspian orders. "I will talk to Onyx: see why he has turned up with this many ships and we will take it from there."

Onyx's ship pulls up alongside ours and he is standing on the deck, leaning against the railings as if he doesn't have a care in the world. Even from as far away as I am I can tell that he's smirking. He's on top of the world and he knows that he's got us right where he wants us. What I wouldn't give to punch him…

"Ah Commander Feioré," Onyx says, still looking smug, "what a pleasure it is to see you out here on such a fine day."

"King Onyx," Caspian says, his voice a little more pinched than normal and I can tell that he's trying to hold back his fury. Onyx has crossed a line with this one. "I was under the impression that we were here for negotiations of peace and yet here you are with a great deal more ships at your disposal than I am."

Onyx shrugs. "When dealing with heathen magic users like you one does have to be prepared, wouldn't you say?"

I can feel myself bristling, righteous anger bubbling up under the surface. How dare this prick say that we're untrustworthy? Not when he's done *this* and we're supposed to be trying for peace!

If Caspian is affected at all, he still doesn't show it. He remains as calm as ever. "Yet we have never proven ourselves to be untrustworthy to you," he says. "We have done nothing to suggest that we are in any way devious or underhanded."

"If you say so," Onyx replies, "but I would beg to differ on that front. Once a lying heathen, always a lying heathen."

"Then maybe we should bury our differences and focus on how we can move on from this without involving our countries," Caspian says. "I don't want to drag the Braxian people into a war and I know you don't want to do the same with your own people."

"So cocky," Onyx chuckles humourlessly. "You think you know better than everyone just because you're named the Commander of the supposed best of the best. The position has clearly gone to your head."

"You imply that your new position hasn't gone to yours," Caspian says coolly.

Onyx laughs. "If you say so."

After a pause Caspian speaks again. "Onyx we need to talk this through. We need to discuss how to move ahead."

"Oh I have already moved ahead," Onyx says with a smirk.

"How so?"

"You honestly thought that we could have a peace negotiation after what you did to our country?" Onyx asks.

Caspian says nothing for a moment. He seems to be thinking over what Onyx has just said and, I must admit, I'm a little confused as well. What does he mean by what we did? As far as I'm aware we haven't directly done anything, although…

"Is this still about the test of skill?" Caspian asks in exasperation. "Because if it is then there must be a better way to settle our differences that doesn't involve both of our countries in a war that may end up costing more lives that necessary."

"And what about what you did to my father?" Onyx asks.

"What?"

What does he mean what we did? We didn't do anything to Zircon—his death was as much of a shock to us as it was to everyone else. Then again after what Amara found out from examining his body and what we heard from the messenger then he's going to keep up this pretence that we were the ones responsible for his death.

"You know you killed him," Onyx says. "There is no point in trying to deny it."

"And what evidence do you have to suggest that we did?" Caspian says.

"You left almost as soon as it was announced that he had died," Onyx says. "I don't need more evidence but what was done to his body speaks for itself."

"And you have been spreading these lies throughout Cimmerian?" Caspian asks.

"What can I say?" Onyx shrugs, smirking. "You made it so easy for me."

"And this is how you intend to lead your people is it?" Caspian asks. "Through scaremongering and lies?"

"As opposed to how you lead yours?" Onyx shoots back in return.

"None of us have ever lied to you or any of the Cimmerian people, Onyx," Caspian says. "If this insult is still from your defeat, then I cannot help that. We won fairly and I have tried to apologise for any insult but if there is nothing I can do to make you realise that then we are going to have to settle this again."

"That's just what I hoped you would say," Onyx says, an unsettling grin spreading across his face.

Caspian shakes his head. "Why do you want this war so badly?"

"Because you and your people need to be made an example of," Onyx says. "Your heathen ways will be the death of everyone if you are allowed to continue. First we eliminated the Draconians to put a stop to their use of magic and now we will eliminate you."

"If there really is no reasoning with you, then we will have to settle this on the battlefield as this is so clearly what you want, but do we really have to endanger thousands of innocent lives on both sides?"

Onyx laughs. "Did you really think that by coming out here to face me you could stop the war that is coming for you?"

"I was hoping that we could talk about this like rational men," Caspian replies. "Are you telling me that I was mistaken?"

"War is upon you, Commander Feioré, whether you like it or not," Onyx says. "There was nothing that you could have said or done that would have prevented it." What? No!

There is a moment of silence, the entire ship holding its breath in anticipation and worry.

This can't be happening—what is he talking about?

"What have you done, Onyx?" Caspian growls.

"As we speak my sister Sapphire and an army of her own are making their way to your lands to start the invasion," Onyx laughs heartlessly. "She will reach the first point of the Braxian Empire before you can even catch up to her."

The first point of the Braxian Empire… Neyara! A high-pitched squeak escapes my lips before I can stop it. I slap a hand over my mouth but it's too late. Both Caspian and Onyx turn to me, Caspian glaring and Onyx smirking. Shit! Now he knows.

"Ah, that's very interesting," Onyx says. "It seems as if one of you is very invested in this invasion."

"Why are you doing this, Onyx?" Caspian asks. "Thousands of lives will be lost if you continue."

"The lives of heathens mean nothing to me," he says. "The invasion is happening and you cannot stop it."

No, this can't be happening! They're going to be reaching Neyara soon if they've had enough of a head start and there is no way that we'd be able to get there in time or get a warning to my parents as Luciana has already gone off to the mainland to rally the troops. My entire body starts to shake and I'm trying to hold myself together but I don't seem to be doing a very good job because that cold sickness is creeping into me again. Tears begin to form in my eyes and my head is spinning.

"Then you leave us no choice," Caspian says, turning his hard gaze back onto Onyx. "If you launch an unprovoked attack on innocent people, then we will hit back at you and yours with everything we have."

"Then prepare for a fight you have no hope of winning, Commander Feioré," Onyx says. He turns his back on us and begins to walk away.

"If that is what you *really* want," Caspian says. He clicks his fingers and a jet of fire heads for one of the ships near the front of Onyx's armada. The fire must hit the gunpowder reserve because seconds later the hull explodes, sending cracked parts of the ship raining down into the sea. Onyx spins round, his face like thunder.

"You son of a bitch!" he spits.

"This is what you wanted, isn't it?" Caspian growls. "If you aren't prepared for the consequences, then you are in for a rude awakening."

Onyx begins barking orders at the sailors on his ship as Caspian stalks away from the bow, shouting his own orders. All I can do is stand there and stare at the ruined ship in front of us. Even if the wind and the waves are on our side there's no way we'll reach the island in time to stop Sapphire. I have to do something; I can't just sit by and wait for my home to be invaded and do nothing to stop it!

Caspian will be so angry if I ask to leave on my own but I can't sit and wait to hear that the worst has happened. I know that there are enough people on Neyara that they would be able to handle themselves in a fight but at the same time what if they can't win against soldiers? I can't stand by and do nothing.

I swiftly come back to life and dash after Caspian. "Commander Feioré!" I cry over the noise as I reach him.

"What is it Sirenia?" he asks, sounding irritated already.

"Please let me go ahead to Neyara," I beg. "If I can get there fast enough, then I can warn them about the invasion before Sapphire gets there and they can prepare for it."

Caspian sighs. "Sirenia, I know this is your family and your homeland that we're talking about but I cannot just let you drop everything and leave. It's too dangerous."

"Commander, please," I beg and I can feel the tears pricking the corners of my eyes again. "Please let me go ahead. I can't stay here and do nothing, otherwise they have no time to prepare and fight back."

"And how do you propose to get there in time?" he asks sceptically.

"I don't know," I almost cry, "I'll swim if I have to! I know that I can get there faster than this ship."

"There's no need for that," Caspian says, almost in despair of me. "Esteria can take you; it will take no time at all with him."

"Thank you Commander," I say hurriedly. I didn't think he would leave me hanging on like that. A couple of days to get back to Neyara and I would be going stir crazy with worry. "Thank you so much!"

"You're not going alone though," Caspian says.

"What?"

"I will allow you to go to warn your family and help them fight off the Cimmerians but I cannot, in all good conscience, send you alone. If Sapphire has reached there already, then it will be much too dangerous and, as the newest of my Neo Warriors, I won't send you to your possible death alone," he says.

"Who is going to accompany me?" I ask.

"I'll go with you," he says. "I'll leave Navroe in charge here."

"Thank you sir," I say, choking back tears.

"Lunest will come with us as well," he says. "If we have an opening for communication back to the ship, then we can work out just how far behind them we are."

"Thank you Commander." I say. I'm still worried that we might not get there in time but if I can leave now then I can at least try and that's enough.

Caspian places a hand on my shoulder. "Go and take a moment to collect yourself," he tells me. "I'll summon Lunest and Esteria. Be back on deck in fifteen minutes to leave."

"Yes Commander," I say and dart back to my quarters.

As I reach my door I pull out my key to unlock it and my hands are shaking so much I can barely get it in the lock. I fumble, trying to get a decent grip on the key but I can't and I end up dropping it. It clatters to the floor and something inside me breaks. Leaning against the door for support the tears begin to fall hard and fast down my cheeks.

I can barely see or breathe. All I can do is clutch the door for support. There are too many questions floating around my head and each and every one of them filling me with dread. What if something happens to them? What if I don't get there in time? I can't afford to fall apart now but I can't seem to be able to keep myself together.

There is a gentle hand on my shoulder and I turn my tear streaked face up to see Dmitri standing behind me. Without a word he bends down, picks up the key and opens the door for me. I allow him to steer me into the room and sit me down on the edge of my bed. I can't even speak: all I can do is cry and wait for the pain and the anguish to stop. Clutching the sides of my head I start fisting my hair in my hands to try and hold some of it in.

This can't be happening. This can't be happening. This can't be happening!

Dmitri gently places his hands on top of mine. The chill of the metal one makes me jump slightly and I open my eyes, looking into his. He gives me a kind, encouraging smile and his grip tightens ever so slightly. I loosen my own grip and let him prise my hands away from my hair. He lets go of one and wipes away my tears with his flesh hand.

"Everything is going to be okay," he says softly.

"How?" I ask, voice quiet.

"I don't have all the answers," he says kindly, "but I know that you can do this. You can be brave and get through this."

"But what if I can't?" I whisper, afraid that if I try to speak any louder, my voice will break.

"You can," he says. "You've passed your training, you've more than proven that you're good enough and you are smarter and braver than you think you are. I know you're still new to this but you will be alright."

"But what about everyone else?" I ask. "What about my family? My home? My friends?"

"I can't promise anything," he says. "I don't want to in case I'm wrong, but I can promise that whatever happens the rest of us will be here to help you. You're so strong Ari; you will get through this."

"But what if I'm not though?"

Dmitri takes my hands again and gives them a squeeze. "You are. You can do this. I believe you can."

"You do?"

"Yes," he says. "We need you at your best and you can't do that if you're letting your head get the better of you."

"Okay…"

"Now, I have no idea how this is going to play out but I can tell you that we are all behind you one hundred percent," he says.

"Okay," I say again, nodding and sniffing.

"You think you're ready to go back up?"

I nod. "Yeah."

"Good." He gives my hands another squeeze before he gets up and pulls me to my feet. "Go and give your face a wash and we'll get you back up on deck."

"Thank you," I say.

On shaking legs, I make my way over to the sink in the corner of the room. Cupping my hands together I conjure some water into them and splash it over my face. I do this a few times before my face is numb from the cold and I feel a little better. I blindly reach for a towel and dry off before looking into the mirror. My eyes are still a little red and puffy but hopefully no one will notice too much.

Dmitri appears in the mirror behind me and I turn and throw my arms around his waist. He's solid and warm and just the support I need. He hugs me back as I try not to start crying again. He drops a kiss on the top of my head and I'm not ashamed to say that that also makes me feel a lot better too.

"You ready to go back out there?" he asks as he pulls away.

"Yeah," I reply, running the back of my hand over my face. "Thank you."

"It's alright," he says, "I knew hearing that was going to be hard for you and I didn't think that you should be left alone."

"All I want is to know that my family are safe," I say.

"I know you do," he says. He places his hand on my shoulder and gives it a squeeze. "Just get home, deal with everything else from there."

I nod. "Okay." I take a deep breath and we leave my room. Dmitri locks the door and presents the key to me.

"I can keep hold of this if you want me to," he says.

"Yes please," I reply. "Not that there's anything in there of any value but I don't want to lose it while I'm away—I'll be so angry if I can't get back in."

He chuckles. "I'll keep them safe for you."

We head back up to the deck where Caspian, Illyria and Orion are waiting for us. Beginning to trembling with nerves again I take a deep steadying breath. I have no idea what I'm going to find when I get home but I won't know until we arrive and I'm going to have to prepare myself for anything. As I reach the three of them I salute.

"Captain Ariana Sirenia reporting for duty," I announce.

"Good," Caspian says. "If the three of you are ready, then we should leave as soon as possible." He turns to Orion. "Esteria, if you would do the honours."

Orion holds out his hand and the colour in his hair drains out, travelling down his arm to form a black hole, just as it had back in Cimmerian. It's still one of the most fascinating things I have ever seen, despite the circumstances.

"Follow me," he tells us before he steps into it. Caspian steps through, followed by Illyria. I cast a quick glance at Dmitri and he gives me an encouraging nod before I take a deep breath and step through myself.

Having never been through a black hole before I can safely say that I would really like to never have to go through one again. It's like being thrown forward at terrific speed but leaving the rest of your body behind. My stomach lurches horribly, my head spins and it feels like I'm being ripped apart and then put back together again atom by atom. It's genuinely unpleasant but I don't really have that much time to dwell on it because it's almost over before I know it (I don't know if that makes it any better or worse though). The effects, however, are not.

As soon as we arrive on solid ground I instantly sink to my knees, coughing and dry heaving as my head spins horribly. I've barely eaten anything so I can't even throw it back up: all there is, is bile.

"Sorry," Orion says, although he doesn't really sound it. In fact, he doesn't sound much better than I feel. "You get used to it the more you do it."

"If you say so," I splutter, spitting onto the ground.

"Do you want me to head back or do you want me to stay?" Orion asks Caspian. "I bought you to the coast as this was the only place I knew how to get to."

"It's quite alright, you head back and rest," Caspian tells him. "If we need you, I can contact you through Lunest."

"Sure sure," Orion says. He steps back through the black hole and it disappears with him.

"You alright Ari?" Illyria asks after a short pause. "Can you stand?"

"Yeah," I say, spitting again and heaving myself to my feet. The world spins horribly for a second but I manage to stay on my feet. Once my head is clearer I look over in the direction of the House. Nothing seems to be out of the ordinary—everything seems just as it always is—but I'm still uneasy. I'll feel a lot better when I see my family. The thought of what could possibly happen if the Cimmerians get here unannounced replaces any sickness. I need to warn my family about what might happen before it's too late. They need to be prepared. I just hope we get there in time…

Chapter 4

"Are you alright Ari?" Illyria asks, her voice breaking through the buzzing that has been filling my head since we hit land.

I give myself a shake. "Yeah I'm fine," I reply but my voice sounds different. The carefree note that's usually there is gone and is replaced with a tremor. I realise I've just been staring in the direction of the House for a good couple of minutes and I know we should head over there as soon as possible but I can't seem to get my legs to move.

Illyria places a gentle hand on my shoulder and she can probably feel me trembling but she's nice enough not to say anything. "Do you need a bit longer?" she asks quietly so that only I can hear her.

Yes... No... I don't know...

"I'm okay," I say firmly.

"Shall we go then?" Caspian asks from behind me. I cast a glance over my shoulder and he has an eyebrow raised at me. "Or did you leave all that fighting spirit of yours back on the ship?" He has a point, I did say I would swim if I had to.

"It's this way," I say and head off in the direction of the House.

My legs feel like lead and it takes every ounce of strength I have to keep moving but I manage it. The gravel of the road crunches under my feet and I listen to the wind rustling through the trees and grass, hoping to hear any sign that something is out of the ordinary. The ocean is restless—I can feel it deep down in my bones but that might just be because I'm restless. I don't want to jump to any conclusions yet, not until I've seen another Neptunian.

"It's beautiful here," Illyria says, breaking the tense silence hanging between us.

"It is, isn't it?" Caspian agrees. "Very peaceful."

"Is it always like this Ari?" Illyria asks and the tension in my shoulders relaxes a little. She has a very soothing voice and I know that she's trying to distract me from thinking too much until we know for definite how far behind or ahead of Sapphire we are.

"It is out here," I say. "The closer you get to the docks and the House there's usually a little bit more going on."

"We should bring the rest of them out here when we're done with this," Illyria says. "I'm sure they'd love to come and spend some time relaxing. I don't think anyone has been out here for any significant length of time."

"I have," Caspian says.

"Really?" Illyria asks. "When?"

"Just after I joined the Neo Warriors," he replies. "Sirenia probably wouldn't remember, you were quite young at the time."

"I was seven," I say absently. I remember a lot of people coming and I remember being told that they were the Neo Warriors but I can't remember why they came or what they were doing while they stayed.

"I bet you were a right cute little thing when you were a kid," Illyria says. "So what do you say? Once all this is over, party at Ari's?"

"Sure," I reply, allowing myself to laugh. "I'm sure my family will be only too happy to…" I tail off, the words catching in my throat. The possibility that there won't be anyone there when we get to the House flashes through my mind and I can't continue. Who knows what we're going to find when we arrive? Why did the only place Orion know here have to be the coast? If he'd gotten us closer then we wouldn't be wasting time walking.

"Sirenia," Caspian says, his voice cutting through my thoughts again. "Which way?"

Looking up I realise that we're at a crossroads and I stare at it for a moment. I've been so lost in my head I momentarily forget where we are and have to take a second to get my bearings.

"It's this way," I say finally, leading them off down the left path. "This will take us to the docks and the House is pretty close to there."

If anything is wrong, I'll know as soon as we get to the docks. While everything so far has looked as normal as ever, we ended up on one of the most deserted parts of Neyara when Orion brought us here so of course it would look normal. The closer we get the more on edge I feel. There seems to be no one in sight. No Cimmerian soldiers (which fills me with relief) but no Neptunians either (which fills me with dread). Everywhere I look and see no one where there should be people has a cold fear creeping down my spine and settling in my stomach. There should be more people around than this.

"Not a Cimmerian soldier in sight," Illyria says as if voicing my thoughts. "We might have gotten here before them."

"Let's not be too hasty," Caspian says. "Just because we haven't seen them yet doesn't mean they're not out there. Keep your wits about you—there's nothing to say that they're not waiting for us to start an ambush and have no interest in civilians at all."

"You think that might be a possibility?" Illyria asks.

"Maybe," Caspian says. "Both Onyx and Sapphire are unpredictable enough to start an invasion without thought when we were supposed to be having discussions of peace so I would put nothing past them. It wouldn't surprise me in the slightest to know that we were their real targets and they only came here to lure us into a trap."

"Knowing that one of us is from here is a handy bit of information," Illyria says.

"Indeed," Caspian says, giving me a pointed look.

Hastily I look away, saying nothing. I shouldn't have made that sound back on the ship but I did and even if they didn't know I was from here beforehand it could already have been too late. There are too many unanswered questions to start placing blame on anyone. If Onyx was just setting a trap for us, I wouldn't put that past him either; if he can find a way to get his hands on Caspian then he'll take it. I just hope that Caspian's right: the Cimmerians do just want us and they'll leave the locals alone.

I'll know as soon as we get to the docks.

The docks are always busy and if they're not then something is definitely wrong. Ever since I can remember there has always been some kind of activity down there: the docks don't stop. Ours aren't quite on the same scale as the mainland but they're pretty close. I can't shake off this feeling that something is wrong but I don't want to voice it just in case I'm right because I don't know what it is yet. I could just be fretting because the ocean is restless.

"Saying that, there don't seem to be any Cimmerian ships around," Caspian says as he casts a glance out towards the sea.

"That doesn't mean anything," I say.

"How so?"

"There are so many coves around the coast they could hide a couple of small ships easily," I reply. "They want this to be a surprise invasion, otherwise they wouldn't have bothered with the pretence of talking; they will have been looking for somewhere to hide."

"Making any invasion have maximum impact," Illyria says, understanding.

"We're the only port between the mainland and Cimmerian," I say. "If they control Neyara, they control a lot of what goes out to Mainland Brax."

"Hitting us where it hurts," Caspian says. "I trust you know where all these coves and hide outs are Sirenia?"

"I know this island like the back of my hand," I say. "If they're hiding in the coves, I can find them."

"We may need you to," Caspian says. "If there is no sign of them anywhere on land, we will assume that they're waiting to ambush us when we arrive by sea."

"Yes sir," I say.

I don't quite know if that's better or worse. Having them wait to ambush us would mean that they haven't started attacking yet, giving me a chance to warn people. This is all too much for me to take in. All I want to do is get to the House and make sure my family is safe—everything else can come later.

"Sirenia," Caspian says as we reach another crossroads.

"Yes sir?"

"Which way now?"

"Down here," I say and lead them down a steep path that will take us to the outskirts of the docks.

When we get there a few minutes later, all of my worst fears seem to be confirmed. The place is deserted. I can't quite see the centre yet but even now, on the outskirts, there would be sailors and merchants running around—I'd be able to hear people talking and shouting at each other as they went about their business.

"Not a very lively place," Illyria mutters.

"Something's wrong," I say. "There should be people, even out here."

"What are you thinking?" Caspian asks.

"I don't know," I reply. "Something doesn't feel right. Even on a slow trade day it's not this quiet."

"Maybe we're already too late," Illyria says.

"We'll know for sure soon," Caspian agrees.

My legs are trembling as I lead the two of them into the heart of the docks and as soon as the sight of it meets my eyes I feel sick and my blood runs cold. Close to where we're standing, lying face down with blood congealing on the back of their head, is a sailor. The uniform is unmistakeable—I stared at it for long enough while on my journey to the mainland—and I now know that this is only the beginning. Tearing my eyes away from the sailor I continue to look around, taking in all the ruined market stalls.

A young woman who sold flowers lies, twisted and broken, among bloodstained petals. Red slowly spreading down the front of her stall and onto the cobble, most of her flowers destroyed in the raid. Crates and barrels have been smashed, some of them containing cargo with their contents left to spill onto the floor; a different kind of blood. One stall owner—a middle aged man who sold knives for cooking—gutted with one of his own blades and left to rot in the sun along with the fish strewn on the ground. It's as if someone has taken a knife to the heart of the Neptunians and has left the blood to flow. I sink to my knees, my legs unable and unwilling to hold me up anymore.

This was them. It must have been. Who else would cause destruction like this? I can't move; it feels like I'm going to be sick but my body can't seem to pull up the strength to do that either. All I can do is sit and stare at the destruction around me. My chest feels like someone has a hold of my heart and is squeezing it, making it hard for me to breathe or even move.

"Sirenia," Caspian says, trying to rouse me into moving.

"Ari we can't stay here," Illyria says. "I know this looks bad but it might not be like this on the rest of the island."

"Lunest," Caspian says, almost as a warning.

"I'm just saying," Illyria almost snaps and I've never heard her sound so firm with anyone, least of all with Caspian. "We won't know until we go and find out."

"Right," I say, shakily pushing myself to my feet again. My legs still feel as if they're made of jelly but I just about manage to take a few steps in the direction of the House. I stumble slightly and Illyria catches me.

"You're alright," she says as I lean on her for support. "I've got you."

I manage a few more steps, desperately trying to fight the spinning of my head and the sickness threatening to envelop me. I don't know anything yet. I keep telling myself that because it's the only thing that is keeping me going.

Deep breaths and the knowledge that both Caspian and Illyria are behind me is the only strength I have.

That is until I hear a soft groan.

It's faint and muffled by a lot of debris but it's there and it's what I need to bring me back to myself—the sign that someone here is still alive. I stop for a second and listen, trying to pick up where the noise is coming from, not even totally sure that I heard it in the first place but after a second I hear it again.

I dart off in the direction of the sound, ignoring Illyria calling after me. Falling to my knees in front of a pile of broken wood and twisted metal I begin frantically pulling it off the person underneath and throwing it away with a strength I didn't know I had. Eventually, under a lot of rubble, I unearth a person. At least I think it's a person, they're so battered and bloody I can't even tell. With everything that had been pressing down on them now off they cough and hazy eyes flutter open. The man, for I can see it's a man now that I've removed the last bit of wood from his chest, squints at me, trying to focus on me.

"I know your face," he says softly.

I have no idea who this man is—one of the sailors that I saw occasionally when I came to the docks but never had the chance to talk to—but I smile at him all the same. He doesn't look that much older than Illyria, he might even be younger than Caspian. I can't tell, his face is covered in too much blood and dirt. Tears fill my eyes as I look down his torso and see a large bit of metal pipe jutting out where his stomach should be.

"Miss Sirenia?" he asks as he reaches a trembling hand up towards my face. I take his hand and grip it tightly.

"Yeah," I say, my voice catching, "it's me. What's your name?"

"Name's Thomas," he says. He doesn't seem in any way put out that he knows who I am but I don't know his name. In fact, he probably expects it: I'm a Neo Warrior now without being the granddaughter of the Head of the House.

"Hi Thomas."

"When did you get here miss?" he asks.

"Not long ago," I reply and that seems to bring him some comfort.

He smiles but it looks as if it costs a lot of effort. "Good," he says. "Don't want you getting mixed up in all this."

"What happened?" I ask but I'm not sure if I really want to know.

"We were taking in ships from the mainland like normal," he says. "Then some merchant ship start coming in, weren't sure who it was at first but the closer they got we realised they were Cimmerians." He stops to cough and blood begins to trail down his chin. "We waved them in, not like their trade ships are out of the ordinary, only to be blown away by a load of cannon fire. Once they'd levelled the docks they made port and Cimmerian soldiers got off and started attacking. Everyone who was still standing tried to hold them back but they were better trained and we didn't stand a chance. Everyone was rounded up and taken further inland so the soldiers could round up more of us."

I clutch his hand, desperate to hold in the tears that are threatening to pour down my cheeks and swallow the lump in my throat, trying to compose myself enough to be able to talk. Turning as I feel a hand on my shoulder I see Illyria. She looks at Thomas and then at me with sad eyes and I know what that means: we can't save him. We might have been able to if we had Amara with us but there's nothing we can do for him as we are.

"Where are the Cimmerians now?" Caspian asks from behind me.

"I don't know," Thomas says. "I got knocked out for a while; they must have thought I was dead and not worth rounding up."

"How long ago was this?" Illyria asks.

"I'm not sure, could have been hours for all I know. I've got a wife and daughter," he says, his voice catching. "Hope they both got out okay. If you see them tell them, I love them."

"Tell them yourself," I say as the tears begin to spill down my cheeks.

He smiles at me and it's the smile of someone who knows their fate. "Her name's Sasha, daughter's called Connie. Will you tell them?"

"We can get you out of this," I say even though everyone knows I'm lying. I want to fight for him. "We can get you fixed and home to them."

Thomas chuckles but it quickly devolves into him coughing up more blood. "We both know this is it for me," he says. He gives my hand a tiny squeeze. "Will you tell them if you see them, tell them I love them?"

"I will," I whisper, unable to make my voice any louder.

Caspian, Illyria and I watch as Thomas' eyes flutter closed, his head falls to the side and he takes one last shuddering breath. His hand falls limp and I clutch it in both of mine, pressing his knuckles to my forehead as the tears begin to fall freely. Everything in me feels as if it's been plunged into icy water, my chest aching. He didn't deserve to die, not like this.

Illyria gives my shoulder a squeeze. "I'm sorry Ari," she says. "I'm sorry but there wasn't anything more we could do for him."

She's right, I know she is, but that doesn't stop it from hurting. I wish I could have done more—if we had just been here on time—but we never stood a chance of getting here before the invasion and Onyx made sure of it. That still doesn't answer where the soldiers are right now though. The docks look like a tsunami hit but there's no telling how long ago that was. They wouldn't have just destroyed the docks and left, they would have continued through the rest of the island until they found the people they were looking for.

No one was ever safe from this.

Caspian kneels down beside me. He reaches over and places his hand over Thomas' eyes, beginning to whisper something in a soft, lilting Martian. I've never heard Caspian speak Martian before, I've never heard anyone speak Martian before, but I expected it to be a much angrier language than it is. I don't know what he's saying but when he has finished he looks up at me. "A prayer for the fallen," he says. He draws his hand back and gets to his feet again.

My head begins to spin and it hurts to breathe as I let go of Thomas' hand. Gently I place it in the centre of his chest along with the other and then push myself up onto still trembling legs. I need to get to the House to see what happened there.

"Ari…?" Illyria asks looking up at me but I'm barely listening. There's only one thing on my mind now and no one will be able to talk me out of it.

Without thinking about it anymore, I turn and run in the direction of the House. I hear Caspian and Illyria calling after me but I don't even think about stopping. I know I should—both of them are my commanding officers, Caspian especially—but I need to know that my family are alive at least. As I run images flash through my mind, wondering what I'm going to find when I get to the House. The worst may have happened—they may all be dead—and I need to know. I need to see that someone here is still alive otherwise Thomas' dying face will haunt me forever.

I run until my legs ache and my lungs burn, twisting my way through streets and back alleys until I finally reach the House. I skid to a halt and double over, placing my hands on my knees as I struggle for breath. It feels like I'm wasting time but if there are Cimmerians inside I need to be able to fight.

I didn't think about that.

Cimmerians could be inside and I don't know if I can take on a whole group of them by myself if it comes down to a fight. I should have waited for Caspian and Illyria and now I don't know if I can go back to look for them. If I do I'll be even further behind the Cimmerians and then who knows what I'll find?

Looking up I see the front doors of the House already standing open and that makes the cold fear in my stomach begin to spread through my body. They don't look as if they've been smashed in but that still isn't very comforting. Just because they haven't forced their way in doesn't mean that they haven't come here.

Taking one last deep breath, I push myself back up, jogging over to the House and up the stairs to the doors. Even when I get closer it doesn't look as if the doors have been forced open or broken into but I'm still sick with worry. Now that I'm inside I can't quite bring myself to run, my legs still shaking with each step. Whether that's from running or from my nerves I can't even begin to wonder. The corridors look completely deserted and I still haven't seen any other people despite how far in I've come.

"Hello?" I call out, slightly breathless, my voice echoing off the walls. I swallow around the lump in my throat, trying to make my voice stick less. There still seems to be no one around as I get further in, sticking my head into different rooms to check. Nothing seems to have been moved and it still doesn't look as if the place has been ransacked but that still doesn't fill me with confidence. I don't know if it would make me feel better to know that soldiers have been through here and destroyed the place.

"Hello…" I call again. "Mum…Dad…Harmony…"

The further in I go the more I realise that the place has been cleared out and if anyone is still here there's only one room I'm going to find them in. My legs are still shaking as I begin to make my way to the council chamber. If anyone's still here, that's where they're going to be. The council should be there and anyone else who retreated for safety. Even though I pretty much know that no one else is here, I still duck my head into the few rooms dotted around until I reach the huge, heavy doors of the council chamber.

The doors are closed and I place a trembling hand against them. My breath catches again and I can't quite bring myself to open the door. I don't know what I'm going to find on the other side and that scares me more than anything. There are still no sounds from anywhere around me and I can't hear anything from inside the room. My hand still stays firmly planted on the door as I try to work up the courage to actually push it open.

No: I came all this way, probably disobeyed direct orders and everything. I can't back down now, not that I'm here.

One more deep breath to steady my nerves and I slowly push the door open. My eyes close as I do, not ready for the sight that's going to be in front of me, and walk in. I take a few steps in and let the door close behind me. It bangs shut a few seconds later, the sound echoing all around me. So far no one has said anything so there is a good chance that this place is just empty but I still don't know if I want to find out one way or the other yet. It takes me a good few minutes of standing there, the unsettling silence pressing in on me before I can work up the courage to finally open my eyes.

The sight that meets me shakes me to my very core.

On the council bench, where they would normally be sat, are the severed heads of the members of the High Council, all mounted onto spikes, some of them even sticking through the top of their skulls. I blink a few times, thinking that this can't possibly be what I'm actually seeing but every time my eyes open the same sight still greets me.

No…

No, this can't be real.

Cold sweat begins to make tracks down the back of my neck as I look at each of them, unable to take in what's happened. They're all dead: some of them even still have blood dripping down onto the stained top of the bench beneath them. They can't have been like this for long. I look at each of their faces in turn—Granddad, Dad, Mum and the rest of them—and feel sick to my stomach. The only people who don't seem to be here are Harmony, Trista's mother and her brother. Clearly they were the lucky ones.

I look down at the floor and see the bodies strewn over it. My mouth goes dry as I look over them. I can't even distinguish whose body is whose, they're all so mangled and covered with blood. The realisation that each of them was probably tortured before they were finally killed hits me like a kick in the gut. My gaze continues down to my feet and I see that I'm standing in a pool of blood that has slowly been making its way over to the door from the pile of bodies. Everything hits me with a shattering clarity and before I know what's happening I'm doubling over, throwing up the entire contents of my stomach onto the floor for the second time today. It feels like I'm dying as I continue to throw up until there's nothing left at all.

Once I've stopped dry heaving I take a few steps back so that I'm no longer standing in the blood but leaving a trail of bloody footprints back towards the door. It all gets too much for me and I sink to my knees. Fresh tears begin streaming down my face as I stare up at the bloodstained face of my mother and my heart burns.

This can't be happening.

This can't be happening.

This can't be happening!

No, this isn't real. I want to believe that this isn't real but the pain that's setting into every single fibre of my being tells me that it is. Everything aches and it's like I've been separated from my body. I knew that there was a possibility that I might find them dead, especially after seeing the docks and talking to Thomas, but I never thought that I would be met with something like this. This is worse than anything I could have imagined.

Through the fog filling my head that makes me wonder if I'm going to pass out, I just about hear the door open and close behind me. I can't even bring myself to look round and see who it is—I don't even care at this point although I doubt the Cimmerians would come back after wreaking this havoc, not unless they're waiting for us to get here. The tears are still falling down my face and all I can do is clench my fists against the floor and try to ride out the pain. I feel a hand on my shoulder and know that it's not the Cimmerians coming back for more—it's far too gentle for that.

"Ari..." Illyria's soft voice says from behind me and suddenly the half formed illusion that I might still be dreaming shatters.

A scream rips itself from my chest and I'm sobbing again. At least I think that sound is coming from me: it sounds like an animal dying. Everything seems to be crumbling all around me and it feels like I'll never be able to pick up all the pieces. My home has been destroyed, most of my family are dead and I don't know what's happened to the others. The screams and sobs racking my chest don't seem to stop, just echo off the walls around me, only serving as a reminder that the horror in front of me is real.

"Ari..." Illyria says again and it sounds as if she's crying as well. "Ari, I'm so sorry."

She wraps me up in her arms and holds me as if trying to keep me from breaking. I scream, sob and cry until my throat burns and no more sound will come out. The world has come to a juddering halt and it feels like I'm dying as well. Illyria holds me, trying desperately to comfort me but I don't think anything will comfort me right now. Finally the screams die down to whimpers and I collapse in her arms.

"Sirenia," Caspian says after my sobbing stops for a second so that I can take a painful, shuddering breath, "we need to go."

"Commander," Illyria says softly, imploringly.

"We can't stay here," Caspian says firmly. "If the Cimmerians have already been through here, then what's to say that they're not still here waiting to ambush us?"

"But Commander…"

"The longer that she stays here the worse it's going to be for her," he says.

"I know but—"

"This isn't a negotiation," Caspian snaps. "We're leaving."

I'm barely listening to them. I know they're talking about me but I can't bring myself to care. If I could move, then I would but none of my limbs seem to be working and I'm pretty sure that if I did stand up I would just fall back down again. I can't bring myself to look away from the council bench, even though the sight makes me sick I just can't take my eyes off their lifeless faces.

"Ari…" Illyria says, her voice close to my ear. "We need to go."

"No," I mumble, shaking my head.

"We need to," she says. "I'm sorry but we can't stay here." I shake my head again, refusing to move. "Ari please, come on!" She takes hold of my arms and tries to pull me to my feet. I feel so numb that I don't fight her, I let her pull me up so I'm standing, tears still streaming down my face. My legs are still shaking so I end up stumbling a little and I have to lean against her for support, gripping the front of her jacket to keep myself standing. If I let go, then I'll just collapse again. I'm still shaking and sobbing but there don't seem to be any more tears left in me, just dry sobs that wrack my chest and make me feel like I'm going to be sick again or pass out.

Illyria tries to steer me out of the room but I don't want to leave. Not yet. I shake my head and try to pull myself out of her grasp but I'm too shaky and she tightens her hold as I feebly try to fight her.

"Ari please don't do this to yourself," she says.

"I can't leave them," I whisper through my sobs, "not like this."

"Ari…we can't stay here," Illyria says again.

"I can't leave." Despite my shaking legs, my feet are planted firmly on the floor and I'm not going anywhere anytime soon.

Suddenly I'm gripped quite harshly and wrenched out of Illyria's arms. Caspian's strong fingers dig into my upper arms as he practically forces me to look at him.

"Sirenia, we need to leave," he says. "If you stay, this will ruin you. There might be more Cimmerian soldiers around and I won't leave you to suffer this same fate. What's done is done and we will deal with it when we find them. I will make them pay for this but first we need to leave and go back to the mainland before they reach there and try to do the same thing."

He's right—I know he is even if every single part of me is telling me to stay. This can't be allowed to happen on the mainland. They could wipe us out if we let them.

"Okay..." I say weakly.

I can't fight anymore. He's right and I know it. There is nothing I can do for my family now, not when they're already dead. The only thing I can do is find Sapphire and Onyx and take my revenge out on them when I stop feeling like this. I don't know how long it will take me to snap out of this but he is right—if I stay here it will only be worse in the long run.

"Then let's go," he says. He gives my arms a squeeze before he drags me to the door. "Do you want me to do anything more here?"

I take one last look over my shoulder at the scene behind me. A wave of nausea washes over me and I cover my mouth with my hand, only just about managing to swallow it down. I don't want to leave them like this but I can't bear to see the alternative; I know exactly what Caspian means when he asks that question and I don't know if I can handle that either. On top of everything else, I can't watch my home go up in flames so I shake my head.

"Then we'll leave it at that," he says and pushes the door open.

As soon as he opens it there is a flurry of activity: voices shouting, guns cocking and blades being unsheathed. I feel myself being harshly ripped away from Caspian, pulled up against an unforgiving body. There is a hand in my hair, forcing my head back, and something sharp being pressed to my throat. I watch as soldiers grab Illyria as well, trying to restrain both her and Caspian but to little avail as the pair fight against the hands trying to hold them. I should be trying to get away as well; I should be trying to help them but I can't muster up the energy to struggle after everything that's happened.

This is probably my fault, my screaming most likely alerted them to the fact that we've been here and where we are.

Caspian throws off the soldiers trying to restrain him and rounds on the ones that have obviously been hiding in the council chambers, ready and waiting to ambush us. His fingers are poised, ready to burn them where they stand but he sees me with a blade at my throat and suddenly stops. The soldiers grab him as he glares at the person holding me.

"How nice of you, of all people, to join us Commander Feioré," Sapphire's voice says close to my ear. Of course she'd be the one to be holding me hostage. I bet she's loving this, having us—Caspian especially—completely at her mercy. "I'm so glad the little siren decided to bring some company with her when she came for a home visit."

"This has nothing to do with her Sapphire," Caspian growls.

"I think it does," Sapphire says. She uses her grip on my hair to force me to look over at the council bench again. "That is your family, isn't it?"

I say nothing. Her grip tightens and I suck in a breath through my teeth. My scalp stings, it feels as if she's trying to rip my hair out at the roots, and my neck is starting to ache.

"If you won't answer me, then I'll make you."

There is a scuffling sound and she turns my head so I can see two soldiers forcing Illyria to her knees, spreading both her arms out so that she can't use her magic. She tries to struggle out of their grip but one of them pulls her arm, hard, and a sickening crack echoes around the walls. She screams and Caspian turns his glare on Sapphire again.

"Let them go Sapphire," he snarls.

"Not a chance," she says. "You think I'm going to pass up the opportunity to bring *you* to my brother? You won't fight back if there is a chance that anything will happen to your precious Neo Warriors."

Sapphire forces my head back even further so that Caspian can see her pushing the blade of her knife right up against my throat. It presses against my skin and I try not to breathe otherwise it will probably slice my throat open. I am leverage. I am still alive because Caspian will do anything to prevent Illyria and I from being killed. If Sapphire wanted me dead, then I would already be dead.

"Now are you going to cooperate and come quietly?" Sapphire asks, the hand that was in my hair suddenly gripping my chin, hard. "I would if I were you, not unless you want to see her pretty little head up on a spike with the rest of her filthy family."

"Let them go Sapphire," Caspian growls again. His eyes are blazing with a fire that I have never seen before: it's a burning hatred that would scorch anyone it's turned on and I'm amazed that Sapphire isn't dying under the pressure.

I should do something. My hands are still free and there is no way that Sapphire would suspect a magical attack from me right now because it would be suicide. My hands are shaking so much and I don't trust myself to do anything even remotely quickly. I can't just let her win though. My resolve hardens: I'm going to do something.

I flick my wrist at one of the soldiers holding Caspian and hit him square in the face with a jet of water. He falls to the floor, crying out in surprise and I'm about to send another jet into the face of another soldier but the blade Sapphire has at my throat is thrown and sinks into Illyria's thigh. Illyria screams again and I freeze. Sapphire's hand is in my hair again and she has another blade at my throat before I can even blink.

"Looks like we have a live wire here," she chuckles in my ear and presses the knife harder into my neck. It's not quite hard enough to break the skin but it's hard enough that it hurts like hell and it will if I make the wrong move again. "You see that?" she hisses forcing me to look at the blade sticking out of Illyria's thigh. "Next time I won't miss. Next time you pull something like that someone's going to pay for it with their life, you understand?"

I grit my teeth. My eyes dart to Caspian, then to Illyria and back again. There is a dark stain beginning to spread across the front of her trousers where the knife is and if Sapphire is that accurate with a blade who knows what else she's capable of. I nod as best I can with a knife to my throat.

"Good," she says and I don't have to look at her to know that she's smirking. "Now here's what's going to happen: we're going to take a little trip down to the dungeons and you're going to be the first guests in the starting point of the Braxian Empire that we hold. When Onyx arrives, we will claim this land for Cimmerian and you will be our first prisoners of war."

"A...and if we refuse?" Illyria asks, her voice breathy as she tries to compose herself enough to speak through the pain.

"I don't think you're in any position to refuse," Sapphire tells her.

"And if *I* refuse?" Caspian asks, surprisingly calm considering how he's looking at Sapphire like he wants to rip her head off. His fingers are poised again and ready to send each and every one of them to a flaming grave.

"Then she dies," Sapphire says. She grips my hair even tighter and presses the knife blade into my throat. I gasp, wincing at the pain. The skin breaks and a small trickle of blood make its way down my neck so I remain completely still for fear of her slicing my throat open.

Caspian looks from me to Illyria and back again before he looks over at the bodies of the council strewn over the room and he seems to realise that Sapphire has us completely backed into a corner. We could fight our way out but it is almost certain that only one of us will get out of this alive. He sighs angrily and holds up his hands in defence.

"Fine," he growls. "You win."

"Commander!" Illyria cries, looking at him in horror.

"It's over, Lunest," Caspian says.

"I'd listen to him if I were you," Sapphire says. "Give us a reason not to kill you where you kneel. Onyx wants him, I have what I want," she gives my hair a tug, "and you we have no real need for."

"That's not part of the deal Sapphire," Caspian growls. "They both live or I kill you all where you stand."

"Fine," Sapphire says sounding smug. "Restrain him and take them away."

It takes four soldiers to restrain Caspian, even though he doesn't appear to be fighting back, before he and Illyria are dragged out of the room. Illyria looks as if she's about to pass out from the pain in her leg and her shoulder and Caspian looks utterly defeated. I want to say something but I still can't do anything without potentially getting my throat cut by Sapphire's knife. We are completely beaten.

Sapphire waits until all the soldiers are out of the council chamber until we are the only two left in there before she forcibly turns me around again so that I have to stare at the heads of my family and everyone else I held dear.

"Take a good look at this, little siren," she hisses in my ear. "Remember that I did this and I will do the same thing to you and every single one of your people. I am capable of more than you can imagine and by the end of the day I will make you scream."

As I look at the bloody face of my mother I'm filled with a strange sense of calm. Sapphire has killed my entire family—I don't know whether Harmony is still alive or not—and she's destroyed my home. What more can she actually do to me? Killing me is the worst thing she could do and I really don't care. At least it would be over, if she killed me. I turn and look at her as best I can. My jaw is set and there is a fire blazing in my eyes that wasn't there a few moments ago. "I'd like to see you try."

Chapter 5

After she apprehended us Sapphire dragged Caspian, Illyria and I down to the dungeons right in the depths of the House, each of us in a separate cell, and once I'd been thrown into mine my arms were forced out to the sides as far as they'd go and chained in place. They angled me so that even breathing hurts as there's just enough pressure on my chest so that it's a struggle and I haven't been able to move without ripping my shoulders or my wrists. I heard the scuffling of Caspian and Illyria being locked up too but as soon as my cell door closed all I could make out was the muffled conversations of the soldiers keeping watch.

At first, I tried to keep track of the soldiers guarding my cell—listening out for when the voices change as I had nothing better to do—but they've all been speaking in Cimmerian and they all sound the same. I've lost track of how long I've been here already. It feels like it's only been a couple of days but it could be closer to a week. Occasionally a guard comes in with food and judging by how infrequently I see them I can only guess that it's about once a day. No point in starving us—you can't torture someone who's half dead. So far a guard (not always the same one) has come in with food six times so it's possible that I've been here for about six days.

It's been a long time since I've been down in the dungeons. When Harmony and I were younger, we used to come down here to explore and play around. Looking back on it now I'm not really sure why; it's not like there's much here. One day Harmony got locked in one of the cells and I couldn't open the door as I was only about five at the time. I ran upstairs, crying because I thought Harmony was locked in there forever, so Dad came and let her out. After that, we never went to the dungeons again but I'm here now and Dad sure as hell isn't coming to save me this time.

For the most part, the dungeons were unused but now that I'm back down here I realise why they were reserved for the worst kinds of criminals. It's dark, dank and there is no natural light, the only thing allowing me to see is a small paraffin lamp hanging from a corner of the cell. There's no water either and it makes my skin burn. Even away from the sea I can still feel the moisture in the air but down here there's nothing and it makes me dizzy. These cells is designed to hold water magic users and keep them from being alert enough to use their magic.

At first, I thought the restraints were simple chains. Uncomfortable, yes, but nothing more. Really after seeing the place after all these years I should have known. Not only do they keep my hands forced apart so I can't use magic (the problem about having to use your hands for casting large scale magic: if those are restrained you're screwed) they're cold, almost freezing. If I'm cold, my water magic doesn't work. I can't conjure anything without it hurting like hell and if I'm too cold it can just turn to ice and be useless. Six days in the freezing cold and the dark and I'm already wondering when someone other than a guard is going to turn up.

I hear the door of my cell unlock and I look up. The door opens and both Sapphire and Onyx step in, looking clean, well-rested and very smug. Of course they would. In their minds, they've won—they've got Caspian and have already taken over a point of the Braxian empire, of course they're smug. I clench my jaw, ready for a fight. I don't imagine that they've come all the way down here just to talk so this is not going to be a fun conversation (for me).

"If there's one thing—and, let's face it, there *is* only one thing—I love about you Braxians," Onyx muses as he runs a hand over the frame of the closed cell door, "is that you're so disgustingly practical."

I don't answer, just glare up at him.

"Magical prisons to hold people with magic," he says when I make no comment, taking my silence as the desire for an explanation. "What a novel idea. It makes holding anyone who would try to oppose us very simple."

"You have made it very easy for us," Sapphire says, a smirk gracing her lips and what I wouldn't give to have the use of my hands so I could punch her in the face.

Still I say nothing.

"She's not very talkative, is she?" Onyx observes, turning to Sapphire.

"There are ways that we can make her talk," Sapphire says. Her smirk widens. "Or at least scream."

She pulls a knife out of her pocket and before I can prepare myself for what's happening she crosses the room and sinks the blade into my upper left arm. I jam my teeth into my bottom lip and squeeze my eyes shut, desperately trying to stop myself from screaming in pain.

If I thought any of the pain I had suffered in my life up to this point was bad, it doesn't even come close. As the blade goes in it seems as if the entire world has slowed down and I can just feel it sinking into my flesh. For a second, I'm out of my own body and I can see it in my arm from the other side, see it ripping my skin apart and tearing the muscle. It's hot and like my entire body is throbbing. My arm is pulsing as if it's trying to force the blade out but it's not coming. I breathe heavily through my nose, trying to stay quiet. I'm not going to give Sapphire the satisfaction of knowing that it hurts although I'm pretty sure my face says just how much pain I'm in.

She leans her face closer to mine. "Are you going to sing for us now little siren?" she whispers.

"Get fucked," I spit through clenched teeth, glaring up at her.

Sapphire laughs and twists the blade. Oh god! My arm feels like it's on fire and I let out a cry without meaning to, needing to relieve some of the pressure building inside me. I didn't want to do that as she wants to know she's hurt me. Sapphire huffs out a soft laugh and gets to her feet, leaving the knife in my arm.

"Now you are going to tell us everything about your king, country and the defences they have around the mainland so that we can continue with our invasion," Onyx says stepping towards me.

"I don't know anything," I say through still-gritted teeth, panting through the agony coursing through my arm.

Sapphire reaches over and twists the knife again and this time I scream, totally unprepared for it. Blood slowly begins to run down my arm to drip onto the floor. I'm glad when she leaves it in there again, it's probably the only thing keeping me from starting to bleed out.

"I can do this all day," she hisses in my ear. "Question is can you."

"I don't know anything," I say again. "I'm just a rookie."

"Hardly call one of the Neo Warriors a rookie," Sapphire snorts. Without warning she rips the blade out of my arm and I let out another cry of pain before I can stop myself. Shit, that hurt! I let my head hang forward, trying to hold in the agony as best I can and trying to prevent Sapphire and Onyx from seeing the tears in my eyes. Blood trickles faster down my arm now and the open wound feels like it's on fire. After counting to thirty in my head, I let out the breath I've been holding, panting through the pain.

Damn…

A shadow falls in front of my line of vision and I just about manage to look up to see Onyx staring down at me. He watches me for a moment as if studying an animal he's just shot but not quite killed yet, working out whether to put it out of its misery or not, before he kneels down so that the two of us are eye-level.

"Now this doesn't have to be as hard as you seem to want to make it," he says softly, his voice supposedly comforting. "All you need to do it tell us how we can get close to the mainland and the king and we'll let you go."

"Like I believe you," I hiss.

"I can make it worth your while," he says. He reaches out and, with a surprisingly gentle hand, brushes my fringe out of my eyes. The smile on his face is anything but comforting though. "Just think about it, I can give you riches beyond your wildest dreams. You can have everything: safety, a life in Cimmerian—provided that you agree to follow us and give me what I want. You can have your homeland back, once I have Mainland Brax I'll have no need for this island. You can have whatever your heart desires and you can have what you crave more than anything in the entire world: your freedom."

"My whole family is dead," I say. "My homeland is in ruins, there are only a handful of people that I care about and I don't know if they're alive or dead or what. You really think I give a damn about my freedom?" Quite frankly it would be easier if they would just kill me and get it over with, at least then I wouldn't have to listen to him talking.

Onyx looks at me, bemused. "Really?" he asks. "There's no one you can think of that you care about other than the people we killed on arrival?"

"All the others are where you can't hurt them," I say. I hope to god that's true. I hope, more than anything, that Trista is safe with Jackson in the House of Pluto. I hope Harmony is somewhere away from all this as well and I hope that they both stay away.

Onyx smirks over his shoulder at Sapphire who opens the door of the cell and leaves, leaving it wide open. I watch her go and wait, wondering where she's going. Onyx offers me no explanation, just continues to watch my reaction. A few minutes later I suddenly hear screams, clear as anything, reverberating through the corridors and bouncing off the walls. It takes a moment for it to sink in and I recognise the voice as Illyria's. I tug on the chains holding me before the pain in my arm hits me again, I get a twinge in my shoulder and I stop.

"You know those tattoos of hers are quite resilient," Onyx says, "even the strongest acid we could find doesn't seem to be burning them off."

"You're a monster," I hiss.

He sneers. "Am I? I'm just trying to protect my people from those who have the power to destroy our lives and everything we hold dear."

"And when have we ever made any move to destroy you?" I ask. "As far as I can tell, you're always the ones who start the wars. You're the only reason people like me even exist. The Neo Warriors wasn't even a division until the Cimmerians first tried to invade."

"So you do know something," he smirks.

"That's all!" I cry. "All I know is what I've read in books about previous wars and I've always been told that they were started by you."

"And the history books are always written by the victors," Onyx says.

"Then why invade at all?"

"Because my kings have known that it's only a matter of time before you and yours realise that you can easily take over," he says. "Why would you not want to take our lands and destroy our people?"

"Because we have enough of our own," I reply.

There is another series of screams from down the corridor and my heart tugs, tears brimming in my eyes as I listen. I can only imagine what Sapphire's doing to Illyria in there and here I am powerless to do anything to stop it.

"Please stop," I sob, my emotions getting the better of me.

"Why?" Onyx asks. "Are you going to tell me what I want to know?"

"I told you I don't know anything," I say.

"You don't know anything about how your army operates at all?" he asks. "You know nothing of your own defences or what your soldiers plan to do in the event of an invasion?"

"No," I reply. "I've only been doing this a few months, I haven't had time to learn everything yet."

"Well then," he says, smirking, almost as if he's happy that I don't know anything as it gives him an excuse to torture me, "it seems as if you and I are going to have a problem."

"Please stop," I say again as the screams from down the hall begin to trail off into pained whimpers that still seem to echo down to me.

Onyx says nothing, just chuckles softly and gets to his feet. After a minute or so of nothing, Sapphire comes back into my cell and closes the door behind her. She takes a handkerchief out of her pocket and wipes the blood from her hands. I want to ask her what she did but I don't think she'd tell me and I don't think I can actually stomach the answer.

"She doesn't seem to want to talk either," she says. "She just keeps jabbering away in that heathen language but she certainly screams very nicely."

Onyx chuckles. "You are having much too much fun with this dear sister."

"Why wouldn't I?" she smirks, looking directly at me, asserting her dominance. I refuse to look away though. She won't break me that easily. "They're so much fun to torture and it's been so long since I've been able to let off some steam."

"Try not to get too carried away though," Onyx says. "Just make sure you leave her alive. It wouldn't do to kill them now, not when we can use them later."

"What do you have in mind?" she asks. They're having this conversation in front of me knowing full well that I can hear and understand. They want me to witness this.

"Well," Onyx says, turning his smirk on me, "there are still nine more of *them* out there."

"No…" I gasp, unable to stop myself. No… They need to stay away. I can't lose anyone else. Both Sapphire and Onyx turn to me.

"And here was me thinking that you had nothing more to live for," Onyx says. "Isn't that what you just said or was that a bluff?"

"It seems our little siren is lying to us," Sapphire says.

She crosses the room and grabs me by the hair, forcing my head upwards so that I have to look at her. I wince slightly, trying to breathe through the pain but her grip is so strong I can't help but give in to the dull ache in my scalp and the stretch in my neck. The angle she's got me at also makes it hard to breathe. I glare up at her, still clinging desperately to not giving her the satisfaction of knowing that she's hurt me but I think she knows.

"Now are you going to tell us what we want to know or are we going to have to hurt more of the people you care about?" Onyx asks.

"I keep telling you that I don't know anything," I hiss as Sapphire gives my hair another harsh yank.

"If you don't want to tell us, that's fine," Sapphire says. "There is more than one way to make the siren sing."

"And I think I know the perfect way," Onyx says, smirking.

"What are you going to do?" I ask, desperate to know even though I suspect they won't tell me.

Onyx says nothing in return he just leaves the cell, this time closing the door behind him. If I strain my ears, I can just about hear the sound of him hailing down a soldier. I'm only half paying attention to him though, all of my focus is on Sapphire.

"You know it's so nice to know that you heathens bleed the same as the rest of us," she says. "Although I must admit, after cutting your friend open, your blood is a lot cleaner than I expected it to be."

I say nothing. I have nothing to say, so I exhale pointedly through my nose, trying to prove a point (I'm not sure what; I don't know what I'm trying to prove to her anymore but I'm going to prove something). She just laughs as she lets my head drop.

"Don't worry," she says, "I won't leave you out, I'll make sure you scream before I'm done with you."

"Like I said," I pant as I try to catch my breath, "I'd like to see you try."

She reaches behind my head and harshly tugs the tie out of my hair and it spills down around my shoulders, sticking to the sweat and blood coating my skin. For whatever reason, this seems to amuse her as she simply looks at me for a while before she gets to her feet. I watch her as she goes over to the door and what I wouldn't give to be able to shoot some water at her, even if it did nothing more than make her clothes slightly damp. She looks out into the corridor before she turns back to me.

"We've got a visitor for you," she says. "I hope you'll be happy to see them."

What does she mean visitor? ...Oh god, did they catch Orion too? They can't have done. We saw him leave before we even knew they were here. They can't have caught him without us seeing; he disappeared right in front of us.

The door to the cell opens all the way and a soldier comes in dragging a struggling Harmony with him. My jaw falls open. She's alive... As soon as she sees me she immediately stops struggling, staring at me in horror, and allows the guard to undo the restraints that are keeping her hands behind her back. Another guard comes down to kneel beside me, undoing the chains keeping me bound and it feels so good to finally let my arms drop once they're undone.

"I think we should let them have a moment alone," Onyx says. "There really is nothing like a touching family reunion, don't you think?"

"Are you sure that's wise?" Sapphire mutters. "What if they try anything?"

"They won't," Onyx says.

"How can you be so sure?"

"There's no way she'll leave the other two," Onyx says, looking pointedly at me. I meet his eyes as I rub my wrists to relieve some of the pain. Damn it, he's right. "Neither of them is powerful enough to take on us and all the soldiers by themselves so we have nothing to worry about."

"That's true," Sapphire says.

"Enjoy your time together," Onyx says as the two of them leave the cell, "it may be the last you have."

The sound of a key in the lock echoes around the walls and both Harmony and I wait before we move. As soon as we're sure that we have been left as alone as we can be she practically runs to me. She kneels beside me and throws her arms around me, pulling me into a hug and holding me as if she'll never let go. It's all too much and I start sobbing into her shoulder. I thought I would never see her again, I had no idea what had happened to her, but she's alive and she's here. Although I don't know how to feel about the last bit, it would be better for her if she wasn't.

"Ari," she says into my hair and continues to whisper my name like a mantra, almost as if she says it enough she'll know that she isn't dreaming.

"I'm so glad you're okay," I mumble into the crook of her neck, hugging her tighter. My arm stings as I tighten my grip but I don't care, I just want to hold onto her for as long as I can. She hugs me back just as tightly for a long moment before pulling back and holding me at arm's length so she can properly look at me. Her eyes fall on the deep gash on my arm, where blood is beginning to stick my shirt to my skin and has started to stain my hair.

She chokes on a sob. "Oh Ari, what have they done to you?" she asks, switching from Universal to Neptunian.

"It's nothing, it's fine," I say, following suit, tugging my shirt over the wound so she can't see it. It's good thinking on her part, switching to a language only we speak—the less they understand of what we're saying to each other the better. Illyria is apparently not talking in Universal so there's no reason for us to either.

"Ari you're bleeding," Harmony says, her tone a little sharper, "it's not nothing."

"It's fine," I lie. "I can barely feel it now."

She stares at me for a moment before she shakes her head, seeming to decide that it's useless to argue with me and changes tactic. "What are you doing here? I thought you were supposed to be training on the mainland."

"I came to warn everyone about a Cimmerian invasion," I say, "but clearly I got here a little too late."

"Cimmerian invasion?" she asks, confused. "What's going on?"

"It's a long story," I reply.

"Then tell me quickly."

"Okay." I take a deep breath. "So you know we went over to Cimmerian for the king's Jubilee?"

"Yes."

"Just as we were leaving, it was announced that Zircon had died and Onyx had been crowned in his place," I tell her.

"What?"

"Cimmerian declared war," I continue. "We went out to meet Onyx to try and negotiate peace so we didn't have to start a war and needlessly lose lives but he'd already sent his sister, Sapphire, over here to invade."

"And this is the first point they'd come to," Harmony said, nodding.

"I left as soon as he told us that Sapphire was heading this way," I tell her. "I was hoping that we would be able to get here before she arrived and warn everyone but we were already too late, even travelling with the help of a member of the House of the Stars."

"Did they capture all of you?"

"No," I say, shaking my head. "Only Caspian and Illyria came with me. He told everyone else to gather reinforcements and follow once we weren't so outnumbered."

"Thank god for small mercies. There's still hope then."

"Is there?" I ask. I know the others will stop at nothing to free us when they find out that we've been captured but that could take ages for word to get back to them.

"It's something," she says.

"So how did they capture you?" I ask. "As far as I knew you weren't on Neyara." I reach over and grab the front of her shirt as if to prove to myself that she is real. She's here and in front of me and alive. Any animosity there might have still been between us is completely forgotten.

"I was away when they got here too," she says. "I went to the House of Pluto with Trista's family to visit her and Jackson. It was just a general visit to see her and see how their trial living together is going before the official wedding preparations begin. Granddad wanted me to go alone as the new Head of the House, even though it's still not official yet." It will be now but I can't quite bring myself to say that yet.

"Then, while we were there, I got a message saying that there had been some kind of disturbance," she says. "I told Trista's family to stay behind with her and I came back as fast as I could. As soon as I stepped off the boat I was dragged back to the House and down here. I had no idea you were here as well. No one's told me anything."

"So Trista's still in the House of Pluto?" I ask.

"Yes." Harmony nods. "She's safe with Jackson and her family is too."

"Good," I say, tears beginning to stream down my face as I bury myself into her shoulder again. I wrap my arms around her and I don't think I'm ever going to be able to let go. "I'm so glad you're both alive. I thought I'd lost everyone."

"What do you mean?" she asks. "Ari…" She pushes me back so that she can look at the tears streaming down my face. "Ari what's happened?"

Oh… She doesn't know! I can't do this…I can't be the one to tell her that we are probably the only members of the Sirenia family left. Who else is going to though? It *is* just us now. That thought completely overwhelms me again and I dissolve into fresh tears, my chest heaving with the struggle of breathing through the sobs. Harmony hugs me as I cry into her chest before she tilts my head up and brushes my hair out of my face, trying to dry some of my tears but it's useless: they're replaced by new ones almost instantly.

"Ari…" she says softly, comfortingly, "what happened?"

"I'm sorry," I sob, choking on my own words, "I'm sorry I didn't get here in time." I cling to the front of her shirt, clenching my fists so tightly I might end up tearing it.

Harmony wraps her arms around me and strokes my hair, trying to soothe me as I cry. "It's okay," she whispers. "It's alright. Just tell me what's happened and I can help fix it."

"You can't fix this," I sob. "They're all gone and I couldn't do anything."

"Who is?" she asks and I feel my heart break again. I have to tell her, she can't find out from Onyx or Sapphire and she certainly can't find out how I did.

"Okay," I say swallowing my tears as best I can so that I can at least try and get the words out. "So after we found out about the invasion I came here as fast as I could with Caspian and Illyria. When we got to the docks, the place looked a wreck so I knew something was wrong." I stop to take a shuddering breath. My throat is burning and talking is becoming more and more painful but I have to get it out. "We found a sailor trapped in the rubble and he told us that the Cimmerians had invaded but we couldn't save him."

"Ari, I'm so sorry."

"That's not the worst of it."

"Go on."

"I went to the council chamber to find everyone and see what had happened but when I got there I found…I found…" I can't even finish the rest of the sentence before breaking down into fresh sobs as I remember the sight of Mum and Dad's heads on spikes. I sound like I'm dying and it feels like it too.

Harmony hugs me tighter, as if she's trying to hold in all my pain and hurt and take it on herself. "What is it?" she asks after a pause, once my sobs have died down, coaxing me to continue. "Tell me."

"They're all dead," I tell her. "Mum, Dad, Granddad, the rest of the council… they've all been killed."

Silence.

The only sound in the cell is my own heavy breathing for a moment before Harmony pushes me back to hold me at arm's length again, her eyes wide. She looks at me, searching my face for something to tell her that she misheard me, that I didn't just tell her that our entire family was killed by the bastards invading our home. When she finds no hint of a lie on my face, she shakes her head in disbelief.

"What?"

"Please don't make me say it again," I mumble. The more I say it the more it makes it real and not just some awful dream that I might wake up from some time. This is actually happening and I have to face it.

"They can't be," she says, shaking her head, her eyes brimming with tears as well.

"I'm sorry," I say.

"No," she whispers softly as the tears begin to spill down her cheeks as well. "No it can't be…"

"I'm so sorry," I say. I wish I wasn't the one who has to do this but it will be so much worse for her if it comes as a taunt from Onyx or Sapphire.

"But they were the most powerful members of the House of Neptune," she says. "How could they have all be wiped out like that by people who don't even use magic?"

"They might not use magic but Onyx and Sapphire know how to work their way around that," I say remembering how Sapphire got Caspian to back down so easily just by using me and Illyria as leverage against him. "But they…"

"If they were ambushed, then there was no way they could have prepared for it," I say. "We didn't know this was happening until it was too late so they would have had no time to get ready for an attack." The words feel like mulch in my mouth, I can barely speak and I'm trembling all over from the effort of not collapsing from the weight of everything that's happened.

"Did they…" Harmony begins but seems to have to stop to compose herself for a second, unable to get her words out. "Was it at least quick?" she asks and my chest aches.

I look away, unable to meet her eye. I'd like to think that it was over relatively quickly but, realistically I have no idea. Knowing Sapphire like I'm starting to and judging by the carnage I saw I don't think it will have been. My silence seems to be all the answer she needs and she chokes back a sob, covering her mouth with her hand.

"Oh god!"

"I'm so sorry," I say again. There is nothing else I *can* say. I shouldn't have to be telling her this; this never should have happened and I don't know what to do to make it better. I don't think there is anything I *can* do…not really. The council is dead, the land is in ruins and both of us are locked in the dungeons like common criminals.

Harmony wraps her arms around me, holding me tightly and the both of us just cry into each other, knowing that we are probably all the other has left. There are a few members of the family who weren't on the council and hopefully they will have gotten away as soon as they heard about the invasion. Then again they might have been killed as well—we have no way of knowing. I cling to Harmony like a lifeline, unable to let her go for fear of her suddenly being taken away from me as well.

"It's okay," she whispers through the tears, stroking my hair.

"No, it's not," I say.

"I still have you," she says. "You're alive and that's all that matters."

"I'm sorry I couldn't save them," I say. "I'm sorry I didn't get here in time."

"It's not your fault," she tells me, pressing a hard kiss to my forehead. "None of this is your fault. You did everything you could and you can't take all of this on yourself."

"But…" I could have done more, I know I could. For start, I could have gotten here in time! There is so much I could have done that might have helped. I have no idea what but I'm a Neo Warrior dammit, I should have been able to do something that would have saved them!

I'll never see Dad smile at me proudly again when I beat an opponent much bigger than me while sparring. I'll never be able to tell Granddad that the gin worked and I got along with everyone so well on my first night because of it. I'll never see my mum again…never be able to hug her or talk to her and it hurts like thousands of tiny knives stabbing me all over my body. All I can do is continue to sob through the pain and the ache and wish that there was some way for me to make it end.

Harmony places her hand on my cheek and I look up at her. The tears have been making fast tracks down her face and she doesn't even try to hide the fact that she's crying. I don't think I can remember seeing her cry after she was about fifteen and it's strange seeing her falling apart as she's usually the stronger out of the two of us. It's comforting though—I'm not alone in this: I still have her.

"You're still here though," she says, brushing a hand over her face to wipe away her tears.

"That's all I care about right now. All I care about is that you're safe."

"Okay…" I say, my voice thick from the tears, the pain and everything crashing down on top of me. "Sorry I was such a dick when I left."

She laughs softly. "I'm sorry too. I was just as much of a dick, maybe more so."

"I guess it doesn't really matter anymore," I sigh.

"Not now, no," she agrees.

I look her over and take in the splotches of my blood that have spread from me to her. Other than that she still seems to look quite clean and not as if she's spending all her time being tortured, which is something. "I got blood on you," I mumble.

"Don't worry about that," she says. "I just want you to be safe, that's all that matters to me now."

"Okay."

"Promise me that you'll do everything you can to keep yourself safe," she says.

"I…"

"Promise me," she says again, gripping me just a little tighter as the door behind her opens with a crash.

"I will," I reply. I don't know how I can when Sapphire seems to want to kill me but I'll try…for Harmony's sake.

Before either of us can do anything, two soldiers grab Harmony and another two grab me and we're wrenched out of each other's grasp. I struggle with all my might, ignoring the pain shooting from my shoulder and down my arm, desperate to get back to her but I'm shoved roughly back against the wall and forced into the chains. All the while I'm struggling against them but to no avail. Harmony's arms are forced behind her back, even though she's struggling just as much as I am, and she's forced into the cuffs again before she is dragged away.

"Harmony!" I scream as they force her to the cell door.

"I love you Ari," she cries back to me.

"I love you too."

"Don't forget that," she tells me. "Whatever happens, I love you."

"I won't," I say but a sob chokes off my voice as I speak so I have no idea whether she heard me or not.

The soldiers leave me and tears stream down my face harder and faster than ever before. I don't even bother to try and hold in my sobs as the door slams closed, there's no point. I can no longer hear Harmony's shouting, the only thing I can hear is my own sobbing and my heart pounding in my ears. I know I'm not alone in here but I can't bring myself to look at whoever is with me, although I know it's going to be one of two people.

Once the sobs have died down to whimpers I hear footfalls against the stone floor and I look up enough to see Onyx's boots walking towards me. I've been staring at them long enough to be able to distinguish him by his boots alone now. He kneels down in front of me and, with a surprising gentleness, he takes hold of my chin and tilts my head up so that I'm forced to look into his eyes.

"Now, do you want to tell me again that you have nothing left that can be taken away from you?" he asks. "Because I truly believe that there is."

"I swear to god if you hurt her I'll…" I begin, switching back to Universal.

"You'll what?" he asks, cutting me off before I can finish my fury filled sentence. Exactly what I'll do to him I have no idea so I'm almost glad he did cut me off. "What can you possibly do to me as you are? I hold all the cards—I have the last living member of your family held captive, I have your commanding officer and one of your comrades and I can easily get my hands on the rest, I have your homeland and, most importantly, I have your life in the palm of my hand. There is so much more that I can do to hurt you."

His grip on my chin tightens so even if I try to drag my face from his grasp I'm stuck and the full weight of my situation hits me.

"Please don't hurt her," I beg. I have no pride anymore—there's no point—I'll grovel on my knees before him if it means keeping Harmony and the others from suffering the same fate as the rest of the council.

"Don't worry," Onyx chuckles, "I have no interest in hurting her. In fact, I think she'll make quite a fine slave with a face like that." He runs the back of his hand gently down my cheek and I struggle not to flinch away. "Such a shame your death will be a wonderful example to your heathen people, I could have had a matching set."

The thought makes me sick but I have to try not to show any revulsion on my face or Harmony will be the one to suffer the consequences.

"Besides," Sapphires says from over by the door (I didn't even know she was here), "there are so many ways you can hurt someone without so much as leaving a mark or even touching them."

"Your other friends though," Onyx says. "Well, let's just say that they won't be so lucky. You have so much more to lose than you think you do. This is no longer about just *your* life anymore. So, with that in mind, will you tell me what I want to know?"

It doesn't matter what I say. I can tell him I don't know anything until I'm blue in the face and he still won't believe me. I could lie, make something up and see where that gets me, but as soon as he finds out none of it was true he'll take it out on someone else to teach me a lesson. It might not be about my life but there is no way I'm going to give him the satisfaction of thinking that he's got to me. Finally my stubbornness will come in useful for something, I just never imagined that it would be to hold fast under torture.

Drawing on as much anger and pain coursing through me and getting as much leverage as I can with his grip on my chin, I glare at him before spitting square in his face. He drops my chin immediately, wiping my spit away with the back of his hand. He laughs humourlessly at the glare I'm sending his way, looking at the back of his hand and then down at me.

There is a moment before he draws his other hand back and the back of it connects with my face. The blow sends me reeling, the rings on his fingers scraping down my cheek, and it pulls painfully at one of my shoulders as my body is flung in one direction but that arm is held fast by the chains. He doesn't give me much time to recover before he gets to his feet and his boot connects with my stomach. I cough and splutter at the sensation and the shock, feeling as if I might throw up, as he stalks over to Sapphire.

"Let's see how a little deprivation does her," he says and suddenly my only source of light is gone. "Maybe she'll be more willing to talk after a few days in the dark with no food or water."

He wrenches the cell door open and stalks out. I look up at Sapphire still standing in the doorway, bathed from behind by the light in the corridor.

"You brought this on yourself little siren," she says. "We'll break you before this is over, mark my words."

She slams the door closed behind her and I'm alone in the darkness. I hear the key in the lock and listen as best I can for their retreating footsteps but with the door closed I can barely hear anything that isn't my own laboured breathing. Only a tiny strip of light from a crack at the bottom of the door gives me anything that isn't pitch darkness. I let out a long sigh. I shouldn't have pissed him off like that; he'll take it out on someone else now.

Dammit…

I try to catch my breath and swallow the pain coursing through my entire body. After the kick to the stomach, I want to pull my arms around myself to hold it all in but if I tug on the chains it only adds more pain. I let out a shaking breath and close my eyes, trying to block out the darkness that feels as if it's pressing in on me. Clearly I'm going to be here for a long time, as long as they think is necessary, and all there is, is nothing.

I suddenly think I hear someone. "*Ari…*"

It sounds like Illyria's voice but there's no way I'd be able to hear her with the door closed. She's too calm to be shouting and that's the only way I'd be able to hear her from her cell. It seemed to be coming from inside my own head so there is a chance I imagined it. I must be losing my mind already. That's not good, it's barely even been a week.

"*Ari…*"

There it is again: her voice inside my head and it's definitely her voice, not anything I've come up with. It's not only her voice as well, it's as if I can feel her presence inside my head too. This is weird…

"*Yeah…*" I say inside my head. If I can hear her in my head, then it stands to reason that she can only hear me when I'm answering with my mind.

"*Can you hear me?*" she asks.

"*Yeah I can,*" I reply. This is so weird. How is this even happening? "*Are you alright?*" she asks.

"*As I can be,*" I reply. "*You?*"

"*I've been better,*" she says and it's as if I feel her chuckle softly. This is so weird…

"*I heard you screaming earlier,*" I say. "*What did they do to you? Sapphire said they tried to burn off your tattoos.*"

"*Yeah they poured acid on my skin,*" Illyria says. "*Mostly just torturing but that was particularly nasty.*"

"*I'm sorry.*"

"*It's fine,*" she says, which is a lie. This is anything but fine but she clearly doesn't want to talk about it.

"*Did they fix your thigh?*" I ask.

"*I'm not bleeding anymore if that's what you mean,*" she replies.

"*How's Caspian?*" I ask, changing the subject.

"*He's faring quite well all things considered,*" she replies. "*I think they've been using both of us to try and get him to crack.*"

"*Yeah that seems to be their preferred tactic,*" I say.

"*How are you doing?*" Illyria asks.

"*Not too bad, all things considered,*" I reply. "*I saw my sister so I know that she's alive at least. Onyx wants to make her his slave.*"

Illyria spits out something in Moonian and I can't help but laugh softly. Clearly that idea repulsed her as much as it did me.

"*We're going to get out of here Ari,*" she tells me. "*I promise you and we'll take back your homeland.*"

"*How are we even having this conversation?*" I ask. I'm still totally baffled that this is even possible (but then again I don't know the extent of Illyria's magic) and I don't know if I want to think about her promise. I don't want to get my hopes up too much.

"Remember when we first met and I made that connection with you?" she asks.

"Yeah."

"I activated it so that we can talk," she says.

"Okay."

"I've sent a message to Kat and the others. Hopefully they'll be here soon with reinforcements and we can get out of here, regroup and work out what to do next. I wanted to be able to have something tangible to tell you before popping up in your head like this."

"Okay," I say again. Even if they do get here and can get us out there is no telling how long that will take but it doesn't matter, as long as they come.

"Ari I'm so sorry for everything that's happened," she says after a pause. "We'll avenge them all and take this land back."

"I'm sorry too," I say. "I'm sorry I dragged you and Caspian into this."

"It's okay," she says. "Any of us would have done the same if it was our family and homeland."

"I guess so..." I hadn't thought about it like that before. The rest of them all seem so calm and sure of themselves, I wouldn't have thought they would lose it like I did.

"Listen I have to go," she says suddenly. "Sapphire and Onyx are coming in for another round. Stay strong Ari, it won't be for long...I hope."

The connection drops and I can no longer feel her. Suddenly I'm all alone in the dark again with nothing more than the tiny crack of light.

"I...I don't know if I can," I say out loud just in case she is still there. I don't want her to hear that. I don't want her to know that I'm falling apart and worry about me. By the sounds of it, she's going to have enough to deal with from another visit from Onyx and Sapphire. I finally stop trying to fight the new wave of tears and just let them flow down my face again. I cry, sobs shaking my chest and hollowing me out until I have no more tears left in me. Eventually I stop crying and let all the fatigue in me take over and I succumb to sleep. At least if I'm asleep, neither Onyx or Sapphire can hurt me.

Chapter 6

I have no idea how long Sapphire and Onyx leave me kneeling there, chained up in the dark, but it feels like forever. The darkness is impenetrable and there's only the tiniest bit of light coming in from under the door that allows me to see when people walk past but nothing that allows me to work out whether it's day or night. There are times when soldiers have come in to let me out of the chains for a short while so that I can eat the barest of meals, which I practically wolf down, only seeing food maybe once every few days, and go to the toilet. Five soldiers come in but the periods I'm left alone are longer than before so it seems as if it's every other day when I get fed. They don't say anything to me and I don't say anything to them. It wouldn't do me any good if I did; I doubt they would say actually anything back if they even understood me.

During the brief stints of time when I am let out of the chains I try to do something to relieve the ache in my arms and legs but I don't get long enough to make any real difference. Sometimes I think about trying to attack them and make my escape but I'm so fatigued from being trapped in here a light breeze would probably blow me over. Occasionally I manage to sleep but it's usually just after the soldiers have left, wanting to be alert for when they next appear. Sometimes it feels like only hours between the times I see them but I know it's longer.

I don't see or hear from anyone other than the soldiers. Occasionally Illyria reaches out to me from her cell and that is keeping me as sane as it can. She seems to be remaining positive, all things considered. When they realised that they weren't going to get anything out of her other than unintelligible Moonian, they gave up trying to get information out of her and basically left her alone, aside from to torture her for sport every so often. Caspian is the same—they use him as a punching bag—and I have no idea about Harmony. Illyria doesn't have the same connection to her as she does to us so she can't find out for me. She keeps telling me that the others are coming but has no idea when. I hope it's soon.

The door to my cell suddenly opens, the sound making me jump and look up. I've slept since the last time I was fed so that could well have been yesterday and I'm not expecting another visit until after I sleep again so this comes as a surprise. Onyx and Sapphire stand in the doorway with a brightly burning paraffin lamp. The light hurts my eyes and I can't look directly at it without my eyes watering. I curl in on myself, trying to hide away from it but it's useless as it even burns when my eyes are closed and I can't move much. I have to keep blinking until my eyes have adjusted, which takes a good few minutes before I can finally look up from the floor and even then the outline of the lamp is still burnt into the back of my retinas.

Wordlessly, Onyx clicks his fingers and two soldiers enter the room, one of them carrying a rickety looking chair. He puts the chair down in the centre of the room while the other begins to undo the chains from my wrists. It only takes one soldier to restrain me now and, to be perfectly honest, I never bother putting up much of a fight anymore. I don't have the strength to. Before I can even begin to work the feeling back into my arms once I'm free, they are forced behind my back and I'm dragged over to the chair.

My legs are so weak from the lack of use, being forced into the same position for so long and for the fact that I've had hardly anything to eat for so long. As I'm barely able to stand on my own now the soldier has to keep a tight hold on my collar after forcing me to my feet. I stumble on my way to the chair before I'm roughly shoved down onto it. It's hard and uncomfortable and they really tug at my arms to get them behind the back of it. The soldier who brought the chair in produces a length of rope and tightly ties me in place.

The rope bites into my skin and I suppress a wince as my hands are roughly manoeuvred so that my palms can't come into contact to conjure anything. Not that I could even if I did have the use of my hands. It's so cold down here my water wouldn't be in any way effective. Onyx is learning. I wonder if he's had any trouble with Caspian—he doesn't even need both hands to use his magic— because he's clearly learnt not to trust us with our hands. I clench mine into fists, feeling the ropes creak and rub at the already sore skin of my wrists. The pain is almost comforting in a weird way—it lets me know that I'm still alive and that I still have the capacity to feel something even if it is just pain.

"How are we feeling after a little reflection?" Onyx asks. "More willing to talk to us now that you've had some time to calm down and think?"

I glare up at him through my lank fringe. My pride won't let me show that being alone down here is terrifying. I highly doubt that this is the worst that they could do to me and, besides, Onyx hasn't broken me yet; I refuse to let him think that he has. I have to be strong for Harmony, Illyria, Caspian and everyone else who he's likely to hurt so I'm not about to give in yet.

"Go fuck yourself," I say, my voice hoarse and cracking from lack of use.

"Pardon?" Onyx asks, his tone mocking. "You're going to have to speak louder than that, I didn't quite hear you." He clicks his fingers again and another soldier appears. "Why don't we give our guest something to drink."

The soldier pulls a hip flask out of his pocket and hands it to Onyx. Onyx unscrews the cap before coming to stand in front of me. A hand in my hair forces my head back and my mouth open. He presses the hip flask to my lips and pours whatever is inside it down my throat. The strong taste of gin hits me as soon as it touches my tongue and I splutter, coughing, trying not to choke. Most of it ends up down my front of my shirt and Onyx doesn't stop until the flask is empty. It doesn't matter—they'll just raid the stores again until there's nothing left.

With the flask empty, Onyx lets my head go. I cough, unable to swallow properly, and I can feel a trail of saliva hanging from my lip to pool on my trousers. After catching my breath, I just about manage to swallow the last of the gin still clinging to the inside of my mouth. My throat burns from the taste but I must admit it feels good to have something more than a mouthful to drink. I look up at Onyx and glare at him as he smirks down at me.

"Feel better?"

"Go fuck yourself," I snarl again. My voice is still weak but I get the venom behind my words so there's no misunderstanding.

Before I have a chance to react (mostly because I'd forgotten she was even here), Sapphire's hand is in my hair, forcing my head back with a grip like steel. She draws a knife, quick as a flash, and for a second I think it's going straight into my face but she stops the blade mere centimetres from my left eye. I stare up at her, blind panic filling me and drenching me with a cold sweat that chills me to my bones in seconds.

I stare down the point, just waiting for it to go into my eye but suddenly it's gone and it's sinking into my thigh. I'm unprepared for it and a scream tears itself from my throat, echoing around the walls and reverberating down the corridor for Harmony, Illyria, Caspian and anyone else unfortunate enough to be down here to hear. Trying to curl in on myself again I attempt to make the pain stop but Sapphire's grip on my hair is too strong.

"You want to show the proper respect for the king of Cimmerian," she hisses.

Swallowing down the bile rising in my throat and the threatening tears I glare up at her. If I can at least pretend that I have all the confidence in the world, then maybe I can make them think I'm more powerful that I actually am. They haven't seen what I *can* do yet so maybe I can keep them guessing.

"I thought I was," I reply.

The knife in my thigh twists painfully and I bite down on another scream before it's roughly yanked out. I can feel the blood, warm and wet, beginning to spill from the wound and run down around my thigh to pool on the chair. Sapphire raises the knife again and I'm not sure where it's going next but before she can do anything Onyx grabs her wrist.

"Temper temper, Sapphire," he says and his voice still sounds as calm and as calculating as ever, "we don't want it to be over before she can give us the information we want." He clicks his fingers and a soldier enters the cell, kneeling beside me to begin bandaging my thigh. Of course Onyx doesn't want me to bleed to death just yet; what would be the point? He hasn't had the satisfaction of breaking me.

"How many times do I have to tell you?" I snap before I can stop myself. "I don't know anything!"

"Still singing that melody are you?" Onyx asks. "And here was me thinking that we might have made some progress since last time. The choice is yours, little siren, you can continue to pretend or I can let Sapphire have her fun with you—and she is ready to have some fun."

"There's nothing for me to tell you because I don't know anything," I say. "What more do you want from me."

"I just want you to cooperate, my dear," Onyx says. "It will only be worse for you if you don't."

"I thought we established last time that I don't care what happens to me anymore," I say, fixing him with a hard glare.

"So you keep saying," Onyx says, running a surprisingly gentle fingertip down my cheek. I flinch away from his touch and continue to scowl at him.

"You going to make me care?" I ask.

"You think that I won't?"

"Not really, no," I say. "You haven't exactly done anything that bad so far."

Sapphire's knife sinks into my other leg, making me bite down on another scream. This time she leaves the blade buried deep in my flesh. I clench my jaw and breathe through my nose, trying not to make a sound. My vision is starting to blur around the edges as Sapphire finally lets go of my hair and I can let my head hang forward, panting heavily as if I've just spent the entire day running training drills.

If she keeps this up, I'm going to pass out and I can't afford to do that…not with them both in here as well. If I do, there's no telling what they'll do to me. I desperately try to cling onto my consciousness as I wait for her next move. Onyx seems content to let her torture me as long as she doesn't kill me, the sick bastard. No matter what he offers me I will never align myself with him. I may not know a whole lot about wars and what goes on between our countries, (no more than what I've learnt in books anyway), but I know when someone is an arsehole and this guy is the biggest dick I've ever had the misfortune of meeting.

Sapphire is suddenly gripping the back of my neck, sharp fingernails digging into my skin, and making me gasp. She forces my head back, making me look up at Onyx who is holding something small as he seems to have decided to stop being a spectator. He's finally decided to get his hands dirty. I probably shouldn't have goaded him on like that. As he steps closer I realise that he's holding a box of matches. He takes a match out and strikes it.

The heat of the flame gets closer and closer as he moves the match up to my face, inches away from my cheek. I try to struggle away from it before it burns my skin but Sapphire's grip has me completely held in place.

"We did think about trying to drown you," he says, calmly watching the match as it slowly burns down further and further, "but it appears on this island you use water magic so it would be pointless. This, however, is much more effective."

Without warning he drops the match onto the leg without a knife in it and I let out a strangled cry as it begins to burn my skin through the crude bandage the soldier wrapped it in. The small flame begins to eat away at my trousers, spreading the burn further over my skin before Onyx slams his boot into my leg, abruptly putting out the flame. I let out the breath I have been holding, long and slow, clenching my teeth as I try not to make any sound.

"Is that enough for you?" he asks. "Are you ready to give up this little act now?"

"There's nothing for me to tell," I hiss through clenched teeth. Tears begin to sting my eyes as he grinds his boot down on the abused skin.

Onyx sighs theatrically. "This just will not do at all," he says, shaking his head. "I had banked on you breaking days ago but you're quite the resilient one, aren't you?"

"Piss off," I hiss through the pain only for it to be replaced by a cry as he grinds his boot down again.

"Maybe a change of technique is in order," he says removing his foot and finally relieving the pressure.

I gasp as feeling floods back to the area. God, that was painful! Blood is seeping through the bandage and it's likely that I'll need a swift patch up again before the day is out. It takes a moment of swallowing down the agony before Onyx's words sink in. What does he mean by change of technique?

"What are you going to do?" I ask.

"You'll see," Onyx smirks before leaving the cell.

Every time I think about what more they could do to me they surprise me with how unimaginably cruel they can be. Apparently I'm way more naïve than I thought when it comes to what they're capable of. Even though she could do anything with Onyx out the room, Sapphire does nothing aside from grip my neck and that in and of itself worries me more than it should. I almost want her to do something just so that I'm not sitting here waiting.

After a few minutes, the cell door opens again and Onyx is followed by a soldier dragging Caspian into the room. He looks like they've been putting him through the ringer as well. There are a few cuts and bruises littering his face and neck, there's dried blood in his hair, he's got a spilt lip and a huge purple bruise forming around his left eye. He takes one look at the state I'm in and sends a murderous look Onyx's way—I must look pretty bad too, although my face has largely been left alone.

The soldier shoves him to his knees on the floor in front of me before leaving, closing the cell door. Onyx closes the distance between them and shoves his boot roughly into Caspian's chest, pushing him backwards and smirking down at him.

"Now this is a sight I never thought I'd be fortunate enough to see," he says gleefully, "the great and powerful Caspian Feioré on his knees in front of me like a dog."

Caspian says nothing. His own answer is to glare up at Onyx, his eyes filled with murder, a burning hatred that I seem to be seeing more and more. Onyx isn't perturbed by this—in fact he seems to take it as a challenge. He removes his boot from Caspian's chest and comes over to stand by me.

"You should be proud of her Commander," he says, running the back of his hand down my cheek. I tense, not knowing if he's going to strike me, but all he seems to want to do now Caspian's here is pet me. "Despite everything we've done to them, neither of your girls is willing to talk. I was rather hoping I'd be able to break one of them; I was so sure it was going to be the siren but she's surprisingly resilient."

He runs his hand gently through my hair and I try to jerk away but Sapphire's hold keeps me in place. She digs her nails into my neck again and I wince. I'm not quiet about it and Caspian notices. He ignores both Onyx and Sapphire and turns to look at me.

"Sirenia are you alright?" he asks.

I open my mouth to answer. I'm not totally sure what I'm going to say because I'm not alright, not really, but right this second I'm not doing as badly as I have been. Before I can say anything, though, the flat of another of Sapphire's blades is pressed to my mouth. My leg pulses around the other as I feel cold steel against my lips.

"Ah ah ah," she cautions as her hand leaves my neck and she grabs a fistful of my hair to keep me from jerking back and away from it. "We didn't bring him in here for a cosy little catch-up. We have other, more important, things to talk about."

"I swear to god, if you do anything more to hurt her—" Caspian begins.

"We've been over this, Commander Feioré," Onyx laughs mockingly, "there is nothing that you *can* do to me. You can't fight back—if you do, one of them will die—you can't escape this dungeon and you can't stop me from advancing my invasion to the mainland. If you do anything to me, Sapphire and the rest of my soldiers will take it out on her," he nods at me, "the other one and the rest of the people on this island. Can you really stomach being responsible for that much pain and suffering?"

Caspian remains resolutely silent. I had been wondering why he didn't just kill Onyx—Caspian's certainly powerful enough—but, in order to deal with the repercussions he would have to kill every single Cimmerian soldier on the island in one fell swoop. I don't think even he is powerful enough to do that, not without taking most of the citizens with him. Caspian knows when he's beaten and, in this instance, we are beaten.

"See," Onyx says with a smirk, "your bleeding heart won't let you. This is why you're weak Feioré, can't even make a small sacrifice for what you want."

"I'd hardly call the murder of thousands of innocent people a 'small sacrifice'," Caspian growls.

"Call it what you will Feioré," Onyx says, "but if you're not willing to do what needs to be done to stop me then I would say that you're at the end of the line here."

Caspian glares up at Onyx and I look helplessly down at the blade of the knife. My breath fogs the surface with every shaking exhale. We're at a standoff: Caspian knowing that he's lost, Onyx knowing that he has Caspian right where he wants him and me as the leverage in the middle of it all. Finally Caspian looks away from Onyx in defeat. With a chuckle, Sapphire yanks the blade away from my lips and lets go of my head. I let it drop forward, breathing heavily as I desperately try to stop myself from shaking.

"I've got to say I'm a little disappointed Feioré," Onyx says, all but ignoring me entirely. "I never expected *you* to be the first to break."

"He's no fun, is he?" Sapphire asks and, looking up, I can see that she's enjoying herself immensely.

"No matter," Onyx says. "It's much more entertaining and profitable if we use him to break someone else." He suddenly turns to me. "Tell me everything I want to know about your king and your army or he dies."

"What?" The word practically drags itself out of my mouth and I'm not totally even sure that I've said anything at all but I know I must have done as Onyx seems pleased.

"I'll say this again slowly, just to make sure that there's absolutely no confusion in the matter whatsoever. You tell me everything I want to know or I will kill him, right here, right now, in front of you. Understand?"

My eyes widen and all I can feel is fear, blind panic coursing through every cell in my body that won't go away, no matter how hard I try to put on a brave face. My head is spinning, I can't think straight, I feel sick and not even from what they were doing to me before they brought Caspian in.

Onyx pushes Caspian forward, so that he is kneeling in front of me, before he pulls a gun out of a holster at his hip. He cocks it and points it at the back of Caspian's head. I can't quite see but I'm pretty sure that it's pressed right up against his scalp, judging by the pained clenching of Caspian's jaw.

"Now tell me everything you know or he dies," Onyx says.

"I…"

"Ten," Onyx begins his countdown.

"Sirenia say nothing," Caspian orders.

"Quiet," Sapphire hisses.

"Nine," Onyx says, continuing his countdown.

"Please…" I begin. I don't know what I'm begging for—that he'll believe me when I say I don't know anything, that he'll drop this and say that he's bluffing or what—but I can't handle the thought of him pulling that trigger.

"Eight," he continues. "What's it to be, little siren? Are you going to sing for me or am I going to have to kill him?"

"I swear I don't know anything," I say for what feels like the hundredth time but my voice comes out as a terrified whimper. I'm trembling all over and I struggle against the ropes but to no avail. Either I'm tied too tightly or I'm too weak to make a difference.

"Seven."

"You must know something," Sapphire says.

"Not anything like what you're asking for," I reply.

"Six."

"You wouldn't want to be responsible for another person's death now would you?" Sapphire asks and my heart stops.

"Wh-what do you mean?" I ask. Oh god…what have they done?

"That sailor down by the docks," Sapphire says. "You couldn't save him but you can save *him*," she says, nodding in Caspian's direction. She must mean Thomas and if she knows about him then that means they were watching us as we discovered their presence here.

"Five," Oynx says and I'm already nearly at the end of my tether.

"Sirenia, there was nothing you could do for him, he was already dead when we found him," Caspian says but it does nothing to comfort me.

"Four."

"Please…" I beg, looking up at Onyx with tear-filled eyes.

"Three," he says in response.

"Last chance, siren," Sapphire says, not even bothering to conceal the glee in her voice.

"Two," Onyx says, eyes locked firmly on my face.

"Sirenia," Caspian warns me.

"One."

Onyx squeezes the trigger and a loud bang fills the room.

Everything begins to move in slow motion and all I can do is sit there and watch it unfold, unable to do anything. Caspian moves backwards and shoves his shoulder against Onyx's arm, making the bullet careen into the back wall of the cell, missing me by an inch or so. Before either Sapphire or Onyx can react, using a strength I'm surprised he still has after everything they've put him through, Caspian breaks out of the ropes holding him by burning through them. He's on his feet in seconds and pressing a hand encased in flames into the side of Onyx's face.

A furious and pained scream rips from Onyx's throat and he kicks out, his boot connecting with Caspian's stomach. The kick sends him sprawling on the floor again and it's suddenly obvious what Caspian's plan was. He saved up what little strength he had to leave his mark on Onyx so that he will never be able to forget him and neither will anybody else. Everywhere he goes Onyx will have to see his last loss to Caspian and Caspian knows how much that will burn him up inside. Pushing himself to his knees again Caspian turns to face me, that blazing gaze fixing me in place just like he has so many time before.

"Don't give in to them," he says. "That's an order Sirenia."

"I won't," I reply softly.

The gun goes off again.

Time seems to stop for a moment and I feel as if I'm underwater, suspended in nothing but crushing silence and pressure. Feeling begins to flood back to my body as something warm and wet hits my face and Caspian slumps forward, his head falling into my lap. The sensation begins to spread over my knees and down onto the chair and the floor. It still doesn't sink in, even as I see smoke coming out of the barrel of Onyx's gun.

And then it hits me all at once, like a blow to the stomach.

Suddenly I'm screaming.

I immediately start struggling against the bonds holding me again and trying to get away from the dead weight of Caspian's lifeless body. I don't even want to think about the fact that his brains are probably all over my face and that his blood is seeping into my clothes—all I can think about doing is getting him off me and that I can't seem to stop screaming.

I scream until I can't breathe and my lungs feel as if they're going to give out. All the while Onyx and Sapphire are standing there watching me with cold, calculating gazes, watching as I fall apart completely in front of them, Onyx holding the side of his face where Caspian's flames burnt him.

Finally, after what feels like hours, my voice gives out and I stop screaming, the sound dying down to pained mewls. Caspian is still on top of me and I can feel his blood slowly running down my legs. I swallow, desperately trying to not make this any worse by throwing up, and bile stings the back of my throat as I force it back down. Trembling all over I just about manage to hold myself as together as I possibly can (which isn't much after the screaming) as I finally raise my eyes to look up at Onyx and Sapphire.

"We'll leave the two of you alone to get reacquainted," Onyx snarls and stalks from the room.

"Let's see how long you hold out after this," Sapphire smirks gleefully. She rips the knife out of my thigh. It hurts but I barely notice. She turns to the soldier still in the corner. "Make sure you get that fixed," she says, nodding to my thigh. "The king won't be happy if she dies."

I don't say anything; I drop my eyes to the floor again as tears begin to slowly make tracks down my cheeks. I hear a flurry of shouting from Onyx as he demands a doctor. The solider does a decent enough job of making sure that my leg won't bleed out before leaving, locking the cell door behind himself but I can still hear people outside. I wait for them to go knowing that they're going to leave me alone with a corpse for god only knows how long. Before the sounds disappear, I distinctly hear Onyx's voice through the haze of fear and anguish.

"You know, I do believe we may have broken her," he says.

"I certainly hope so," Sapphire says.

"You're too cruel," Onyx laughs but it's a pained laugh.

"I would very much like to see just how much more she can take," Sapphire says.

"Later," Onyx tells her. "Let her have some time alone with her beloved Commander first."

There's suddenly silence and I'm left alone with Caspian's body. At least this time they left me the light. I guess that's so I can see what's happened and be reminded of the fact that I got him killed.

There was nothing I could have said that would have saved him. Onyx wanted to kill him and they'll probably kill me and Illyria as well, if not any time soon then eventually. The tears continue to slowly make their way down my face and it only becomes more apparent that I don't think I'd be overly sad if they did kill me.

"*Ari...*" I hear Illyria's voice inside my head and feel her presence just touching the edge of my consciousness, like last time. I push her away, using every last bit of mental resilience I have to keep her from getting inside my head. I don't want her to see me like this. I don't want anyone to ever see me like this.

"*Ari...come on, talk to me...*" she presses again but I stay firm. I'm not letting her in...not yet. "*Please...tell me what happened,*" she says trying once more but I refuse to let my walls down. I feel the edges of her magic leave and I let out the breath I've been holding. I can't deal with it now, I need time to calm down before I can talk about this.

Tears stream down my face, dripping off my chin and falling into the shattered back of Caspian's head. The man I thought was impossible to kill, the strongest of the Neo Warriors and the fiercest man I've ever met, is now dead in my lap and I wish I could join him.

I'm sorry…

I'm sorry I couldn't be stronger.

~ *** ~

I slowly lose track of how long they leave me alone with Caspian's body. Could be hours, or closer to a day. I have no idea. All I can do it sit here and hope that the torture ends soon. I look down at the congealed blood in the back of his head and contemplate if there are any ways for me to kill myself while tied to a chair. I think I'd rather die by my own hand than by theirs but the more I think about it the more I can't quite bring myself to actually do it.

There's nothing I can *do* to end my own life either. I can't use magic because I don't have the use of my hands and I can't do anything else either. I toy with the idea of biting my tongue so that I bleed out but, again, I can't actually bring myself to do it even after all the pep-talks I give myself to gear me up to it. If I angle myself just right, I could rub my wrist against a sharp part of the back of the chair, slit my wrists that way, but I can't quite get the angle right and as I try I realise it's not as sharp as I thought. It would take me a while to get through.

I could tip the chair back and hit my head on the floor…hopefully it will be enough to kill me or a least knock me unconscious for a few hours. Then again, if it isn't I'm just on the floor with Caspian on top of me and it's bad enough that

I've still got him sprawled out on my lap, although he seems to have stopped bleeding now. Another option is straining hard enough to burst some kind of blood vessel in my brain and bleed out that way. Refusing to eat is always an option; I'm practically a skeleton anyway so that won't take very long. I need to do something other than wait for them to come and kill me, I just need to work myself up to it. In all honesty, I don't even care if they do kill me, I think I'd even welcome it…

The lock suddenly clicks open and I look up to see Sapphire enter flanked by two burly soldiers. No Onyx this time, probably nursing his face. She looks over at me and that nasty smirk of hers is playing about her lips again. I don't even bother glaring at her this time, I just look up with dead eyes. The smirk on her face twists, clearly pleased.

"Take him away," she tells the soldiers, nodding at Caspian. "The little siren and I are going to have some alone girl bonding time." That sounds ominous. Hell, even without the undertones of the impending torture in there that would sound ominous.

The soldiers wordlessly each grab one of Caspian's arms and drag him from the cell. With the weight gone from my legs, I stretch them out slightly, tensing the muscles to try and get some of the feeling back. I can't even remember the last time I got to properly move around and to be honest I don't even know if I'd be able to stand even if Sapphire did let me. I haven't changed my clothes for so long either, which are covered with both my blood and Caspian's. God knows how long I've been sitting in it as the material of my trousers is dry and cracks with the slightest movement, caking the skin underneath too.

Sapphire steps closer to me and takes hold of my chin. With a gentleness, I wouldn't have thought possible from her she tilts my face upwards so that I have to look at her. She stares down at me for a moment, studying me before she lets go of my face. My head hangs forward. I don't want to look at her just in case I start crying again, although I doubt I have any tears left in me. I still don't want her to see me if I do.

I'm so pathetic! Why can't I be stronger, like Caspian was.

There is a rustle of her clothing and then something hard and heavy hits me round the side of the head. I feel the skin split open and blood begin to trickle down my face from it as my head is thrown to the side like a rag-doll's. I retch, dizzy and sick from the blow but one of her hands is in my hair, forcing my head back roughly so that I have to look at her. The other hand carelessly drops whatever it was she hit me with. It hits the floor with a metallic thunk and she covers my mouth with her hand.

"Don't throw up," she orders and I pinch my lips together to try and stop myself from doing so. It would be a nice slice of revenge if I did throw up all over her face but she'd probably make things worse if I did. I'm genuinely struggling to think of what 'worse' could be though. I breathe heavily through my nose, feeling the warm, wet trickle of blood down my neck to soak into the top of my shirt. I'm not even sure what is my blood and what is Caspian's anymore unless it's fresh and the thought makes me swallow another retch.

When I finally feel the urge to be sick lessen to the point where I can open my eyes to look at her, everything around her face is hazy. She's bathed in a halo of light from the lamp still hanging in the corner and with my vision still blurry it makes her look almost ethereal, like some kind of angel. The hard line of her jaw and her scowl, not to mention the pain in the base of my scalp, tell me otherwise though.

"Didn't think he was serious did you?" she asks, removing her hand from my mouth. "Didn't think he'd actually kill him?"

I cough and take a shuddering breath in. "I have no idea what you're capable of," I finally say, my voice hoarse and scratchy from screaming and then lack of use afterwards.

Sapphire lets out a soft, breathy laugh. "And that's just the way I want it," she says. "If you have no idea what I'm going to do to you, then you can't predict anything or be ready for it when it comes. It's the perfect way to keep you in line."

"Have you always gotten off on torturing people or am I just lucky?" I ask. I should probably keep my mouth shut and not give her the satisfaction but, in a strange way, I still want her to think that she doesn't have any power over me. I want her to think that she can't break me and that I'm not afraid.

I *am* afraid and she probably *will* break me soon but if I keep up the facade then I can keep her guessing: I can keep hold of what little power I have left.

She huffs out a laugh again and yanks my hair until it feels like she's going to rip it out. "My, my, someone's certainly started to grow a backbone," she says. "It's a little late in the game for that don't you think? Or did all that crying and screaming from seeing your big, strong Commander put down like an animal in front of you finally make you decide to fight back? Do you feel like you have something to lose now?"

"No," I say, "because I don't have anything to lose."

"You keep saying this," she says, shaking her head, "but, you forget, I've still got your other friend *and* your sister locked up in chains here as well."

"Considering that Onyx wants to make Harmony his slave and you're going to kill Illyria regardless, what does it matter what I do anymore?" I say, looking up at her as defiantly as I can. "I'm going to die eventually either way so what does it matter?"

"This is true," she says. "You are going to die but that doesn't mean I can't still have all the fun I want with you in the meantime."

She lets go of my hair and pulls a knife out of a sheath at her hip. For a horrifying moment, I think it's going into my leg again but she reaches behind the chair and cuts the ropes that are holding me to it. She doesn't cut the ones binding my hands so I have nothing to stop myself from hitting the floor as she pulls me off the chair and throws me onto the ground. The side of my head that isn't bleeding hits the stone with a sickening crack that reverberates in my skull and that wave of dizziness crashes over me again.

I don't have a whole lot of time to recover from the fall before she kicks me, hard, in the stomach. The blow makes me cough and splutter, fighting for breath as she lands another kick. My entire body feels like it's on fire as she continues to deliver blow after blow to my stomach, back, anywhere that she can reach and I can't fight it, can't stop it and can't do anything to defend myself. All I can do is ride out the pain screeching through me and hope that she gets bored soon.

"Had enough yet siren?" she asks between kicks, giving me just enough respite to spit some blood onto the floor before I can answer.

I glare up at her. "Not a chance," I wheeze. I'm lying. In reality, I have had enough and I wish she would stop but she doesn't want to.

"Consider this payback for what Caspian did to my brother," she says as she continues to kick me.

I have no idea how long she beats me as I lose track of time after the first few rounds. All I do is lie there and wait for it to be over. She occasionally stops beating me into the floor to shove my face into it, making sure that she drags it across the stone and causes as much pain and damage as possible. At first, I try to stop myself from crying out in agony but then, when I can't take it anymore, I just give up and let her, and anyone else listening, hear me scream.

Finally, after what feels like hours, she seems to tire herself out and get bored. By now, I'm barely conscious, every muscle and bone in my body is in agony and absolutely burning. Blood stains the floor, and I'm vaguely aware that I'm lying in not only my blood but Caspian's as well, although his is probably long dry by now. She gives me another swift kick to the gut and I let out a sharp cry. Trembling and barely able to see her through the blood and sweat in my eyes, I look up blindly in the direction I think she's in.

"Don't worry," she tells me, "this is far from over. I'm only just getting started with you and I'm going to make this as long and as painful as possible."

With that, she slams the cell door and locks it again, leaving me lying, bleeding on the floor. If I'm lucky, I might actually just bleed out now. My body feels heavy, everything aches and I'm willing it to come to an end. Closing my eyes I let myself fall into blissful unconsciousness, praying that I won't wake up again.

Chapter 7

The sound of angry voices shouting outside my cell door finally brings me around and back to consciousness. I have no idea how long I was out cold for, the last thing I remember was Sapphire beating me then locking me up so I have no way of knowing how much time has passed. I don't even want to think about what Sapphire, Onyx or anyone else could have done while I was unconscious but I don't feel as if I have any new injuries and I don't appear to have moved since I passed out so that's something I suppose.

The shouting in the corridor is fuzzy at first but the argument seems to get more and more heated and finally the sound begins to properly pull me back to reality. One of the voices is a lot louder and a lot more shrill than the other and it's this one that I catch first.

"…can't treat people like this, Sapphire!" the voice shouts.

What…? There is a spoken response that I don't quite hear through the heavy door but I can guess that it's probably Sapphire. I strain my ears, trying to guess who the other person is but I can't place their voice.

"This is sick!" the other voice shouts. "You can't do this to people! It doesn't matter what you think of them, you could end up with an entire army on your door if you carry on like this. For god's sake, she's barely older than Diaya!"

I don't hear Sapphire's full response (although, judging from that last part, I would guess that they're talking about me) but I just about catch the name 'Emerald'. Obviously the whole family doesn't share Sapphire and Onyx's penchant for torture.

"No!" Emerald shouts. "That doesn't excuse *this*."

"Onyx is trying to protect us!" Sapphire shouts and I can now hear her through the door as well. "You'd know that if you spent even a second listening to him."

"This is not about listening to him or what he thinks, this is about basic human rights!" Emerald shouts back.

"Then it's clear where your loyalties lie!"

"Who said anything about loyalty?"

"If you're not willing to work with us then you're against us," Sapphire tells her.

"Then I guess I'm against you. You want to be a ruthless dictator and follow Onyx blindly then you're not the person I thought you were. If our father were alive to see this—"

"Well, he's not!" Sapphire shouts.

"And for the first time I'm glad!" Emerald shouts back. "I can't even imagine what he would think of you if he could see you like this."

"They are the reason he's dead!"

"I don't believe that for a second," Emerald tells her. "Feioré and the rest of them have always been friends to us, why would they suddenly change that now?"

"So they could start a war!"

"The only people who seem to want this war are you and Onyx!"

Emerald's quite fierce when she's angry. I'd barely even heard her speak when we were in Cimmerian, we may have had one conversation, nothing more, but she's clearly a force as she's laying into Sapphire.

"Onyx is trying to protect the Cimmerian people!" Sapphire shouts, her own rage beginning to show through. "Why can't you see that?"

"If this is protecting us, then I don't want his protection!"

"That's your affair," Sapphire snarls. "If you want to leave, then leave. If you won't follow your king, then leave before he decides to charge you for treason."

"I'm his goddamn sister! Is he going to kill me as well?"

"Just don't get in our way," Sapphire snaps at her, knowing that she has lost that argument. "Onyx will do as he sees fit and the other two will do as their king commands."

"Like hell I'm leaving them here!" Emerald shouts. "I'm taking Diaya and Ruby and I'm taking them as far away from the two of you as possible!"

"We'll just see what Onyx has to say about that."

"Sapphire!" Emerald shouts. "Sapphire, we're not done!"

The shouting continues but grows fainter and fainter until I can no longer hear either of them. Well…

It's interesting to know that it only seems to be Onyx and Sapphire who want to start a war. I wonder how long it was before Emerald found out about this. I would guess recently considering the screaming match. I let my head fall back against the floor; now that I have nothing left to listen to, straining my neck up to hear is too much effort. I let the exhaustion envelop me again and allow myself to fall back to sleep.

~ *** ~

Being asleep offers no more comfort than staring at the wall or the ceiling. Fitful dreaming is no more of an escape than being left alone with my thoughts. I dreamt about Mum, seeing her as she was before I left for the mainland and then seeing her head on a spike in the council chamber. I dreamt of Caspian too. The image of the light leaving his eyes as Onyx shot him in cold blood is one that will haunt me for the rest of my life. All I can see when I close my eyes is death. I can't take this anymore…

The cell door opening brings me round again. I don't even bother to open my eyes as I hear footsteps against the floor, I just wait for Sapphire to start the next round of beating. Hopefully this time she'll kill me and get it over with but I think she still wants me alive to torture…for fun if nothing else. I clench my gut, waiting for the first kick but it never comes. She's going to make me wait. Every muscle in my body tightens to the point of pain, just waiting for the blow that never comes. When I am finally touched, the hand that brushes my sweat and blood soaked fringe out of my eyes is the gentlest touch I've felt in a long time.

With a lot more effort than it should physically take, I open my eyes and I must be dreaming because it looks as if I'm staring up at Diaya. I blink at her, trying to decide if she is real or if I'm just hallucinating. Did I dream that argument between Emerald and Sapphire or is there an actual chance that Diaya is here on Neyara as well?

She leans over me, gently turning me onto my side so that she can reach my hands and begins to untie the ropes that have bitten my wrists raw. This has to be real. This can't be simply my imagination; I can smell her clean clothes and feel her hair brushing against my cheek. I can't be hallucinating this much. After a moment or so, the ropes begin to loosen so it must be real and, eventually, they come away completely letting my hands fall free.

"Diaya?" My voice sounds awful; raspy and scratchy, as if I've died and been brought back again in the most painful way possible. To be honest, if feels as if I have as well. "What are you doing here?"

"Shh," she says as she rolls me onto my back and slowly, so I don't get too dizzy, helps me up into a sitting position, "try not to talk too much." She picks up a cup from the tray she must have brought in with her and holds it to my lips, her other hand cradling the back of my head. "Drink this, you'll feel better."

The liquid inside hits my lips and, oh my god, it's water! I drink a little too fast and end up coughing, unable to swallow it all at once. Diaya takes the cup away and rubs soothing circles on my back while I catch my breath. She picks up a piece of something and presses it into my hand. It takes a while for me to register but my fingers close around it. It's food… It's food! And not the stale stuff the soldiers have been bringing me. This is real, fresh food.

"I brought what I could," she says as I tentatively lift my hand to my mouth and take a bite. It's cheese and my stomach aches as the taste hits my tongue. I can't even remember the last time I ate anything. "I thought the protein might be good for you. Don't eat too quickly or you'll make yourself sick."

It takes all of my self-control not to just wolf the whole thing down in one bite but I do as she says and nibble it so that I can swallow it and keep it down. There isn't that much and I want to make this last—who knows when I'll next get something fresh?

"What are you doing here?" I ask again as she reaches into a bowl, also on the tray, and pulls out a dripping cloth. She wrings it out before lifting my chin up so that she can get a better angle and begins to clean the dried blood off my face. The cloth is warm and wet, but a much nicer warm and wet than anything else I've felt recently and, more than anything, it's clean. It stings a little on the open cuts but her hands are gentle and it doesn't ache as badly as it could do. It even starts to feel rather nice after a while.

"Are you alright?" she asks, ignoring my question.

"Peachy," I reply, letting out a hollow laugh.

"What happened to you?"

"Your sister." I say, bluntly.

"Right," she says.

Diaya looks away, a little sheepish and I instantly wish I could take it back. I open my mouth but I can't quite get the words to come out so I close it again and dutifully sit still as she continues to clean the blood off my face. I wonder if Onyx or Sapphire know she's down here? I doubt they do and I doubt they'd be overly thrilled to find out either.

"What are you doing here?" I ask for the third time. Hopefully she'll actually give me an answer now.

"Came with the rest of them," she says as she dips the cloth into the water and wrings it out again. I can't quite see the contents of the bowl in this light but, judging by the colour of the cloth, I would guess it's pretty red by now. "Onyx sent for me, Ema and Ruby once he and Sapphire had laid their claim here. Got here the day before yesterday."

"Okay…" That much I could have guessed on my own after that argument between Sapphire and Emerald. "What are you doing *in here*?"

"Cleaning you up," she said. "Close your eyes."

I do as she says. "But why?" I ask before I can stop myself. I don't know what the answer is going to be. I doubt it's going to be some kind of new torture tactic, Diaya always seemed way too nice for that, too kind. That might get her killed one of these days.

"Just because I came here with Onyx and Sapphire doesn't mean I have to act like them," she says.

"Right…" I mumble. "Sorry…"

"And besides," she says, ignoring me, "you're my friend, of course I'm going to come down here and help you."

"Thanks," I say weakly. I try to smile at her but everything aches, even more so after having the blood rubbed off, and it comes out more as a grimace.

"I sent you letters," she says after a pause.

"Never got any," I say. "I sent ones of my own too but it makes sense that you didn't get any of them either."

"That's Onyx for you," she says sadly. "I imagined that he'd intercept any letter I tried to send to you but I still wanted to try."

We both fall into silence for a moment; her cleaning the blood off my face and neck before moving on to the exposed bits of my arms and my wrists, me too exhausted to actually think of anything to say. It's not until she gets to the rope burns around my wrists and she chokes down a sob that I look at her face again. Tears are slowly making their way down her cheeks and she looks like she's really struggling to hold it together.

I reach up to try and brush them away with the back of my hand but, just as I do, I get a twinge of pain ripping through me from one of my many stab wounds and I have to drop my arm back down, wincing.

"I'm sorry," she whispers through her tears. "I'm so sorry."

"What are you sorry for?" I ask.

"I'm sorry they've done this to you."

"Hey," I say, reaching over to place my hand on top of hers, "this isn't your fault. Besides," I add after a pause, "this is nothing."

"Really?" she asks sceptically. "It doesn't look like nothing."

"I've had worse."

"You liar," she laughs softly.

"Trust me."

"Really?"

"You should have seen me after training with Caspian, now that was hard," I joke although it feels very hollow. "I'll be fine, I promise." I try to smile at her but, again, it just comes off as a pained grimace.

"Will you though?" she asks and I have a feeling I know what she means by that. There is a good chance that either Sapphire is going to kill me when she's tired of playing with me (which may not be that long away now) or Onyx is going to kill me as an example to the rest of the Neptunians and a message to the rest of the Neo Warriors. Either way I doubt I've got that much longer left in here.

"So what happened since I last saw you?" I ask. "Seeing as Onyx didn't let any of your letters get through." I can't quite bring myself to answer her question so I'll just change the subject and hope we can gloss over the fact that her brother and sister are murderous raving psychos who are going to kill me soon.

"Right…of course," she says, shaking herself out of her thoughts and picking up the cloth again. "After you left this, doctor came and pronounced that father had been murdered by various different times of Braxian magic."

"You know we wouldn't—" I begin.

"I know," she cuts me off. "So Onyx, using this to his advantage, starts this hate campaign against you all—telling everyone that the Neo Warriors were responsible for the king's death. He said it was obvious you had done something by how fast you left but the doctor's report only confirmed it. Then, once he'd got people listening and actually believing him, he started talking about a war and teaching you all a lesson."

"You know we had nothing to do with that, right?" I ask although I doubt she'd be here if she did.

"Of course you didn't," she says. "I mean I know *you* certainly didn't because I was with you the whole time and I can't imagine any of the others doing anything like that either. Father trusted you all and you all wanted peace as much as he did. There was no reason for you to start a war and you have magic. I imagine if you *really* wanted to start a war it wouldn't be by sneaking around and murdering the king."

"Not going to argue with that logic," I say. "So then what happened?"

"Onyx rallied his troops, got an army together and started his invasion," she says. "He went off to meet you and the rest of the Neo Warriors like he said he would and sent Sapphire over here to take this island. She had a huge head start on you so there was no way that you could possibly have stopped her unless you already knew this was what Onyx was planning on doing from the beginning."

"Right…" Of course that would be how he would have this play out. "What do you think of the island by the way?" I ask.

"I'm sure it's very nice when it's not crawling with soldiers," she says and I let out a soft, weak laugh.

"Yeah it's less crowded and you get to see more of the landscape," I say. "Although I haven't actually seen daylight in…a while."

"My guess is probably about three weeks now," she says.

"Wow…" Nearly a month. I've been in here that long. I wonder how long it's been since Caspian died, how long since my family died…

It crosses my mind that the others might not come. If it's been this long, maybe they'll leave the island and focus on keeping the Cimmerians off the mainland. It does take a while to get here from where we met Onyx and from the mainland too. The likelihood is that once Illyria told them that the Cimmerians had taken Neyara they went back to the mainland for reinforcements and if they're coming by sea that could easily take them a month. The sea would be the only way they could get here to make a sneak attack as well, coming in all guns blazing with a Mercurian airship might not work so well. Still, it's awful knowing just how long I've been locked up.

"That's pretty much the whole story," Diaya finishes when I don't say anything else. "Sapphire took the island and Onyx came to reap the benefits."

"And Sapphire disposes of anyone in the way," I mutter darkly. It's out before I can stop it but I know Diaya heard me as her hand stills a moment.

"I'm sorry about your family," she says. "Caspian too."

"What about the other two?" I ask, wanting to change the subject again.

"Who?"

"Emerald and Ruby?" I ask. "I heard Emerald and Sapphire going at each other at one point. She said that she was going to take you and Ruby and leave."

"They have," she says, sniffing and I can tell that she's trying to hold back tears again. "Have what?"

"Gone," she clarifies. "As soon as Ema found out what Onyx and Sapphire had done to you and the other woman in here she was furious. She told Onyx that she wouldn't stand for this and that she was going to take me and leave for somewhere else with Ruby. She said she wanted to put as much distance between us and him as possible so they're probably on their way to Eriadal or somewhere else on the other side of the world by now if she's not going back to Cimmerian. God, I wish I could have gone with them."

She bites down on a sob again, obviously not wanting to fall apart when she came here to care for me but she can't seem to hold it in an longer. I reach over and take her hand again. This time she laces her fingers with mine and gives my hand a gentle squeeze, trying to keep herself from breaking down as tears silently roll down her cheeks.

"Why didn't you?" I ask when her shoulders seem to have stopped shaking with her silent sobs.

"I'm still under-age," she replies. "By Cimmerian law until I turn eighteen, I'm under the care of my oldest living blood relative unless a judge rules that they're unfit to look after me. In my case, that just so happens to be the king and Onyx so there was even less chance of him letting me leave even if it was with them. Both Ema and Ruby fought their corner to take me with them but in a situation like this the king will always have the deciding vote. Onyx said that I stayed with him and if they wouldn't follow his rule then they could either leave or stay and die with the rest of you. Obviously they chose to go. If there was any way that I could have gone with them, I would have done."

"I'm sorry," I say, my own eyes filling with tears. If that's the case, she's just as trapped here as I am.

"Don't be," she says, wiping her face with her free hand. "None of this is anyone's fault but Onyx's and Sapphire's. I don't know why but he always hated the fact that father enjoyed the company of Braxians, especially Caspian and the Neo Warriors. I don't think anyone ever realised just how deep his hatred went until father died and now that he's out of the picture Onyx is going to take out every last bit of hatred he has on those of you he's managed to capture. I'm just so sorry that it had to be you."

"It's fine," I say. "I was the one who darted over here without thinking as soon as I found out he was gunning for my homeland."

"So what are you going to do when you finally get out of here?" Diaya asks. "Are you going to try and get back to the mainland and the rest of the Neo Warriors or are you going to stay here? You can't take on Onyx's entire army by yourself."

There is a longer than necessary pause before I speak again, choosing my words carefully. "Let's be realistic here I don't think I'm getting out." I don't want to say it and she doesn't want to hear it but it has to be said, there's no point me lying to myself or her.

Diaya's eyes fill with tears again. She shakes her head and her voice is thick as she speaks again. "No."

"Diaya…"

Tears begin to slowly make their way down her cheeks. "You can't just give up," she says, her voice barely a whisper now.

"What is there that I can do?" I ask. I try to reach over, manoeuvring myself into a different position so I can better comfort her but my wrist gives out the second I put pressure on it and I fall back to where I was. "Look at me, I can barely stand, let alone fight anyone. I'm outnumbered and even if I was as powerful as Caspian or Kat or any of the others I still wouldn't be able to do anything."

"But…"

I give her hand another squeeze. "It's okay," I say even though the both of us know that it's really not. I've made my peace with it and that's enough. I'm not scared to die anymore. The longer I've been in here the more I've been welcoming it, I just never really thought about how it might affect other people.

"Is there anything I can do for you?" she asks after a pause, the weight of my words having sunk in.

"Nah," I say and weakly wave her off, "just keep doing what you're doing. It's nice and now I don't feel quite so bad."

"Okay," she says and does her best to smile at me.

"If there's a bit more of that cheese going that would be great," I say in a vain attempt to lighten the mood. It earns me a laugh and she passes me some, which I accept and try not to inhale for fear of making myself sick.

She continues to clean me up, making sure to get all the blood out of the wounds as best she can without actually taking my shirt off before she does her best to clean the dried blood around them off. The two of us silent, her cleaning and me watching for a moment. If I close my eyes, I can forget that I'm in a prison cell having been beaten and tortured.

Some of the cuts hurt more than others as she cleans them but those are the fresher ones. The water in the bowl she brought is basically red now and so is the cloth but neither of us says anything about it. I feel much better and much cleaner; this is the closest thing I've had to a wash since I got here. This is the closest I've been to water in so long… After having spent my entire life around it I can't be without it now. It's made me weak, frail and shaky, like I'm trying to fight off the effects of addiction.

Diaya is just finishing with one of the wounds on the top of my thighs (she can't get in there as much as she would like because of my trousers and the bandage) when the door of the cell suddenly clangs open. I open my eyes and look towards the door to see Sapphire in the doorway. Great…I was just starting to feel better as well.

"Sapphire!" Diaya cries as she glances over her shoulder and sees her. She immediately drops the cloth back into the bowl, water splashing over the sides. I can't even begin to make myself move other than to look over at Sapphire; everything feels heavy and I realise that I've stopped caring about her being near me now. She's going to hurt me anyway so what's the point in avoiding the inevitable?

"Diamond, Onyx wants to see you," Sapphire says calmly, much too calmly for someone who has caught her sister helping the enemy.

"Okay, I'll just…" Diaya begins.

"Now," Sapphire tells her, her voice much firmer.

"Yes Sapphire," Diaya mumbles. She lowers her eyes to the floor, her face flushing as she gingerly puts the bowl back on the tray. Swiftly she picks up the tray and practically darts from the cell. As she reaches the door she casts one last glance at me and I give her a small smile of thanks. This time I actually manage it even though smiling makes my face hurt at the moment…hell, everything makes my face hurt at the moment.

Once Diaya's gone Sapphire closes the cell door and locks it from the inside. I try to push myself to my feet, she's going to kick the shit out of me again but I should at least try to fight back this time. It's hard: my wrists keep giving out and my arms keep trembling but I slowly begin to stagger up onto even shakier legs. Sapphire just watches me the entire time, waiting until I'm on my feet before she makes her move.

I'm just about upright when Sapphire strikes. She crosses the room, grabs me by the hair and forces my top half down so that I'm bent double as she brings her knee up to meet my stomach. I cough, spluttering, as pain rips through me again along with the urge to be sick. It's not like I'm a stranger to pain anymore but getting kneed in the stomach, especially when I wasn't expecting it, still knocks the wind out of me.

I don't even have time to retch before she lets go of my hair, dropping me so that I fall to the floor, clutching my stomach to try and hold in the agony. I feel like I'm going to be sick but try to control it; I've barely eaten anything so it will suck plus Sapphire will make it worse for me if I do throw up. She doesn't waste time before she delivers the next blow either—a few more good kicks to my stomach, one after the other in quick succession and all I can do is ride it out. I just have to wait until it's over.

Once she seems bored of kicking me she looks down and realises that I'm holding onto myself too much to even try to fight back. Clearly this irritates her as she grabs me by the hair and yanks me to my knees. I cry out in pain, clutching her wrist to try and alleviate some of the ache but to no avail. Her grip is like a vice and I'm not breaking out of it any time soon.

Before I can do anything to catch myself, I get thrown against the wall like a sack of potatoes. Another cry rips from my throat as my back hits the cold, hard stone and I fall to the floor again, completely limp and totally powerless to do anything in retaliation. I wait for her to strike me again but it doesn't come, I look up and see her heading towards the door. She opens it, letting it bang loudly against the wall.

"Lock her up," I hear her snarl at a soldier, "and make sure this time she stays locked up. No one but myself or Onyx goes into this cell, do you understand?"

"Yes Ma'am."

I hear her stalk down the corridor and the solider who has been standing guard comes into the cell, closing the door behind him. He comes over to me and I don't fight him as he takes hold of my wrists and with my arms limp and pliable he's easily able to get them back into the chains. The cold iron grates against the rope burn from before and I wince—after that I probably have new wounds on top of the ones that Diaya just finished cleaning.

"Sorry," the soldier says softly as I wince in pain, so softly that I'm not even certain that I heard him correctly. "What?"

"Are you alright?" he asks.

"What?" It's all I can ask because I can't believe that a *Cimmerian soldier* is asking me how I am.

"Your sister is safe," he tells me.

"How do you know?" I ask. Discovering that he seems to care about my well-being is all too much for me to wrap my head around. I have too many questions for the amount of time I know we don't have—it doesn't take that long to lock up a skeleton and he will be expected back outside at any moment, either by Sapphire (although I think she left already) or the other soldiers.

"I've been guarding her as well," he says. "She's being kept in one of the rooms upstairs, Onyx is trying to convince her to join him."

"She won't," I say, totally confident that Harmony would never alley herself with the likes of him, not after what he's done.

"He offered her your safety," the soldier says. "He said that if she cooperated then he would let you live."

"Oh…" That changes things. Given the circumstances, Harmony would probably do anything to keep me safe, even if that does mean going along with Onyx and his plans for the mass genocide and enslavement of our people.

"I'm sorry," the soldier says, dropping his eyes to the floor.

"Why are you telling me this?" I ask.

Now that I look at him, he doesn't look all that much older than Harmony herself. He's probably a little younger than Caspian was at the very least. The light in the cell is still as awful as it's always been but my eyes seem to have adjusted quite well to the dark. He's obviously never seen any action until now as his face isn't ravaged by scars so we're in the same boat although I probably look a lot worse than he does.

"Because I have a sister your age," he says, "and the thought of her being chained up and tortured is more than I can bear."

"Why are you helping them then?" I ask. If he's so outraged by this, why did he join up with Onyx in the first place?

"I don't have a choice," he says. "I joined the army years ago, before the idea of a war was even thrown around, and now I can't leave without being shot for desertion."

"Do you have a family?" I ask.

"My sister plus a wife with a baby on the way," he replies. "My sister lost the use of her legs when she was young, our mother died a few years ago and our father left when she was small. My wife and I are the only ones she has left to care for her."

"Then make sure you get back to them," I tell him. I have no idea if this is true or not. It could just be a sob story so that I feel sorry for him and don't hate him for chaining me up in here but I have to believe there's still some good left in the Cimmerian people. They can't all be like Onyx and Sapphire—Diaya has shown me that more than anyone. Wars aren't black and white: there is no good or evil in this, just people following orders with the threat of their own death hanging over their heads.

"Thank you," he says and gives me a small smile. "I'll try and bring some more food for the both of you next time I'm on food duty."

"Isn't that a really dangerous thing to do?" I ask. I don't even know this man's name and he's offering to put himself potentially in the firing line so that Illyria and I can have a bit more food once in a while.

"Probably," he chuckles softly, "they do monitor what we bring down here but I'll see what I can do, especially as I won't be able to let the princess down here again."

"Thank you," I say. Part of me still can't believe I'm even having this conversation but I know this is real, the dull throbbing in my wrists tells me that I haven't just fallen unconscious again. "What's your name?" I ask.

"Nick," he replies, smiling.

"Nick can you give Harmony a message from me?" I ask. I don't know if I can trust this man or what but so far he hasn't done anything to try and hurt me. Getting me to trust him could be what he'll do to hurt me but I won't know that until it's too late. I probably shouldn't trust anyone on the Cimmerian side but that would mean making Diaya my enemy as well and I don't want to do that. I don't want to think the worst of people and, when all is said and done, it doesn't matter anymore: I can't have much longer left to live.

"Of course," he says.

"Tell her not to give in," I reply, "no matter what Onyx promises, don't give up and don't give in. I'll be fine."

"Miss..." he says. Both of us know that's not true—hell, he probably knows that better than I do because he might have some idea on when they're planning on killing Illyria and me as an example for everyone else.

"Tell her," I say. "Tell her that no matter what happens to me she mustn't give in, she must not surrender because I know deep down that she doesn't want to. Will you tell her that for me please?"

He seems to think this over for a second, clearly unhappy that I'm planning to sacrifice my life but I knew what I was getting into when I became a soldier. "Okay."

"Thank you."

"I'll do what I can for you while you're here," he says.

"Don't get yourself killed for me," I tell him.

"Don't worry," he say giving me one final smile, "I won't."

Unable to do anything else for me, he leaves the cell and locks the door behind him, leaving me alone again. I let out the breath I didn't realise that I've been holding and sink into myself. That was a lot harder than I thought it would be: actually saying out loud that I'm prepared to die in order to protect people. Since I became a Neo Warrior and since I started training as a soldier, I knew that I might have to one day but now I'm actually going to have to and *be* a soldier. Caspian shaped me into the person I am now and I'm going to have to learn how to continue to be a solider without him. If by some miracle I do survive this, then I have to be prepared to do this again and again and again until this war is over.

Chapter 8

The door of my cell opens and I lift my head up to see who's come to visit me today. I've realised over the last few visits that I no longer care who it is, not even if it's the prospect of a meagre meal. It's only ever likely to be one of three people: the guard who brings me food (not Nick, I haven't seen him since we talked and that must have been a week ago judging by the number of times the other has come in), Onyx or Sapphire and I'm only ever happy to see one of them. I'm surprised this time as Onyx enters followed by two guards dragging someone else in with them. I can't see who it is at first because one of the guards is in the way but it's either going to be Harmony or Illyria. I haven't seen Harmony since she was allowed into my cell for a reunion and I haven't seen Illyria since we first got captured. How long ago that was now? I can't remember; it could be close to half a year for all I know.

The two guards force the person onto the hard floor of the cell in front of me and when I look at them properly I see that it's Illyria. She looks terrible: thin, gaunt, with a haunted look in her eyes from lack of sleep and the outside world. The usual glow that surrounds her gives off a faint light in the darkness but it's dull, barely shining at all, and I can see marks on her skin where Sapphire said that she tried to burn her tattoos off with acid. I know I probably don't look much better here but I'm still taken aback. Like when I first saw Caspian, it's a shock to the system to see someone you know looking so different. It's the first time I've seen Onyx since he killed Caspian and he's got bandages covering the left hand side of his face where Caspian burnt him. I'd be amazed if he can still see out of that eye.

I open my mouth to say something but Illyria sees and instantly her eyes bore into me, still managing to keep a faint glow as she activates the magical link between us, and I hear her voice inside my head.

"*Don't say anything,*" she tells me and I close my mouth.

"*Okay,*" I reply. It's strange having a conversation inside my own head but the more I do it the more I get used to it. We haven't talked like this much as it must take an incredible about of strength on her part to maintain the link through the cells and she doesn't look as if she has much to spare for idle chit-chat.

"*Are you okay?*" she asks, eyes still staring straight into my soul.

"*I've been better,*" I reply. "*You?*"

"*They haven't killed me yet so I'm counting that as a bonus,*" she says and she's right. Neither of us are dead yet so there's got to be something said for that, right? Obviously that's not going to last—we're going to die here eventually—but the longer we're left alive the more that tiny flicker of hope that we might be rescued still holds within me.

"*I'm glad you're still alive,*" I tell her. Under normal circumstances I would have said 'I'm glad you're okay' but there's nothing okay about the situation we're both in.

"*Right back at you sugar,*" she says and I just about see the tiniest of smiles tug at the corner of her lips.

I have no idea if Onyx knows that this silent conversation is going on or if he thinks we're just staring intensely at each other. He hasn't ordered the guards to strike either of us so my guess is that he doesn't. To him there aren't different kinds of magic, there's just magic. To him there's no difference between what I can do and what Illyria can do but he has at least learnt well enough not to try and drown me because it wouldn't do any good. I can only imagine the look on his and Sapphire's faces if they tried and I suddenly sprouted gills. It would be hilarious for about all of ten seconds and then they'd probably try and jam something in there.

"What's the matter?" Onyx asks and I'm not sure which one of us he's talking to so I'm going to assume that it's both of us. "I thought you'd be happy to see each other—after all you are comrades and now that three has gone down to two…"

Illyria hisses something at him in Moonian that even I don't understand. Onyx smirks before he closes the distance between them and backhands her across the face. After reeling from the blow, she turns back to glare defiantly at him. Illyria takes no nonsense from anyone, not even someone trying to kill her and I only wish I could be half as strong willed as she is. I'm just about holding it together under the torture they're putting me through but I don't know how much longer I'm going to be able to fight back before I just beg them to kill me.

"Does it speak Universal or do I have to get you to translate everything?" Onyx asks me. I don't answer. "Come now siren, you don't want to be responsible for another person getting a bullet in their brain now do you?"

"I told you I didn't know anything!" I snap before I can stop myself.

Onyx's eyes glint maliciously and he knows that he's getting to me. I wish he didn't because it gives him power over me but there's no point trying to hide it. The best I can do now is try to make him think I'm not as angry or desperate as I actually am. Realistically I know that if he was going to kill me without making it a public execution he would have done so by now; it's when he finally decides to take me outside that I'm going to have to worry. For now, I settle for glaring at him again, maintaining eye contact until he finally looks away.

He strolls over to Illyria, her eyes on him the entire time, and bends down so that he can tuck a lank lock of her hair behind one off her ears before grabbing a fistful and pulling it harshly. She winces but doesn't make any other sound. He turns back to look at me.

"I asked you if she spoke Universal," he says, his voice low and dangerous. "You can either answer or I can cut out her tongue and it won't matter either way."

"I speak it," Illyria hisses at him in Universal, finally breaking her silence, "I just have nothing to say to you."

"That certainly is good to hear, I'm so glad you'll be able to understand me," Onyx says, smiling. It's a smile that makes me very nervous—why would he care if she understands him or not? He lets go of her hair and gets to his feet. "I must admit I was planning on saving this as a surprise for later, maybe when you're in front of everyone on the island," he says.

Illyria looks directly at me and I hear her voice inside my head again. *"Loves the sound of his own voice doesn't he?"*

I just about manage to stop myself from snorting with laughter. He really does—that much was obvious when we were first on Cimmerian but, after having to listening to him going on, it's even more noticeable. Laughing about it now wouldn't do either of us any good so I manage to keep my face as straight as possible.

"Then I thought I really should have revealed this before I shot Feioré," he continues. Hang on, revealed what? "It would have been so much fun to see the look on his face when he found out that you were such a disappointment." That last part is spoken directly to me but I have no idea what he's on about. Why me specifically?

"What?" I ask before I can stop myself.

"It would have been much more fun that way but this will have to do instead," he says as if I hadn't spoken.

"What are you talking about?" I ask.

Onyx doesn't say anything. He simply reaches into his jacket and pulls out a small envelope, an envelope with some very familiar handwriting on it and I feel the bottom drop out of my stomach.

"Now this came into my possession not long after you all left Cimmerian," he says holding the envelope up. "Addressed to my youngest sister and bearing the mark of the Braxian Neo Warriors."

Oh no… No, please tell me this isn't happening.

"So I decide to open said letter and have a read of the contents," Onyx says. "Obviously once I did I decided to keep the letter for myself as it contains some very helpful hints inside after all of the polite drivel."

"What's going on?" Illyria asks aloud, not bothering to use her magic or to speak in Braxian just so that he can't understand her.

"Please don't," I beg, knowing full well what's about to come out before he even says it. I can't believe I was so stupid! Out of everything I could have said in those letters I didn't even think about the prospect that they wouldn't make it to Diaya. Obviously begging will do me no good though. He's going to read it out and then whatever opinion Illyria has of me will be shattered and if I ever get out of this I'll probably get a court martial and be stripped of my rank. What am I thinking? Like I'll ever get out of here…out of this. At least before I could have died with her thinking better of me.

"I think this is my favourite part," Onyx says as he opens one of the folded pieces of paper. "*When you finally get the chance to come to my home island, I'll take you round all of the coves. They basically cover the entire right side of the island and you can hide there for hours without anyone spotting you. I'm pretty sure you could get an entire ship in there but obviously never tried, I've stuck a rough drawing of a map and all the best places to go in with this letter and we can cross them off as we do them. I used to play in the coves as a kid 'cause there's one that takes you directly to the House if you go in far enough. So willing to be helpful without even knowing.*" Onyx turns to me and I want to be sick.

Every single word out of his mouth is like a blow to Illyria's opinion of me and I can't look at her. I don't want to see the disappointment in her eyes. Without even realising it, I basically gave Onyx and his army everything they needed to successfully invade. I'm the reason that everyone is either dead or has been captured.

This is all my fault.

"There is more," Onyx says still smirking at me, "shall I go on?"

"Please don't," I beg, my voice barely above a whisper. I don't think I can hear any more of what might be in that letter. The docks took up a paragraph of my letter to Diaya and, thinking about it, I'm pretty sure I even told her about down here when I was describing the House. I'm so stupid, I should have thought that this could happen. Hot, angry tears prick the corners of my eyes and I'm still fighting the urge to be sick.

"But there's so much more in here," Onyx says with a nasty smile. It's the kind of smile that immediately makes you know that you've messed up and I've messed up big time. I only manage to hold his gaze for a second before I look away and let the tears just spill from my eyes. It's all because of me…

I hadn't thought that this would happen, never imagined something like this otherwise I would have stopped to think about the consequences. Now they're all dead and it's because of me: Mum, Dad, Granddad, the rest of the council, Caspian and countless others. I unwittingly gave Onyx exactly what he needed to make this invasion possible. Revulsion and self-hatred bubble up inside me and it feels like I'm never going to be able to stop crying. Whatever ends up happening to me, I deserve it.

"*The docks are easily the best place to go,*" Onyx continues and it sinks in that it isn't over yet.

"Please…" I beg again but it falls on deaf ears as he carries on.

"*There's so many people there and they literally have anything you could possibly want. I've been able to get food, fishing supplies, drink, they even sell gunpowder and stuff that they get for the ships and fuel for everyone's homes. I'm pretty sure that they even sell weapons and things like that there as well…*"

"She said enough!" Illyria snaps, making me look up. She's glaring at him and I don't think I've ever seen her looking this angry before.

Onyx turns to her and raises an eyebrow. "Oh, jumping to her defence, are we, or have you had enough knowing just what kind of person your fellow soldier turned out to be?"

Illyria doesn't say anything to him; she turns to me and I drop my eyes to the floor. I can't face all that anger turned on me. It should be and I deserve it but I'm not ready to face it yet. Onyx chuckles and I hear the rustle of paper and fabric as he folds up my letter and slips it back into his jacket. I don't want to face either of them so I keep my eyes locked on the floor, cheeks burning with shame.

"Are you sure I can't convince you to hear more?" he asks Illyria. "It really is a fascinating read."

"How about you go fuck yourself?" Illyria snarls, too preoccupied with being furious to bother speaking in a language he can't understand.

There is silence for a moment before I hear his boots on the floor and a loud crack as he strikes her again. I look up just as the force of the blow knocks her sideways to the ground and I can't help the gasp that escapes my throat. All I can think is that I'm the reason she's here, I'm the reason that this has happened to her and I'm the reason that eventually we're both going to be killed here.

"Take her back to her cell," Onyx orders and the guards each grab one of Illyria's arms and drag her to her feet—not that it looks as if she needs much strong arming; both of us are incredibly weak so probably only one of them would have done.

As they begin to drag her away our eyes meet for a second and I don't see fury or anything else that I know I deserve there. All I see is disappointment and that hurts more than any anger or hatred ever could. I don't blame her though—I wouldn't even blame her if she hated me: I hate me right now. Breaking our gaze I let my head drop and keep my eyes to the floor until I hear the door close and see Onyx's boots come into my line of vision. He kneels down in front of me, his hand coming up under my chin so that he can tilt my face upwards. I look into his eyes and all I see is a sadistic killer.

"Don't you see now," he says softly, "it never mattered how fast you got here or how long it took you to find out that you couldn't stop us—you gave us everything we needed in order to make this possible. Every single person on this island who has died: it's your fault. The countless more that will die are also your fault and when I finally put you down in front of them all you will have their faces, knowing that you did this to them, burnt into your memory as the last thing you will ever see."

"Does Diaya know about this?" I ask, finally finding my voice although it's thick with tears and self-loathing.

"Why does that matter?" he asks, his voice still soft and silky as if he were telling me something that I wanted to hear rather than handing me my fate as an accessory to his invasion and massacre.

"I just wondered if she knew what kind of person her brother really is," I say and despite everything I hate about myself I can't disguise the hatred I feel towards him.

"When I give this letter to your sister, she will know what kind of person you are and she will gladly watch you die," he tells me.

It was bad enough having Illyria hear that; I hadn't thought of the prospect of him giving the letter to Harmony as well. He's probably right: she would hate me for the rest of my life, knowing that I gave them the information to invade our home and kill our family. I wouldn't blame her at all, if it were the other way around I'd probably feel the same way. Closing my eyes I let the tears that have been building slip down my face again.

His hand keeps my face up for a moment as he watches me fall apart but eventually he gets bored and lets my head drop. I don't open my eyes or even bother trying to look up at him, I just wait for him to leave. It seems as if he watches me for ages but it's probably not all that long before I hear him leave, bolting the cell door behind himself.

Once I'm alone I let out the breath I didn't even realise I was holding. I can't believe I was so stupid! At least the saving grace here is that Caspian didn't die knowing what a poor excuse for a solider I am. I don't think I could have taken that. I've never been responsible for the suffering of so many people before. The only thing I can really hope for now is that my death might act as some kind of penance.

~ *** ~

I'm stuck inside my own head for hours, even possibly closer to a day; I'm not really sure but I don't think it's longer than that. Occasionally I think about trying to reach out to see if I can explain myself to Illyria but I don't. Even if she did let me in, what the hell would I say to her? 'Hey sorry I know I messed up big time and you're in prison and most likely going to be executed because of me but can we talk?' I don't think so somehow… If I were her I wouldn't want to talk to me so I just leave it.

It genuinely does surprise me therefore when I feel her presence pushing at the corner of my mind. For a moment, I think about pushing her away, unsure if I'm ready to deal with her anger yet, but then I decide to relax and let her in. If she has something to say to me, then she deserves to say it and I need to face it rather than take the coward's way out.

"*Ari,*" she says inside my head after I've relaxed enough to let her in "*can you hear me?*"

"*Yeah I can hear you,*" I reply, also inside my own head so that she can hear me too.

"*Are you okay?*" she asks.

Don't ask me that. Don't ask me how I'm doing in all of this, I don't deserve to have anyone's sympathy. "*Fine,*" I lie.

"*Ari this is me you're talking to,*" she says. "*I can tell from your thoughts that you're not.*"

"*Oh…*"

"*I could practically hear you screaming from the other cell,*" she chuckles softly. "*So do you want to tell me the truth or are we going to keep dancing around this like we don't have something to talk about?*"

I sigh audibly so she probably doesn't hear it. "*Honestly,*" I say "*I'm not fine. I'm so far beyond fine at this point.*"

"*That should be a given,*" she says. "*That was a huge bomb to drop on you and you're going to need time to process it.*"

"*I don't deserve time,*" I say.

"*Maybe you don't,*" she says, "*but time is the only thing that you and I do have at the moment.*"

"*Do we?*" I ask. I was under the impression that our days were numbered it's just that neither of us has been told what that number is yet.

"*Well, we haven't got anything else to do,*" she chuckles derisively. She's right about that I suppose: time alone with our thoughts is the only thing that we have going for the both of us. "*You can't keep thinking about this right up 'til the end Ari,*" she adds.

"*Why not?*" I ask. "*I deserve to.*"

"*You think you do and maybe you do, who am I to judge, but it won't bring them back and it won't undo what's been done,*" she says.

I can feel hot tears making their way down my cheeks again. "*I can't believe I was so stupid.*"

"*We all make mistakes,*" she says.

"Not like this."

"*You can't blame yourself forever.*"

"Can't I?"

"*No,*" she says firmly and it's a tone I've never heard from her. The usually soft-spoken Illyria is sharp and businesslike now. "*I know you think that you deserve to and you shouldn't forget this but you can't shoulder all the blame. Don't get me wrong: this is your mistake, you made it and you're the one who is going to have to live with these consequences but you can't let them rule you. There are currently only three people that you know of who know about this, right?*"

"You, me and Onyx," I reply.

"*And I would guess Sapphire too so if you continue to feel sorry for yourself about this they will be able to use that against you for the rest of the time that you're locked in here.*"

"I guess..."

"*They can threaten to tell everyone but as long as you make peace with yourself about this, they can't hold it over you right up until the point when Onyx decides to kill you,*" Illyria says. "*Don't let him do that, if he does then he wins and you're nothing but his pawn to do with as he pleases.*"

"*How can you be so understanding?*" I ask in frustration. Her words are starting to get to me. I know she's right but that doesn't make it any less difficult to hear when all I want is for her to scream at me. "*I gave him everything that he needed to get here and take over.*"

"*You couldn't have known that the letter would end up being used like that,*" she says.

"But I should have done!" I cry as more tears make their way down my face. "*I should have thought more before I wrote down everything that could possibly be known about this place and sent it off to our enemy.*"

"You were writing to a friend," she says.

"*This is all because of me!*" I practically scream, my own thoughts making my head hurt. "*If it wasn't for me, then you wouldn't be in prison, neither would my sister, what's left of my people wouldn't be slaves and neither Caspian or my family would have been killed.*"

I leave that to hang in the air for a moment and Illyria doesn't say anything in response. She seems to be waiting for me to talk again but I don't know what else *to* say. It's all been laid out and that is how it is. This is my fault and eventually I'm going to pay for what I've done. I won't complain, I'll take it and I'll know that I deserved this all along.

"I just want to die," I say aloud in the hope that she won't hear me.

Clearly my head is screaming it too loudly for her not to because I hear her voice again, as softly as it always has been. *"Don't think that way sugar."*

"But..." I start to protest but I don't know how to continue.

"If you die, then who is going to save all those people out there?" she asks.

"The others?" I offer.

"Maybe," she says, *"but they need you to be their champion."*

"Do they?" I ask. I don't see how on earth having the person who put you in this mess saving you would be of any consolation.

"It would help you put things right," she says and I will grant her that. If, by some miracle, we were able to get out of here and to a point where I could save my people then it would at least help with the guilt eating me up inside.

"Hey Illyria?" I ask.

"Yes sugar?"

"Can I ask you a couple of things?"

"Sure thing."

"How are we able to talk like this?" I decide to lead with this first, mostly out of curiosity more than anything else, but also because I don't know if I'm ready to face the answer to the question I really want to ask yet. *"I know it's because of the mind link you made with me when we met but these prisons were made to block out the use of magic."*

"I can't use new magic," Illyria says. *"The only way I can describe it is that I can use old magic—magic that I had already activated before we were put in here."*

"What do you mean?"

"I set up this link with you long before we arrived here, same as I set up links with Caspian and all the others, so I can still use those. The others not so much anymore, I'm not strong enough to reach that far away now" she says. *"New magic I can't use so I couldn't force Onyx to see what I want him to or to enter his dreams. Much in the same way I imagine that if he tried to drown you those gills of yours would still pop out because that magic is part of you but you can't conjure water anymore."*

"That makes sense," I say. Talking to her is comforting. At least I know that she still will talk to me and that I haven't lost my lifeline to everyone. Even when neither of us are talking I can still feel her presence inside my head, just another part of this link between us while she still has it activated.

"What was the other thing you wanted to ask me?" she asks when I don't say anything more.

"If this ever got back—what I did—I would be stripped of my rank and get a court martial wouldn't I?" I ask, starting off with that.

"Probably," she replies. *"I don't really know. This kind of thing has never come up before and I've never actually known anyone to get a court martial or dishonourably discharged, despite the fact that it was Caspian's favourite threat to make sure that no one was late to training in the mornings."*

"Are you going to tell Kat about what I wrote in those letters?" I ask.

There it is: the question I don't want to get an answer for but the one I desperately need answered. It's not that I am under any misunderstanding that we are getting out of this alive, but Kat is the Commander now and she deserves to know. Even if it means they all hate me, even if it means that I'm dismissed posthumously, she should know.

"No," Illyria says finally.

"Why not?" I ask.

"Because having to see your family be killed, your homeland destroyed and your only living relative a prisoner is punishment enough," she says. *"What you're going to do to yourself every day for the rest of your life is much worse than anything that Kat or the Braxian government could ever do to you."*

I've never felt more grateful to anyone in my entire life before. Keeping this to herself could potentially put Illyria at fault as well but she's prepared to do that. She is right though: no punishment (save death) could be worse than having to live with the knowledge that I gave Onyx everything he needed in order to come here and destroy everything I held dear. *"Do me a favour though,"* she says.

"Anything."

"If, by some chance of fate or luck or the old gods finally deciding to listen to prayers again for a change, whatever, promise me that you'll put things right," she says. *"It was a mistake, there's no doubt about that, and you couldn't have known that this was going to happen but you have to take responsibility."*

"I will."

"*That's your new goal in life: you free these people and you fix this,*" she finishes. "*If you want to tell Kat about what happened with the letter, then I won't stop you, that's your decision to do so but I won't.*"

"*Thank you Illyria,*" I say and even in my head my voice is thick with tears.

"*We've all got to look out for each other sugar,*" she tells me, "*you and yours more than anyone.*"

"*Okay.*"

"*So make sure you look out for these people and get them their home back someday,*" she says. "*I'm not saying that it's going to be easy and it sure as hell won't be any time soon but if we get out of this I'll help you. That's a promise.*"

"*Thank you,*" I say again. I don't really know what else I can say to that.

"*Of course this is provided that Onyx doesn't kill us within the next few days and we're actually able to be saved and save others along with us,*" she says with a soft laugh.

"*This is true.*"

"*Sit tight sugar, the others are coming,*" she tells me. "*Hopefully soon, I don't know—I lost the strength to find out a while back.*"

"*Okay,*" I say.

"*Just try to get some sleep and not think about it too much.*"

"*Okay.*" How likely that is going to be is anyone's guess.

"*If you need me just reach for me and I'll hear you,*" she says. "*I've got enough strength in me for this.*"

"*Thank you.*"

I feel the link drop and I no longer feel her presence inside my head. It's strange, talking to her made me feel both better and worse in equal measure. She is right about one thing though: if I do manage to get out of here and get my freedom back again, I have to spend every waking second of my life trying to get Neyara back its freedom from the Cimmerians.

~ *** ~

It's been a while since I've had a visit from Sapphire, and it's barely been two days since Onyx was last here, so it's a bit of a surprise to see her come through my cell door. She doesn't say anything to me at first, just looks me up and down as she locks the door behind herself. She stands there for longer than usual, putting me on edge. I know that she's here for a reason, probably to kick me while she and Onyx think I'm down. Eventually she crosses the room and roughly grabs my hair. She forces my head backwards so that I have to look at her. I'm getting rather used to being in this position so it's not as much of a shock as it was the first time it happened. The crick in my neck is almost normal now.

"It's been a while siren," she smirks.

"Come back for another round?" I ask, my words slurring a little from the new waves of nausea of no food and the sudden onslaught of pain. "Don't you get tired of beating up someone who can't fight back?"

"Don't you get tired of antagonising the person who can kill you in a second and not feel a damn thing about it?" she asked.

"Touché," I reply, just about managing to smirk up at her. I have no idea where this newfound confidence is coming from, because I know she can kill me and not feel any remorse for doing so but I can't seem to stop myself. I can't fight back with magic or my fists so I might as well get the barbs in while I can. It's about the only thing I can do to unnerve her and make her know that she hasn't won yet. It actually seems to work as well as a low growl rumbles in her throat and she turns away.

"You know I would have thought you would have learnt your lesson by now," she hisses, "but apparently not. Apparently you're quite content to keep pissing me off more and more."

"What is it that you're so angry about?" I ask. "You could take out your underlying frustration on anyone in this prison so what is it about me that makes me so lucky?"

"You really want to know?" Sapphire asks, turning to look at me. The smirk on her face is becoming increasingly unpleasant but that does nothing to deter me.

"God, I really do," I reply. It's been niggling at me for a while now. Sapphire could have chosen to focus on Caspian, Illyria or Harmony. She could have chosen anyone to make her main victim but for some reason she chose me from the beginning. There's got to be something to it other than she just doesn't like me and the longer I keep her talking then the longer I can go without a beating.

"Fine, you people sicken me," she says sounding relatively calm.

"Charming," I mumble.

"The pure and simple fact that my father even used to entertain having you anywhere near us was disgusting," she says as she pulls up the chair I was tied to ages ago, which has just been left in here with me, and sits down in front of me. "You're a race of heathens and you don't deserve to live."

"Why do you hate us so much?" I ask. I'm genuinely curious. I know there has always been this underlying hatred between the two countries but when we went over there most people were so friendly it's like it wasn't an issue. There will always be militants on both sides but I don't know where this has come from.

"Isn't it obvious?" she asks.

"Not really."

"Then you're stupider than I thought."

"Enlighten me then."

"You lord it over those of us who don't use magic," she says.

"How?"

"You know how," she spits. I have no idea what she means so I'll let her continue. "You can destroy a city in a second and you don't seem to think that it's a problem. Criminals with that kind of power shouldn't be allowed to roam the streets."

"We have ways of dealing with our own criminals," I say. "As it might have escaped your notice we have magically enforced prisons to hold people who might use their powers *to* take out a city."

"That's not the point," she snaps. "If one of you heathens decided to, you could wipe out my entire family."

"Like you've wiped out mine?" I ask, sounding surprisingly calm.

I shouldn't have done that. She gets to her feet and that earns me a kick to the stomach. I fall forward, groaning in pain as everything clenches tightly.

"You let this threat hang over our heads, making believe that everything is peaceful and that's what you want while, all along, plotting to take us out," she says as she sits back down.

"Where are you getting this?" I ask. "As far as I know the vast majority of the wars between us have always been started by Cimmerians."

"Because someone needs to stand up to you," she snarls. "Your race will be the death of all of us if you're allowed to continue living."

"So what is it about *me*?" I ask. "You could have focused on anyone—Caspian, Illyria, my sister—but you seem to have fixated on *me*. Everything you have done to them has been to get to me. Not you and Onyx, just you and I want to know why. What on earth could I have possibly done to you?"

"You wouldn't understand, it's beyond your comprehension," she says.

"Try me."

"Fine, for one thing I thought you'd be the easiest to break," she says, "but it appears that I was wrong on that front."

"Then I'm pleased to have disappointed you," I say defiantly. "What would you have done if you had broken me?"

"Used you to get to Feioré," she says, shrugging as though bored. I should have guessed that one. "Although using him to get to you was even more fun than I thought it would be and Onyx got his desired outcome."

"Still haven't quite broken me though," I say.

She laughs humourlessly. "There's still time little siren. There are so many wonderful things I can do to you before I truly break you."

"You still haven't answered my question," I say after letting that hang in the air for a moment. "Why do you seem to hate me so much?"

"Because you're a Braxian heathen," she replies.

"No, this has nothing to do with being Braxian or Cimmerian," I say. "This is about you and me."

"You really do think the world of yourself, don't you?"

"Not really," I reply, shrugging as best I can. "In the grand scheme of things, my life doesn't really matter that much but you seem to be giving me a reason to think that I matter to you and I think I have a right to know why before you kill me."

She gets to her feet, growling with disgust before the back of her hand connects with my face. I'm sent reeling from the blow and my shoulder gets tugged the wrong way but a smirk spreads over my face as I look back at her. I've gotten to her. She's losing it; that calm collected exterior is already starting to crack and that makes me rather happy. I continue to smirk up at her until she turns away, fuming.

"I cannot believe that my father was even remotely interested in you and your so called talent," she hisses and it's almost as if she's isn't even talking to me. "You must have some pretty enthralling magic to make a king fall for the doe-eyed angel look."

And it suddenly dawns on me why she hates me so much. "That's it, isn't it?" I ask, unable to stop myself. "You're jealous."

"What?" she snarls rounding on me.

"You're jealous because your father said that I was a better singer than you at the banquet," I say.

"Shut up," she growls, glaring.

"That's really petty when you think about it," I say. I know I shouldn't because I'm going to get another beating, judging by the murderous look on her face. "You, an accomplished princess of Cimmerian in your own right, with a good few years on me, are jealous of an eighteen-year-old heathen who is basically still a child."

"I said shut up!" she screams and the next thing I know she has me by the hair, her knee coming up to connect with my face. I turn my head as best I can at the very last second to stop my nose from being broken but I can feel the blood starting to trickle down my face from a newly reopened wound again. When she finally lets me go, I spit a mouthful of it onto the floor along with the rest.

"God, it must really burn you up just *how much* I get to you," I pant as I glare up at her.

That was a bad idea.

She aims a swift kick to the chair, sending it across the room before she pulls her knife out and sinks the blade into my shoulder. I scream in pain as she twists it in deeper, as deep as it will go making sure to cut up as much of me as possible. Okay, upon reflection that was not one of my finest ideas. That was probably about the stupidest thing I could have said to her.

"One of these days, little siren, I am going to take so much pleasure in killing you," she snarls. "For now, I will settle for doing everything I can to make your entire existence miserable. You think it hurt when I beat you? You think it hurt when you saw what was left of your filthy family lying dead at your feet or when Feioré was shot in front of you? Even when Onyx read out that letter to the other one and you realised that all of this was made possible by you? That will be nothing compared to what I can do to you now."

"And you think that's what your father would have wanted?" I ask, gasping through the burning in my arm. "You think he would have wanted you and Onyx to start a war that will endanger millions of innocent lives?"

"Onyx has a vision that doesn't include our father," Sapphire says, "and now, with him gotten out of the way that vision can finally become a reality."

I think that over for a moment, the cogs in my lethargic brain trying to put two and two together and then it suddenly clicks. "You killed him."

The smile that spreads over her face is boarder-line psychotic. "How astute of you," she says.

"You killed your own father?" I ask, unable to wrap my head around it. "Why?"

"Onyx knew that the only way he could start this war would be to get rid of our father and pin the blame on you," she says, "and you gave us the perfect opportunity at the Jubilee by leaving as soon as you heard that he was dead."

"I hope it was worth it," I growl. "Putting the rest of your family through that for the sake of revenge. If they find out about this…"

She grabs my chin harshly, her fingers digging painfully into my skin as she forces me to look at her. I try to wrench my face away but her grip is like a vice that I can't seem to shake no matter what.

"You won't ever have the opportunity to tell anyone," she tells me. "You'll never see the light of day alive again."

"You can't keep me silent," I hiss.

"Oh but I can," she says. "I can hurt you in ways you've never imagined. I can drive you mad, until all you see when you close your eyes is my face. I will make sure that you are never free from me. I will be the star of your nightmares for the rest of your very short life. You think what we did to Feioré was the end? It was only the beginning. Imagine seeing your friend in the other cell murdered before your eyes, your sister fucked by as many Cimmerian soldiers that will follow the order and your precious homeland completely and utterly ravaged."

I close my eyes, trying to force her away by taking away the image of her but she's still there burnt on the inside of my head, taunting me with her words and the picture she's painting. I think of Harmony and Illyria and anyone else she could use to get to me. God there's even Diaya! She surely wouldn't do anything to her own sister just to get to me? She might do though, they murdered their own father so I have no idea what they're truly capable of. She gives my head a fierce shake and I open my eyes again.

"I will make you understand what real pain is and it doesn't even have to be things I do *to* you," she tells me. "There are thousands of things I can do to you without even touching you. You will know what real pain feels like and you will beg me for death before the end."

I believe her.

She lets go of my chin and I let my head hang forward, utterly defeated. There's no point fighting it. She will hound me until there is nothing left inside my head but her. Hell, I'd beg her for death now if I didn't think she would still do everything she promised just because she can and wants to. She wants me to break and, after a threat like that I can't fight back anymore and she seems to realise it.

"Where's all that fighting spirit from a moment ago?" she asks.

I can't even bring myself to lift my gaze from the floor to face her, let alone answer her. I can feel the tears pricking my eyes again and I don't want her to see.

"That's what I thought," she laughs humourlessly.

I hear her footsteps and look up to see her walk away before letting my head drop again. I listen to the door slam closed and lock. The tears slowly make their way down my face and I don't do anything to stop them.

I'm sorry Caspian…Illyria…Harmony…Mum…I'm sorry I couldn't be stronger. I'm sorry I couldn't do anything to save you. I can't even save myself, let alone do anything to save anyone else. I'm so pathetic. I wish Sapphire would just kill me.

Chapter 9

Time is not a concept I have anymore. Not that time has meant much to me since being imprisoned but I was vaguely trying to keep track of what day and what month it was. I've tried counting the guards who have bought me food again but only three have come and I know it's been longer than that since Sapphire last came to break my spirit. Neither her nor Onyx have been in during the time I've been alone and I gave up any hope of seeing Diaya again—all I can wish for is that neither Onyx or Sapphire has done anything to hurt her for trying to help me.

Illyria has only been able to contact me twice after we last spoke, both of us being too weak to maintain any kind of connection for very long so most of the time I'm alone with my thoughts, which is no longer the comfort it used to be. Each day all I think about is what's happened since we were imprisoned and hope that the next morning will finally be the day when Onyx decides it's time for our execution.

When the guard left last time, he took my lamp away so the cell door opening and a sudden onslaught of light makes my eyes sting. Looking up blearily, I see Onyx and I can't help but feel dread and relief in equal measure. The best I can hope for is that this is the end but, knowing Onyx, he's probably going to drag it out for as long as possible.

"Good morning, little siren," he says and I grit my teeth. I hate that nickname so much. "I trust you've had a pleasant stay." Stay?

He clicks his fingers and two soldiers come into the cell. Wordlessly they unchain me from the wall before forcing my hands behind my back. They barely need to force me: I've only been fed enough to keep me alive and I don't have the strength to do anything on my own anymore, let alone try and fight them off. A new pair of chains tighten around my wrists and once the soldiers are done they let me drop to the floor and step back, waiting for their next set of orders.

Ah… Yeah, that means it's time.

Slowly, Onyx crosses the room and kneels in front of me. He tilts my head up, taking hold of my chin and studies my face. I have no idea if he's happy with what he sees or not or if he's just feeling smug as he smirks down at me. I must look an absolute state: dried blood on my face and in my hair, lifeless eyes with huge purple bruises under them from lack of decent sleep, gaunt and hollow from not eating.

"It does seem a shame to have wasted such a pretty face," he says as he runs his thumb over my cracked lips. "The things I could have done with you…" He sighs at the thought and I feel bile creeping up the back of my throat. I swallow it down but I'm sure the disgust still blatantly shows on my face. He clenches his grip and I wince. "No matter though," he continues, "I have one sister to do my bidding and while having the two of you would have been such a treat, I need to have one of you to use as an example for your filthy people."

I don't reply, simply look up at him with blank, lifeless eyes. If I wasn't so dehydrated I'd spit in his face but, as it is, I can just about manage a scowl. This seems to amuse him greatly. "What? Nothing to say?" he asks.

I don't reply.

"You really don't have anything to say to me?" he asks again. "No last words, no pleas for your worthless life to be spared? Nothing for your friends, your home, your people?" I continue to stare at him. Please, does this mean it's going to be over soon?

Onyx chuckles softly. "I expected better from you, siren."

"Sorry to disappoint," I finally say. My voice sounds like someone grinding rocks together, hard and gravelly, and speaking hurts my parched throat.

"So she does speak," Onyx says with a raised eyebrow.

"Means I don't have to listen to you anymore," I say. I might as well get at least one more barb in before he kills me.

"I am going to miss that fighting spirit," he chuckles humourlessly. "There was me thinking that Sapphire had finally quashed it for good. No matter. The sight of your sister in chains, seeing her screaming as she watches you die will be enough to do it. Well…that will be the last thing you ever see so it really doesn't matter the effect it has on you. It will be a very nice way to break *her* though."

Every time he brings up Harmony, it's just another wonderful reminder that she's caught up in this too. He's going to kill Illyria no matter what I do but Harmony still has to live with him after this.

"Please…" I say softly and I can feel my breath catching in my throat like I want to cry but there are no more tears left in me.

"Please what, siren?"

"Please don't hurt her."

"I have no intention of doing any *physical* damage to her," Onyx says, a nasty smile on his face. "Besides, once you're gone and I take her as my slave, I'll be the only one that she has. I can rip the magic out of her and make her into a proper Cimmerian slave."

I drop my eyes to the floor, I can't take this anymore. "Just hurry up and kill me already but please don't hurt her."

Onyx laughs softly. "Sapphire will be pleased," he muses. "It seems that we've finally broken you." He places his hand on my cheek, his touch suspiciously gentle, and smiles at me before drawing his hand back and slapping me, hard, across the face. The blow knocks me to the floor and my head hits the stone. I watch as he gets to his feet and stalks out of the cell. As he reaches the door he stops for the briefest of moments.

"Take her away," he tells the soldiers without a second glance back.

No one moves until Onyx has disappeared and his footsteps have faded away completely. I let out the breath I didn't realise I had been holding just before both soldiers roughly grab me and haul me to my feet, dragging me out of the cell. They needn't have bothered—one of them could have flung me over his shoulder and carried me. It probably would have been easier as well. I try to fall into step with them but my legs feel like sand, not having been used for so long so it's a struggle.

As the feeling begins to come back to my legs, so does the pain. Every step is agony and every so often I stumble and fall to my knees if the soldiers don't catch me first. Each time I do fall, I'm roughly forced to my feet again as they lead me out of the dungeons, through the House and outside. It's a long way so it takes quite a long time and every single step of the way feels like I'm walking on broken glass. At first, I try to look around—see what they've done to the place since occupying it—but my eyes sting, having been in darkness for so long, and I can just about see a few feet in front of my face.

Finally, after what seems like hours, they lead me out of the doors at the front of the House and the first thing that hits me is the light. Sunlight…natural sunlight that burns my eyes and I screw them shut trying to curl in on myself, away from it. I can't remember the last time I saw sunlight but, judging by how hot and bright it is and what I'd worked out from guard counting, it's been about five weeks since we first came here. One of the soldiers gives me a harsh shake and I force myself to stand and open my eyes. I focus on the floor, blinking rapidly until I can see properly. It's not only being out in sunlight but the feeling of being outside as well that makes me feel so overcome with emotion.

The fresh air is like a gift from heaven, having only been breathing the stale air of the underground for so long. I smell the salt of the sea on the wind and my head begins to spin. I'm glad that I can at least die outside, near the ocean, rather than in the dungeons. The feeling of being hit with so many smells and feelings that I had forgotten makes me a little light headed but I fight against the sensation. This is the last time I'm ever going to see daylight and be out in the open again so I don't want to waste it by passing out. I close my eyes and pretend that I'm free, even if only for a second.

Another rough yank tells me that my moment is over. The soldiers drag me up to a large wooden stage that has been erected in front of the entrance to the House. I look over and see Illyria already standing there. She looks as thin and gaunt as I probably do, the dried blood standing out against her white hair. She's tied to a post with a small pile of kindling at her feet and there is another post next to her with its own kindling pile.

That must be for me then…

I didn't think they still burnt people at the stake but Onyx obviously wants this to be a very showy affair so of course he would resort to an old method of execution. Also it won't be quick, it won't be painless and it will have the biggest impact on the crowd.

I glance over to the other side of the stage and see Harmony sitting chained to a chair, her feet fastened to the legs and her hands behind her back. She looks a lot better than either Illyria or I do, although there are a few visible bruises, none seem to be on her face and that's probably because Onyx wants to keep her looking pretty. She's the slave, I'm the example. We lock eyes for a second and I notice hers fill with tears when she sees me. How long ago was it that we last saw each other? She was shocked at my appearance then and I looked a hell of a lot better than I do now. Finally, I look away and sigh to myself.

I'm sorry, Harm.

I let the soldiers drag me over to stand in front of the post next to Illyria's. The chains are undone for a second so that the soldiers can chain me to it. The wood of the post is splintered and harsh against my already sore skin but being able to lean against it feels alright. It gives me something to ground myself to so I don't fall over as soon as the soldiers step away and it looks as if Illyria has done the same thing.

The soldiers leave and I look out into the crowd beginning to form in front of the stage. My eyes are still a little hazy and adjusting to being in such bright light for the first time in over a month is painful but I can still see that a lot of people are here already. Word must have gotten down to the docks (if the docks are even still the place where everyone congregates anymore) as more and more people seem to be turning up by the second. I can't look at the sadness on their faces when they see me and realise who I am and turn away, looking off towards the gardens, only to discover that that was a bad idea as well.

A little way away from the stage, hanging by the neck from a sturdy looking tree branch is Caspian. At least I'm almost positive it's Caspian. After being shot in the back of the head at point-blank range, there isn't a whole lot of his face left. The rest of him seems as the same as ever and I wonder if Amara's magic has something to do with that. I have no idea how long it's been since he died but I would hazard a guess at a few weeks at least so he shouldn't still look like that. I'm glad the worst is the bullet's exit wound otherwise I'd probably be sick even with how little there is in my stomach.

The bodies of the council seem to be nowhere in sight and I'm very thankful for that—they probably don't have magic from a member of the House of the Sun keeping them from decaying and they already looked pretty bad when I first saw them. I don't think I could take seeing that again and I don't want to end up crying today. If I'm going to die in front of all of these people—*my* people—then I'm going to do it on my own terms (as much as I can under the circumstances) and not give Onyx or Sapphire the satisfaction of seeing me cry and beg for my life in front of them. I'll die with as much dignity as I can muster.

Soldiers line the crowd but more people are arriving, desperate to watch what's happening. I let my gaze flick over the entire crowd briefly but not long enough to pick out any faces. At the very back, there is someone in a hooded cloak but they're probably another soldier, ready to strike if someone tries anything so I pay them no mind. Why they would need someone like that here I have no idea, with the amount of soldiers standing around I doubt anyone would try anything.

Onyx and Sapphire step out onto the middle of the stage and a hush falls over the crowd, the chatter dying down to nothing.

"People of the House of Neptune," Onyx says, his voice ringing out over the crowd, "you have been defeated. Your council is dead, your House is in ruins and those left alive now belong to us. You will bow down to us and acknowledge us as your supreme rulers."

There is a murmur from the crowd. Whether the people will accept this or not is another matter entirely but the soldiers are all very heavily armed and as I take a closer look I realise there seems to be a lot of women and children in the crowd. Even if some of the women did think about taking on the soldiers they'll aim to protect the children. I look around again and suddenly spot a familiar face. Levi is staring at me in anger and confusion, probably wondering what the hell happened to me. I hold his gaze for a moment—*please, whatever you're thinking about doing, don't do it, it's not worth it, not for my sake*—before I look away. I can't stomach the look in his eyes any longer and if I continue to look at him, I'll break down.

"As a show of goodwill I will take the head of your House, Harmony Sirenia, as my personal slave," Onyx tells the crowd. "Your Neo Warrior though…" He smirks over at me. "She will not be so lucky. Any of you foolish enough to stand against us will suffer the same fate so let this be a lesson to you all."

There is another murmur among the crowd, this one slightly louder. The surrounding soldiers all clutch their weapons tighter in order to show their strength which seems to give a lot of people pause. Even with our magic, we're still pretty outnumbered—we've always been a small House so there was no way we would have been able to defend ourselves against this many armed men and there's nothing Illyria and I can do now either.

"Silence!" Sapphire screeches and the murmuring stops.

"As you can see," Onyx says, gesturing over to where Caspian's body hangs, "the leader of the Neo Warriors, Caspian Feioré, has already been bested by us so it would be in your best interest to cooperate unless you want to receive the same treatment."

Another murmur and a few gasps come from the crowd, some of the people only just noticing Caspian hanging there.

"All that remains now is for us to make an example of the other two we have captured and send a message to the Braxian king—that the Cimmerians are here to stay and we will best his armies no matter how many he sends," Onyx finishes.

"Hey Illyria," I mutter aloud as Onyx begins talking about the plans he has for Neyara now that he owns it. (He really does love the sound of his own voice.)

"Yeah sugar?"

"I'm sorry I dragged you into this."

"It's okay," she replies. "This was inevitable. Onyx wanted a war too badly for it not to have happened."

"I should have just come on my own, then this never would have happened," I say.

"They would have killed you instantly."

"No, they wouldn't," I reply, casting a glance over at Onyx and Sapphire. I know exactly how they think now. Sapphire looks over in our direction and catches my eye. She smirks at me before turning back to the crowd. She's got what she wanted now so she's feeling very smug. I turn back to Illyria. "I'm much more valuable to them as an example for anyone who tries to cross them than I am just being killed on sight."

"I think we both are," she says.

She's not wrong. The Neo Warriors have always stood as a symbol of hope for all of Brax, especially when it came to defending people against the Cimmerians. Now the Commander has been killed, a particularly famous Commander at that, and they're about to watch two of the others—one of whom is the daughter of their own House and barely old enough to stand as a proper Neo Warrior—die horribly. This is what it's always been about: showing their strength by making an example of the two of us.

"There is nothing you can do to defeat us, this is our land now," Onyx says and I'm actually starting to get a bit sick of him talking; I wish he'd just get on with it and kill us so I don't have to listen to him anymore. Looking back over at the crowd, I see some movement from the very back, just in front of the Cimmerian soldiers. It's that hooded figure again and they seem to be weaving their way through the crowd, into the centre.

What…? The figure turns their head and I just about catch a sharp flash of crimson against the sea of blue before it's covered with the hood again. Was that Remy…? No… No, it can't be. I must be seeing things. I think that in the back of my mind I want someone to come and save us so badly, I'm starting to see things that aren't really there. If it is him though…

"Your king and your Neo Warriors will not save you," Onyx tells the crowd and the glee is evident in his voice. "Kneel before us."

The crowd remains still.

"Did you not hear what he said?" Sapphire screeches. "Show some respect and kneel!"

Slowly, reluctantly, each member of the crowd begins to kneel down, showing their submission to Onyx and the Cimmerians. All save two: once the entire crowd is on their knees, the only ones left standing are Rich, the man who was a Harmony supporter and gave me a hard time when I was first named as Neo Warrior, and the mysterious hooded figure. A few of the people around both of them try to gently pull them down but both stay resolutely on their feet: Rich looking at Onyx defiantly, the other's hood is pulled down too low to see their face.

"I will never bow to the likes of you," Rich says calmly. "Not while there is still breath in my body."

Onyx laughs humourlessly. "It seems there are more examples to be made than just your fallen captains," he says, his eyes never leaving Rich for a second. "Kill him first."

A few of the soldiers closest to us pull out guns, cock them and open fire. I can't look. Turning away, I squeeze my eyes shut and wait for the screams but they never come. The gunfire stops and I slowly open my eyes, looking back to where Rich was standing. In his place seems to be a huge cocoon that looks as if it's made out of thick tree roots and melts back into the soil as soon as it becomes apparent that the soldiers won't start firing again.

Murmurs start up again, most people looking at Rich in shock, he himself looking more than a little surprised as well, but I know better. I look past him to the hooded figure who is holding their hand, palm outstretched, towards him. My breath catches in my throat.

Oh god... It is him!

"Who are you that dares to challenge me?" Onyx snarls.

The figure reaches up and pulls their hood back to reveal that shock of crimson hair standing like a beacon of hope against the blue surrounding it. "I am Captain Renton Remelston, Neo Warrior of the House of Venus, and I'm taking back what's ours."

For a second, I feel my knees buckle. I'm amazed that I've been able to stand for this long but the shock of seeing Remy—actually seeing him and knowing by the reactions of everyone else that it is actually him—shakes me. They actually came...it wasn't all for nothing.

Onyx's bark of laughter rings out through the crowd. "You honestly think one Neo Warrior is enough to stop me and my army?"

"That's why I brought reinforcements," Remy says. "Now!"

His shout echoes over the heads of the crowd and for a moment, nothing happens but then suddenly, there is a flurry of movement everywhere. Seven other people get to their feet. More hoods, hats, wigs and magical glamours are removed to reveal the rest of the Neo Warriors kneeling in and among the crowd. Everyone turns to look at them in stunned awe, including the soldiers who just stand there staring. Onyx looks wildly around at the soldiers who all seem to be frozen in place, not knowing how to react.

"Don't just stand there," he shouts at them, "kill them!"

I turn to Illyria and she looks as surprised as I do; clearly, she'd given up hope of being rescued too. Looking back out at the crowd, I see Remy, Ellis and Dmitri fighting with some of the soldiers, trying to keep them away from the crowd while Orion, Samuel and Penny try to evacuate the civilians from the area. Being outnumbered is taking its toll on even them though; their focus is too split between the crowd and the soldiers. Penny seems distracted, half her attention on hurrying the crowd down to the docks and the other half constantly flicking from where Illyria and I are to the other side of the stage, looking for something. I've no idea what she's looking for but she doesn't seem to be paying as much attention to the crowd as she should be. She'll get herself injured at this rate if she doesn't keep an eye out for the soldiers.

Suddenly, there is a fierce beating of wings from above and I look up to see Luciana diving down towards the crowd. I can't quite believe all this is happening. They're here…they actually came when I thought that there was no way I'd ever see any of them again! Onyx and Sapphire are completely unprepared for this as well, along with all the rest of the soldiers, so whatever plan was formulated for this has worked. Obviously, the Cimmerians hadn't been expecting any resistance once they took Neyara so it's interesting to see the tables turned. They clearly don't know what to do other than leave the fighting to their soldiers.

Both of them turn and try to run back to the House, under the misapprehension that they'll be safe in there. I just about manage to turn my head to watch them leave but before they can get very far, a cage of lightning seems to appear out of nowhere, surrounding them. I look over at Penny again to see her holding out her hand, a look of abject fury on her face that I've never seen before. Sapphire and Onyx are trapped for fear of getting fried if they put even the slightest foot wrong and, judging by just how close they are standing, there isn't a lot of room for them to move.

I continue to scan the crowd until I see a flash of orange dart over to the tree where Caspian is hanging. Kat pulls out a gun and shoots through the rope Caspian's body is hanging from. Remy, forgoing the soldier he has been fighting with by knocking him out with the butt of the soldier's own gun, joins her. He heaves Caspian's body onto his shoulder and Kat turns, making the ground tremble beneath us, drawing everyone's attention before she shouts over the rapidly diminishing crowd.

"Orion, now!"

Orion sprints past a few soldiers who all lunge for him at the same time, weaving his way past them. He's too fast for any of them to grab and he manages to get past them and all the others who try to catch him. He sprints to the very back of the crowd, behind where the line of soldiers had been and I can just about see the colour drain out of his hair as he casts a black hole in the space next to him.

"Luciana, cover him!" Kat shouts up at her, taking control of the situation as second-in-command.

Without a second's thought, Luciana flies over to Orion. She pulls two new guns out of holsters at her hips and opens fire again, her aim fixed on any soldiers that try to get close to him. Remy runs through the last few people heading for the docks, although he's moving much slower now with the extra weight of Caspian's body. Finally he reaches Orion and I watch as he goes through the black hole and disappears.

"Shoot her down!" Onyx screams at the soldiers, still unable to move because of Penny's lightning cage. "Don't let them get away!"

With their new orders, some of the soldiers leave the fights they have been engaged in and draw bows, pull arrows from quivers and cock guns to try and shoot Luciana out of the sky. None of their weapons can touch her however as Samuel is there with strong winds to blow them all off course, keeping her able to protect Orion.

I'm so busy watching the scene unfold in front of me that I don't notice the chains around my wrist tightening for a second before they loosen and become non-existent. I bring my hands around to my face, slumping against the pole behind me. They're suddenly free and I almost don't know what to do with them.

All I can do is stare at them for a minute before I cast a glance over my shoulder to see Dmitri pulling the metal of Illyria's cuffs away from her wrists so that they fall to the floor in a crumpled, melted mess.

As soon as her hands are free, Illyria also slumps against the post behind her, both of us so drained of everything. I'm still too much in shock to move but Illyria tries to recover herself quicker and goes to take a step forward. She immediately falls backwards and Dmitri moves to catch her. She places a hand to her head, what little colour there had been in her face suddenly draining from her cheeks.

"Are you alright?" Dmitri asks.

"I think so," she replies.

"Can you stand?"

"Not very well."

"Okay," he says. He turns to me. "Ari, are you alright?"

"I think so," I reply. I'm on my feet and that is enough at the moment. Adrenaline is keeping me standing right now and there's nothing that will stop me until it burns out.

"Don't let any more of them get away!" Onyx shouts and I look back up at the black hole to see Samuel slip through it, Kat helping Luciana defend Orion.

"We need to go," Dmitri says.

"But what about the rest of the Neptunians?" Illyria asks.

"We can come back when we have more of a plan and we can bring more people," Dmitri says. "Right now, we're outnumbered and we need you two back to full strength."

"But…" I begin.

"That's an order," Dmitri says, pulling rank on the both of us. "I promise we'll come back and drive them out of here but for now, we need to stop any more of us being killed."

His words hit me like a punch in the gut and I can feel tears welling up in my eyes. "Okay…" I mumble.

"Good." He places Illyria's arm around his neck and is about to pick her up when a heavily armed soldier climbs onto the stage.

The soldier raises a weapon but Dmitri raises his hand, taking control of the metal in the soldier's armour as he does, and clenches his fist. The soldier's arms and legs snap to his sides and he loses balance, toppling face first to the stage. As he falls, a set of keys clatter to the floor. I stare at the keys and then I look up at Harmony at the other end of the stage. I turn back to Dmitri for a second to see him gathering Illyria up in his arms.

I have a choice to make—go with them or try and save Harmony.

Without even thinking, I dart to the soldier struggling on the floor against the armour holding him, grab the keys and dart over to Harmony.

"Ari!" I hear Dmitri shout after me but I don't pay any attention.

I'm not losing another member of my family to them!

Skidding to a halt next to Harmony, I fall with a thud to the floor behind her. I begin trying keys in the lock of the chains binding her hands. There are so many and no indication to which one I should use so I pick one at random but I can't get it to fit so I start trying the next one, jiggling it in the lock, desperate to get it to fit.

"Ari, what are you doing?" she cries.

"What does it look like?" I reply with my own question, my fingers fumbling as yet another key fails to fit into the lock. I'm beginning to wonder if I don't have the right key at all but there's no way I can give up now. "I'm taking you with me."

"Ari, you can't!"

"Why not?"

"Because someone has to stay here and protect Neyara and the House."

"But why does it have to be you?" I cry, frustration at another failed key and everything going on around me getting the better of me. I stop suddenly. My chest is aching and it gets difficult to breathe. Tears begin to fall down my cheeks and I sit back on my heels, unable to do anything more.

"Ari," she says softly, leaning her head back so that she's closer to me, "it's alright. I know there aren't enough of you to save everyone here."

"But…" I sob, the tears falling faster down my face now.

"Ari, I'll be alright," she says.

"I can't leave you with them," I sniff. "I don't want to lose you as well."

"It's alright," she says. "Please don't worry about me, just get yourself out of here safely. That's all I care about right now."

"No, you're coming with us!"

With renewed vigour, I desperately try the next key. It slips in the lock and sticks, I try turning it but it won't budge. I'm just about to scream in frustration when I turn it the other way and it opens. With a strangled gasp, I pull the chains off and push myself to my feet to start on the chains around her feet. My hands are shaking even more now and the key that fit the back lock doesn't fit these ones so I have to start from square one.

There are gentle hands on my face all of a sudden and I look up into Harmony's eyes to see that they are brimming with tears as well. She leans down as far as she can and presses a soft kiss to my forehead.

"It's alright," she says again. "You go, get out of here while you still can."

"I don't want to leave you," I sob, breaking down and crying into her knees, still clutching the keys in my fist.

The next thing I feel is a strong hand grabbing a fistful of my shirt and I turn around, not ready for the inevitable fight with a soldier, but instead come face to face with Ellis.

"Come on, we need to go," he tells me. "Penny's hurt, she can't hold that cage much longer and we need to get you out of here."

"Just give me a second," I say turning back to the chains, trying the next key and beginning my struggle all over again.

"Ari, go with him," Harmony tells me again. "I'll be fine."

"No!" I can barely see through the tears streaming down my face. All I can think about is getting these chains undone but the keys just won't fit! I wish I had metal magic, like Dmitri! Harmony takes hold of my face again, forcing me to look up at her while she prises the keys out of my hand.

"Ari, I won't see you back in prison," she says. "I'll be fine, go."

I stare at her for a moment and I can feel my heart breaking. I can't leave her but I can't stay either.

A loud crackle and then a boom rings all around us as the lightning cage that had been keeping Onyx and Sapphire trapped disappears. I turn frantically to the black hole to see Luciana dragging the injured Penny through it. Now, the only ones still left here are Kat, Orion, Ellis and me. Before I can do anything else, Ellis picks me up in his strong grip and throws me over his shoulder.

"Ellis!" Harmony cries as he turns to leave and he turns back to face her.

"Yeah?"

"Take care of her, okay?"

Tears slowly trail down Harmony's face and that only makes me cry even harder. Ellis could carry her and I could run—we don't have to just leave her here. If I could only find my voice, I could say this but I can't seem to breathe properly.

"I promise," Ellis says and begins to carry me away.

"Harmony!" I scream, reaching out for her and struggling against the grip Ellis has on me as Onyx advances on her from behind.

She leans forward and manages to undo the chains a lot faster than I could as her hands are a lot steadier than mine and she seems to have no trouble finding the right key. I'm willing her to hurry so she can come with us. The chains come free and she jumps down from the stage, following Ellis and I, Onyx at her heels. I begin to struggle even harder, wanting to grab her and pull her along faster so we can take her with us. I can feel Ellis' grip slacken slightly as he throws off a soldier and I manage to wriggle out of it. Hitting the floor almost face first, I push myself to my feet, running towards her.

"Ariana!" she cries, reaching out her hand for mine.

"Harmony!"

The world seems to slow down for a second. Just before I reach Harmony and take her hand, I feel Ellis' huge arms wrap around my waist again and he heaves me up onto his shoulder. At the same time, Onyx roughly grabs Harmony from behind, pulling her away from me. My fingers clutch around air, just a few centimetres away from hers, and there's nothing I can do to stop us from being parted again.

I see her scream my name once more but I can't hear it from the furious pounding of my heart in my ears and I barely hear myself screaming to her in response. The next thing I know, the distance between us grows larger and larger as Onyx drags her back to the House and Ellis carries me over to the black hole. My throat is raw from screaming and I keep struggling against Ellis' hold, desperate to get back to Harmony. All I can focus on is her until the world around me starts to darken and I feel a rush of nausea pass through me.

No…

No, this can't be happening!

I can't just leave her like this.

I need to do something to save her!

But I can't…

The bright sunlight of the outside world begins to fade into the gloom of what looks like one of the basement rooms back at headquarters. The black hole sickness hits me once again but I try to swallow it down so that I can still struggle against Ellis even though his grip has tightened around me. He stops running and I watch as Kat steps through the black hole, followed by Orion, and it begins to close.

No!

No, I need to get back!

I need to get to Harmony!

I need to save her!

Finally, the effort of holding me seems to be too much for Ellis to handle along with the effects of passing through Orion's black hole and he drops me. I just about manage to land on my feet and dart over to where the black hole is getting smaller and smaller. Once again, time seems to slow down as I run to it and I watch it shrinking. It closes just before I can reach it and my fist connects with the cold, hard stone wall where it had just been, and I know it's over.

No... Please no, it can't be over. I can't have lost her. Why can't I just be stronger and actually be able to save someone that I love for once in my fucking life?

I pound on the wall repeatedly, tears streaming down my face as sobs and choked screams wrench my chest. Oblivious to everyone around me and not caring that I'm still alive, I cry out my anger, pain and frustration.

It wasn't supposed to end like this...

TO BE CONTINUED